# LEGEND OF CAEMERIS

# DESCENDANT'S

# THRONE

## BOOK THREE

# CLARE L ROLFE

First published by Clare L Rolfe in 2022

Rolfe, Clare L.

Descendant's Throne / by Clare L Rolfe

Legend of Caemeris

Paperback ISBN 978-0-6450880-3-8

Ebook ISBN 978-0-6450880-4-5

Printed and distributed by Ingram Spark

A catalogue record for this
book is available from the
National Library of Australia

# Contents

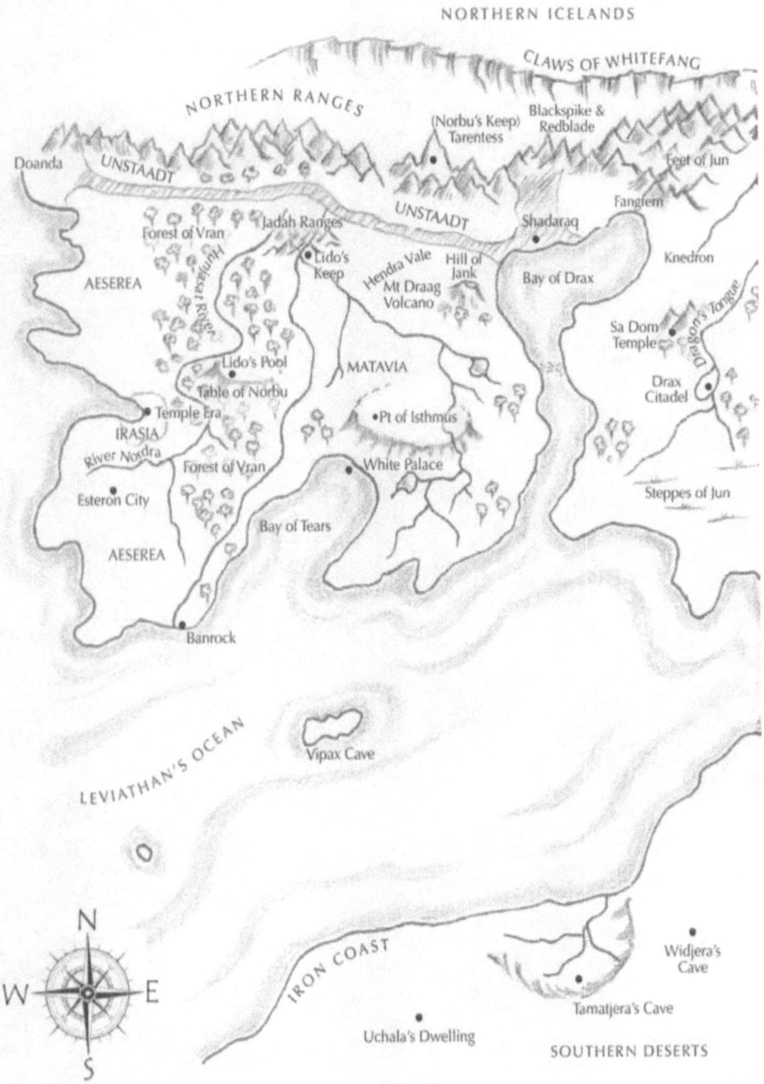
NORTHERN ICELANDS
CLAWS OF WHITEFANG
NORTHERN RANGES
(Norbu's Keep)
Tarentess
Blackspike &
Redblade
Feet of Jun
Doanda
UNSTAADT
UNSTAADT
Fangfern
Shadaraq
Forest of Vran
Jadah Ranges
Hunjassat River
Lido's
Keep
Hendra Vale
Hill of
Jank
Knedron
AESEREA
Mt Draag
Volcano
Bay of Drax
Sa Dom
Temple
Dragon's Tongue
Lido's Pool
MATAVIA
Drax
Citadel
Table of Norbu
Temple Era
•Pt of Isthmus
IRASIA
River Nordra
Forest of Vran
White Palace
Steppes of Jun
Esteron City
Bay of Tears
AESEREA
Banrock
Vipax Cave
LEVIATHAN'S OCEAN
N
W
E
S
IRON COAST
Widjera's
Cave
Tamatjera's Cave
Uchala's Dwelling
SOUTHERN DESERTS

The World of ARGLETHIUM

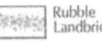

Rubble Landbridge

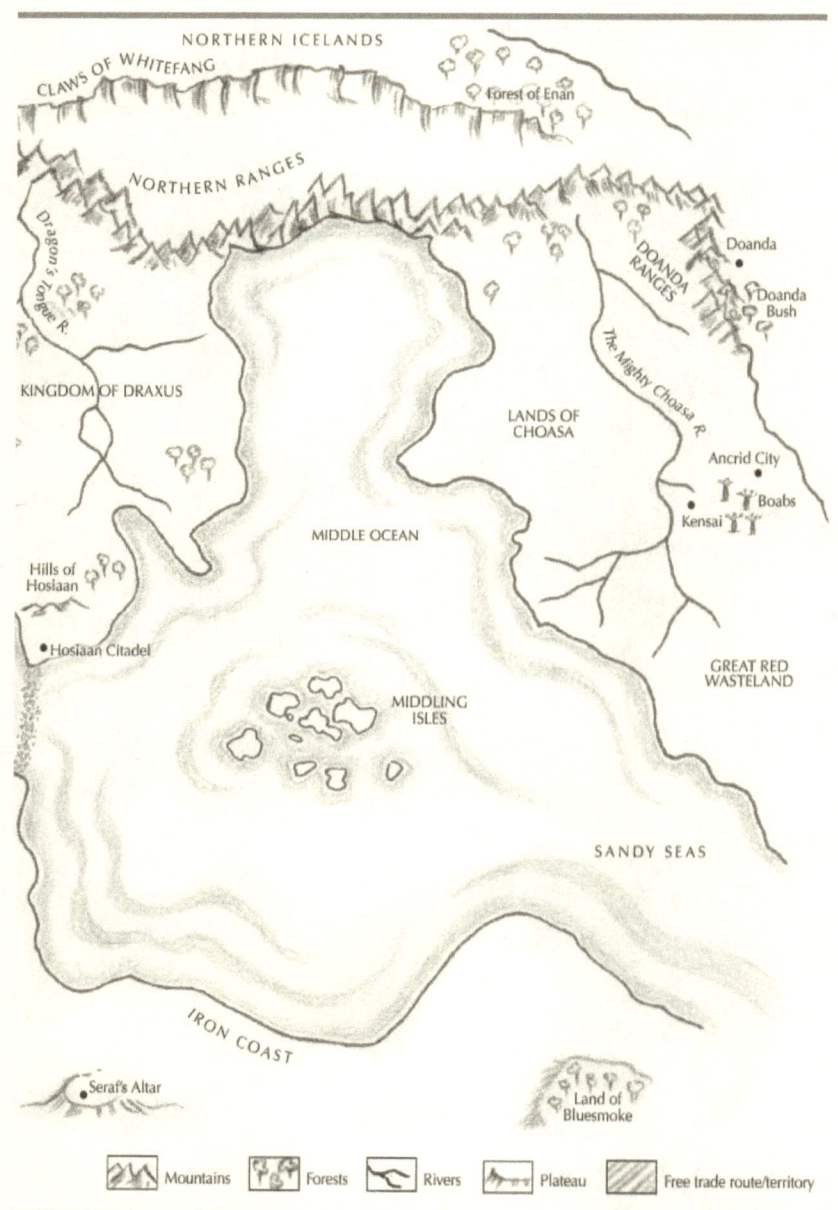

NORTHERN ICELANDS

CLAWS OF WHITEFANG

Forest of Enan

NORTHERN RANGES

Dragon's Tongue R.

DOANDA RANGES

Doanda

Doanda Bush

KINGDOM OF DRAXUS

The Mighty Choasa R.

LANDS OF CHOASA

Ancrid City

Boabs

Kensai

Hills of Hosiaan

MIDDLE OCEAN

Hosiaan Citadel

GREAT RED WASTELAND

MIDDLING ISLES

SANDY SEAS

IRON COAST

Seraf's Altar

Land of Bluesmoke

Mountains    Forests    Rivers    Plateau    Free trade route/territory

# PART ONE

# QUICKENING
## of
# BLADE AND FIRE

# Uchala's Dwelling

Sa watched the horizon bob in front of her as she and the Aracnine made their way further into the red desert. As she sat perched on top of First's shoulder her mind wandered back to the farewell with Kado. She had seen a tear form in his eyes as she said goodbye to him. His words clear in her mind almost as if he were speaking to her right at this moment.

"Sa-Tuc, I do not know what purpose you have in this war or where your destiny lies but know this, I intend to rebuild the Drax dynasty, and I want you to be seated beside me when they hand me the Sceptre of the Dragon." He had held her arm fiercely not wanting to let her go.

"I cannot stay Kado, I must find a way to break the bond with these creatures or they will never set me free. Do not let your heart lie in fields of false hope. I desire also to see the Banner of the Dragon flying and restoration of Drax City, but too much now lies in ruins. I go to a place of one of the ancients far to the south. When I return, I will know more clearly where my fate lies. Restore your Kingdom and unite to defeat the shadow that seeks to conquer our world. Bring our people together under the Dragon's might again Kado Ko Drax."

"I will not let you go Sa-Tuc. We belong together."

He had grabbed her and kissed her so vehemently that she was stunned by his passion. Always confused with the feelings which were roused with Kado, Sa did not know how to respond. Deep within a longing for the bond of her only friend since childhood stirred but quickly it was overridden by the urge to finish this quest that she had been thrust into. She had pulled away feeling helpless at what to say to him.

"Rebuild your Kingdom son of the Dragon. My destiny lies elsewhere." Sa remembered the fear and pain she had seen in Kado's eyes as she had uttered them.

Suddenly First stopped, jolting Sa's attention back to the desert they now crossed. It screeched across the red plains as it lifted its massive talon pointing to black glistening rocks shimmering in the heat. An image came to Sa's mind of an underground cavern. Inside lay a body. Sa looked more closely and realised it was Ange.

"First, we must go there and rescue Ange."

She hopped off First's shoulder and stood in front of all the Aracnine.

"I command you all to go this place and take the girl. We can protect her until she is healed from her wounds."

"No, you are not our Queen until the Crown of Uchala is worn. The flame of Belmaris shines within the shadow and it is by the First Star that the Shadow will live or die. It is no longer our burden."

First scooped up Sa and continued into the desert. Sa struggled desperate to go to Ange but in the end, it was futile as the great talon remained firmly clamped around her torso.

The Aracnine began to make a steep descent into a ravine. It was full of verdant ferns and palms amongst trees in full blossom. A scent of lemon was carried on the breeze as the contingent climbed down the rocky ledge.

"What is this place First?"

"Its name here is unknown to us, but it is where the web of Uchala lies most heavily in this world and is scented with the memories of Stonthrax."

"Who is Stonthrax?" asked Sa

"Our maker" replied First.

Sa wanted to ask more questions, but she knew there would be no answers from the guardians.

First began to walk in a stream of crystal-clear water that seemed to originate on the far side of the ravine. Sa saw the pristineness of the flowing water and licked her lips feeling how dry they were.

"First I am thirsty."

The talon released Sa. She jumped down to the water. The sun was just beginning to rest on the tip of the escarpment above. Sa guessed it was a turn of the glass until twilight and they had walked towards the west.

She drank heartily and savoured the sweetness of the water. She saw some berries on one of the shrubs on the edge of the stream and decided she would try some. Walking over she plucked them off and smelt them. There was a slight hint of blackberry, and the skin was purple. She sucked the juice, expecting it to be bitter but instead the taste was sweet. Growls from her stomach responded to the berries. She realised it was the first food she had eaten in almost ten dawns.

"First this food will not be enough for me. I will need to find something else a pheasant or rodent."

First did not respond to her. Finally, Last of the Aracnine had scaled down the cliff and was approaching First and Sa. In its arms lay the mangled the remains of the two Aracnine which had been destroyed by Voloc.

First screeched at the sight of Six and Seven. Its call rebounded off the walls of the ravine and up out to the far reaches of the desert that surrounded them. The other Aracnine joined in the cacophony sending their chorus of grief echoing into Sa's heart forcing her onto her knees in the water. Unused to grieving for anyone, the pain of the Guardians sorrow for their brethren made Sa's heart stop. Taking life was only a means to earn her keep. The depth of the loss it caused had never concerned her or penetrated the steely façade. For the first time, Sa-Tuc saw the face of sorrow, and crumbled at the sight of it.

First picked her up and called for the others to continue to the other side of the valley. They headed through the bushes and eventually came to the mouth of a cave. Some janabaals were sunning themselves in the last of the day's rays. They watched lethargically as the creatures approached. Sa was surprised they did not run from them but instead seemed at ease with the creatures. The stream's current was stronger here as it spilled over a ledge at the entrance. The interior could not be seen from the outside and was mostly obscured by flowering shrubs of vibrant reds and blues. First, stooped down low to avoid hitting its corona on the roof of the entrance. It put Sa down to let her walk behind it. The others followed. As the group walked further into the cave; silence blanketed them as the trickling stream dried up. The tunnel soon became completely black so that Sa could not walk without stumbling. She scanned the darkness and saw the red eyes peering at her from the Aracnine: eight little specs from each of them bobbing in an ocean of darkness.

"First I cannot see."

The talon picked up Sa again and continued for what seemed an age. Suddenly they stopped. Sa could not see if they were still in a tunnel. The air feels different she thought. First glowed red casting a dim light around them. Before them was an empty cavern. They stood on the edge of stone bridge that extended halfway towards the other side of a rock wall broken only by one jagged gap in the stone. The bridge spanned across a massive abyss which repelled any light back as soon as its surface was touched by it. First suddenly leapt across the chasm onto the ledge and continued to the gap on the opposite wall. The tunnel they walked through was illuminated by light filtering from the far end. It was a pale translucent blue and Sa wondered what would cause that sort of light.

Entering the chamber, the blue light suddenly became so bright that it blinded Sa and the Aracnine.

"Bind thy blood Uchala and let your brethren enter" spoke First. The light dimmed just enough allowing them all to step into the chamber and see clearly.

In the middle of the domed shape room hung a small tear drop shaped pouch. It was from here that the blue light emanated. Around the walls lay markings unknown to Sa. They were not just random scratches but seemed to be a language. As she walked around inspecting the walls, she noticed something crunched underfoot. Looking down she saw the shed exoskeletons of spiders.

"What is this place First?"

"It is where our kind are first birthed in this world. It is the dome of the wanderer Uchala."

"What is this Uchala? Is it's form like the Aracnine or like the creatures we call spiders?"

First ignored her question as Last entered with the remains of the two Aracnine. The others except First knelt as Last placed the torsos and limbs gently on the floor directly beneath the pouch that hung from the roof.

The Aracnine all stood and clasping hands began to chant again. First made Sa hold its talon as well. Instantly a surge of power coursed through Sa, but the talon held her firmly stopping her from fainting.

"First please it is too much. Let me go."

"See thy servants be born and know your dominion for once the crown of Uchala is worn this shall be your sceptre of rule."

First lifted its claw and pierced the sack above them. As it did it chanted,

"This sacrilege is sought by all the Aracnine as a boon to restore the eight again. Let the blood of the wanderer now fill this flesh that lies torn by the destroyer of the First Star. Let the blue of the first light that stung the dark now fill the red that formed these guardians here in this place. Our bonds are broken from the usurper and our Queen lies in readiness to bear the bite of the great spirits made before the wars of creation. We claim the spirit of Uchala the wanderer to heal the eight guardians of Stonthrax."

As the sharp nail pierced the sack something moved slightly but was obscured by the light bursting forth even more brightly than before. At the same time a pulse of energy shot through from First's talon into Sa's arm and gripped her tightly not letting her move. Sa felt a presence clawing her mind like it was sifting through her thoughts and memories looking for something.

A drop of blue liquid squeezed through the tear First had made in the sack and dripped onto the torn chest of Six and then Seven. Following the tear drop a set of tiny legs and body emerged almost indiscernible as the blue skin was the same colour as the light the sack emitted. As the spiderling pulled its way out it eased itself down on a fine thread towards the bodies. It began to spin a web across the open wounds in the heads, chest and legs and arms. The blue of the spider contrasted brightly against the red of the Aracnine bodies.

Sa could hardly breathe as the presence in her mind overwhelmed her. She felt the sharp pricks of the spider's web pierce the hide of the Aracnine on the ground as it began to heal the body.

"Please First help me," Sa pleaded but it ignored her.

Then the spider rose off Sixth's chest and climbed towards the sack. Crawling back into the pouch it wove a web across the tear to close it once more. Then the blue light dimmed leaving the Aracnine and Sa in semi darkness and complete silence. They continued to sway in unison and the presence in Sa's mind remained as she drifted into unconsciousness.

Sa woke and found she was floating. Then she was aware of First's grip on her arm pulling her forward. She looked for the others, but they were nowhere to be seen.

"Where are we First?"

The guardian did not answer. Suddenly a voice exploded in her mind.

"One who seeks the suzerainty over the Aracnine, you will be tested for your worthiness to assume the crown of the Wanderer."

"I seek nothing, I have been chosen by these creatures but do not know why they have chosen me."

"Your blood is mixed with that of the first born. It calls to them."

"Who are you?"

"You shall see."

A doorway in the shape of a circle pulsed with blue light appeared before them. First did not move to open the door.

Sa pushed it and found it opened easily. Behind it lay all the colours of the world swirling together in a silent penumbra. First and Sa walked into the womb of the mother of the ancients.

"Welcome First of the Guardians and Sa-Tuc of Uchala and Clayborn."

The voice came from nowhere and everywhere and was the same as the one in her mind.

Sa felt herself suddenly pulled into a maelstrom of blues and indigoes. The ribbons began to lacerate her with thousands of tiny cuts until she could feel herself being shredded. She screamed out to First, but it did not come for her. The assassin of Ko screamed in agony into the silence of the rainbow that surrounded her. She heard the door shut leaving her at the mercy of this unknown spirit. Kado came to mind, and she clung to his face not wanting to slip into a fevered madness from the pain of her flesh being torn off her limbs.

Suddenly it stopped. Sa gasped for air waiting for the flaying to begin again. Slowly she raised her arm, but nothing was there. Her body was not there.

"Am I dead?"

"Sa-Tuc, I am Uchala, the wanderer. I am one of the first created at the time of the light reaching the void. My blood flows with the blood born of the blue. My spawn crawled inside your mother's womb and laid an egg there. From this rape came the being now before me, you who are known as Sa-Tuc. Your creation screamed union of the caemexa and oblyquixiton across the expanses of time and into my dwelling. I felt your birth and your power born of two eggs and not the seed of a male spawning but as it was deemed that I sleep until the coming of the shadow, so I did not suckle you with my fangs to bring your blue light to its fullness. Instead in my sorrowful dormitions I saw my youngling suckled on the teat of one not worthy. To watch my youngling be turned into a scorned and warped creature that could be as fierce and lethal as my off- spring but perverted in her destiny and purpose. Your life has been dogged with the acts of debauchery and with the stain of Uchala. During your life you have brought death and misery to others of your kind for no other reason than the glory of masters maligned by their desires. I have watched you from afar my youngling with no way to bring you to me. Not until the Shadow came with the custodian. It was here I saw my death and a time for my youngling to rise and take her crown."

"What have you done to me?"

"You are now just essence. The blood of the clayborn has been removed and only the light of the ancients remains."

"What will happen to me?"

"Do you accept the crown of Uchala, your mother and ruler and restorer of your life?"

"I do not know. What will become of me?"

"That will be your decision but in taking the crown you will drink of ancient power not the dirt of your world. Your life will be to rule a force greater than yourself and watch until the darkness of the Oblyquixiton seeks the ending of the light. You will become one of the ancients but stronger for your heritage will allow you to exist within the clayborn realm as one of them."

"If I choose not to take this crown?"

"Then the sacred blood in your veins shall be drawn out as I would draw the juices of my prey; leaving you hollow and nothing more than the decaying flesh, that becomes the destiny of the clayborn who seek nothing beyond their own glory and needs. They live with no memory and no future, and none is therefore given. Those blinded by the skin of their flesh which covers their sight denied to them. But the breach has happened and now these memories are revealed and one of your kind sits on the precipice of memory and the future. For this you shall watch and wait to see how the wars of creation shall proceed, if they will begin once more or end."

"Then what choice is this, when my world lies in peril from the very thing that devours all the light including those of the ancient?"

"It is for you to decide. The fate of this ancient war that now rests in the dying realms is unclear to all. I see the face of the one you call Kado in your mind. His heart seeks the warrior Sa-Tuc to give him the strength to rule the Dragon. The Spider and the Dragon united. You shall never be bonded in body but only in the heart and the power to call for obedience to your sceptres of rule. Choose Sa-Tuc."

"Before I choose, who are the Aracnine? Are they your younglings?"

"Nay they are my brethren, born of the same but separate. Their destiny lies unknown even to me, but they have asked for a ruler of their ancient memories and now it is given. Beware of their wrath Sa-Tuc if you forsake the crown of Uchala. They wield a power akin to that of the First Star that has not yet been awoken. They are the guardians, born from one called Stonthrax who lies in the memory of time and shadow. Remember also they are chained to the shadow."

"Will my rule not free them?"

The voice did not answer Sa as she floated in the miasma of colour around her. Kado's face came to mind; was his desire only for her strength; a strength not of her own making but a perverted coupling because of her mother's own dilapidated existence. Would Kado want the Sa-Tuc she would become if she forsook the crown; the sewer rat once more, a perfect weapon to fight the battles that would face them even if the Dynasty of the Dragon was restored. Her mind pondered these things. In her heart lay sorrow, pain and grief, things that had been denied to her because of her heritage. Pain which she had never endured before, but its presence would never leave without her strength to protect her.

"Is that the choice before me to gain the same as Ange or loss of my strength and skill as the predator assassin?" she asked into the emptiness of the swirling colours.

She thought of Ange and the doom that now lay on all the lands. Sa-Tuc had only known service, the feelings she had endured in the time with the Aracnine would continue even in bondage to them as their Queen. What choice did Sa-Tuc ever have, her fortune had always been at the hands of others? And now whether as a ruler of ancient power or as a weakened warrior attempting to thwart the demon that grew in strength every day, her life was forfeited to powers which she did not make or control.

"If I take the crown can the Spider and the Dragon rule in legion together beyond the defeat of the shadow?"

"Uchala only knows the power that lies within at the time of my creation. The dragon is unknown to me. But once the sceptre is taken and the bite of my fang felt then it will be you who chooses how it is wielded and whose destruction or glory is decided."

"I choose the crown of the one called Uchala; my mother and restorer."

Instantly Sa felt a tremendous pain followed by bolts of sheer energy consume her. Everything went black as the venom of Uchala stripped away the last of Sa-Tuc, assassin of Ko.

In the cavern beneath the red desert, Six and Seven suddenly breathed and woke to see their brethren standing over them. Inside their chests the blue strands of webbing had thickened, puckering their red hides. Standing they took their place amongst the eight and began to sway in unison. Soon a small dot of blue formed and slowly grew in the cavern. So slow in its formation it was almost impossible to see it growing larger. It formed the shape of a person then a spider then back to the person until sitting in the centre of the domed chamber sat a woman. She was an incandescent blue, lighting the chamber and the empty cavern that lay outside its walls.

The eight guardians stood in unison with joy and sadness erupting in their empty forms as their Queen grew before them. Slowly everything stilled and the Aracnine stopped their swaying. The woman opened her eyes. Seeing with the vision of the ancients she pierced the very hearts of the Aracnine and seared away their scars of bondage that had spanned the eons of time since the dawn of creation. First and Last screeched joined by the other six guardians and shook the foundations of the earth. As the walls of the dome cracked from the cry of the Aracnine's liberation the cavern began to fill with rubble.

"Enough!" commanded Sa. "Bow before me servants. See your Queen and ruler. Obey me or die; for your glory or destruction is bound to me."

Slowly a chain began to form; beginning in the heart of Sa and snaked its way into each of the eight guardians. Gathering the slack of the chain Sa-Tuc reefed it towards herself forcing the Aracnine to their knees again.

She opened her mouth, and two great fangs slowly came out dripping thick blue liquid.

"Be reborn of the blood of Sa-Tuchala, mother and restorer."

First screamed, as the pain of the venom chorused its baptism through its body.

# 2

# The Charm of Change

Flashes of raven black and alabaster wove in and out of the hedges of rose bushes. The feel of the grass was fresh and pricked the sole of her feet just enough to make her dance rather than run. She easily missed the clutching thorns of the roses as she glided past them.

"Watch me father, as I fly" the young girl called as she leapt across the small pond. She barely touched the ground before leaping into the air again. Her hair trailing like the plumes of peacocks.

"Sing the charm of the raven Giandra." Her father's voice floated across the air. Giandra looked briefly toward the black tower of her birth home.

*"Whip the air under my feet*

*Lighter than frozen breath of dawn*

*Stronger than the storms at sea*

*Sharper than beak and thorn*

*I call upon the black eye and feather,*

*Break my bones and let me fly like raven spawn."*

Suddenly Giandra could see the top of a tree and then over into the wheat fields. A mouse scampered and her eye spun toward its movement. She darted toward it, but it disappeared. Her voice rasped into the air.

She woke. She was lying on the grass; broken and alone.

Her father's sharp rebuke pierced her mind. "You will learn the charm of change, or you will never inherit the sceptre of Adria. Pick her up and take her to the apothecary."

Giandra screamed with pain as the old man, Ingaad, picked her up off the grass and took her to the small house at the bottom of the walled in fortress.

"Ah you again young witch. You ever disappoint your father and ancestors. I don't know what I can do this time to make the sickle of shadow awaken in you."

"It is under pain of death Apothecary if you do not succeed." Her father's voice echoed through the hut.

"I cannot make the bloodening awaken in your spawn. You have defiled your gift by your coupling with one not of your kin."

The apothecary felt a sharp claw in his face.

"Awaken her!" echoed the fierce command.

Giandra lay in pain on the litter watching the flames dance. How she wanted to fall into them and end it all. She had endured humiliation at her failures to take command of her ancestral powers so often that she had lost count. Her father's insistence brutal at times. He never understood her mother's tainted blood ruled her flesh more than his.

"Why did you choose her father, if she was so unworthy?"

"Wealth and my kin were barren from so many generations of coupling. There was no choice."

Zvanach was looking at a parchment through an eye glass. A knock came to the door. Giandra watched paralysed on the litter with her contorted limbs splayed as the old monk opened the door.

"Yes?" asked Zvanach

A young girl stood at the threshold. Giandra looked at the tiny figure draped in the shrouds of the sisters of the Temple. Her skin was white and fragile like hers. The hair covered by a veil.

"I have brought the alms from today's sacrifices." The girl bowed and gave the old monk a sack tied with rope.

Zvanach took it and opened it.

"Hmph. The old warlock won't be happy."

Zvanach eyed the girl thoughtfully.

Run thought Giandra as she lay feeling the pulsing heat of the fire over her flesh. Run from here.

"Come in. How old are you?"

The girl bowed but did not move.

"Come in. I will send a note to your mentor that I delayed your return."

"Run" whispered Giandra.

The novice stepped into the small hut.

"How old are you?"

"I am 1 cycle."

She looked furtively at Giandra lying on the floor. Giandra could see her swallow her fear on seeing the broken body on the bed. Am I smiling wondered Giandra? But the girl could only see a face mangled from the crashing fall to the ground with clots of blood entangled in the hair.

Zvanach looked at both girls and rubbed the place in his arm where the witches mark had been placed so long ago. He could feel the flame of Adria in the young nun and knew she would be suitable.

He took a bowl and poured some soup into it.

"Here drink." He ordered as he handed the bowl to the girl.

She took it and sipped.

Zvanach leafed through the parchment. He stopped and tapped his finger on a page.

His eyes glistened in the shadows of the room made by the dancing light of the fire.

"I am not worth it Zvanach." Giandra wheezed through her broken teeth.

"I know but your father would never let me die. I would remain tormented for as long as he lives. You are beyond repair this time. It is the only way."

He took the knife from his table and walked behind the little girl as she sipped the soup. Gently he slid it across her neck and let the blood run into the bowl.

She lay down gently on the floor lifeless. Giandra could see her eyes.

"Into this blood I call forth the inheritance of Adria, forgotten in this one but remembered here now. Let it fill what lays empty just as shadows fill the night and the sun fills the day. Bring it to life in this half-blood stained, take it from this one slain."

He cradled Giandra's head, and she drank the bowl filled with blood. Then he poured it into the wounds.

Giandra screamed with pain as her body healed.

"You curse me for I will always crave the blood of children."

Zvanach watched Giandra be remade.

"Yes, but your father will be happy." He spoke aloud to Giandra. I have healed and had my revenge he thought.

Giandra woke as she heard Noab grizzle in her chest. She had fallen asleep near the window. A wind had risen off the bay and made her shiver. She took the baby to his cradle.

What made me think of things so long ago she wondered. She undressed and slid into bed. She felt Piotr Faad's body next to hers.

Giandra lay silently on the bed. She left her body and searched once more for Voloc. You still lie in your lair dark one. She peered deeply and saw the desert-dweller lost but aware of her. They looked at each other through the mind of Voloc. The chasm of emptiness broken down with the presence of the clayborn of caemeris.

"It seeks you desert dweller. I have your kin near me and shall devour you all. Why does the dark one desire you so much? Show me what you see as well."

Ange looked at the stabbing glare of the Queen. Another flame lay behind it, the same flame as the sun but tinged with a shadow like that of Voloc.

"Your light brings death, while this one brought life, but it is the same light."

"Yes, you are right and when I rule both then I will be mightier than all."

Ange watched Giandra delve into the memories of Voloc. Why do you let me peer so deep dark one? Surely you could drive me out and send me to my grave, to become ashes for the worms to dig between.

There was no answer as Giandra watched the history of light and dark. The call of undefeatable power surged in her blood calling to the curse within her. The crystal contained it and the dark could not conquer it. Others would have crumpled as the emptiness engulfed everything, but Giandra saw the possibilities the untouched vastness held.

"I shall have it. You are the key desert dweller for you shall draw the bonds made at the beginning of our world to me and I shall bind them to my crown. Teach me ancient and powerful one. What can

Giandra of the Adriaan Fire learn? Do you understand what you hold within your hands maimed servant of the red wastes of your land?"

"You still do not understand what lies here. None of us do but it is given to me, and I shall restore the mighty Norbu and his brethren to defeat Voloc once more."

"I have what you hold dear and more. I shall call the blood-kin of the Keeper of this stone, and I will ask for allegiance with me. When enough of the covenant strands are gathered, I will snatch it from your hands."

"I have been entrusted to keep it. You will have no victory here. This battle was begun long before you or I and it is only the custodians who made the stone can defeat Voloc. Leave here or you shall be destroyed as well. My sister knows my duty and understands I must fulfill it. The memories of Caemeris forged long ago shall protect her and her children. The covenant was forged by Norbu, the bonds cannot be unmade by any other than their maker. None shall give you the power you crave when we know you shall destroy us anyway. You are a wretched fool blind to all things" spoke Ange

"Creatures who dwell here. You both seek a way to destroy Voloc the destroyer. But it is already dead and seeks the same. You will never find victory within this vastness of time. Youngling of the clayborn give it up now and let the end begin. For the Caemeris usurped the dark and now it is time to contain the light once more" spoke Voloc.

"Dark one. What if I could persuade the clayborn youngling to let go of the stone you seek. Surely you will let me sip of your emptiness to enflame my dying flesh once more if I convince her to give it to you."

"Be gone sorcerer of dim light. You are dead with in and soon your flesh shall join you. The power you seek is ash and shadow compared to the memories of Voloc. Drink of me and know your death."

Giandra smiled as she woke. She gazed across her chamber. She saw herself in a mirror and saw her dark eyes peer deeply inside herself. She had aged a thousand cycles as the emptiness invaded her. She drank the dark and let it consume her.

"I will control you" she spoke into the silent chamber.

Faad woke to the sound of the ocean, a soothing salve to the shadows which constantly dwelt within the palace and his mind. His gaze was caught by an image of Giandra in the mirror. She appeared as a withered old woman and a young girl at the same time. He stared at her eyes and his flesh tingled at the deadness inside them but strangely it seemed seductive to him. She did not see him as she stared at something else, he could not see. The image suddenly disappeared as Giandra woke.

"What keeps you awake Giandra?" mumbled Faad.

"Memories of my childhood Piotr."

"I know nothing about you."

"I was born of the order of Adria Sorcerers. Ancients from the time of first peoples in Westresse. I am the last. Queen Nene Des Vries is also one, but her people chose to move away from the Adriaan order in favour of their forests and cats. My mother was of wealthy nobility and my father seduced her to obtain her land titles. But the coupling broke my inheritance, and I was not worthy of the heritage my father had been given. Many times, he tried to make me as powerful as him but each time it failed. I used to sit and watch the temple sacrifices and learn the charms, but nothing could mend my stained blood. An apothecary who dabbled in all the banished brews was forced to work under my father to make me heal."

"And did he heal you?"

"Yes, he did and then I killed my father for making me who I am and my mother for being who she was."

"Why did you marry Ranik? You could have ruled without him."

Faad heard a hiss and the Queen's skin go colder.

"I was not strong enough to rule a Kingdom on my own even with my knowledge of fire and blood. His depravity fed and disguised my curse and between my land holdings and his we ruled Matavia. Through our children I would have ruled it all. But for..."

"But for what Giandra?" Faad stroked her arm and then her thigh.

"Did I tell you I killed the old monk who healed me as well?"

"No. Why?"

"He cursed me. He brought the condemned blood of a half-breed to the fire of Adria and made me drink of a pureblood not yet stained.

And it cursed me. He broke the sacred covenant and it cursed me to crave for blood ever more. To remain alive, I must feed. What stronger lust than for my own."

"Your children?"

"My sweet are always with me now."

Faad wondered if Ranik had ever known about his children.

"Is that why you never had anymore?" asked Faad.

"Perhaps. It was as if I would be tormented with one memory of ecstasy of devouring my own children and then never be able to repeat it again nor redeem myself with more children. The price of my curse was paid by rendering me barren."

Faad understood now what happened to the children, the heirs. Not even Ranik had known that their mother had killed them because she could not resist the fatal lust in her flesh for their blood.

Silence pervaded the room. There was no moonlight and only the cold light of a white crystal used as a bed lamp which captured a reflection off the embers in the fireplace.

"We will need to gather our armies soon to meet with the Clansman" spoke Faad.

"I have seen what the shadow desires and I want it as well. It will make me stronger than any Adriaan flame. It lets me see what I cannot."

"But how?"

"The children. They have the same blood. It calls the shadow here. With their blood and the desert dwellers I can summon the power of Adria and take the jewel for myself."

Faad did not answer. Deep within he knew Giandra would not be strong enough to conquer Voloc. And to make an enemy of Gildas would see the destruction of the Matavian Kingdom once and for all.

"I see your thoughts Piotr." Giandra rolled over and moved herself onto his body. He began to stiffen as her soft flesh massaged his.

"I will build a new realm. One ruled by flame and light. I will make it as I see it. I will remove this curse laid upon me by a vengeful servant. Together we will sire new heirs to our throne. I will never die."

"How old are you?" he asked

"Much older than you" she replied. She mounted him and let Faad see her age. He groaned with the pleasure and pain of the lust for control and power. He felt himself fall into her black eyes. It was like the heart of a volcano, dead but still spewing lethal heat and venomous ash. He felt his bones melt inside her.

You are my Queen and lover Faad thought. Giandra held him tight between her thighs and he groaned deep within her body.

"We will never die Piotr. We will never die." Giandra whispered into his ear as she slowly drew her body away from his.

They both lay near one another not asleep but half-awake dreaming together as the sun slowly rose across the bay. Soon its rays pricked the sight of the captain. He got up and ate some of the breakfast plate left near the window. He watched the boats as they were loaded with more captives from lands of Drax and Aeserea.

"Captain, the messengers from the Keeper of Tarentess have arrived."

"Take them to the main hall. I will be there shortly."

Faad sipped the wine and ate more of the beef on his plate.

"The clansman's men are here to parlance over readying to head south. What shall I tell them?"

Giandra walked over to the window to watch the ocean. The sun was turning the black waters to red vermillion. Noab grizzled in her arms as she held him.

Faad wondered if she would devour these children as well.

"No, their blood is not of Adriaan fire" Giandra smiled as she answered Faad's thought. "They are my bargaining coins. They are my path to conquer this shadow who is thwarted by their ancient heritage from the bonds made at the time of the making of the world."

"What of this alliance with the Graanar? What is your command?"

"I only desire the other child and shall use Gildas to help us escape."

Faad felt the wound Gildas had inflicted on him as a mark of allegiance to Tarentess. He will not let me go Faad thought.

Giandra touched the scar and Faad instantly felt his flesh freeze beneath it.

"I own you as much as this newly made sorcerer. The stain in his blood flows of the deeper strength which made us all. This barbarian of the north will be easily manipulated by his new strength. Lure him here Faad we shall draw the fire of rage into the air and release it upon the world. It feeds the shadow and lets me bring the warrior closer to its lair."

"They fight for nothing Giandra, so why do they bother?"

"Ah Piotr, do you know why I keep you as a lover?"

"Because you can Giandra. Since when has any Matavian known or understood freedom."

Giandra smiled at his answer.

"True because I can, just as I could with any of our people. But why you Piotr? You are handsome yes, one of our best fighters. You have won many battles against our enemies. Yet none of these reasons matter to me. It is because you see no other way, no hope beyond the approval of disapproval of your masters. You have no vision no sight beyond this instant and seek no glory for yourself only to be allowed to exist one more day because your ruler allows it. It is good, you neither threaten the king and queen and do not resent them either. You ask only to be allowed to live until tomorrow. While the barbarian of the ice and now the ruler of stone seeks a new dawn. He runs to battle not for glory but in hope that there is something better. There is nothing to say there is and all sense will say it is only death he pursues. But they see something else beyond the rule of their master. While their vision is not clear it is this hope that urges them to fight and not lie down to accept the judgement of their masters. Servants are of no use to a ruler if they desire something else besides them. It causes division in the hearts of their people and threatens to unseat their loyalty from their king and queen. Death or nothing Faad this is what I see in your heart, and you sit waiting for me to say which one is your meal for today."

"I would not be Matavian to be any other way."

"I know and now you will lure the warrior here and I will play with the fire in his flesh. I will bring the children to me, and we shall seek out the shadow in its lair. Once there I will bargain with them all for my right to rule."

Faad got up and went to the water bath. He splashed his face and looked in the polished metal mirror. He saw his withered grey flesh. I am being eaten alive like those children of hers. Was there a time Matavian when you knew freedom? He touched the scar once more of Tarentess. Is this where my hope lies in a tyrant of stone and ice. He smiled at his fate. Once again, I will do my master's work and not dare to wonder who I am and why is it I am here at all.

The Queen rose and went to the cradle where Noab slept. She placed him inside it. His blood power flowed with the strands of history that drove the shadow now to destroy this world.

She looked across the bay through the window and saw herself sitting above the ocean and lands. She was staring directly at the sun and knew the same spirit lay in her warring cursed heart.

"Father watch your daughter now and see how she will conquer the charm of change, the sea and land and skies above. Desert Dweller and mother, where are you? Your child calls to you. Can you hear him cry in the doom of night and another hopeless dawn? Come to him. He sorrows for his kin. You have abandoned your child. Come."

Giandra felt the terror bloom in Tessi's mind as she thrust the images of Noab screaming into his mother's dreams.

Faad strode in and saw the red glow around the Queen.

"I will tell the Northmen to meet us on the Vale of death. I will ready the soldiers for battle. We will have the advantage on the vale as they descend. The ones not killed will be easily captured. They need our ships, but we will weaken them so that they will become our captives."

"Good. I will ensure Gildas pursues me."

"I do not understand why they did not take the land bridge made from the ports of Hosiaan?"

"Gildas seeks revenge, his lust drives him as does mine. He also knows the blood of the desert dwellers flows in these babes, and it is the shadow who wants those last fleeting threads of power to be consumed as well. We are the same beasts Gildas and I. It will be a battle who shall rule in the end. He will try to protect the younglings from Voloc, but it will be in vain."

"Gildas will destroy this place when he understands our scheme."

"Yes, Piotr he will, but we are on the dawn of a new age and it inevitable that some things must die for the new to be born. Besides would you miss the walls of this palace so terribly much? Lure Gildas here we will weaken his forces and while he is distracted with rage and destruction, I will take the children." Giandra stroked her lover's cheek. He felt the drop of blood form and run down his cheek.

"Why not escape with the concubine and her babies before the westerners and graanar arrive. It will make no difference to have Gildas here if you have ensorcelled the girl to bring her child to you? Is this not your desire to barter them with this demon?"

"Piotr, the shadows do not run deep within you, my love. You do not understand power and its many faces. One thing is certain that Gildas' failure to maintain his rule was his blind fury. It killed his wife and son, and it will give victory to me. He will not hesitate to thrust his sword into me. Seeing me escape with those babes will ensure he chases directly to Voloc's den to seek one more chance to kill me and if possible Voloc. It will bring the strongest potency of the blood covenant together in one place between Gildas and the desert dwellers for me to draw upon so I may steal the jewel from Voloc. It will be sweet also to twist a thorn into this raw spot and watch his agony at the sight of my escape with the younglings to remind him once more of his failure. Ever he seeks redemption for the death of his son by his hand."

Faad did not answer. He knew the might of Gildas sword and the clutch of the demon in his mind. The Queen would not gain victory over either of them, but the pleasure of violence and relentless warring bound him to follow her schemes.

# 3

# Tarentess

Tessi sat with Angette bouncing on her knee. Her shrill giggles of delight rang through the empty chambers of the Keep but were quickly lost as they floated out into the clouds surrounding the mountain. The alert brown eyes of the baby saw Gildas climb up over the edge into the entrance along with Tyl and Axl. She squealed with excitement at seeing them. She reached for the large graanar as they stood heaving from the long climb up.

Gildas nodded at Tessi and the child. He was in a good mood pleased that they had returned from their scouting trip without any skirmishes.

Tyl threw some pheasants down on the floor while Axl and Gildas arranged large bundles of twigs and branches to make a fire.

Nekoda and Kado wandered over when they heard the arrival of the three clansmen.

"What news Gildas?"

Gildas sat down on the opposite side to Tessi and began to make a pipe. Nekoda wandered over and sat next to him.

Kado rolled his eyes waiting impatiently for an answer.

"The claws of the eagle and vulture has spread far and wide. But more so the forests of Vran have been razed to the ground. The scums of Matavia are still trying to flush out the rest of the Westerlings from Aeserea and your people seem to fare no better."

"I must journey east to the Feet of Jun. I know there will be allies there we can use. What of your people? The shadow's poison begins to work its way north Gildas. If the Icelands melt then not even the great peaks of Tarentess will hold the ocean that will flow south, drowning all in its wake."

"Ay Prince, I see all that you see but we need to be strong to confront the demon."

"Something thwarts the demon though; all would be smoke and ashes by now had the beast been able to draw the power from within the jewel. Has this place revealed any secrets to defeating the enemy?" asked Kado.

Gildas blew a few curls of smoke from his pipe. Angette crawled over to him mesmerised by the patterns formed from each puff. She balanced herself on his massive thigh and reached up wanting to catch the wisps of smoke as they disappeared. Gildas helped her nestle into his lap as he continued to look out across the clouds.

"We need to conquer this little battle first Prince. Girl you can stay here until our fates are decided. I think even if the lands around us begin to fall into ruin, then the places of these spirits will be the last standing and will remain our refuge."

"What of my son, Noab? The Queen will kill him as she did her own."

"I need the Matavians on side and do not wish for two battles. It will weaken our forces. When the chance presents itself we will pull him from the clutches of the Queen."

Tessi got up trying not to burst into tears again. She picked up Angette off Gildas' lap.

"What if he is dead already? What if a chance does not come?"

"Do you feel it in your heart mother that your son is gone?" asked Gildas.

She hesitated not expecting the clansman to say that.

"No."

She stormed off to where her litter lay. Angette began to cry wanting to go back to Gildas, but Tessi wrapped her into a swaddling clothe and lay down with her. She knew the great iceman was her only hope of saving Noab and staying alive, but the terror that would rise in her heart whenever she thought of her son in the Queen's arms made her want to run there now and save him. Angette still struggled wanting to go back to Gildas, but Tessi hugged her even more closely

Soon the smell of roasting pheasant and fish smoking filled the chamber. Kado went to see if Tessi wanted something to eat but he saw they were both asleep and left them.

"We need to meet with the leaders of the lands of the west and the Graanar. We will bring them here and form our alliances" spoke Gildas.

"Should we risk showing them this place, remember it was only at the invite of the spirits that we have this sanctuary" replied Kado.

"Ay but I see no other way. The secrets of this place were shown to me. I will not bring the banner of the eagle here. To reveal the secrets laid bare to us will bind the Graanar and Westerners more strongly as a show of trust. This Lord Jiang, will he be easy to persuade to follow our lead or will he want his own glory first?"

"Lord Jiang could be persuaded but as with all these men, they are not fools, and my father was a tyrant rather than a ruler. He did not inspire true loyalty and kinship. There may be bloodshed. But you have my word that once I am restored as the heir, I will follow you into battle Gildas."

"Then it is settled. We will bring Jarrod and the Aeserean generals to the Keep.'"

"But how graanar?" asked Tyl.

"I have been thinking about that. Time presses too quickly for us to send for them with scouts and they will not come without some persuasion."

Tessi silently came out from the darkened area of the chamber with Angette. Her eyes were still red from crying, but she saw the food and felt ravenous.

"Here Tessi."

Kado gave her some slices of breast meat on a thin slab of granite. She smiled tentatively at the prince. Angette squirmed restless. Tessi put her down and she went straight to Gildas. He scooped her up in the crook of his arm as he took another leg of the bird.

"You have found another place for you graanar when this battle is finished; a wet nurse for the clan wives who have dried up" chided Axl.

"Hmph."

Gildas finished eating and walked toward the chamber where the basin stood. Nekoda followed him and Angette cooed in his arm playing with a leather choker he wore around his neck. He touched the rock wall until it began to tremble revealing the passageway into the secret chamber.

The well stood as silent as the stone it lay in. Gildas went to it and tilted Angette forward to peer into the mirrored surface. It rippled just slightly and formed the face of another child. Gildas guessed it was the boy Noab.

He stared into it "Is the child alive?"

An image formed of a child in a bassinette. Near him stood the Queen of Matavia rocking it ever so gently while she stared out the window across the Bay of Tears. Gildas noticed in the far horizon a red glow in the sky towards the south.

He pulled away and chucked Angette under the chin. "Your brother lives."

Angette giggled and continued to chew on the leather knot in the choker around his neck.

He looked again and this time a face formed of an eagle. "Come to your brethren's roost."

He turned away and took Angette back to Tessi.

"Your son lives mother."

"Did you see him in your magic well? Can I see him?"

"Only I may look into the basin of Norbu. But believe me your son lives."

"Thankyou" whispered Tessi.

"Believe this too mother when the time is ripe, the Queen's blood will paint the walls of her white palace."

Tessi smiled at Gildas' gesture of revenge but inwardly she shivered at the ferocity of the world which surrounded her.

The sky slowly darkened as the night fell. Just briefly the clouds separated showing the ice laden northern reaches. The black line that snaked its way through the white had become so large that the ocean beneath could be seen in places. Gildas smoked his pipe as he waited in the dark keeping watch.

Men will not be enough he thought as the image of the massive opening in the icesheets came back to him. It was like a python eating its way across the face of Arglethium.

Kado came over to him unable to sleep.

"I am keen to begin my journey Gildas. I cannot linger here indefinitely."

"I know Prince, leave when you wish. When it is time to draw out the demon we shall meet again and die in battle together."

"Yes, I agree, I do not think men will defeat this thing Gildas, more than just us will be needed."

"Ay, the girl lives but she is not in this world. But I fear that her battle will be harder and longer to endure then ours. When you leave which path will you take?"

"I will follow the feet of the mountains directly east."

"There is another refuge like this one. It was the water spirit's Keep. A mighty serpent came to us there. It spoke to us and told us to look for allies in the sky and water. It may be better to head there and then East across the bridge made from the ruins of your city. It will be dangerous to venture along the trader route. It is overrun."

"All will be needed Gildas. Where is this place found?"

"It lies at the base of the great valley in the northern most tip of the Forests of Vran. It appears these woodlands are protected as the fires of the Matavians did not spread there. The Keep's entrance is found at the end of the stream where the trees become so dense that the sun never enters there. Call for Vipax."

"Where I go my father kept a wealth of weaponry and supplies in case he ever needed to lie in siege against another enemy. But it may still not be enough. I will send word once I have seen this cache for myself."

"I would spare Tyl and Axl, but I will need them to rally the graanar."

"I need to do this on my own Gildas. I plan to wield the sceptre of the Dragon when I meet the demon on the battlefield. If I cannot win back what is rightfully mine, then what use am I to you?"

"Ay that is true Prince."

"If there is not enough hidden in my father's armoury, what will we do for battle gear? The Matavians cannot be trusted. They are in legion with the demon and will stand with it."

"I bide my time with that scum until the girls' child can be taken. I know where I can find more blades and arrows. Even that witch that bought us all into this war told me her brethren, these custodians, were not unmerciful."

"What else did you see when you went below?"

"We saw the Unstaadt soldiers and Matavians heading south. Not only this, your people Kado, and desert dwellers like the girl and Westerlings, were being forced onto those ships south. We will go to battle against our own who are enslaved. It shall be the free fighting the captured. How would you kill one of your own?"

"Cunning!" Kado thumped his hand against the rock wall. "Will the Graan follow you? Will Jarrod bring all the clans to fight with you?"

"I have a thousand already loyal that lie now in the Vale below preparing for battle. I will bring Jarrod here and show him what is needed. If they choose not to fight, then we will go to battle without them. At least we can die as honourable men, eh."

"I will leave on the dawn. Will you remain here? How will I send message?"

"Let me think on these things Kado. I have never waged war against a demon before. Even I never knew how to fight me. Much needs to be considered" Gildas half smiled at the prince as he settled in again to keep watch. "Rest Kado Ko Drax. I want to see the banner of the Dragon above your head as much as you."

The dawn crept into the Keep slowly. Angette was the first to greet it along with Nekoda. The dim rays reached inside the Keep just enough to illuminate the throne of Norbu. As it did so it cast a silhouette of five eagles roosting on its headrest and arms along the western side of the chamber.

Nekoda barked when it saw the Orynth asleep on the throne which roused everyone. Gildas got up first. He had fallen asleep and had not heard their arrival. Kado, Tessi, Tyl and Axl gazed in awe, astounded at the birds and their size. Suddenly the eagles spread their wings to their full span and began to transform into the Orynth. Tessi gasped in fright and fled behind Tyl.

"Do not draw your weapons brothers, they mean no harm" Gildas commanded. He knelt on one knee with his sword laid flat on the ground. He motioned for the others to do the same.

"Mighty brethren and servants to Norbu, welcome back to the throne of your father. I trust your grief for the death of YU has waned and your hearts have healed."

"Yes, they have Ice Lord and much has passed in the time of our mourning. Rise you are not our servants nor are we your masters."

EY walked towards Gildas and then began to inspect the others.

"You have the same scent as the other, from the desert, you are her kin. She lies elsewhere now."

Tessi looked at the large bird god with questioning eyes but was too afraid to ask out loud if it knew where Ange was.

"Have you seen the girl gifted with the jewel of the gods?" asked Gildas.

"Nay it is not shown to us these things and Voloc's shroud ever blinds us."

EY stood in front of Tyl and Axl. It was a head taller than the graanar. "You are like the Ice Lord; fierce in your brow and feathers."

The clansmen stood back perturbed that such creatures existed. They sensed the hidden strength that belied the gentle speech and soft plumage.

"Dragon master, one such as you have never walked with the Orynth."

"No indeed we have not, magnificent one. I am Kado Ko Drax of the Ko Dynasty. Are you here to aid us in this dark hour that faces all creatures that tread this world?"

"We were summoned for a reason and in doing so a sacrilege has occurred. Did we not warn you Ice Lord?"

EY looked at Gildas. The other Orynth bristled as well with breasts puffed out and legs spread apart defensively.

"The god gave me permission, the god of our spirits and when all stands on the abyss of ruin, we have been abandoned by these gods to finish this battle begun against the demon. I have been granted leave to seek a path to victory. My blood now flows with the blood of the earth from my blade born of Norbu's well. I have been given stewardship of this Keep until the mighty Lord returns and throws me from its heights.'

XI came towards Gildas and pecked him on the cheek. He tightened his grip on the blade but did not lift it for he needed these creatures to help them.

"Understand the blood of the earth now calls to me and not that of the Ice Mother. I could no more walk away from here and this battle that stands before me than my own skin."

"We must defend this most sacred place. It cannot be usurped by a clayborn unless sanctioned by the power of Norbu."

EY stepped forward and pecked Gildas on the cheek but with such force that his cheek bone was exposed.

Gildas reacted by hefting his sword to EY's breastbone.

"The Orynth cannot forsake their Lord and brethren now or ever."

"Ay so it must be" Gildas threatened.

"Only you, and all of us" provoked EY.

"Gildas you cannot. They will tear you to shreds" warned Kado.

Gildas looked at Axl and Tyl and then Tessi and Kado. Nekoda whined in anticipation of what was to come.

"This is the least of what we will endure in the days ahead. I need these creatures to fight for us and I must prove to them that I have been granted rule of the sacred well of Norbu. Take the child and mother Kado and shield them from this."

Kado grabbed Tessi and Angette "Come this is something Gildas must do."

Tessi ran to Gildas "Remember Noab, his life rests on you."

"That and more; I do not forget."

"Orynth, I ask one boon if I am to be defeated and thrown from the heights of this Keep, that this girl and her children may have sanctuary until the fate of the fate of the world is decided."

"So, it shall be" responded XI.

Axl and Tyl stood away from Gildas as he and the Orynth took their stance ready to battle. He gripped the sword and felt its energy surge into him lighting the Keep with its rays. EY flew at him in the flicker of an eye and thrust Gildas into the wall of rock. He rebounded off it but keeping his footing he turned with a wide sweeping arc connecting with EY's arm. PO, AX and VA stood behind Gildas sending a barrage of punches and blows at the clansman until he was too winded to stand. XI stood over him and taking his head in his winged hands, he pulled Gildas up and threw him towards the entrance of the cavern. EY clawed at his face and torso, Gildas tried to deflect the blows with his sword managing to dislodge feathers and flesh from the powerful creature. Amongst the feathers and screeches from the Orynth, Axl and Tyl went to his side to defend him.

"Nay graanar, stand down. I am not defeated yet."

Standing he raised the sword of Norbu and gestured for the Orynth to come to him.

EY gripped the blade of the sword and twisting it down to the ground almost snapping Gildas elbow.

"By the strength of Norbu I will defeat thee!"

He managed to release the sword and bring it to full arc and down onto the Orynth, but EY shot forward and grabbed Gildas by the chest to thrust him off the ledge. Gildas seeing what the creature was going to do he twisted his leg into that of EY's causing them to tumble from the Keep. Instantly EY's wings unfolded controlling the free fall. The others followed as EY darted back and forth trying to dislodge the clansman, but Gildas thrust his sword into EY's shoulder stopping him from letting go of the Orynth. As they broke through the layer of cloud cover, the icy blast of the northern lands hit them. Gildas could see the white of the ice coming towards them closer. VA caught them and attempted to reef them apart, but Gildas was latched to the sword stuck firmly into EY. Suddenly they were on the ground. Gildas stumbled and pulled the sword out. VA, XI and PO grabbed him from behind as AX and EY came towards him with talons bared to slice open his belly.

Gildas placed the blade into the ice and shouted through the maelstrom of the snow around them "Mother of the ice pour your power into your forsaken son. I ask this now through the gift of your sacred brethren Norbu."

AX swiped at Gildas chest and exposed the flesh just near his heart. EY transformed back into an eagle and flying directly at Gildas with talons ready began to flay the skin off his chest.

"Ice Mother I plead to thee!"

Suddenly the sword flared into life, he wrenched it out of the ground and with three swift strokes a spray of blood and feathers lay on the snow as all five of the Orynth were cut, not lethally, but enough to show who wielded the might of Norbu.

"Come brothers, darker days and longer battles lie ahead. Do you concede?"

EY stood and then bowed to Gildas.

"You have shown that the favour of the earth now lies in your hand and blood. The mighty Norbu has sanctioned you."

AX, PO, VA, XI and EY all pecked Gildas on the cheek as a mark of camaraderie. Blood dripped from all of them, including Gildas.

VA took Gildas and lifted him back up into the air.

"Before we go back to the Keep, take me to the place where the ice has broken."

VA flew across the skies with such speed that the snow began to sting Gildas. He began to shiver as the cold seeped into his skin.

"There! Take me down."

VA alighted just on the edge of the chasm that had formed in the ice sheet. Gildas and VA were completely dwarfed by the width and the size of the cliffs that reached all the way down to the black ocean.

Gildas could barely see the water crashing against the icy walls. Further along he saw two large white shapes floating in the current.

"Brethren, take me down there."

VA lifted him again and effortlessly took him to where the shapes were floating. As he neared them, he saw they were the large white fish that the clans hunted in the eastern oceans. The graanar called them the Ice bears of the ocean. Rammed in between them were two fishing boats; they still had the bodies of graanar in them. All over the bodies of the fish and the men were pustules. The plague had begun to reach the northern lands.

"Take me back to the Keep."

A thundering crack resounded across the chasm as a mountain size chunk of the cliff face fell into the waters. It sent a tsunami of water over the fish and the boats forcing them under the surface of the ocean forever.

"Rest in the claws of the Ice Mother graanar" called Gildas as VA took him away towards the Keep.

VA gently dropped Gildas onto the floor of the cavern. Immediately Tyl and Axl went to him to inspect any wounds. Gildas began to shiver uncontrollably. Tessi fetched his cloak and offered it to him.

"Ay, mother."

"I will get a fire going" she spoke.

Gildas nodded at Tessi as she busily gathered the twigs for the fire.

The Orynth stood in front of Norbu's throne, their chests were puffed out and their plumage and wings were preened to a smooth glistening affect. It was as if the battle had never happened.

Nekoda thinking that they were going to attack again stood in front of Gildas snarling.

"We now begin our time without our honourable brethren, Norbu and YU. The Orynth stand in league and service with the Iceman known as Gildas the great, surrogate bearer of the blood of the earth and most precious rock and stone that stands here; Tarentess, Keep of Norbu. New memories shall be scored into the hearts and legends of the Orynth from this moment. To battle the shadow called Voloc. To prepare for a mighty clash that will test feather and flesh."

All the Orynth screeched their allegiance inside the Keep and across the skies.

"Mighty warriors I only ask that the sky and turf you have guarded and fought for since the beginning days, which lives and dies only because of this world's existence be defended once more alongside us, the ignorant ones but who are made of the same dirt and stone as the Orynth."

EY strode forward and Gildas raised his sword. EY grasped the sword as well and both he and Gildas felt the energy bond them as blood brothers. EY's brindle feathers shimmered with golds and rich ambers as the power of the sword flowed through it.

Gildas sat down before the fire trying to warm himself. Kado staunched the bleeding from the wounds using an undershirt to make a bandage.

"I call a war council to begin our path forward to defeat the demon called Voloc."

Suddenly a squawk came from PO. Tessi ran over quickly and grabbed Angette. In her chubby hands she held a clump of sleek black feathers.

"I am sorry" spoke Tessi as she scooped Angette away. PO bowed slightly not saying anything.

"I have seen a great sadness befall my lands. Below not only does the ice begin to break but the plague that ravaged the eastern deserts now afflicts the Graan and the great fish that dwell in the Eastern Oceans. The poison of the demon spreads."

Tyl and Axl, bristled "Our clansman Gildas?"

"Ay, graanar, no time can be lost now. We must rally all the peoples that remain free of the yoke of Voloc, hunt the demon and destroy it. Orynth the reason I have asked you here is firstly to assist us in bringing the leaders of the free lands to this Keep. To show them they must join us in this battle and fight. I want the Queen and General of Aeserea and Elder Chieftains of the Graan to be bought to this Keep. Here we will form a treaty to unite and go to battle against the demon's legions. Orynth we will need your wings to bring them here, even if they resist. They must be shown the truth of our world and the things that have lain hidden to our eyes."

"What of the Matavians?" asked Kado.

"I place no real hope or aid on their treacherous shoulders. I have seen their ships laden with weapons and slaves, captured to send to the south to defend the Keep of this demon. It may well be, we will have two enemies to fight. I think this Captain Faad and Queen desire their own rule now that Ranik is dead, and this desire fools them into thinking they will rule the demon. But I will attempt parlay with them as we proceed south. Perhaps the bond I placed on the captain will keep another battle at bay. Prince will you wait until this meet takes place or will you depart before?"

"You have my allegiance Gildas. I will depart on the morn and begin uniting my Kingdom. If I may ask a boon of these magnificent creatures, that they could carry me some of the way to the edge of the Forest of Vran, to hasten my journey."

"We will aid you in this request" replied EY.

"I also ask that three of the Orynth take Tyl and go to the lands of my people to bring Jarrod, Polax and Olac of Clotte here" spoke Gildas.

"What of the other chieftains Gildas?" asked Axl, slightly disappointed at not being asked to go.

"The other clans will follow these three chieftains, Axl. I will need you to go with the other two Orynth to find the Queen of Aeserea and her General."

Axl nodded with a grin on his face, excited about flying in the air with one of the bird gods.

The chamber began to darken as night approached. Tessi, Nekoda and Angette sat near the fire listening to it all. Angette played with the feathers from PO's leg. Tessi fingered one of them amazed at their silkiness. She felt a small kernel of hope rise in her chest at the sight of these creatures. Perhaps they had not been completely abandoned.

"It is decided then, all shall leave on the dawn. Kado be safe and strong. Remember the Keep of the water spirit. Tell the serpent that the Well of Norbu has been entrusted to one whose flesh runs with the blood of Arglethium."

Taking the sword Gildas nicked a cut in the palm of his hand and then Kado's.

"You walk with the brethren of Tarentess now Prince. The serpent will smell it."

Kado nodded as he looked at Gildas. He saw that the clansman's skin had begun to change resembling the slate rock of the Keep.

# 4

# Homage to Vran

Nene sat upon the rock quietly stitching a soldier's torn tunic. She had managed to remove most of the blood stains from the front, but some remained leaving light brown shadows on the yellow and green cloth. Nene had stopped shedding tears over the loss of her Kingdom and her brothers, but her heart remained heavy with grief and bitterness. The hatred that would well in her heart whenever another of her soldiers lay dead at the feet of Lioness, was more potent than the venom of the snakes that lived in the forest of Vran. Bile rose in her throat from the anger at the destruction of the sacred trees and animals.

"My lady, I have finished these" spoke Jocelyn.

"Good, I am almost finished dear and then can you take them to the southern entrance. There are scouts ready to deliver them to the battle fields in the western territories."

"We have almost run out of thread, my lady."

"I know. I will begin sorting the tunics and trousers from the pile over there. We can repair what is not too worn and use the others to pull the thread and re-weave it."

Nene looked at the uniforms and thought of all the soldiers that they had been taken from. Then the memory of her dead brothers by the hands of those beasts came to her. She squeezed her hands together making the wounds of her fingers reopen and bleed. She looked at them; she had worn her flesh to the bone washing Draved's blood from the rock where he had fallen. She was so engulfed in her grief Jocelyn had had to pull her off when her own blood began to mingle with Draved's.

"This is an annihilation" she spoke to herself as she began to bind the open blisters on her fingers again.

A scream followed by a group of young attendants running through the entrance on the western side of the grove roused her from her thoughts. A high-pitched whine echoed into the vault of the grove. It was familiar to her. Then it came again. Nene stood her heart beating fast.

"It cannot be."

She ran towards the entrance, almost tripping over in her haste. As she sprinted along the ledge the large dirty yellow head poked through the entrance.

"Ushan my pet."

The large cat snarled at first but then tentatively walked towards the queen. Nene got down on her haunches and waited for her beloved pet come to her. Then behind Ushan came four more cats equally as ragged and run down by the battle fields they had so valiantly defended.

Ushan sat down in front of Nene, winking at her in a gesture of friendliness. Nene threw herself forward and sobbed heavily as the lioness licked her hair. The smell of rotten flesh in the lion's breath almost made her pass out.

"Goodness, you have feasted well Ushan."

The other lions meandered their way down to the stream to drink. The servants and villagers stood around the ledges at a safe distance as the lions made themselves at home in the sanctuary dedicated to their kind.

"It is ok people; they will not attack you. Let them be, this is the home of their sacred mother. This is an omen, I am sure. The Lioness sees our suffering and tells us she is watching over us."

As reassuring as Nene's words were intended to be no one moved from the safety of the ledges.

"Come Ushan."

Nene led the great cat towards the pool to sit with the others. They snarled as she neared them, but Ushan quietened them with a roar.

"Jocelyn, fetch me some soap so I can wash Ushan."

Jocelyn stood frozen not wanting to go near the cats.

"Hurry girl."

Coming back, she threw the soap to the Queen and bowed apologetically. Nene sat near the lion as she scrubbed the fur stiff with blood and gore.

"I will send a message to the General to find a Lion seer to come and tend to you all."

Nene knew the Lions would grow hungry again and may not wish to go out to feed.

Once she had finished cleaning Ushan, Nene went back to her grotto writing messages and edicts to send by kites to battle. Ushan and her pride had moved to higher ground on a ledge halfway up the mountain wall and were basking in the moonlight as it streamed into the grove.

Nene was concerned with two of the messages she had received from a scout to the north. A large contingent of the northern graanar had been seen sparring in what appeared to be readying for battle. They could not afford another enemy. Then the other message came from the coast telling of the villagers being herded onto ships in chains. *"The Matavian soldiers are frenzied like dogs with rabies, nothing can thwart them. No treaty will be forged with them."* were the last words written on the scroll.

She did not want to relinquish her lands, but she risked the local people being forced into slavery if they continued to try and fight. If they withdrew then at least some of the people could be saved. Nene finished writing to Cotus requesting he return for parlance. Never in the history of the Aesearean Kingdom had they witnessed such brutality and lust for destruction. There were no allies to be had, the Ko Kingdom had fallen, the desert lands, too far anyway, had succumbed to a plague and the northern ice clans were belligerent to all but their own.

Nene sighed heavily knowing what she must do but not wishing to; to relinquish their lands and live like cave folk until the Aeserean people could rise again.

She thought of her grandfather after he had returned from battle with Matavia over the land of Irasia. He had taken her on his knee.

"You know the Matavians and Aeserean's descend from the same sires. Two brothers who had been loyal to each other until a feud over a woman began. To quell the hatred and jealousy each felt for the other, their father divided the Kingdom of Westron into Matavia and Aeserea and Irasia. The King retired to rule the territory of Irasia and left the sons to rule their lands as they wished. Since that time, the two peoples have always been at war with one another."

Nene remembered saying we must descend from the fairer son, for we are kinder to our people.

Her grandfather said yes it was that brother the Princess wanted not the other. He also warned that both brothers were prone to vanity and let their desire to rule bring war many times between the two lands.

Nene attached the scrolls to the kite requesting Cotus return. She lay down on her bed and hoped her dreams would be restful or at least give her answers about what to do.

More soldiers arrived over the following days. The dead ones began to fill the crypts to where no more could be buried there. Cotus was on his way, a lion seer had been found with relief as it was growing more difficult keeping Ushan and her family away from the sick and dying. The lions were coaxed into a grove smaller and secluded which could be blocked. Food was left every day to keep the great cats appetites satisfied.

Nene would go there to think with her pets and pray to the Lioness to help defeat the brutality that now subjugated them to living in caves. She heard Cotus arrive on one of these days she had been contemplating all the problems that now beset Aeserea. His great booming voice echoed through the tunnel into the new dwelling place of Ushan. Her heart and mood lifted hearing the great Knight of the Aeserean Throne arrive.

She stood, her hair was barely kept in place now and her dresses were thread bare.

She took the sash from around her waist and tied it around Ushan's neck. She regally strolled through the tunnel and into the sunlit sanctuary to greet her Knight.

"My Lady"

Cotus Medret bowed deeply seeing his Queen and her beloved pet.

"My General, is it not a good omen that the great cats of Aeserea have returned to us?"

"My lady, I believe that at least it shows the ferocity and tenacity of the Aeserean spirit to keep fighting an enemy which can only be described as a wraith from the underlands."

"We will go to the Den of Ushan and speak in solitude. Jocelyn, do we have something to offer our Lord Knight?"

"I think so my lady" the girl ran off to fetch some food as Nene led the soldier to the entrance.

Once seated Nene sat stroking Ushan as she perched herself on a boulder. Cotus looked at the other lions lying above them and then checked how far the entrance was to the den.

"How bad is it Cotus?"

"We are defeated but not completely destroyed. I have ordered all the remaining soldiers to withdraw to the wild lands of the west provinces. They are to rally the townsfolk as they go and take them with them until this war ends or our lives. The coast lies almost deserted as the remaining people are enslaved and sent on ships to the south."

"To what purpose is this enslavement? What lies in the south that draws the Matavians there? Any wealth from the soil and rocks lies with the Drax Lands, which they lay claim against now anyway?"

"I do not know my Lady, we managed to capture a General, but he gutted himself before he would speak. One thing though he laid allegiance to the Queen of Matavia and not Ranik. I have heard rumours from the men that Ranik was killed by an enemy wielding great power."

"Cotus, are you aware that a thousand Graan sit in the valley west of Doanda. I still do not know if they mean harm or not, for they have been there for many moons and do not seem to make any posture of aggression towards us or the Matavians."

The knight got up and stretched his back. His mind raced. What was happening? They had all but lost their territory and now existed as bandits in the dark mountain caves.

"This is grave news my lady. I do not know. We are defeated and another battle with those barbarians will see the end of us all."

He sat with shoulders slumped. The mighty soldier, veteran of many battles and victories looked old to his Queen's eyes. Nene went to him and spoke.

"I have not seen complete shadow in my dreams, a small glimmer of light remains in the darkness. We need to find a way to it."

"They are pretty words my queen, meant to inspire hope but I have faced many enemies, and none have I seen such as this. The general we captured, just as he took his last breath, he looked at me with eyes that were redder than the blood that flowed from his body."

"What of these Graan? They are enemies of Ranik as much as us. Could we not ask them for alliance?"

"Hmm, I will need to consider this. I cannot see the Graan being willing to fight for the Matavians, and they hardly need them. Argh, it's like the world turned upside in its last throes of life."

Jocelyn came into the grove with a plate of food for the Knight. He accepted it graciously.

"This has just arrived as well, my lady and lord."

She handed Nene a scroll. The kite sat in a cage with a green piece of cloth tied around its leg. It was used to guide the birds to their destiny, a scent to follow.

Nene unrolled it and read it quietly. Cotus threw Ushan some scraps. The great cat ate them in one gulp.

Nene stood and handed the soldier the message.

*"A parlance is requested by those who are avowed enemies of the banner of the Eagle and demon that now walks this world. We seek the Queen of Aeserea and her Knight General. The Keeper of Tarentess."*

"Is it the light we have been seeking Cotus?"

"Or is it a trap to flush us out of our sanctuary?" he replied.

"Tarentess, I have never heard of this place. The demon though, it may be as we thought. My dreams have been filled with those red eyes that you spoke of Cotus. I think we must take the chance and meet this Keeper of Tarentess. It is the twilight of the Aeserean Kingdom, what choice do we have?"

"Let me rest this eve and I will decide by the dawn."

Cotus saw the scrawl on the message and noticed the lettering. It was that of the Graan script. The distinctive curl and dots above the letters 'a', something the common trader tongue, the native tongue of Aeserea, never used. Perhaps these Graan in the valley north of them were here to seek to allegiance. Cotus had heard rumours of the battle that had seen the death of Ranik. Was this Keeper the enemy that had slain the tyrant?

He looked at the stars in the sky and for the first time the Knight General pined for the days of his retirement from the service to the throne and spend his days with his beloved mare. He had always wanted to explore the eastern lands more. To see the riches delved out of the ground and beautiful silks of the lands of the Dragon. But instead, the end of his life was to die slowly as a renegade and brigand in a mountain keep. The Queen was right, what choice did they have but to meet this unknown suzerain of Tarentess. It would not be long before the Queen would altogether descend into insanity. The death of her brothers and the loss of her throne had been too much for her and had finally caused her iron will to crack. The last message he had received from her, the one meant to summon him here, spoke of the legends of long ago, and fairy tales told to children against the Matavians. That was when he sent the order to withdraw to safety. Lord Warick was to lead the people and soldiers away and act as protectorate until further orders came.

"You will be remembered as a wise and fair but formidable ruler of the Aeserean people, my Queen, but I fear that you will be the last" he whispered in the silent moonlight.

Cotus Medret managed to find sleep and this time his dreams were of him running freely on his mare towards the cowering faces of their eternal enemy.

Upon the dawn he was woken by the growls of Nene's lions feasting on another deer. The Queen herself was busily sorting out trousers and tunics into separate piles and then instructing a group of servants to begin pulling threads from another heap.

"Ah Knight General, I hope you are rested. Jocelyn, bring some porridge for his Lord."

"I am my lady. What is this?"

"We will salvage what we can and use the rest as yarn to repair it."

Cotus nodded but thought it was all in vain, there would be soon more clothes than soldiers.

"When you have eaten and washed, I will meet with you in Ushan's den."

On entering the den, he saw Nene darning a tunic, her fingers had begun to bleed again and were staining the material. He went to her and got down on one knee and took away the tunic and the needle and thread. Taking her hands, he looked her.

"You have been my ruler and friend as was your father before you. But I fear my Lady our lands are gone and the kingdom we have both cherished lies in a shadow so deep that it no longer feels the kiss of the sun or the stroke of the morning breeze. I see your wisdom even in this time of your fragile wearied mind. We will meet this Keeper of Tarentess and if it is a trap then we shall pay our homage to the great Vran and then this Keeper of the unknown shall feel our blades in his flesh. Instruct your people to barricade the grove after we leave. Send a message to this Keeper that we will meet on the morrow at the Field of Vran. It is open and all paths lead away from this place. We will see for many leagues any enemy coming and if needed then we can flee to the labyrinth of mountain paths which border the grasslands."

Tears streamed down Nene's eyes as she nodded. Then suddenly she shot forward and hugged the huge knight fiercely.

"I have lost my father's Kingdom and now I am losing my mind. You know if I had ever taken a husband, it would have been you. But I could see that your heart always lay in the battlefield and it was this devotion that made our throne and kingdom remain strong. I feared if I made you choose between your soldiers and me that perhaps it would have weakened the kingdom and lessened you. Cotus, I will follow wherever you lead and know that more than my gratitude goes with you."

She lay on Medret's shoulder her sobs racking her body. He gently pried her off unsure of what to say.

"My lady..."

They stared at one another not wanting to let this stark fragile moment of truth crumble like the world around them. The Queen pulled away rousing herself.

"It was wrong of me to be so bold, Cotus. But my words are true. I will write the message and instruct the guards. We will be riding I presume. I will need britches to wear."

"Yes, I will gather our supplies."

"You know there is a secret passage that leads to the eastern path of the Field of Vran.'

"Yes, my lady I do."

He took a corner of her apron and dabbed her eyes and face. She winced still from the scars of the creatures that had taken her brother's lives.

"It was more than duty to a crown that made me want to protect you so fiercely my fair lion-hearted Queen."

Nene smiled at the words as she dipped the Lion claw and dipped it into the ink well to write the message.

The moonlight shone on the mare of the Knight as he led them towards the meeting point. They had had been silent most of the way through the maze of passages in the mountain. Nene felt embarrassed by her words to Cotus but if this was to be the end then it was better he knew her feelings. If not, then he would be honourable and not hold them against her or take advantage either. His words had not surprised her but instead of joy at hearing them a vague regret clouded her heart. She remembered many of the young suitors that had been arranged by her father all seemed fair but of course her need for an equal in her learning and single mindedness seemed to bring out the failings of each of them. Either they would buckle and cower or take it as a challenge that she needed to be controlled in some way. The meanness of one Prince remained in her memory; he had thrashed a servant almost to death for his offence at Nene's refusal to follow his directive on a trade agreement. It was after witnessing this that she had gone to her father.

"I will become Queen but will take no Prince Regent and when I am gone Draved or Dronagh or one of their heirs will assume your crown. I would despair if I were to tarnish the throne with a poor husband or produce an heir that was not worthy."

"Is there no-one daughter that you would take as your husband?"

"There is one father, but to curtail his life to one of standing in my shadow and at my whim would diminish him and with time my love."

None of them compared to Cotus Medret she thought to herself.

"My Lady the fields are just over there upon the rise. We will camp here and wait until our invitee arrives. We will have a clear view while under cover. It is not even a quart turn of the glass til dawn, it is hoped they will not be late."

They unpacked their things and made a camp under two large oaks that towered over thick mulberry bushes and myrtles. They tied the horses to the trees and made them sit down amongst the bushes to remain hidden. The dawn crept slowly, pale with barely any sign of the sun as the clouds seemed to thicken as the day grew. Suddenly they heard voices rise with the dawn.

A group of Unstaadt mercenaries were headed directly towards the trees. Nene and Medret crouched as low as they could and held the horses firmly by their bridles so they would not whinny.

The group stopped just on the other side of the islet of trees. They were making camp.

Cotus rolled his eyes in frustration. He could see through the bushes how close they were. One move and they would be found. Nene stared at him directly shaking her head. She gripped the sword at her side. She could defend herself if needed. She cursed herself for not bringing Ushan; she would have made short work of them. Just then one of the horses sneezed, instantly three massive Unstaadt men came crashing through the thickets.

Cotus drew his blade as did Nene and began to back away out onto the open fields.

"My Lady, they are slow witted these ones, so be quick and deadly with your blows."

Nene nodded her heart thudding in her chest. One of them came at her teasingly saying something in their ugly tongue. His underestimation of her being a woman helped her land a swift jab at his sword arm making him drop his blade. As he stooped to grab it, she thrust her sword down his back and shaved a bit of flesh off his shoulder. Then one of the others grabbed her. She screamed and began to kick trying to get away, but his strength was so great she could not move. She took her blade and slashed wildly managing to cut his leg forcing him to collapse. She whipped around and plunged her sword into his neck.

Cotus was in full thrust and parry with the other heaving soldier. He was making ground on him and soon managed to beat him down and with one final blow decapitated him. The knight saw the last one remaining, roaring he threw himself toward him.

Nene ran to help Medret and then a sight made her heart sink; a dozen more soldiers were running towards them.

"Get your horse Nene. Flee!"

Medret quickly leapt onto his mare.

"Go towards the mountains, we will try and lose them in the passes."

Nene shot off, as her black mare snorted in fear. The Unstaadts were gaining quickly.

They reached a full gallop, but the arrows began to land all around them. One of them caught in the front flank of her mare, laming her so that her gallop became a fast trot. One of the mercenaries seemed to be able to run at an unnatural pace caught her stirrup. She thrashed at him with her blade, Cotus ran his own horse into the man, but he would not let go. Suddenly Nene's horse collapsed throwing her into the air and causing her to land on her back. Cotus lunged down as he neared her.

"Get up now Nene, get on."

Dazed and winded she stood and almost fell over, but Medret grabbed her and hoisted her behind him.

He took off across the fields of Vran hoping to outrun the Unstaadts. It was almost a league to the nearest tunnel into the mountains.

"Hasten wife, let the wind carry you and us together."

He spurred on the great white mare but to no avail as another band of soldiers came from the south towards them; they were a cavalry outfit and could not be outrun.

A hundred warriors of the Vulture swiftly surrounded their prey as it tried to flee. Soon the knight's horse frothed blood at the bit and nostrils. Nene gripped Cotus fiercely not wanting to give up or let go of him.

Suddenly a dark shadow gathered over the racing horses and their quarry. Nene felt something sink into her back and found herself being lifted into the air. She looked down on Cotus and saw a massive eagle pick him up. The eagle held another man in its talons.

With her heart in her throat, she looked up at the feathery underbelly of the creature carrying her. The soldiers below stopped their chase and let off a volley of arrows, but they simply bounced off the plumage of the birds. Catching her breath, she managed to speak.

"Are you the Keeper of Tarentess?"

The bird squawked loudly into the sky.

Nene looked down watching the white mare of the Knight General bolt away unfettered, as the she was carried higher into the clouds.

# 5

# Giants of the Sea

"Heave!" shouted Polax.

Forty graan pulled in unison on the twelve ropes that were attached to the seabear thrashing in the ocean. It was in its death throes, blood mixed with the foam of the wash of the black water.

"Heave!"

The large tail of the fish began to pull up onto the side of the Graanar vessel. The boats were massive and made from the ancient timbers of the forest of Enan; black gnarled wood that had withstood the blizzards of Raajn. Timber that could rise upon the crushing waves in the northern ocean without splintering or rotting. The vessels could last ten generations of the graanar as well as the mighty fish thrashing and biting as it neared its death.

"Tie her up!"

Twenty of the crew ran over to the edge of the ship. Each of them thrusting an iron hook into the white scales. It thrashed in ebbing contortions to release itself but to no avail. Soon the blood that mixed with the black water was greater than what flowed inside the massive fish. The grappling hooks secured the creature to the side of the vessel causing it to right itself against the weight of the seabear on the other side. The hull sunk further into the black water as the sails were unfurled and the graan took their oars to begin the journey back to the shore.

Polax had sailed so far into the reaches of the eastern edges of the ocean that had the light of day ever dawned they would have seen the western lands of Aeserea, but such was the darkness that remained, all the fishers saw was an endless horizon of black ocean and white ice.

"Chief, a storm's gathering to the south."

"Ay, make to the north and we'll wait her out from the tip o' the Teeth."

The waves began to grow larger washing up over the bow of the ship rocking it from side to side so that the carcasses were immersed under the heaving surface with each impact.

"Hold ya, poles. Now heave!"

Polax roared across the ship as a mountain of water came directly toward the bow of the vessel. At its fullest height it dwarfed the mast. Polax gripped the rudder keeping a straight route directly into the slip face of the wave. A surge came as the clansmen in unison stroked together hefting the ship up onto the wave and over it as it crashed down underneath. White frigid foam hit Polax in the face momentarily blinding him.

"Hold em, heave."

The deluges battered them one after another, a dozen times over. As they teetered on the top of the last wave the sound of rolling thunder came with it. Polax could feel it shake the timbers. He almost lost his grip on the rudder as the boat tipped and descended the steep back of the wave. He looked through the spray and a sight ahead made his heart sink. The calmness that followed the last of the waves lasted only a few hundred strokes as the sight of a huge whirlpool met his eyes. He reefed the rudder hard to the east to try and steer around it, but the ferocity of the watery vortex began to drag the boat towards it.

"Release the bear on the western side."

Instantly the clansmen wielded their axes to cut the hooks loose. The ship suddenly shot to the east pulling it away from the maelstrom ahead.

"Now heave, fro, heave, fro, heave."

Polax screamed above the noise of the ocean's tempest as he kept his full weight on the rudder to steer the ship. Up ahead vaguely he saw three massive ice bergs moving towards the hole in the ocean. The current was so great the white behemoths tipped on their side and in equidistant precision began to spin around the edges until their tips hit each other, forming a roof over the centre of the pool.

"The bitch has let go now push forward graanar, a thousand strokes to the teeth. We will find shelter there."

Soon the outcrop of the cliffs that extended into the ocean from the land came into the view. The graan called them the Teeth of Raajn, as they were in fact the end of the claws of White Cliff formed eons ago. For a league, the ice shelf hung over the waves in cloister like formation providing a haven for ships when the ocean raged against itself. They arched around for leagues back onto the western ridges of the Doanda territory.

Polax and his crew eased the vessel in amongst the spires of ice and headed towards a gap in the cliff. The water was calmest here and they could get off the ship and stay in a small clutch of huts built for times like this. Above them, for almost a league extending towards the sky was the edge of their homelands. Polax watched as the bow of the ship gently glided in amongst the spires. A shrill crack pierced the sky above them. The graanar watched in the distance the great icebergs sink beneath the surface and into the funnel of the maelstrom.

"What makes the seas so angry, Polax? I have never seen the great bergs be eaten in one bite before" called Chalo the chief of oars.

"Nay, neither have I Chalo."

Suddenly the loud cracking sound broke the sky just above them and with it the vortex of another whirlpool formed just ahead of them. Out of the centrifuge of the current came the icebergs with such force they were rammed up and into the cliffs. The tidal wave that followed from the impact pushed the graanar ship up into the roof of ice splintering the masts into a thousand pieces. Then as the wave subsided the ship crashed onto the water sending six graan over the edge and into the churning current. They disappeared in an instant as the water sucked them under.

"Grab the hooks and throw them into the cliffs, abandon the ship."

Polax raced down to the main deck and helped pull the hooks from the seabear. He thrust the lasso with the iron hook at the icy mountain before him. He could feel the ship being tugged towards the whirlpool. Three more hooks caught in the ledges of ice. Polax leapt onto the rope and tested; it held fast. Then the graanar began to heave themselves off the vessel and up onto the cliff. As the last of them climbed the ropes, the vessel suddenly shot into the current and sped into the centre of the maelstrom and disintegrated.

Polax pulled up each of the crew as they neared the ledge. He saw that the iceberg tip had blocked the ledge where they could walk to the gap in the teeth and make camp.

"What'll we do Polax?" called Chalo.

"We'll have to scale the berg and try and get around it to the get to the camp. We'll freeze here or get washed off."

The Chieftain had noticed the tide line in the ice and knew by another night or two the waters would be higher than they were now. He took his axe and dislodged the grappling hook. He walked towards the iceberg and noticed that the ice grated against the mountainside, pushed by the force of the ocean. He threw the hook again as hard as he could. Testing it was secure he climbed up over the massive spear of ice. He saw that it was at least seven hundred paces to the ledge before it re-emerged. The gap was only a few hundred further beyond.

"Come Graanar, nearly home."

The men followed their chieftain in single file using their axes and hooks to carry their weight. Over the length of the slippery face, their steps would faulter as the maelstrom beneath kept pushing the iceberg deeper into the cliff and then back out again.

"Hurry" Polax shouted back to his clansmen.

Polax stared up at the chunk of cliff close to being dislodged. It would crash directly onto the graanar below. The grating sound of ice on rock ascended into a higher pitch as the earth could no longer stop the urging of the ocean. Finally, the last of the crew reached the edge of the berg just in enough time as one final surge splintered the cliff sending an avalanche onto the iceberg. A ripple tore through the icy surface and with the churning water beneath, the iceberg tore in two.

"Hurry!"

Polax bolted his way forward as he saw the ripple make its way toward their side and into the narrow ledge they stood upon. With great strides he made it to the end spearing the grappling hook into the ledge he swung around the side and down onto the outcrop of rock. He looked up and swinging the rope back threw it to Chalo. Chalo caught and passed it back to along the graanar behind him. A dozen more graanar latched their axes and scaled the cliff face to where Polax stood. Only half had made it through when the full force of the avalanche cascaded along the cliff propelling the remaining crew down onto the ice sheet below.

Polax and Chalo bolted straight down to them to dig the ice off the buried men. The thundering boom of the iceberg finally sinking into the water propelled them onto their backs.

"Graanar, answer the call of the chieftain!" shouted Polax

He counted twenty-five voices out of the forty that set sail.

"We shall camp here and make for the lands above when the blizzard clears."

They all stood watching the maelstrom grow larger in the ocean forming a sink hole in the surface.

"It's as if the ice mother sucks the water into her belly. It is the same curse that brought the pox to our lands."

"Ay, Chalo, never in my fifty winters and summers nor in my father's memory had the clan Timmo lost a boat to the giants of the sea. My grandfather often spoke of the seas this far to the north. They are at war with the ice mother and seek any chance to destroy those loyal to her milk. I see now why he was loath to fish these waters."

"It is full turn of the moon's face Polax to our lands. If the wrath of Raajn finds us, then it will be the end of Polax and Chalo of Timmo."

"We will rest when we reach the huts and repair the ropes for the climb up. If we die trying brother, then at least it will be on the ice the great mother treads not this cursed water."


Jarrod watched the three great birds alight onto the ground and transform into the Orynth. Tyl stood next to them watching the Gol Lord ready to attack with little provocation.

"Hail Elda Chief. We mean no harm and come on mission from your brother Gildas, Keeper of Tarentess, the dwelling that lies to the north of the great ranges that border our lands."

"Who are these creatures that now beset us?" asked Jarrod agitated.

EY strode towards Jarrod.

"We are the servants and brethren of Norbu, Lord of Arglethium. We have given allegiance to your kin Gildas, Keeper of Tarentess, who seeks a council with you and your equals."

"We are here to take you to the mighty mountain Keep called Tarentess, along with Polax of Timmo and Olac of Clotte" spoke Tyl.

"I have made my ruling on the wars in the southern lands. Those who wish to fight the Matavian, scourge and its demon may do so, but the Graan will only fight on their lands if the war comes here."

"This request is made to unite the peoples that remain unchained from the demon. More will be needed Elda. The Orynth have dwelt here since the dawn of our world and fought many battles against this enemy. The world will die the longer the beast remains unchallenged. Our mighty icelands are already succumbing to the power this demon draws from the earth. Come with us and you will see" replied Tyl.

"Nay, graanar, I will not, and I forbid Olac and Polax to leave as well for this war council. The graanar will fight here and die here if we must. Let these creatures fight their own battle against this ancient enemy. It is beyond the graanar to fight these spirits."

Tyl knew this would happen and taking a deep breath "Orynth, by the command of Tarentess, and its blade wrought from the blood of Arglethium."

Tyl looked at EY who squawked loudly into the air, wrapped its huge, feathered limbs around Jarrod and lifted him into the air. VA gathered Tyl and XI followed them into the air.

"Go south EY" commanded Tyl.

Jarrod struggled to get out but gave up when he felt the strength of the bird god. Caelwyn, Jano and Han watched as their husband and father was carried away into the sky.

"Tommo and Jank, take a sled and follow them, they are headed south" Caelwyn shouted at the stunned graan.

Tommo shouted across the village "Get the dogs and the axe blades ready, feather and blood is to be spilt."

In the distance from the direction of the kennels could be heard the baying of the dogs as they saw the sleds being prepared.

Jarrod watched the land beneath speed past as they flew south. His face had begun to bite from the ice that hit it.

"Tyl you will be quartered for this" he shouted across to the graanar. Tyl did not respond.

Soon the huts of the Clan Clotte came into view.

"Down there EY"

They descended smoothly, towards the unsuspecting graanar and gently landed away from the village. As soon as EY released Jarrod, he took his axe and swung it at the bird. EY did not flinch, and the blade merely bounced off. Jarrod then turned his rage at Tyl but XI stood in front of him to prevent the Chieftain from attacking.

Olac and the rest of the village came running towards them.

"Stay back, these creatures seek to steal you away Olac" warned Jarrod.

"Gildas seeks a meet with you and Polax. You know your lands are now being devoured by the evil that grows in the south" shouted Tyl.

"Your brother once again brings division to the graan. You mean to carry me to his hideout Tyl of Timmo. I should have killed him on the plains when I had the chance. Take me there so he may finally feel my blade in his belly."

"XI, gather the chieftain."

"No!" shouted Jarrod, but his voice was lost as EY collected him again and joined XI and VA.

The Orynth and the graanar flew directly east. Soon on the horizon the black line of the eastern ocean could be seen. Olac and Jarrod stayed limp in the talons of EY and XI. Jarrod's mind raced. If Olac met Gildas and tried to kill him then these gods would not let the Chieftain live a moment longer. War would come of it. Gildas was smart though, he knew if he got these three chiefs onside then the clans would unite.

"Curse you Gildas, war and death follow you wherever you tread" Jarrod swore under his breath.

Tyl guided the Orynth down towards the village below. The people began to gather as they saw the strange creatures alight with their cargo.

Tyl's mother and younger brother Sami came racing towards them. Tyl embraced them relieved that they were still alive.

"I have come for Father."

"He is not here brother. He fishes in the northern seas for the great sea bears."

"Sami, I cannot explain all that has come to pass but it is with haste that I seek our father. Has the pox afflicted the village here?"

"Ay but only the fish that come from the south. That is why the ships were sent north to seek food for the winter. What are these?" Sami asked pointing to the Orynth. He suddenly saw Jarrod and Olac standing behind him.

"Elda Chief. Hail the Elda- Chieftain Graanar of Timmo!"

 Immediately the villagers bowed as Jarrod walked away from EY to where Tyl stood.

"Stand Clan Timmo. What is this news of a pox?" asked Jarrod.

"Gildas saw it with his own eyes Elda, graanar and the mighty fish of the eastern shores bloodied and blistered, lying dead in the waters. The war has come north to the lands of the Ice bear. The ice breaks and splinters as the world beneath crumbles. Come to Gildas, he has been blessed with the blood of the earth and seeks an army to fight the demon and relieve it of the power of the jewel" spoke Tyl.

"Is this true of a pox besetting Timmo lands? Why was news not sent to Gol Village?"

"Elda, we tried to send messengers, but the storms that have beleaguered our shores have hindered us leaving. Many of our clan are now hunting in the north for food" spoke Huna, Tyl's mother.

"We have no time to waste. EY we will go north to find Polax. XI will follow to search as well and VA stay guard here until I return. Chieftain's, I ask thee to wait" spoke Tyl.

"Ay lad, I wait my chance to set eyes upon Gildas of Gol again" replied Olac.

Tyl hesitated sensing that Olac had only one intention when he saw Gildas again,

"I warn you Olac, Gildas is no longer bound to the milk of the ice mother, a deeper power flows in his veins. He asks for peace so all the lands may unite. You are not his match. Lay down your weapon before it is too late."

Olac stared at Tyl as he spat on the ground.

"I will wait Tyl of Timmo until you fetch your father back."

"I think we have no choice" spoke Jarrod eyeing the Orynth that stood guard. A few children had gathered and were growing game enough to go near the huge gods. VA stood watching silently like a sentinel.

EY lifted Tyl into the air and began to speed along the coastline, XI followed. The loftiness of their position allowed Tyl to see far out into the ocean. He noticed how the waters churned in great whirlpools rather than the usual massive icebreaker waves that would engulf their shores. He scoured the waters looking for his father. He searched for the distinctive white carved bear's head that stood at the bow and stern.

Further they flew, Tyl began to shiver as they went into the heart of the ice mother and felt her frozen breast touch his skin.

"Where are you Chieftain of Timmo, your son seeks you?"

Polax and his men slept in the huts. It was warmer here then outside but only by a hair's breadth. The Chieftain stirred slightly as he felt a mild shudder under his back. He felt it again and sat up. The roar of the ocean outside remained the same or was it louder? He got up and peered through a gap in the wall of the humpy. There was nothing. The tremor came again but it was stronger.

"What is it chief?" called Chalo

Polax wrapped his fur hood across his face. Standing outside he saw that the churning ocean that had swallowed his boat was even larger and was now beginning to abrade the rocks and packed ice.

"Get up Graanar, we need to begin the climb to the lands above."

Chalo saw it as well. Then the tremor returned along with a cacophony of crashing rocks as another row of the teeth fell into the waters beneath.

A dozen iron hooks flew into the air and bit into the cliff above. Polax heaved himself up. Everything around them began to reverberate with the force of the ocean. It was as if the water had found its strength to eat the earth and had begun its final meal. Polax looked up, it was half a league to the top, but he knew there were ridges which sloped to the top of the plateau. If they could get to them, they would be able to walk the rest of the way.

He felt a splash of frigid water hit him. Below the waves had crashed over the ledge and washed away the huts. The clutch of humpies had been built by his great grandfather were taken by the water. The ice mother curses and blesses he thought. He heaved himself up again straining his leg on a rock protuberance while digging his pickaxe in to lever himself up higher. A scream cut through the noise of the tide crashing as three Graanar fell into the churning waters.

"Ice mother bless these loyal cubs of yours" Polax prayed as he climbed.

The mighty Chiefs of the Graan were always chosen in the first place by their strength and battle prowess and it had been the greatest of these Graanar that all others had descended. Polax led his graanar closer to the safety of the ledge with arms and legs as powerful as any Chieftain that had preceded him. His mind blanked out the cold and the pain of the exhaustion that seeped into his bones. He thought of nothing except each powerful blow into the cliff face to get away from the ocean and winch his clan to safety. Suddenly in time with the heaving of his chest his axe struck the top of the ledge and sunk into the granite beneath. Polax reefed himself up and lay panting.

After only a moment he took the grappling hook and smashed into the rock to anchor it. He threw the rope down to Chalo. He looked out across the ocean and the sight made his heart chill like his flesh. As far as he could see the ocean churning in a gargantuan maelstrom. The roar at the epicentre subsumed by a high-pitched whine as the force of the swirling waters sucked the air into the channel it formed in the centre.

"Mother of the ice save us! Hurry Graanar, heave to now!" he yelled.

Chalo and two other graan anchored their own hooks and let the ropes fall to the remaining graanar below. The ocean roared up the walls towards them clawing at their feet to drag them back into its belly.

Polax noticed that the water was reaching the lip of the ridge they stood on in the direction where they could climb to the top.

"Cursed beast who taunts us. I will go ahead and find the path. I will knot the rope along to follow."

Polax began to make his way along the ledge, Chalo watched the chieftain get washed with wave after wave until he disappeared into the darkness and slurry of snow and water.

The graanar began to follow their Chieftain until the ocean flung itself at the cliff with such ferocity it took the ledge with it. Chalo slipped down and barely clung to the hook that remained embedded in the rock. Kyl, brother to Chalo grabbed Chalo's hand before it slipped off the hook, but it was too late, the ocean surged again and snatched Chalo into the waves. Kyl watched his brother be sucked into the centre of the whirlpool.

"We can't go any further!" Kyl screamed at Polax.

Tyl looked down and saw Chalo's body disappear into the heaving ocean.

"There EY!" Tyl pointed to the stranded graan on the ledge

EY and XI sped into the flooded alcove and grabbed three of the crew.

The Orynth flew through the whipping ice and snow and dropped the graanar to safety on the large plateau of ice.

"Where is Polax?" Tyl shouted to Kyl.

"He walked ahead along the ridge then the wave washed it away."

"XI bring the others up here. EY we will search for the chieftain."

Speeding back over the edge of the cliff EY dived straight down. Tyl could barely see as the snow flew into his face. In the frenzy EY suddenly darted down then up as a wave threatened to catch them. Suddenly Tyl saw his father.

"There EY."

EY shot towards Polax who was hanging onto his rope desperately trying not to fall into the water. Just as EY's talons went to grab the Chieftain a wave rose and swallowed Polax, knocking the Orynth into the cliff.

Recovering EY and Tyl saw the flailing arms of Polax as the water carried him towards the maelstrom.

EY followed trying to snatch him out but each time the ocean played with it, sucking Polax under then thrusting him up just out of reach.

Suddenly the high-pitched whistle of the centre of the frenzied whirlpool could be heard. Polax spun around the edges and down into the channel.

"EY, after him!" screamed Tyl.

EY made a wide arc and with razor precision dove directly into the heart of the churning sea and into the funnel. The noise made Tyl's ears bleed, and his chest felt crushed by the forces. Down and down, they went. Polax flew around like a limp rag. EY's claws reached him and latched on, digging into his flesh reefing the chieftain out of the centrifuge.

EY hesitated slightly as the strength of the oceans churning did not want to release the clansman. EY wrenched hard almost tearing Polax in two, but the water relented, and the trio spun up into the sky.

Landing back on the plateau Polax fell onto the ice unconscious but was breathing. EY shot off suddenly, but Tyl did not react as he tended to his father.

"XI take some of the others back and return with VA to help carry the crew back home. I will wait for EY." XI nodded and collected three graan and flew off. The remaining graanar stood around Tyl watching if their Chieftain would live or die.

EY returned and gently collected Tyl and Polax.

"I will send the birds back." Tyl shouted to the remaining graanar. The cheers of his brothers made Tyl's heart rise with pride at their strength to defeat the cursed ocean.

Polax roused and looked at Tyl and then the Orynth that carried him.

"So, what trouble dogs you now son?"

Tyl smiled at his father "It wasn't my fault this time Chieftain."

# 6

# Scaletryx

The forest breeze was refreshing after the foulness of the burnt and desolate remains of the battle fields of Aeserea. The Orynth and Tyl had left Kado on the edge of the remaining forest to begin his journey home. EY had assured Kado the path to the Keep was only a day's trek into the forest. The sweet coolness of the forest had revived him somewhat after restless nights of thinking of what lay ahead. The shadow of failure hung heavily around him but the need for what he had to do was greater still and spurned him on. Sa came to mind, but he blocked the image of her face quickly to hide the pain at her leaving. He knew that deep down even if Sa-Tuc returned she would not be the same person he knew. He arrived at the cathedral of fig trees and vines that led to the Keep of Lido. Silence surrounded him making him feel like he was deaf. Even the leaves of the majestic trees did not rustle with the breeze. The crunching of his footsteps was magnified from the debris of the forest floor rebounding off the buttressed roots of the trees. The sunlight faded gradually as he walked further along until it became completely dark. His breathing became more difficult as the air thickened. He was expecting the odour of decay to greet him, like in the tunnels of the Ranik's palace. Instead of death it was as if the very essence of the forest had disappeared, leaving only the outer skin of the trees and shrubs as decoration.

Soon the trickle of running water broke through the oppressive silence. Kado quickened his pace finding hope in the sound. The stream was crystal clear and the taste fresh as he scooped handfuls into his mouth. He followed the stream along until the waterfall which signalled the entrance to the Keep appeared. He stepped through the cascading flows expecting solid ground to be on the other side but instead he fell into the rush of the water and was carried down into the cave. He was thrust into the cavern walls by the stream as it swirled into the heart of Lido's dwelling.

Grabbing an outcrop of rock Kado managed to find an anchor and pull himself up onto a ledge out of the turbulent water. Panting from the sudden commotion he looked around him. The cave was unremarkable except for the chambers of the creatures. He noticed some of them had begun to rot making the water murky. Little bits of flesh and bones floated in the columns. Strewn on the floor were thousands of shells of tiny crab like creatures.

"The world is truly dying" he spoke.

His voice echoed throughout the empty caves. He took the sword Gildas had given him and cut his hand. He let the blood drip into the water.

"The blood of Arglethium calls the mighty serpent Vipax for parlance. Hear the cry of the cradle that has been your home since the dawn of time and answer its call."

Kado sat down and began eating some roasted root he had cooked along the way. He thought he would wait three days and nights. If this serpent god did not appear then he would leave for the Feet of Jun.

He fingered the blade Gildas had given him. It was as light as a feather but stronger than the stone of the mountainside of Tarentess. Time passed slowly as he sat thinking of what he would find in the Hills of Jun and the remnants of his people. Lord Jiang would not forgive him easily for his transgression with his daughter, nor would he be likely to trust him. The lingering memory of Kado Kodrax to the people of the Dragon Dynasty was a weak addict seeking pleasure and self-destruction at every turn.

Kado fell asleep as he thought of the last Harvest of the Moon festival and the face of his father's rage. He also remembered Lord Jiang's anger being assuaged by the generous payment by the emperor as an apology for Kado's conduct.

Vipax woke. The smell was an old smell, ancient and potent. It was one drop not even pure but mixed with the scent of the dragon and a clayborn.

Gliding through the water the serpent felt the tugs of the northern waters and wondered what caused the tumult in the icy reaches. It had not ventured there in many moons. It licked the water but nothing familiar came to its memory. Continuing towards the scent, the ancient power that had been brought here and cause of the all the death pricked its scales. Power left unfettered growing in strength. The time grew close when this invasion could no longer be ignored.

It would need to be destroyed like those who brought it to this place where it should it never have come. Norbu, stone forger, made it in the last days of the dying light of Caemeris.

Vipax entered the cave and rose to the surface of the water. The skin that covered its sparkling yellow eyes retracted slowly revealing their facets as they caught the faint light that penetrated the cavern. The eyes watched Kado asleep on the ledge. Whipping out its tongue it tasted the creature and instantly recognised the blood of Arglethium flowing in its veins. Vipax retreated under the surface so that only its eyes were visible.

Kado stirred feeling rested but hungry. He took some more of the root began to chew. He went to fill his water cask but stopped suddenly when he saw the two massive eyes staring at him.

"Vipax, mighty keeper of the oceans."

He gulped hard as he bowed realising how large the creature must be. It rose and filled the open expanse that sat above the pool of water.

"Who are you clayborn, that you dare call this sentinel from its slumber?"

"I am Kado Kodrax, heir to the Kingdom of the Dragon. A kingdom now in ruins and on the precipice of falling out of time and memory, waiting to be devoured by Voloc."

"How is it the blood of this world flows within you?"

"It was given by the guardian of Tarentess, Gildas Gol from the north. Norbu has bestowed the fountain of Arglethium to Gildas, so that a way to defeat the shadow can be found."

"This shadow fills my nest with sickness and my tongue with the taste of death."

Kado noticed the yellow eyes glower with rage, lighting the cavern with their shine.

"It is for this reason great one, that I have called you. I seek an alliance to defeat this shadow. Its power is beyond us, the ones you call clayborn. We merely hope to win the source of its growing strength back to weaken it."

"How can Vipax aid a clayborn? It eats the ones that try to take my fish from the waters in which I dwell, and now I wait until a way is clear for me to destroy the destroyer. Vipax battles are not with those of the last born."

"Help us defeat the shadow. We will lure it to your waters to be eaten by the mighty viper of the deep ocean."

The serpent did not answer, and its eyes were unreadable to Kado. He decided to continue.

"I journey to the remains of my people to unite them under the banner of the dragon. We will gather with those of us who are not enslaved by the Shadow's servants and with the Keeper of Tarentess's gifted blade, we will unite and battle this shadow. Would not the mighty serpent Vipax desire to battle and show the world its beauty and majestic strength."

The eyes glimmered slightly at the flattery as the serpent remembered the early days of creation when the shadow had come before to destroy the earth. The ancient memories rose of how it would master the might of the untamed waves and its scales would illuminate the darkened depths showing the hidden treasures of the sea. It looked at Kado once again.

"The scent of the dragon stains your blood clayborn."

"The dynasty I was born into pledge its fortunes and strength to the myth of the dragon."

The serpent remained silent. After what seemed several turns of the glass Kado wondered if it had fallen asleep. He got up to stretch as his legs began to cramp. He walked into the chambers that contained the creatures held captive by the Keep. He touched the columns of water and felt them ripple but not give way. It seemed to go on for an eternity as he walked further into the cavern. The dark wall that had frightened Ange and Nekoda rose before the prince. He peered into it drawn by its impenetrable emptiness. It reminded him of the nightmares that would crowd his mind when he starved himself of the lily. Suddenly behind him in the lake of water Vipax hissed. Startling Kado he turned and nearly slipped in a pile of dead crabs.

"Do you smell the scent of the dragon clayborn?"

"No. It is not real. It is only a legend that my people have held as a superstition. Our wealth and strength were born of the riches in the earth; formed there by the ancient rocks."

Vipax hissed but did not argue with Kado.

"Where is it you wish to go?"

"To a place where my father hid his wealth, and weapons for times such as these and to claim the sceptre of rule for my own. It lies to the east of here under the great stone that juts out from the mountainside, called the feet of Jun."

Vipax hissed and at the same time its eyes shone dazzling Kado. He squinted trying to block out the light.

"Your eyes are like yellow diamonds, brighter and more glorious than the sun itself, mighty serpent" spoke Kado.

Suddenly Vipax' tongue shot out and grabbed Kado by the legs and pulled him over. His heart almost stopped when he noticed the fangs of the serpent protrude out of its jaws. A droplet of venom hung on the tips. It slipped off and fell onto the sandstone and melted the rock into liquid.

"Blasphemy clayborn. Nothing is greater than Belmaris, offspring of the First Star. My eyes are its gift to me as my nest lies far away from the benevolent one's gaze."

The fangs retracted and the tongue let go. Kado slid back as far as it could. His heart thudded in his chest so much he thought his rib cage would break. Plucking up his courage he stood.

"Are you friend or foe to the clayborn as they go to battle against the ancient enemy?"

Vipax slid its tongue past Kado and delved into the wall of darkness behind Kado. As it touched the shadow its eyes flared red and then all the colours of a rainbow. Kado moved as far away as he could.

His mind raced. It was a power and rule unto itself and would not lay its loyalty to any other.

"What do you see in there colourful one?" Kado asked.

"All that has come before and now waits to be unleashed. Vipax is no servant to the clayborn but the death that dims the gift of Belmaris must be destroyed."

"When the time calls, and the Keeper of Tarentess calls his army to war will Vipax, mighty serpent of the sea, answer?"

"Yes" came the lisped whisper.

Kado breathed a barely audible sigh of relief.

"I must go now great one, for time passes quickly and I have yet to take my place as ruler for my people. It is many days journey from here to the feet of Jun."

"I will take you. My ocean has many hidden paths only known by the mighty Vipax."

"But I cannot swim that far, gracious serpent, I will die."

"All the ancients have the gift of restoring life. It is not wise to use but when we were birthed like the creatures of the void then the breath of re-creation was given to us to restore the offspring of Belmaris. Come I will show you where the waters tickle the feet of the Jun. The warrior Jun was turned to stone after the spine of the beast pierced its hide and laid waste to it."

"I am most grateful mighty and beautiful serpent, but I fear that I have received a boon enough for my people with your alliance."

Vipax hissed slightly. Kado's heart began to beat faster as he realised that the serpent would drown him. There was no escape and even if there was, he would offend the god.

"Come, I will take you. Vipax grows weary of its solitude. No more younglings hatch around me as the Voloc's curse eats them before they are strong."

A tear formed in the viper's eye and trickled down onto the rock. Unlike the venom the tear turned to crystal. Kado looked at it mesmerised. Was this how the jewel of Ange's was made? Would it contain power? He automatically went to pick it up but pulled away as it lay close to the serpent's mouth.

"Take it, a rare gift indeed for a clayborn. To tease so many gifts from the flesh of the mighty Vipax sings of blessings bestowed on your hide by more than just this world. I will call you Scaletryx, Fang Master of Serpent and Dragon."

Kado picked up the crystal and gazed into the facets. Each edge perfectly formed in every bevel and corner.

"When Belmaris' great light shines upon it you shall see the ages of Vipax life and deeds. I grow weary of this Scaletryx. I shall take you now to the place you seek."

Suddenly the serpents tongue shot out and wrapped around Kado's legs and dragged him into the water.

"Vipax, no!"

"You do not trust the mighty Vipax. I shall show you Scaletryx for our allegiance shall be bonded. The serpent and the dragon together."

The snake withdrew under the water with Kado in its mouth. The frigid water engulfed Kado, he struggled to get free as the air in his chest began to run out. His heart thudded like it was going to explode. He felt the weight of the ocean crush him as Vipax glided down into the unseen depths of its kingdom.

Kado could no longer bear it and expelled his last breath. The sudden darkness became complete as his life was snuffed out. He lay limp in the mouth of the ancient leviathan, swimming gracefully but oblivious to the fragility of the clayborn that lay within its mouth.

Vipax swam effortlessly thinking of the battles that had drawn it here at the time of this world's creation, especially of the time the dragon had come. So long ago now it had forgotten the empty silence of the ocean here, devoid of any of Belmaris' grace.

A squid as white as alabaster lashed out towards Kado floating in Vipax mouth looking for food. Vipax eyes glowed yellow blinding the eyeless creature. It screeched at Vipax.

"Be gone this one is bound to your mighty forebear."

On the horizon of the limitless depths blacker shapes than the water moved closer towards the serpent. They were large spires of rock rising from the floor of the ocean. The pressure became so great here that Kado's bones were crushed by the forces. His arms and legs flailed at perverse angles. His eyes burst sending tiny blooms of red into the murky depths.

Vipax swam between the spires, the light of its eyes guiding the way through the massive stone structures. It swam down into a ravine and into an elongated cave.

"Do you remember me, your ancient enemy of the first days?" it lisped into the empty chamber. Its voice echoed for what seemed an eternity. Vipax remembered the battle when it, the Orynth and Norbu defeated the white behemoth of the void in the first wars of creation.

Exiting through a small opening Vipax began to ascend. It could feel the light of the sun touch its scales. Its' rainbow scales and diamond eyes shimmering in glory to the great star's heat. Swimming faster and faster, its tail flicking forcing the great serpent up out of the ocean and into the daylight, towards the sky. Roaring its praise to the sun, its massive jaws opened, and the golden fangs shone out for all the world to see the beautiful but terrible Vipax. Kado fell from the gaping mouth and into the ocean; his lifeless body falling hard onto the surface of the ocean then sinking beneath.

Vipax began to frolic with joy and vanity reliving its glory days and the oneness with the world and the colours of the Caemeris. In great heaving turns and arcs the snake splashed upon the waves of the eastern ocean. Tsunamis rose with each contortion and flip, sending them towards the east, west, and south. Finally, as the sun sunk beneath the horizon Vipax finished its' revelling and sank into the water.

Tasting the water again its mind began to grow foggy as it tried to remember what had awoken it. Then just as the sadness of the decay that now poisoned its mind pervaded all its senses, the smell of the earth came to its nostrils. Following it through the water it found the body of the Kado. Licking his flesh, it remembered.

"Ahh, Scaletryx!"

Vipax scooped Kado into its mouth and swam towards the belly of the Jun. Finding the large spires of rocks again Vipax entered the empty chamber but instead went down even deeper until it found a small opening. It squeezed through and flowed with the water as it channelled down into the earth. The water began to taste sweet rather than salty as the jet stream reached far under the northern ranges. Soon Vipax swam in rivers that careened through a labyrinth of caves. Suddenly slowing its pace, it eased itself towards the surface to emerge at a table of flat rock. It gently placed Kado onto it.

Its eyes and fangs sparkled as they reflected the great mounds of gold and silver jewels which lay sparkling on the floor of the cave. Vipax's hide changed to a cold steel glitter as its eyes scanned the walls peering at the ledges carved from solid black granite in precisely ordered rows; each of them stacked with caches of swords, shields, crossbows, and catapults. It was so high that not even the serpent's head would reach the top.

A tear formed again in its eyes as it knew that the world's end was near as the vanity of Vipax craved for the battles that once raged in the beginning days.

"Destruction has come again and with it my ancient enemy will awaken. The stain of the void will baptise the dragon to life once more. Our bond will be to destroy the shadow and what it desires the most, the stone forged by Norbu. For I remember the times before light when it ruptured the void. When Caemeris burned all living things to ash and only with the chains of shadow did that searing power relent. So it is that Vipax brings the shadow and light together in Scaletryx, progeny of Draxanus Deathflame and the clay wrought of shadow and light by Norbu of Caemeris. And if victory is not won in this age, then it will be your curse, Scaletryx, to dwell between light and shadow until the gates of Stonthrax are closed and an end to all things come."

Vipax opened its great jaws and let its fangs drip their poison onto Kado. His skin began to melt leaving the pure white of his crushed bones on the stone. Then it watched as the venom began to knit the chalky fragments together with flesh and sinew and then the skin. Lastly Kado's face reformed until the heir of Draxanus Deathflame gasped his first breath.

He looked at Vipax with fear and gratitude.

"What have you done mighty one?"

"Wrought glory and death Scaletryx."

# 7

# War Council

Pellets of ice fell onto the stone floor of Tarentess as the Orynth landed and shook their plumage free of the frozen land beneath. Polax, Olac and Jarrod stood warily inside the throne room still dazed from the flight.

Gildas bowed to EY, VA, and XI in gratitude and then embraced Tyl. Axl walked over and slapped his cousin on the back and then bowed to Jarrod and Polax. Nekoda sniffed around their legs excited that new people had arrived. He barked his approval and went back to the entrance standing guard. The dog had been watching some vulture-owls nesting in a crack in the cliff.

"Tyl cause another fight, uncle?" asked Axl seeing the bruises and frostbite on Polax face. The Chieftain grinned but did not answer still stunned at everything that had happened in the last two days.

Gildas bowed to Jarrod and then moved to embrace his brother in greeting but Jarrod did not respond. As he stood away to greet Olac, the three Chieftains suddenly grasped their swords. Gildas looked behind him and saw Tessi, Angette and the Queen and Knight General emerge from the other side of the Keep. They had arrived the day before. Having rested they were not so overwhelmed at the

Orynth and the place they had been bought to. AX and PO flew down when they saw the Chieftains' posture of aggression.

"Steady, this place is for friends not foes."

"You are no friend or Graanar any longer!" shouted Olac as he flew at Gildas to strike him down in one blow.

Gildas raised his sword to block the hefty swing of the clansman. His blade sliced the thick iron of the graan blade cleanly in two leaving a sharp edge on both pieces of broken axe. Turning he grabbed Olac in a headlock and made him kneel.

"I should have spilt your blood on the ice, cursed son of whore!" Olac bellowed as he struggled under the arm of Gildas.

"Careful Chieftain, you curse the mother of the Elda Chief also. You shall not defeat me Olac of Clotte, nor my blade. I am guardian of this place and have been given passage to be its ruler. Bow before me graanar. I and the Ice Mother stand eye to eye now."

"You blaspheme, Gildas!" Olac spat back.

Jarrod walked over to his brother and taking his arm pulled on it insisting he let go of the clansman's neck.

"Then be worthy of the throne you have been given brother."

Gildas looked at Jarrod and knew he was right. The strength he now bore placed him outside the league of his clans. He could no longer deem himself one of them. To defeat one such as Olac would be a hollow victory.

"Ay, brother, your words are heeded." Gildas let go cautiously expecting Olac's temper to get the better of him again.

Olac stood back holding his neck seething but taking notice of Jarrod's glare not to cause any more trouble.

"Come, gather around the Throne of Tarentess. I call the war council to begin" spoke Gildas as he sheathed his blade. He took his place on the throne while the others sat on the rugs thrown down to soften the stone floors. The Orynth gathered behind in perfect line and solidarity while Nekoda sat proudly at the feet of Gildas.

"Elda Chieftain Jarrod of Gol, Chief Olac of Clotte and Polax of Timmo, I ask you to acknowledge the Queen of Aeserea Nene Fey Des Vries and her Knight General Cotus Medret. These creatures are the Orynth, servant and brethren to the god Norbu. Unknown to us as our allegiances and devotions as peoples have been to other gods and spirits passed down by our ancestors. Believe me when I say that Norbu is real and has been the Lord of rock and stone since the time of creation. This is his throne and Keep. I have been given stewardship of this seat until his return."

"Where is this god?" asked Polax.

"I believe he is trapped in this jewel of power that the demon now possesses along with his brethren. One of these brethren was the spirit that summoned me and Kado Kodrax, Sa-Tuc and Ange Tsaed from the eastern deserts. For what purpose this has happened remains un-clear, but the demon seeks to destroy these gods and us. The jewel which the Queen and Knight have not yet seen, contains the remnants of an ancient power. One of our companions, Ange, was chosen to safeguard it until the gods return. However, the shadow has imprisoned her to gain the power contained within the jewel. But I believe that she still lives despite her capture."

He saw Tessi reach forward wanting him to tell her the fate of Ange.

"This is Tessi Tsaed of the lands of the Mighty Choasa, sister to Ange."

She shrunk back shyly as everyone looked at her and Angette. The baby pulled away from Tessi and crawled to Gildas. It reached his leg and motioned to be picked up. Gildas stooped and placed her on his knee.

"Your sister lives but I do not think it is in this world. I believe that she has entered the realm of the spirits that called us."

"How do you know this?" asked Tessi.

"I have seen her only once in the sacred well. That is all I know of your sister's fate."

"What is it you want of us Gildas? As I ruled when we last met, if this war meets the Graan on its land we will fight to the end for victory or death" spoke Jarrod.

"This is not a war over territory or wealth. It is about the destruction of us and everything around us. It is true the power that has come to our lands is beyond our strength, but I believe Ange has seen a way to victory. She needs us to fight until she returns. Something thwarts the shadow from not annihilating us now."

Tessi had tears in her eyes as she looked at Gildas "You believe the demon has not killed her?"

"I do. I think that all would be ash and smoke by now. She spoke to me before the jaws of the Shadow locked around her. She wanted us to go south. It was from here the pale god of death and this demon came and I believe is where the shadow's lair lies and the breach which allowed these spirits into our world."

Queen Nene stood, as she began to grow stiff from the hard stone they sat upon.

"All of this explains my suspicions that more than the ambitions of the despot Ranik drove his desire to invade and conquer. Was it this jewel that he searched for in the Irastian temple leading to its destruction?"

"Ay and the last piece had been hidden by the Lord of this Mount, Norbu. It was when the jewel was reformed that these gods were trapped together. But none explained the purpose of this or why they did not wield its power to destroy the demon. Something else lies at the heart of their quest. It also tells me that we may be on our own and need to battle the shadow ourselves regardless of the fate of these brethren."

"It will be our destruction either way" stated Nene.

"I believe there is hope while ever the girl remains in the world of the spirits. So why have I called you here? A small party could make it their quest to retrieve the girl from the demon and hide away until the gods are brought back here to do battle."

"Ay Gildas, it cannot be ours to fight if it be spirits that have never shown themselves to men. It is their battle and while our fate maybe tied to their victory, we have no part to play in this" spoke Jarrod.

"I believe that the spirits fight not to defeat the shadow but to restore their covenant with one another. I also believe that if they return then they come not to remain in the world but to relinquish it. So even if the shadow is defeated it will remain if we do not drive it to its death."

"I do not understand any of this but if there are enslaved Aeserean subjects then it behoves us to free them. The Matavian scourge needs to be killed and if it means that we must unite to defeat them then so be it. My lady, do you follow your knight to battle?" Medret spoke feeling frustrated at the vagaries of Gildas' explanation.

"Of course, General. It cannot be borne that any of our people will be left to a fate of slow and painful deaths at the end of a Matavian whip. If at the very least they see the flag of the golden lioness as their last memory before death takes them, then it is some comfort for their souls to run to the heart of the Lioness."

Gildas nodded satisfied that the Aeserean's were onside.

"Graanar, I ask you for your allegiance. You will be needed. I have the word of the heir to the Drax Kingdom that they will fight alongside us."

"I do not understand what we will achieve other than death and ruination to leave the women and children defenceless for when the demon does defeat the world" spoke Jarrod.

"I have not lost all hope, I believe this place and the Orynth and the fact that the world has not turned to dust that we have a chance to salvage ourselves from annihilation. We must try, the mighty Icelands are dogged with plagues and the great ice sheets crack.

Once they have melted then, the lands beneath will be swallowed in the melt waters" replied Gildas.

"Ay the northern ocean stirs in great churning maelstroms. Something beneath drives the waters to a frenzy I have never seen." Polax spoke.

Jarrod nodded and then looked at Olac. "Olac, will clan Clotte follow my decision?"

Olac did not respond for a long time. Gildas gripped his blade expecting more trouble from the Chieftain.

"Clan Clotte have seen the scourge of this beast infect our lands. A great ravine now lies across the sheet that once led to our hunting pools. The sound of it ripping through the ice woke us from a thousand leagues away. We will follow the Elda Chieftain only. You know our blood yearns for vengeance against Gildas of Gol, but a greater enemy threatens the hides of the Graan. The axes of Clan Clotte will stand with their Chieftain."

"So, brother, will the ice bear fight alongside the lion and the dragon?"

"Where will this battle be fought?"

"In the southern lands of the Iron Coast. The demon's lair is found in the heart of the great desert."

"Yes, I believe I know where" interrupted Nene "A monk from the order of Ira told of the legends of their founder travelling from the lands of the Iron Coast. They speak of an ancient gate to the spirit world where a covenant was made with the first peoples. Is this where the demon lives?"

"Ay Queen, it is. Not only that, it builds a fortress around itself. The Orynth brought back news of this. The slaves are being herded deep into the desert and are being made to dig rock and stone to build the walls. Not only that they are being made into creatures, perverted and deformed by the power it now draws."

"What weapons will we have to fight it?" asked Polax.

"Weapons forged from the blood of the mountains. The Drax Kingdom also holds vast caches of blades and shields."

Polax looked at Jarrod "What choice do we have Elda, I have seen some of the destruction and felt its wrath upon my skin. I have seen the power of these winged gods who rescued me and the blade that is wielded by your brother. We have allies that I believe can match the strength of this beast. We either fight or die like broken ships upon the raging seas."

"Ay Polax, your even-tempered use of the axe has always been the strength of Clan Timmo. The Graan fight. The Rule of the Ice Bear will bow this one time to the rule of Tarentess and this god Norbu, who has seen fit to bestow his gifts on Gildas of Gol. Stand Chieftains."

Olac, Polax and Jarrod each stood before Gildas. They clashed their axes together and then on the ground. Kneeling before Gildas upon the throne they pledged their blades to the Keeper of Tarentess. Cotus Medret came up beside them and knelt. He pulled his sword from his hilt and offered it to Gildas.

"Tyl take all their weapons including yours and the Queens and hurl them into the sky to be lost in the clouds that surround us" commanded Gildas.

Tyl hesitated unsure of what Gildas intended to do. Gildas smiled at the sudden alarm he could see in the four men and Queen.

"Do as I ask Tyl of Timmo."

Tyl took the blades and axe from Polax, Jarrod and Medret. He reached Olac who would not let go of his axe only grunting in agitation at such a brazen gesture to humiliate warriors who have pledged their allegiance. Tyl pulled harder and managed to dislodge the axe from the huge hands of the Chieftain.

Gildas walked towards the stone wall that hid the basin of blood. Pressing, it shimmered allowing him to go into the chamber. Standing over the basin he touched the metal liquid. It transformed into an axe followed by another and another until the room was filled with them. Then Gildas looked again and a sword almost the same as the one he now wielded formed and then another until the chamber became overfilled with them.

He plucked the first eight of each of the weapons that had been made and brought them out into the throne room.

"Graanar stand before me."

Olac, Polax, Jarrod, Tyl and Axl lined up in front of Gildas, all equal in height but dwarfed by Gildas. Gildas lay the swords down on the floor and gave each of the graanar an axe.

"These are made and washed in the blood of Arglethium, swear an oath to the Keeper of the Blood that you shall die and defend the world from death and destruction. Swear it in blood and by the Ice Bear that now lays fealty to the mighty Norbu."

The graanar each took the razor-sharp blades and sliced their hands, Gildas did the same and grasping each of his brothers their blood mingled with the blood of the earth.

"Queen of the Lioness and Aeserea, and her Knight General stand before me. These are made and washed in the blood of the earth, swear an oath to the Keeper of the Blood you shall die defending the world from death and destruction. Swear it in blood and by the Lioness that now lays fealty to the mighty Norbu."

Once more the blood of the earth mingled with the blood of the Aeserean Queen and her Knight General. Cotus Medret grimaced at the primitive nature of it, preferring their own system of bestowing allegiance and fealty.

"Tessi Tsaed, stand before me." Tessi came over with Angette.

Gildas took a smaller blade and dagger. He gave them to Tessi.

"Woman and mother and last of the desert dwellers to the east, take this blade and swear an oath to the Blood of Arglethium, that you shall die to defend the world from death and destruction. Swear it in blood and by the blood of your children that now lay fealty to the mighty Norbu and his brethren Ange Tsaed, blood born to you and now custodian of the world's sorrow. Keeper of the Tears of Ascendant."

Gildas cut his hand and waited while Tessi placed Angette on the ground. Taking her dagger, she pricked her palm and grasped Gildas. His massive hand completely covered her slender fingers. Tears welled in her eyes as the fear and sorrow of everything that had engulfed her life and was still to come, rose in her heart and claimed her.

"You are strong Tessi Tsaed. I feel your blood in me. You ravaged desert wife, birth mother of flowers from sand, fruitful even in the bed of malice, your fecund flesh is ever green and flows with the breath of the mountain, gives strength to stone and is now one with Arglethium's blood" Gildas spoke to her.

"Remember mighty Lord, it is the desert dwellers who grow flowers from sand. And it is by their loyalty to dirt and their kin that you may have your victory and by no others." Gildas knew she spoke the truth. All their fates rested upon Ange now.

"Orynth, I ask a boon, can you fetch some pheasants and fish to feast upon so that our alliances and oaths can be celebrated over a hearty meal" spoke Gildas.

"Ay and some ale brewed on the east coast" winked Axl at EY.

They flew out and within a half a turn of the glass they had returned with talons full of pheasants and large fish but to Axl's disappointment no ale.

Gildas and Tyl had barely got the fire going for the spit as the others inspected and tested their blades.

Jarrod swung his axe to test the balance. He nicked the edge of one of the walls. He noticed that the slice was clean and smooth like it had been polished, but he had barely felt it pass through the rock. It was like slicing through the flesh of a carp.

Soon the smell of flesh roasting filled the throne room.

As they ate Nene, cradled Angette who sat happily cooing in her arms.

"Gildas, what will happen with this little one and her mother. I noticed the scars on the poor thing's arms. She was sold as a slave at one point."

"Her other child lies captive with Ranik's Queen. He will need to be rescued but I hold them to an oath, a tenuous one, to join in battle when the time comes, and they hold me ransom with the child."

"Since when will Ranik hold true to any word. It is said he was taken by this demon" spoke Nene.

"Ranik is dead. My blade cloved his head in two."

Nene and Medret and the clansmen stopped eating when they heard the news.

"This is good news indeed but who leads the scum now?" spoke Medret.

"His Queen and Captain Piotr Faad. He once saw the folly of allowing the demon to seize the jewel but after the news of how destructive the Matavians have become, I wonder if he has succumbed also to the power of the shadow."

"We will find no ally there, Gildas" spoke Medret. "They have been our enemy for as long as the throne of Aeserea has existed, driven by an evil spirit or not, they seek only their own glory and death to all others."

"Ay" replied Gildas, thinking how well he understood his enemy.

"So, what is the battle plan? If we are to travel to the Iron Coast, then there will be a battle just to get to the oceans that will take us there?" asked Jarrod. "A thousand Graan lie beneath in the forests above Unstaadt. We can rally the clans to another ten thousand if we include the free clan wives who have come of age."

"Yes, our army has been decimated by the Ranik's scourge, but we have maintained the western provinces and three legions of soldiers lie there under the command of Lord Warick" spoke Nene.

"How many does the prince from the middling lands intend to bring?" asked Jarrod.

"He hopes to rally at least ten thousand, maybe more, if all the feudal Lords will unite. They are skilled fighters the warriors of the Drax lands, their blades will be useful. First, we need to secure the ports and harbours to get to the southern lands. A path has been found by the Orynth where we can traverse from the coast to the interior with little hindrance from the army of the enslaved. I will seek parlance from Lord Faad and the Queen but if they resist then we will annex their ports also and cleanse the lands of the scum once and for all. It will cut off the supply of slaves to the demon. Once we have secured the ships then we assemble in the lands of the Iron Coast to begin the final battle. Jarrod, Polax and Olac, gather your clan warriors, and I will send word to the prince, that you and his forces are to meet on the coast of the Hosiaan Province. A land bridge was formed there when the mighty Norbu erupted from the ground. We will land on the Iron coast from the West and you and the Princeling from the east. We will meet at the fortress of Iron to face our enemy."

"How long?" asked Jarrod.

"By the next full moon and a quart, I want the legions of Tarentess battle ready at the walls of the demons lair."

"What of the weaponry?" asked Medret.

"Send word to your legions in the west to gather with the Graan. I will bestow the gifts of the mountain to all then. The other Graanar supplies will be sent in readiness for you as you near the pass of the Blade and Spike. But the prince's cache will be also overflowing ready to be plundered for battle."

"What if the prince is not ready or is unable to regain control of his Kingdom?" asked Tyl.

"Then plunder the Hills of Jun for its riches and weaponry and kill any that resist. The Legions of Tarentess will not be thwarted from their purpose. The prince knows this is my order and he will obey."

"The Queen will use Noab as a weapon against you if you threaten her or her kingdom. She killed her own children. She is mad with bitterness and evil" spoke Tessi.

"I have not forgotten your son."

Gildas looked at Tessi and knew she was right. The child will need to be rescued before any attack can begin.

"I will not stay here alone when you go to battle fretting over what may be happening and be left to be driven mad by my loneliness."

"It is not safe anywhere else. You will have to wait here. You will have to trust me."

"It is safe in the grove of the Lioness. She may come with me to the safety of the grove. There will be others there and work for her to do to keep her mind from being tormented with fear" spoke Nene.

"It is true Gildas, the grove is impenetrable except from the very tips of the Jadah ranges. No man can climb those heights only the red beasts that have been unleashed by the demon. Or perhaps these winged gods" spoke Medret.

"I guess it will be safe there. These creatures you speak of were bound to the demon but are now loyal to the assassin, Sa Tuc. She still may yet be called upon along with these Aracnine. An unknown boon of their strength may await us" replied Gildas.

Suddenly the Orynth flew from the roost they had been resting upon when Gildas spoke the word Aracnine.

EY strutted forward and spoke for the first time since arriving back from the Ice Lands.

"The sacred Aracnine, unseen before to the Orynth but they are the mightiest of all the creatures born of the first light which broke the gates of Stonthrax. Blessings upon the Orynth if we battle only once alongside the most sacred of all creations of the Oblyquixiton."

"These are the creatures that killed my brothers and decimated our brave soldiers. How can they be our allies?" spoke Nene, barely suppressing the anger and sorrow that had been stirred.

"Are they beholden to the light or the dark EY?" asked Gildas.

"Neither. They were unleashed at the bidding of the first stars and can lie within the eye of Caemeris and in the cradle of the void. Their true purpose is forgotten now. The gaolers of the shadow must bear the strength of the First Star. There are few created things who can hold the power of the First in their breast and not be destroyed by it."

Gildas nodded feeling more hopeful. He would send EY to search for the assassin and her pets.

"So, it is decided we shall leave here upon the second dawn. I will send word to Kado, and Knight General send word to your people to rally with the Graan. Queen and Tessi you will be taken to the Grove of the Lioness for safety until our fate is decided. PO will take you there when we leave."

Gildas stood and looked at his clansmen. He walked towards them and embraced Tyl, Axl and Polax. As he neared Olac, the chieftain stepped away and held his blade to stop him.

Gildas acknowledged the gesture and moved towards Jarrod.

"Brother do you follow me willingly like the days of old?"

"I never followed you willingly but out of the loyalty to a brother whose pride led him to folly and destruction at every turn and threatened to take the people of the ice mother over the same path.

The spirits have chosen well Gildas. I follow you knowing that your lust for battle will now be used for the sake of all of us and not your own glory. The ice mother both curses and blesses."

Gildas stood looking at his brother with his hands upon his shoulders. The image of the witch threatening to snatch away the memories of Jarrod and Jesse, and their unconditional loyalty to him remained vivid like it was only yesterday. Their loyalty the one thing in his hate filled heart that thwarted the demon from consuming his mind and soul entirely. He would be dead but for them. He owed them everything.

"Ay, such is the fury and battle lust of Gildas of Gol, that it takes the destruction of the world to see how blind his eyes and heart were to those around him."

He stood back and yelled "Graanar!"

The clansmen responded 'Graanar!" with clashing swords and blades echoing through the Keep and out into the icy winds.

# 8

# Hill of the Jun

Kado stood and surveyed the cavern. He was overwhelmed by the wealth which bombarded his sight.

"So, father, you were making sure that no one would take the sceptre from the Ko Drax rulers."

He turned and looked at Vipax

"Mighty one, I have my weapons, can I rule the people needed to bring war to Voloc?"

"You have the blessing of Vipax, Scaletryx. You will find a way to victory, now and even beyond. Remember the memory of sentinels is long and we see far into the beginning of time and far into the future."

"What do you see for me Vipax?" asked Kado sensing that the serpent was not telling him everything.

"You will see Scaletryx. Do not let the doubt I tasted in your blood cloud what must be done. Conquer your fear and finish the quest. I will go now. I grow weary of this air and wish to glorify Belmaris once more before I am called to do battle."

The yellow eyes stared deep into the mind of Kado. His resurrection from the venom of Vipax had given him the resolve he needed to seek victory at all costs. Slowly Vipax slid under the surface of the water and disappeared.

Kado picked up a sword and dagger and inspected the ornate carvings of ancient script of the Draxus. The precision of the engravings was exquisite. The steel glistened even in the semi darkness. Scanning the walls, he saw a doorway carved out of the rock. He placed the weapons in a halter and put on a chain mail vest over a silk shirt, and trousers. There was a pair of boots with the same intricate stitching as the dagger. He took a firebrand from the wall and stepped into the passage.

A long winding staircase rose before him. He climbed for what seemed an eternity in silence. Soon he could hear muffled voices. He came to the end of the stairwell. Stopping at the door he let his breathing settle. Once he stepped through the door he would not return. Gripping the blade, he unlatched the lock as quietly as he could and opened the door.

Inside two guards, stood ready with spears pointing at Kado as he entered an antechamber. There was nothing in the room but two torches on the wall and passageway on the other side.

One of the guards rushed him and forced him up onto the wall with the point of the spear tickling his throat. One firm thrust would kill him instantly.

"Who are you?"

"Stand down guards. I am Kado Kodrax, Heir to the throne of the Dragon Dynasty. Which master do you swear allegiance to now?"

Kado felt the spearhead retract just slightly at the words but then the disbelief of his claim took over the solider again and this time the tip pierced his skin.

"Emperor Ko and his son are dead. How did you get into the caves beneath?"

Kado rolled up his sleeve and showed the guard the tattoo of the royal seal given to heirs of the ruling family. The guard looked at it and stepped away.

"Take me to the Lord who commands you" ordered Kado.

The other guard came up to him and took his dagger and sword off him and turning him around bound his hands.

"Stay here I will take him to Commander Poat" the guard spoke who had bound him.

Thrusting Kado forward the guard directed him up another passageway. The climb was steeper this time with no end. Kado could hear the guard's breathing becoming more laboured as they ascended. His body was not tiring. Eventually they came to the end of the stairwell and a stone wall met them.

Everything suddenly went black as a sack was placed over Kado's head. He heard grating over rock as something heavy was pushed open. He guessed it was the wall moving. He felt the guard tug his right arm making him walk forward. He instantly felt the air change from a stale earthy smell to one of spice and roasting meats. The guard guided him for another twenty paces and then made him sit on the floor. The sound of the rock wall closing behind him echoed more loudly indicating the place was larger than where he had come from. Suddenly the sack was removed from his head. Blinking, he saw Lord Jiang and his son, Lon, sitting upon a dais. He got up but was pushed down again.

"Sit before the ruler of the Jun Mountain or we will make you crawl to him" snarled the guard.

"Everyone is to leave except the guard and my son" ordered Lord Jiang.

Lord Jiang clapped his hands to signal that everyone was to obey. The room emptied immediately leaving Kado and Jiang, Lon, and a dozen guards.

"So, the son of Ko, lives" spoke Jiang as he got up and walked towards Kado.

Kado stood again. Jiang waved the soldier away.

"I do Lord Jiang, and I have come to re-claim my right to rule the sceptre of the dragon. I have also come to gather the remains of our people and do battle against the armies that destroyed the Drax City and our lands."

Jiang looked at Kado for a long time and then slowly a smile crept along his face as he stared into Kado's eyes. Kado did not flinch but realised that Jiang would not give up power without a fight. He began to inch a tiny blade down out of his sleeve.

"A lily addict and vagrant dog ruling these lands and then doing battle against Ranik's hoards and his demons. Your father should have drowned you at your birth, Kado Kodrax, dying ember. I will have you hung from the eerie above and watch the buzzards pick your flesh, indolent leech. Take him and string him up!" Jiang barked at the guards.

Kado cut the rope that bound his hands and flew at Jiang in an instant. He sliced the blade across Jiang's neck, but it only glanced off a leather choker that protected the Lord's throat. He thrust Kado off him and onto the ground. Three guards swooped onto the Kado and pinned him to the floor so hard, that he could barely breathe.

"Think of the riches beneath Jiang. It is yours as well as mine."

Jiang sat back on the chair and began to laugh.

"It is mine as are the weapons. You are as unnecessary as ever Kado."

The guards hoisted Kado up and began to drag him towards a tunnel. Kado struggled to get free but could not get the leverage he needed to attack.

Taking him out onto the ledge on the eastern side of the mountain they tied Kado to four pegs hammered into the rock wall. He lay flat on the ground with each limb stretched akimbo. One of the guards spat on him and then kicked him in the groin. He then shredded Kado's tunic leaving his belly exposed. The guard noticed Kado wincing in pain, but there was no blood from a cut on his bottom lip or cheek.

"That is for my cousin Min, your father flogged him to death for bringing back your stash of hash."

Kado lay on the granite rock straining with all his might to pull his hands free, but the leather strap merely tightened more. Kado felt the sun begin to burn. It was nearing midday and soon the stone would heat up as well. He let his arms go completely limp hoping it would loosen the bonds just a little. He heard a swish of wings and a foul smell of rotten flesh hit him. He looked up and saw a buzzard pecking at an arm of the previous prisoner. It eyed Kado briefly and then continued to tear the flesh from the limb. Then another of the carnivorous birds landed and began to fight over the dead meat.

Kado's mind raced. By another few days, the birds would smell death on him and attack him alive. He thought of Vipax.

"Mighty Serpent, Scaletryx was able to draw a tear from your sun kissed eyes. Surely he knows the means of freeing himself from these bonds."

"My gifts do not bleed" came the voice across the breeze.

Kado thought of the cryptic words and wondered what they meant. The hours passed and the only noise that broke the monotony of his situation was the sound of the birds pecking at the bones of the meal they had found.

One of them flew down and started to peck at a hand that had fallen near Kado to remove the last morsel of flesh. It hopped near Kado's hand as it speared a finger bone splintering it. It pecked again but hit his hand instead. He winced and then noticed the bird staring at him. He knew it had found a feast. It squawked at him calling the others.

Soon six of the beasts sat near him on the ledge. Kado began to struggle but he was bound fast. The first tested his hand again and ripped a piece off his palm. He shouted and flailed as best he could to scare the birds off. They hopped back twice and waited. Kado watched the buzzard gulp down his meat. It came back and tore again at his hand this time most of his palm disappeared down its craggy throat. Kado looked at his hand horrified at seeing the white bone and tendons but noticed that there was no blood, not even from the piece the bird had in its mouth. Suddenly one of them went for his cheek and tore the skin away from his eye. He screamed at them to go as two more pecked at his torso through the slits the soldiers had made. He heard laughter echoing from the tunnel.

"Mighty heir to the dragon throne, scream for your father prince and see if he will kill the birds for you" a guard taunted.

Kado felt tugging at his hand again. This time most of the skin on the knuckles was torn off. He reefed in futility trying to get his hand away from the sharp black beak. Suddenly the bones and tendons of his hand collapsed and slid through the bonds. He rolled over swiftly and undid his other hand. He grabbed one of the beasts and wrung its neck killing it. He threw it over the cliff. Three of them flew off after it while the others stayed. He hissed at the remaining ones as he undid his feet. He quickly got up and flattened himself against the cliff face waiting to see if any of the guards had seen him get free. He looked at his hands, white bones replaced his fingers. There was no pain and this hand felt as strong as the other one. He touched his cheek and felt the bone was exposed there as well.

Creeping into the tunnel he waited until his eyes adjusted from the bright daylight. He could not see anyone and began to test the ground looking for the knife that he had dropped along the way. He soon heard a slight chink and bent down and felt the blade then the handle. He grabbed it and began to walk towards Jiang's chamber. Voices echoed down the passage. He steadied his breathing. He needed Jiang alive to acknowledge him as heir. Most of the people here would never have seen him unless they had been at the palace. He inched forward and peered into the chamber. There were still the twelve guards, Jiang, and his son Lon. He looked at his hand and thought of Vipax words, my gifts do not bleed. He wondered for a moment what he had become. Taking the dagger, he launched himself at the first two guards and garrotted them. Instantly the rest of the room flew at him. Jiang pulled his sword out as did Lon. Kado kept up the momentum and took out another guard and then suddenly felt the force of massive blow to his back. He landed on the ground winded but managed to get out of the way of Lon's foot as it went to crush his head. He darted up and brought the dagger down and into his thigh. Lon collapsed with a roar. Kado managed to grab the sword from his arms and held it tight against Lon's throat.

"I will slice it off Jiang, put down your sword."

Jiang stood looking at Kado and his hand.

"You are not a man. Look at you. The spirits have dredged you from the stinking pits of the underworld."

"Nevertheless, I will remove your son's head and make you beg before the people to save yours."

"You know I will not lose honour like that Kodrax. What do you want?"

"The Sceptre of the Dragon in my hand."

"You will not rule the people. Your father almost broke them with his tyranny. They will not live under the bonds of another Drax Emperor. Give up now."

Jiang darted a glance behind Kado.

Kado tensed waiting for an attack and felt the spear enter his flesh. He gasped feeling his lung puncture, but he remained standing. He sliced across the throat of Lon and thrust his body to the floor. Turning he flew at the guard with a high kick and snapped his neck and again at the next two that came towards him. His frenzied attack left one guard alive and Jiang standing on the dais.

Jiang's face was apoplectic with rage as he drew his sword. Kado stood ready to meet him. Their blades clashed ringing around the chamber. People had heard the ruckus entered the chamber to see what had happened. More guards began to fill the room. Their captain told them to wait. Soon Jiang began to fatigue as Kado matched his very blow but did not land any lethal ones.

"Give up Jiang, I will spare your life if you bow to the heir of the dragon once more."

"I will not bow to the murderer of my son."

Jiang swung down heavily and caught Kado's arm. The blade sliced the flesh away. Kado smashed the hilt of his own sword into Jiang's head and knocked him out.

Kado stood over the Lord looking at the soldiers and people.

"Do you know who I am?"

No one answered, horrified at the state of Kado's macerated body.

"I am your ruler. Bring me the Sceptre of the Dragon."

He dragged Lords Jiang's body over to the dais. Two of the soldiers rushed at him but he deflected their spears easily.

"Find it!" he shouted.

Lord Jiang began to rouse. Kado hoisted him up and onto a seat.

"Take Lon and place him outside for the feeding."

No one reacted. Kado's mind raced, how was he going to convince them he was the ruler?

Jiang sat back against the wall and looked at Kado.

"They will not swear their service again to the Drax Empire. It is finished and buried beneath the rubble of the citadel" croaked Jiang.

"We are all dead anyway Jiang. Hope lies with the allied that now wait to go to battle in the south. The spirits called me for a reason. The blood that courses through my veins was among the first to walk these lands. It is by this right that I am here to seize control and lead us into battle against the shadow that seeks to destroy us."

"Hmph, seek a treaty with it Kado. You are more akin to their kind than that of the dragon."

"Kado Kodrax, you live."

Princess Yun stood at the entrance of the chamber. She was followed by Lords Han, and Quodac. They walked into the room and stood before the dais.

"Your face and hand!" She went to touch his face, but Kado flinched away. "They said a spirit raised from the underworld had come to kill us. Sent by the demon who commands the western tyrant. But I see it is the heir to the throne father."

The princess stood looking at Kado with a quizzical look on her face and Kado noticed she did not acknowledge her father.

"What has happened to you Prince?"

"Many things Princess, too much to tell here. I asked for the Sceptre of the Dragon. I have come to reclaim my throne and Kingdom."

"Well father won't be very happy with that" she giggled.

The memory of the night came back to Kado. The girl was still alluring but he had also seen that a sharp sting belied the coquettish demeanour; a mischief which once matured could be dangerous.

"Perhaps if you fetch it for me, I will tell you of all the things that have happened to me Princess."

He inclined his head in honour of her status. Suddenly Lord Jiang came up behind her, turned her around and slapped her. He went to do it again, but Kado's had shot over and with lightning speed his dagger was sitting at the Lord's throat.

"I want the sceptre of the dragon now!" he commanded to all in the room.

Jiang relented and nodded to his aid Una to find it.

"Shall we sit while we wait." Kado gestured to Jiang and the Princess to the chairs beside the central throne upon the dais. "Bind Lord Jiang to the chair."

Kado walked around inspecting the chamber.

"How many of our people remain Lord Quo?"

"We have three thousand dwelling in the mountain, Kado and many thousands are scattered. But they are dwindling fast as the Matavians and Unstaadt are capturing any they find and sending them on ships to the south."

"Yes, this is happening in the western lands as well."

"You will need to fight for your hand to rule the sceptre again Kado. The people have not forgotten the tyranny of your father and have sworn loyalty to Jiang" spoke Lord Han.

"You waste your time Prince; they will not follow you" Jiang retorted once more.

"I will show them who rules these lands and who it is that we must fight to save them. I will show them the new enemy and make them forget my father."

No one responded but he saw the looks between Jiang, Han and Quodac.

"What is it?" He asked.

Princess Yun began to giggle.

"Word was sent this morning; we have capitulated and offer allegiance to the ruler of Matavia in place of war. Three thousand farmers, peasants and concubines will be sent as offering for whatever purpose they seek."

"Why would the Matavians agree to this, they have already destroyed the kingdom and now occupy our lands?"

"They seek the wealth that lies here as well. They know if we rally, we will kill ourselves while trying to defeat us" replied Jiang. "You know how impenetrable this place is and we could bury the treasure depriving the Matavians of their spoils. It is not the right time for the dragon to raise its head with flame. Their passion for conquest will slow as their soldiers weary" replied Lord Han.

Kado sat quietly trying to figure out why Faad would have agreed to such a thing. Perhaps he would hold true to his oath to Gildas.

"This wealth is not theirs, nor yours Lord. Have the people been sent already?"

"They have."

"This will not be borne. The scum that has ravaged this land still lie in the demon's claws. They serve only its will, and it seeks only to kill this world. You have betrayed your people and lands Jiang, foolhardy coward. It is not Ranik or his Queen that we fight, but the shadow and it will not grow weary. I will raise this army and with the northerner Gildas we will gather to destroy this shadow. Lord Quodac, will you lay fealty to the Drax Magisterium once more."

The Lord stood looking at Jiang and Kado. He loathed both for different reasons and to live again under the yoke of a Drax Ruler filled his heart with anger. But he looked at the wounds Kado bore and knew that something more powerful had blessed or cursed the prince and it had also sanctioned him to live. His hatred of the Matavians ran deeply as they had killed his family and razed his lands to quagmires of mud and rubble for the sake of the minerals that lay beneath.

"Lord Jiang is a coward. I follow the breath of the Dragon once more. Your father was not well loved Kado Kodrax, a cruel and unjust man but strong. Strength is needed now not capitulation."

"You will not command the army Kado. They are loyal to me" Jiang had stood defensively.

Kado saw the look he gave to the guards.

"What payment did you take Jiang?"

Jiang looked at Kado; the indolent brat had matured since their last meeting he thought. Kado fingered his sword.

"Now!" shouted Jiang as the palace warriors flooded into the chamber. The head swordsman and his liege took Kado instantly and held him.

"On his knees. I will give you no honourable death."

Jiang raised his sword to decapitate the prince. Kado looked up at him and smiled. Unnerving Jiang slightly he hesitated. Suddenly Princess Yun ran in front of her father to protect Kado. She held the sceptre of the Dragon in her hands.

"Father, I will not let you kill him."

"Get her out of the way. I will deal with you later."

A soldier dragged the Princess along the ground. She flung the sceptre at Kado. He reefed his wounded arm free and managed to pick up the bejewelled gold rod. He felt the weight of if in his hand and was suddenly struck by a moment of doubt, would he have his father's determination to rule for its own sake and no other. But then the whisper of Vipax tongue echoed in his mind and the quest he was now called to fulfil. As his resolve returned his hand gripped the sceptre and he thrust it into the guard's chest. Then heaving it out blocked the blade of Jiang and swung it so hard the snap of Jiang's neck could be heard above the dead thump of the gold rod hitting his skull.

"String his body up for the birds. Everyone who is loyal to Jiang is to be paraded before it. Bow now before your ruler. Swear fealty once more to dragon blood and breath."

No one moved as he spoke, and the aching doubt almost resurfaced until Princess Yun bowed before him followed by Quodac and Han.

"Bow before your Emperor" Princess Yun commanded.

Slowly the warriors and servants followed Princess Yun's order. Kado saw the look of fear in their eyes and knew it was not just the memory of his father which weighed on their hearts and minds but the creature who now stood before them.

Kado looked at them and then the Princess. She looked up at him and they both knew where the loyalty of the people lay. She tilted her head coquettishly at him with a smile. He wondered what had made the Princess want to protect him and swear fealty to him.

Kado knew he would never inspire love in the hearts of the people of the dragon but at least for now in this dark hour his tenuous rule had been reinstated.

"Gather all the soldiers and begin to ready for war."

He strode to the dais and sat. He looked at his hand and arm and noticed the new bits of pink flesh reforming. The wounds were already healing. What had Vipax turned him into?

His heart ached for Sa-Tuc as the fear and doubt began to nibble again at his mind.

Princess Yun came towards him and bowed.

"I will fetch some food and water for you Emperor."

Looking at her he nodded his head.

"You must have hated your father as much as I disliked mine, Princess?"

She looked at him smiling and giggled at his words but did not answer his question.

# 9

# Nightmares & Nettle Tea

Nene and Tessi watched Medret and Gildas race through the forest as PO flew higher towards the Sanctuary of the Lioness. Angette was wrapped in a swaddling cloth tied around Tessi's chest.

"It's wonderful isn't it dear. Imagine these beautiful creatures hidden from our eyes for so long." Nene held her face up to fully catch the wind as they sped through the air.

Tessi nodded but every beat of her thudding heart longed to be back on the ground. She hugged Angette tightly, terrified that she would fall out of her halter.

Soon the grey peak that signalled the location of the grove came into view.

"Down there, PO" called Nene "Watch out for my cats when you land, you would make a fine feast for them."

PO gracefully aimed for the opening in the mountain. Tessi could see the spec of green from the grove that lay at the bottom of the cave. A bloom of pain welled in Nene's chest as she watched their approach realising this was the last view Dravad had seen before he plunged to his death.

People gathered ready to attack PO as it landed near the pool, gently depositing Tessi and Nene.

"Lower your swords my people, this is our friend, PO of the lofty and valiant Orynth."

Tessi took Angette out of her halter and let her see the beautiful oasis in which they had arrived. Her heart eased a little at the welcoming sandstone and green ferns compared to the coldness of Tarentess. Angette reached for PO to play with its glossy black plumage, but it startled slightly and gave a warning squawk remembering the tuft of feathers that Angette managed to remove last time. Transforming into the eagle again PO flew to a ledge above and perched itself there to keep watch. It began to preen itself only giving the people below a momentary glance.

"My Lady, you are safe and well?" asked Jocelyn.

"Yes Jocelyn, this is Tessi, and her child Angette. They will be our guests for a while."

"What news comes from outside?"

"I will call an assembly to announce to everyone of what has passed since I have been gone. But first I wish to eat and wash. Jocelyn, please find a place for Tessi to sleep."

"Yes ma'am."

The girl gestured for Tessi to follow her and led her up to one of the carved chambers in the wall.

"I know a perfect place that will be safe for you and your baby. How old is she?"

"Just a little over one and half summers."

Tessi struggled to hold Angette, she was so eager to crawl and explore the grove.

Jocelyn guided Tessi to a cave that sat inside the cliff wall. The cave was obscured by a small outcrop of rock which gave it the effect of a petition.

"There ye are, it is quiet here and you can keep the baby safe by blocking this gap off. Now I will ask the boys to bring you some hessian blankets to make a bed and fetch some food for you. I am Jocelyn."

Tessi looked at the girl and thought they looked the same age, tears brimmed in her eyes at the kindness of the girl.

"I am Tessi, and this is Angette. I have another child Noab, but he is held captive by the Queen of Matavia."

"Oh, they are a scourge our neighbours of the sea. They have destroyed our lands and are as cruel to their own people as they are to everyone else. Rest, dearest, you must be so sad within your heart to have been torn away from your child and lands like us. We are all bonded in sorrow from these demon-folk, who drown tree and rock with blood. All my family are dead now so this must be my home until a brighter dawn comes."

"I have only my sister, but she has been called to another quest. My mother and father died in the plagues of the deserts."

Tessi stopped herself from saying anymore, the sadness of it threatening to engulf her again.

"You are here now, and the Queen and her Knight will protect us and the creature that bought you." Jocelyn hugged Tessi. As the girl walked off Tessi's heart leapt with the warmth and affection of Jocelyn. She placed Angette on the ground to walk. She heard a faint roar coming from over the far side of the grove.

"Ahh, the Queen's pets have seen the bird god." Jocelyn called back to Tessi giggling. She gestured to Angette like a lion with its paws up ready to pounce. Angette mimicked Jocelyn giggling as well.

Tessi smiled but as Jocelyn left, she suddenly felt the weight of everything return. Tessi took her swag off and rolled out the blankets and made herself a bed. She took Angette and cradled her to breast feed. As they lay together, they both fell asleep.

The Queen's face stared at her. White upon white, so luminous it almost shone. Her eyes pierced Tessi's mind and she could not turn away. She could hear a child crying, it was Noab. Tessi tried to run to him, but something held her. Then she saw the white claws of the Queen digging into her arms.

"I want the other child. This one grows weak now and I thirst for more. Bring your children together. They cry for each other, young mother so foolish, how can you give them a life? Everyone will be dead soon who remain an enemy to the shadow. Let me give your children a life that you cannot."

Tessi ran towards the shrill crying to find Noab and save him. She was in the tunnels where they had imprisoned Ange. The screaming became more distressed. Tessi ran faster and faster, but she could not find Noab in the pitch-black. The panic burning her throat as it rose with every scream. Suddenly the alabaster skin of the Queen met her. She held Noab, he screamed for Tessi, but the white claws cut his baby flesh. She licked the blood off her fingers.

Tessi screamed aloud. She woke saturated with perspiration. Angette lay grizzling in her arms. The grove was lit by moonlight through the open roof of the sanctuary. There was a small lump of bread and a bowl of milk near her. She took a piece of bread and ate it sparingly as the fear from her dream still gnawed at her stomach. She sipped the milk and set the rest aside for Angette. Looking around the grove she remembered seeing Queen Nene wander into a passage to the right side. She trod carefully to avoid stumbling and waking anyone else up. She eventually found the passage that lay hidden directly from the main part of the grove. Silently she walked into the small cavern that housed Nene. The corpulent body of the Queen was sound asleep emitting stifled snores on her litter.

Tessi nudged her arm to wake her. Nene did not respond. She tugged more urgently this time at her sleeve. Nene startled at being woken.

"Tessi, dear what is it? Is there something wrong with Angette?"

"Yes, she is fine, but Noab is in danger. I saw it in a dream, the Queen will kill him. We must go there and rescue him."

Nene got up seeing the very real fear in Tessi's eyes. Angette woke as well and began to grizzle. Nene went to cradle her, but Tessi would not let her go.

"What happened? Gildas has promised to rescue the child. He and Cotus will be true to their words."

"It will be too late. My little Noab will be lost in the destruction that threatens this world. Please my lady, we must rescue him before he is devoured by the Queen." She dug her fingers into Nene's arm so distraught at the memories that lingered from the nightmare.

"But how my dear? We cannot break into the Palace of the Bay of Tears and not be discovered. Please rest until dawn. Your mind will seem clearer in the daylight. I have been afflicted with these nightmares as well, but it is only the fear and sorrow that lies so heavily on my heart that makes them seem real."

Tessi looked at the Queen. Anger then frustration rose in her heart. She did not understand thought Tessi.

"I will go myself. It will be easier that way. I will be able to hide. I will take Angette with me. The taint of battle already lies upon her spirit, she will be fierce of heart when she is older. I would prefer to die with Noab safe in my arms, knowing that I came for him then leave him alone at the mercy of that witch. The echoes of his screams pierced my heart. I will not abandon him."

"You will surely die and leave the babes to a fate unthinkable if you attempt this Tessi. Now you must rest. On the morn I will send word to Gildas and Cotus, to tell us their plan to rescue Noab. It will set your mind at ease. I will ask Jocelyn to prepare some nettle tea. It will settle your mind and body."

Nene noticed Tessi's eyes go blank like she had come to a decision in her mind. The Queen placed her hand on Tessi's arm.

"You must trust us dear heart. I cannot imagine the pain and sorrow you have endured in all this time. But nothing will be gained by doing something rash now with a fevered mind and heart from the shadows the night brings. Why was your child so precious to Queen Giandra? Why did Ranik tolerate a slave girl who was with child in the first place? His cruelty knows no limits to his own people, little that of a slave child, sold to satisfy his demented perversions."

"Noab and Angette were sired by Ranik. They have been named as heirs to the kingdom. To the people of Matavia they are known as Tias and Mordraag."

Tessi began to sob as the memories of living in the palace came back to her again.

"My dear sweet child. I see now. Oh, the suffering you have endured" Nene hugged Tessi closely.

"But I do not believe it is for this reason the Queen wants the children. I believe she has been driven to madness first by the loss of her own children but also the other servants whispered that she was a sorcerer who used evil ways to maintain her beauty, including drinking the blood of children."

Nene sat looking at Tessi

"You are right dear. When the news came of the death of her children many years ago now, I offered my condolences as way of garnering better relations with my neighbours. But my offer was rejected by Giandra. It was after this that I noticed that the Queen would never accompany Ranik, and she was never seen outside the palace. Rumours on the winds spoke of a white wraith that would haunt the villagers, maiming or stealing children" spoke Nene.

"I think though now that I have seen everything with Ange and Gildas, she wants the children because the same blood that flows in Ange flows in them and me. The shadow has laid its claws on everyone in the palace my lady, including the Queen" replied Tessi.

"The more reason to trust Gildas. The spirits have emboldened him to fight this battle. Let him do it. It is too much for one such as yourself, as valiant and courageous as you are my darling. This is a war against which no ordinary man or woman however ablaze their heart is with passion, can win on their own. You must promise me you will not do anything foolish. I will send word tonight so your mind may be put at some ease that Gildas has Noab in his sight."

Tessi relented a little more reassured.

"Please now wait here while I fetch some nettle tea and some ink and parchment to write on. I will send PO. That will be the quickest way of sending a message."

Tessi sat back against the rock wall with Angette cradled securely in her arms. Noab's face kept coming into her mind. Then the last night she had seen Ange in the battle on the plateau. She remembered the strength her sister had shown as she neared the demon and plunged her sword into its massive thigh. She never hesitated regardless of the fear she must have felt within her heart. The same choice was before her now. Would she have the courage of her sister to fight for her child? Looking at her daughter she saw the same beautiful eyes as Mata and Ange. Tessi knew in her heart what she must do. Ange and Tessi were the last of their peoples. She sung gently to Angette as she watched Nene return with a pot of steaming water. The faint scent of grass met Tessi bringing back the memory of the evening Hanni betrayed her and Ange. The memory of the Queen holding Noab, threatening to harm him with her poison. The image of Ange's sword plunging into the demon's thigh was clear as the eyes of her baby. Nene handed Tessi the tea and began to write on the parchment.

"Will you stay here until the dawn dear heart. I am sure we will have an answer by mid morn at the latest."

"No, I will go to my bed. I feel better just talking to you lady. Jocelyn is close by if I need anything."

Nene hugged Tessi.

"Please call me Nene."

She walked with Tessi out into the grove. PO stood ready to take the message to Gildas. Nene handed it to the Orynth and after the bird had flown out of the grove, she looked across at Tessi and saw she had settled back into her bed with Angette.

She looked at the tiny figure and wondered how such a fragile beauty had withstood such ravages and evil.

"Would the Queen of Aeserea have survived that much terror and despotic callousness? I have barely managed to keep my mind from fevered states so haunted with the images I have seen and the loss of my brothers. Rest little one, your strength shall be my strength also."

The light cascaded into the grove waking the remnants of the people left to serve the Kingdom of the Lioness. Nene stirred feeling out of sorts after her interrupted sleep. She wondered if PO had returned with good news for Tessi. She placed her dress and apron on, noting how the hems were beginning to fray. She thought to herself that she would spend the afternoon mending all her garments. She had missed her embroidery and thought it was time to begin a tapestry to herald all that had passed. It would occupy her mind while they waited for the war to be over. Even if it were not a victory, in time people would find this dwelling and discover the last story told of the Aeserean people on the tapestry.

Walking out into the cavern she went to the stream and scooped a bowl full of water and drank it heartily. Sitting on a rock she began to brush her hair and braid it. Will, a serving boy came up to her with a bowl of oatmeal and warmed tea.

"My lady the leaves are old. We have sent a group, including Jocelyn and your guest, out to venture into the fields to pick some more. The soldiers needed to raid a stash of weapons and we all thought it was best if everyone went together."

"That is good Will, wise decision."

Nene enjoyed the oatmeal and stale tea. It was good Tessi went with them; it would keep her busy until PO returned.

The sun moved its way across the sky signalling the afternoon was arriving. Nene's fingers were sore from darning her aprons and the few dresses she had managed to salvage from the palace. Suddenly a shadow obscured the sunlight. She looked up and saw the graceful Orynth alighting on the mossy area of rocks. It held a scroll of parchment. PO walked over to Nene and handed her the scroll.

Opening it she noted it had been written by Cotus.

"Dear Nene, Keeper has set heart to finding the flower of the desert. It is requested that the Orynth return to assist its brethren."

Nene nodded satisfied.

"Thank you, PO. Did your eagle eyes see anything else on their flight?"

"No, it seems the battle moves south to the coast. Long caravans of your kind walk to their doom as they board the vessels that rock on the great waters of Lido."

"I will let you go PO. Gildas has use of you now. Thank you for your allegiance. We lesser ones must seem clumsy indeed compared to the grace and beauty of the Orynth?"

"It is not for me to say why you were made to dwell here, in lands that seem to barely give enough leaving you at the mercy of their whim. But ever since the time of things created so has it always been, that light and dark hold sway and all beings made from them must run their gauntlet. The ground dwellers while ugly to our eyes have valiant hearts like the Orynth. We are proud to place our feather and your skin together in battle if it thwarts Voloc and its progeny."

PO bowed as did Nene in return. Flying up and out of the grove Nene's heart ached as she lost sight of the magnificent creature. How much more lay hidden in this world of theirs?

Nene looked and saw the party return with baskets full of nettles, nuts and sheaves of wheat that had been left untended. There had been over thirty sent and the bustle of the return felt almost festive.

"We should have enough to last at least the next six moons and the colder months. There is more coming to ripeness in another cycle. We can venture out again to gather it on the turn of the leaf, my Lady" beamed Jocelyn.

"That is splendid Jocelyn. Almonds, goodness we can grind it to make the milk and flour, along with the oats and wheat. I think we could allow a small celebration as thanksgiving to the bountiful harvest."

Nene sighed as the scene lifted her spirits. Soon more of her subjects returned with so many sacks that half of the cavern floor was covered in baskets spilling over with grains and nuts. She began to look for Tessi, thanking people as they sat to rest on the ground around her.

"Jocelyn, have you seen Tessi?"

"No, I have not ma'am. She came with me this morning, but I lost her once we were out picking."

Nene began to grow nervous.

"Send Will and the other boy Jack to look for her in the tunnels. I will go with one of the soldiers to see if she is in the forest."

"Yes Ma'am. Jack and Will." Jocelyn ran off calling the two boys.

"Captain, I think we have lost the girl and child from the desert people. Come with me and bring two of your men, we will search the forest."

Nene led the soldiers back through the maze of tunnels and into the forest.

"Which way did you come from?"

"From the western edge Ma'am"

"We will meet back here in the turn of the glass. She will not have gotten far in the time since they left. We should be able to find her."

Nene went in the direction of the almond tree grove and began to search frantically for Tessi. In the back of her mind, she knew what Tessi was wanting to do, but it would mean her certain death or worse to be enslaved once more. Soon she realised that the shadows grew longer and that it was nearing the twilight. She felt a tug on her sleeve and saw that it was Captain Kyle Yonan.

"My lady it is not safe to linger here particularly at night. We have not been able to find your guests."

"Yes Captain, we will return and send a search party in the morning. She would be on foot with a child. She will not get too far."

"Beg my pardon ma'am but where does the girl journey?"

"She seeks her other child, in the Bay of Tears."

"Then she is lost to you ma'am if I can be so bold to speak. If we have not found her by eventide tomorrow, then she will not return to your care."

"I know Captain. That is my fear."

"Would you like me to send a message to the Lord Knight?"

"No, he has much more to than this to occupy him, but he also is aware of Tessi and her baby. Battle is nigh Kyle, an alliance has been struck between us, the Graan and the easterners of the Drax

Kingdom. An army never seen before in our time or my father's, gathers to wage war here first and then in the great lands to the south. It will be to the death."

"Ay ma'am, it has been whispered such a bargain has been struck and that a mighty warrior from the mountains has been called down to seek the shadow and destroy it. I know ma'am it is not the time to ask, but I seek one boon from you my fair and gracious Queen?"

"Yes Kyle, ask."

"I ask to go battle alongside my brothers with the banner of the green and gold flying high above us and emblazoned on our chest and rid the world of Matavia. The Keep is safe, nothing only the birds of the skies and their gods may enter it."

Nene looked at the soldier, her heart bursting with pride and sadness. She had remembered Cotus often speaking his praise, but a battle wound had shortened his career, relegating him to the palace guard. A post worthy of itself for any Aeserean but for Lord Yonan it had been a blow to his prowess as a soldier and a loss to the cavalry.

"Kyle, having you go into battle for my crown and lands is only second to the mighty Cotus Medret. Go with my blessing and decree. Fight valiantly and fearlessly. And if death should find you run with all your strength to the bosom of the Lioness, whose grace now lies with the Lord of Tarentess."

As Nene and the Captain entered the sanctuary Jocelyn ran to her hoping the Queen had good news but when the Queen shook her head she burst into tears.

"Oh, my lady it is my fault. I should have stayed with her. But she looked so happy to be going out."

"Do not blame yourself Jocelyn. I saw the look of resolution in her eyes last night. She had set her mind to seek her child regardless of what would become of her. Would you expect anything less of a mother?"

"No ma'am."

"Go now and prepare the feast for the people to enjoy their spoils. We will search again in the morning. If we do not find her then we will begin to blockade the entrances. I have granted the captain and any soldiers who wish leave to go and join the legions that now gather for the last battle. We will be safe here until the fates of our lands and peoples are decided."

Jocelyn nodded and left, her sobs still echoing around the cavern. Nene got up and went towards the place Tessi had made her bed. She looked at the bare spot where her blanket had lain.

"Oh, brave heart I fear I cannot have your death on my mind regardless of how much longer I may live."

The sanctuary became dark quickly as the sun dipped below the cliffs above them. Nene watched the villagers and servants gather around a tiny cornucopia of nuts, dried fruit, and wheaten cakes. They looked happy and contented but their bodies were gaunt from living on such meagre portions and their eyes hollow as the sorrow of their plight bore down on their hearts.

"Feast my people. Fair and full of love for one another has ever been the way of the Aeserean people. My gratitude to you cannot be told adequately. Hold strong for darker days are yet to come but the grace of the Lioness has not forsaken us. I will take my leave to rest. Please enjoy this while you can."

Everyone hesitated not wanting the Queen to leave but realised they would not dissuade her. They suddenly burst into cheers and toasted to their fair and gracious queen with bowls full of goat's milk.

Nene went inside to sit with Ushan. The great cat had been out hunting and was full on deer meat.

"How can I sit here, plump and protected while that girl stands ready to walk into the pits of the demon's lair with only the thought of saving her child and none to the danger that she knows awaits her. Does Queen Nene lay here like a fattened lamb ready for the spring slaughtering or does she fulfil the call of the heart of the Lioness, her strength, her ferocity and fight for those placed under her protection."

Nene sat in the dim light of Ushan's cave. An anger welled inside her once more at the destruction of her land, the great forest of Vran and her brothers. The anger pushed aside the fear once more. She looked at Ushan.

"Are you ready for an adventure Ushan?"

The cat purred heavily as the Queen stroked the large head thinking of what she would need for the journey.

PART TWO

# ASCENDANCY

## CUSTODIAN

### of

## MEMORY AND DEATH

# Fear and Courage Part II

The wind whipped around her head cutting straight through her cloak. It clawed at her face as if it were trying to scratch away the flesh. Ange's lips were scabbed and bloody from the trek across the barren rocky plateau. She had no sense of time. She had vague memories of walking across another place like this somewhere else, but she could not remember where that place was.

Her name was Ange Tsaed. She was here to find the lady again and her brethren. She peered far into the distance towards a hazy outline of black rock. It was in that black shape which speared straight up into the sky; that was where she would find the lady. Then all this would be explained, the reason she walked here alone and why she was in this place.

She scrambled down a ledge onto a roughly hewn path of gravel. Her footsteps crunching on the stones was magnified by the walls of slate towering either side of the path. At least here she was protected from the wind. The wind had a name as well and it had something to do with the lady she was searching for.

She licked her parched lips. She drank from the cask which hung from her side. The liquid was rich and thick. There was a god of the water Ange thought. She remembered a place that was cool and green. She had lay down and rested once. The water would come to life around her. But it seemed like a dream. The gulp revived her, and she continued into the maze of rocks. Her body was weary and did not seem to work very well. One of her legs was crooked and would give way. She could not understand why it was like that. Looking ahead she saw that the jagged rocks began to close in on each other so that the path was lost under foot. She had to step on the steep edges of the boulders. Her shins soon began to bleed from the scratches as she slipped and fell on the sharp edges of the stones.

A roar came across the air and Ange lay down as she knew what would happen next. Everything began to move, the rocks pulled apart and then reformed. The ground shattered beneath her, but she did not fall. The wind stilled and the light seemed to intensify. She hung suspended over shattered stones waiting for the roars to end. The light was strange colour Ange thought. It was yellow and reminded her of the light in her dreams. It was fast light not slow light like the images that would come to her. In one dream she remembered lying in tall green plants and her eyes were stinging as she was looking at a yellow circle in the sky. It stayed in the one spot all the time and never changed. She fell asleep thinking of this moment wanting it to be real. She drifted to the ground as she dreamt, as the rocks reformed beneath her. But soon the silence woke her. She got up and began to walk. Deeper into the labyrinth of rocks Ange trod with only the sound of her footsteps to keep her company. It did not seem strange to her that she should be alone like this. It was as if looking into the world from the outside instead of feeling a part of it. She stopped suddenly as she heard something momentarily disturb her musing. It was tiny whispers. She waited and listened. Silence. She took a few steps. The whispers returned, only louder this time. She jumped thinking there was someone behind her.

"Who are you?"

There was no reply.

"Who are you?"

Nothing.

Ange continued to walk along letting her mind drift from listening to the intermittent whispers and then to images in her mind. She imagined chasing a creature; it was brutal looking but seemed to want to be friends with her. She kept chasing it through green plants and along a stream of water. It tried to speak to her, but she could not understand anything it said. It ran to her and pushed her over and she began to laugh. She stopped though as she realised her laughter was booming around her. She waited for it to stop. As the echoes of laughter dissipated, she saw that she stood in a large hall. It was carved from the mountainside and the ceiling was a curved arch so high above that she could barely see the buttresses of the stone roof. In the distance a miniscule glow of blue green light broke through the gloom. Her heart began to thud in her chest as she knew she had finally reached the tower. The whispers returned. She seized her sword and made sure the dagger she carried also sat inside her sleeve, ready to be snatched out it in an instant. She wondered how she had known to put it there. In her mind she ran through what she would do if she were attacked. Walking closer the glow soon crystallised into two specs shining in the darkness. Ange began to feel sick as she realised, they were eyes peering at her.

"I feel your fear and courage and taste the dimness that veils your mind. I can feel the confusion and doubt that consumes your heart. I know that only a silent place like this can ease the chaos those lost fragments chewing at your mind cause. The utter annihilation that brings peace is all that sustained me when the bonds were strong. You have entered the realm of the Caemexa, clayborn. You now know that each moment is what lingers not the sum of all that has been. No memory, that is the curse of the immortal and their blessing."

Baachelaus sat looking at the tiny creature sent to steal back what the god desired. She was a wretched thing but cleverly chosen the god thought. It sensed the iron will to live and fight and the lust to pursue its purpose. A will honed and tested in each day it had to survive in the face of derision and scorn by all around it. Her contorted and deformed shape a reminder of her enemies' own fragility.

Ange had felt each of the words the monster spoke plunge like knives into her. Her hand ached where it clenched the sword looking at the malevolent god rise from its throne and come towards her. Its face screamed of agony endured for eons and in its chest lay a broken chain link, shredded from forces so strong that it would be unbearable to a body such as hers.

"I have come to find the lady."

"I know."

"I will not be stopped. I have no other purpose than this. My body may look broken and my mind foggy, but I can still wield a blade."

The hand reached out to Ange. She saw the long white fingers as sharp as claws tainted with dead black flesh at the tips reach for her. Ange could hear the whispers that had followed her on the journey here. She ducked away to flee the talons bearing down on her. She pulled out her sword and swiped at the emaciated thigh of the god. The blade cut and instantly the flesh sizzled at the edges of the wound. She slashed again but this time the hand caught the hilt of her sword, and she was instantly hoisted up into the air. She was pulled up to the face of the monster. She stared into the eyeless sockets and the gaping mouth. The foulness of decay made her gag. The face cracked into a grin and the blue green specs of light shone brighter.

"Keeper, you are brave. Bring my brethren to me and you shall be rewarded. Fail and you shall know my agony."

"I seek the lady for my own purpose. It shall be made clear when I find her."

Ange felt the claws dig into her flesh. Her heart felt like it was going to explode until a thought came to her.

"You cannot kill me."

Instantly the hand tightened even more and thrust her into the air. She landed on the stone floor with a thump. She was winded and gagged for air.

"Find the lady yourself. I have my own quest" she panted.

Baachelaus walked back to the throne in the centre of the dais. Ange heard chains dragging behind the creature.

"Who are you?" she asked.

"I am Baachelaus."

"Who is Baachelaus?"

"I am the changer of light to dark to light. Without me all things remain the same until death takes them. From me came more colours to make the many paths of Caemeris."

"Why are we here in this place?" Ange stood feeling braver.

"Find your lady and you shall know."

"Why do you not find her? If you know she is here, then why do you not seek her?"

The specs which were the god's eyes glowed in anger at Ange's questions, but she persisted.

"You cannot harm me."

Then the large, cavernous room became filled with yellow light. Ange's heart lifted as the gloom of the granite hall was pushed away reminding her senses of the bright hopeful feeling of waking. What was it called when each time new things would begin, and the gloom of night would lift? Another spirit entered the throne room of the creature.

Seraf looked at Ange and flared brilliantly, hurting Ange's eyes. She shielded them with her arm and tried to desperately cover her face with her hood, but the searing heat washed over her.

"Enough Seraf, she cannot be killed."

Baachelaus lifted his hand and instantly the flames dimmed.

Ange rose and looked around her. She blinked and for a moment felt knives pierce her eyes where the flames had burnt them. She stared trying to see. Slowly the world came into view. She looked at Baachelaus on the throne.

Seraf stalked around her threatening to flare at any moment.

"You are another of the brethren" she said to the fire god.

"What creature is this that stains this realm? How do you bear to dwell here and not die? I have made your eyes dim and yet they still watch me."

"I am Ange Tsaed and I seek the one called Assumpta."

Ange took her shield out of its holster in readiness for the god of fire to attack. She noticed as she strapped it to her arm her reflection. Her eyes were white where the flames had seared them.

Seraf stopped and turned directly towards her.

"Clayborn you are unworthy to walk in the realm forged by Caemeris."

"My quest is not with you fire god." Ange strode towards Baachelaus.

"If you cannot kill me or stop me then I will leave and continue my search."

Baachelaus looked at her. The god felt the chains pull again and wondered where Voloc was. His mind still reeled with mists of memories long ago and now this realm where he existed as its ruler unknown and never seen before. He sat upon a throne made for a god mired in shadow.

Then a roar came across the wind. Ange fell to the floor waiting for the stone cathedral to collapse but nothing moved. The shudder came again with the rumble of the voice closer this time.

"Bring it here" Baachelaus spoke to Seraf.

Seraf flew out of the hall in a flash.

"I am ruler here clayborn and none shall command me."

Ange stood looking at the god her heart beginning to thud again. She wanted to flee to find the lady. Ange realised that while the god could not kill her, she would never be able to escape its hold. She needed to find Assumpta otherwise she would remain caged here with Baachelaus.

The sound of chains scraping on stone echoed from below and filled the chamber. Ange turned and saw a god, mightier than the others and stronger. It was bound in thick heavy black chains, which dug into is body, sparks fractioned against its skin as if it wanted to destroy him. She knew this god, but from where?

"Come brethren, Norbu, forger of stone from light." Baachelaus motioned for the custodian of Arglethium to come forward.

The mighty god stood halfway to the roof and his massive body blocked the light of Seraf placing Ange and Baachelaus in shadow.

"Descendant, you shall release me. Our places are as equals not as ruler and the ruled."

"I have no memory of our time before now brother. And it is I who sit upon a throne as ruler of a failed realm."

"Keeper, why are you here? Do you not know that you must find her, the world awaits her to make us strong again? While we are sundered from one another Voloc's poison seeps ever deeper into the wounds."

"Who are you? I have seen you before."

"I am Norbu, forger of stone and bringer of clayborn to birth. I lie here chained by my brethren whose purpose has been corrupted. His gaoler the shadow, destroyer of the light, known as Voloc rules your lands unfettered and shall devour all that has been wrought since the time of the great Star."

Ange stared for a long time her opaque eyes unreadable. None of the world Norbu spoke of remained in her memory. Was this what the dreams were, her life before this place?

Baachelaus clenched his claws and instantly the chain that hung in his chest reformed and the ones around Norbu's tightened sending the mighty god to his knees. Norbu roared as the links cut and burned him.

"You do not rule here Brethren." Baachelaus thundered across the chamber. The stone walls and floors shook but did not break or shatter. Ange felt her heart miss a beat as Baachelaus' voice rippled through her body.

"I already rule you and the custodians of creation. I shall not be defeated and nor will my throne. Know my wrath and despair as the millennia spent in the shadow of Voloc. None came to tear the bonds. None came to release me from the searing heat of the shadow's malice. None came to quell the sorrow or fear that became the light of my existence. I am Baachelaus, God of death and malice, reborn of the darkness of Voloc. I now sit here upon the throne of my kingdom and shall not be usurped. Light now lies at my mercy. I am both Caemexa of the first stars and reborn from emptiness where light is destroyed. I am ruler of the remnants of Caemeris vision. I usurp the rule of the first star and shall bring all under my dominion. Even the shadow Voloc will crumble in my sight."

Baachelaus and Seraf surrounded him and then Aerean appeared in a maelstrom of wind. Norbu crumbled under the weight of the chains as they glowed with the heat of Seraf and the wind of Aerean tore his flesh. Baachelaus eyes shone with the blue and green of Uchala and Vipax. The power so great that Norbu was pounded into the stone floor. The custodian's flesh began to blister as Descendant's malice poured forth.

"Lido, Ascendant, bring the new custodian of shadow and memory forth. Bring the six together and restore the Caemexa of light." Norbu raised his fist and thundered his plea for help into the corrupted realm.

Ange watched the mighty god fall. She remembered falling once, when stones had hit her making her body collapse as others had stood over her spitting and deriding her. They had left her bleeding. A man walked past her and ignored her. She remembered one of the people speaking "That is her pata, even he doesn't want her."

Ange looked at Norbu and saw his eyes. They were the same colour as the stone of the floor but shimmered with green and brown. They were rich and deep with welcome. A wave of love and warmth washed over her. For the first time she felt the safety of being cradled by something that wanted her to be here and part of its heart. Tears welled in her eyes. She crawled over to Norbu. In the noise of the wind and the heat, she grabbed his face and kissed it. Tears fell down her cheeks and stung the burns of Seraf.

"I will find them and bring them back so that this may end."

"Hurry Keeper, time moves faster in your realm than here, and I grow weaker the longer the chains of Descendant lie upon me. Find the water spirit Lido as well. She hides herself in hope that it will weaken Baachelaus. Take them to the gate of Magmeris. You must bring us together and destroy us. The new custodian of shadow and memory must rise. It is the end of the Caemexa. If Baachelaus is not destroyed, then we cannot die. His rule lay in death and memory."

"Who is the new custodian of shadow and memory? Where do I find them?"

"You are."

"I don't understand. I will free you."

Suddenly everything stilled. Baachelaus stood watching but did not seem to hear what Norbu had said. Seraf and Aerean stilled.

Ange stood and strode directly toward the pale god.

"I will seek Assumpta and the water spirit."

"Seraf and Aerean will follow you clayborn. And then all will be under my dominion" spoke Baachelaus.

"And have me free?" replied Norbu. "You keep me bound by all your wills alone brother. You have not conquered me yet Descendant. She is to seek them on her own."

It was true on his own Baachelaus could not conquer Norbu or Voloc. Something still thwarted him. Was it Voloc? Had the gaoler not freed its prisoner? Only with the power of all the others was there a chance for Descendant to rule Caemeris. Voloc had taught Baachelaus how to exist within death and now the custodian would rule the chaos of light's creation once all the caemexa were together.

"You will seek the Ascendant and Lido. Bring them here and you shall have your freedom, clayborn."

"What of your brethren what will become of them?" Ange looked at the emptiness behind the specs and desperately wanted to flee.

"That is not your concern clayborn. We were made before your world was even a thought. Our time has been, and it is this that is forgotten by Baachelaus. The tear, the stone, you hold was forged so the memory of light and its power may be held by others. By the clayborn if they are to be the custodians for the next age of light" spoke Norbu.

Ange wondered about Norbu's words, if the clayborn are to be the custodians of the next age of light.

"Go Custodian! Do not let the sorrowful and bitter depths of Descendant distract you or addle your resolve with doubt. My brethren has forgotten its purpose" spoke Norbu behind her.

She turned and looked into Norbu's eyes. She felt their strength restore hers.

"Where shall I begin?" Ange asked.

Baachelaus felt the power of Norbu flood Ange's spirit and exploded with rage.

It wrenched on the chains strangling Norbu and knocking over Ange. The god snatched Ange and drew her close. Fear consumed her as the god filled her mind with its own, draining her will.

"You shall begin in the pits of the Ondraack. These creatures were born before me, and their hearts beat with the shadow there. My vision is dim within their reaches. You are strong clayborn and wisely chosen but to know true fear will strengthen you even more for your quest."

Baachelaus eyes flared blue and pierced Ange's body. She convulsed with the force of the gaze of the custodian.

"Know who I am and who you attempt to thwart. Out of all that has been created only I have stood and looked at the endless void and not be destroyed by its malice. Bring me my brethren or you shall know my wrath."

Suddenly Ange was flying through darkness so fast she could hardly keep her breathe. Fear hung like a boulder around her heart and would not let go. It was if the god had marked her to keep her bonded to its mind and own desolation.

She stopped. It was silent. Ange could hear her heart beating against her chest. She could see nothing. She tentatively took the first step. There was nothing underneath that she could feel. It was not stone but was solid. There was no light. Ange thought she was walking forward but as she kept going a doubt grew that she was not moving. A wisp of air brushed her neck. She turned to see if anything was there but only more darkness met her.

"I am here. The god of the brethren, known as Descendant, has sent me."

Her voice did not echo but seemed to be swallowed by the shadow around her.

"Lady and water spirit, Ange seeks you. I call you now like you called me. Answer me if you are here."

She got down onto her hands and knees to feel the ground in front of her. Her hand touched the edge of something. She moved forward trying to find another edge. There was nothing. She moved to the side and found a wall. She grasped something solid and loose. She threw it hoping it would connect with something. Nothing. She tried another and nothing again.

"Lido, Assumpta!" she called in a hoarse whisper. There was no sound not even her own echo. She moved along the implacable wall of darkness slowly finding her way. She felt along the base of the wall and noticed it ended suddenly. Her fingers felt down to where her knees sat and moving forward noticed the ledge ended as well.

Ange felt her foot touch another object. She picked it up and threw it. The sound of it hitting something made her heart skip with some hope that she was nearing an end to the abyss. She crawled over the edge and slowly eased herself into the empty space. She dangled making sure her grip was good before sliding along the ledge. Her hands began to tremble as the distance seemed to go forever. Then her heart froze when two red eyes appeared in the darkness where she had come from. She stopped and tried not to breathe hoping the creature would not see her.

The gaze of the eyes did not move and seemed to peer over her head. It disappeared. She continued until her hand felt the end of the rock she was hanging from. She put her leg out and found there was nothing there. Panicking she searched again and realised that it was the end of the wall. Her arms and legs trembled as she began move back the way she came. But after a few moments the ledge ended there as well. She stretched hoping it was just small gap but there was nothing. She sobbed with frustration and exhaustion as she dangled in the darkness alone, not knowing if she would plunge to her death if she let go. Then something grabbed her leg and yanked her down. She screamed but it was swallowed by the impenetrable darkness. Suddenly she landed on something solid. She heard sniffing. She covered her nose and mouth to stop gagging. The fear in her mind at whatever hovered over her grew so much it seemed more real than the foul breath that met her.

"Show yourself creature! You know I walk your realm. Begin the battle so I can see what I must fight. Hiding in the dark like scavengers is not a worthy enemy."

Only silence answered her call. Her heart began to slow as nothing happened. Why doesn't it attack? It knows I am here. She stood breathing until she began to feel like she was sucking in the black abyss around her. The panic rose as she began to believe she was drowning. It bloomed into full belief. She tried to find who she was and where she came from but there was nothing only more emptiness. She began to flail in the darkness trying to stop the void engulf her.

"I am Ange, clayborn, chosen to find the Ascendant, called by Norbu…"

The words stopped as she realised, she did not know why she had been called.

"I am here, I am Ange. Answer me!"

Her voice wailed into the shroud of black surrounding her.

"Answer me!"

Then the vaguest whisper passed near her.

"Know my pain clayborn. Search the depths of my prison and find what we both desire."

The vicious cold eyes formed in her mind. Ange stared back at them. Anger rose in her heart.

"I will not become you, rotten and lost to your purpose. I walk with a broken body and still live; you have been given the power of gods and lie in the depths of sorrow and despair."

A monumental spear of heat shot through her body thrusting her into the void. She hurtled so fast that her chest felt crushed under the weight of it. She kept going; nothing was going to stop her in this endless space.

"Where are the custodians called Assumpta, and the water spirit Lido?" she called.

Suddenly an image of the ugly creature licking her face and them both lying near a pool of water came to her. The grass was soft and comforting and the sunlight danced around them in the dappled shade. It reflected off the water, like jewels. The water gave everything life and the sound of its flowing pervaded her mind and body. She dove into it and flowed over the bright stones on the bed of the river and across vistas of red sand until the ocean met her. Ange fell into the heaving waves and felt her body bend with the ebbs of the tides. The happiness of the image in her mind burst forth smashing the darkness around her and stopping her flight. Getting up dazed her eyes focussed slowly, stinging from the pale gloom that now surrounded her. She stood on a plain of grey rocks again. Water dripped down slabs of slate studded with black glossy bushes. The largest of the rocks only rose a few lengths above her head. She saw that the path she stood upon ended in a tunnel.

She walked forward knowing that something watched her. The prick of its gaze stung the flesh of her back. Walking into the tunnel Ange gripped her sword and shield tightly waiting for the attack. She saw that the tunnel ended in a cage carved out of the slate.

"You are here" a voice in the gloom drifted out. Ange's heart lifted when she heard it. Running to the bars of rock her heart nearly leapt out her chest.

Inside stood a translucent figure barely visible against the wall. It caused the wall to ripple as it moved towards Ange.

"Lido" Ange called.

"Hasten now it comes, Ange."

"The dead god has Norbu in chains. I am here to find you and Assumpta."

Ange tested the stone bars. They were solid.

"Can't you escape between the rock?"

"I cannot. Ondraack contains me and the cage protects me."

"Ange!" Lido shimmered with fear.

Then Ange felt a breath touch her neck. Not wanting to turn but knowing she must, she gripped her sword and shield. She whipped around ready to face whatever stood behind her.

She sobbed when she saw the creature behind her.

"Your strength shall not fail you now sister" whispered Lido.

Ange felt the watery hand touch her shoulder.

The creature hissed. It was long and skinny and had glossy skin that was as dark as the vault that she had been thrust into by Baachelaus. Its eyes were beautiful discs of indigoes and violets endless in their depth and age. It opened its mouth and razor-sharp fangs appeared. A claw suddenly shot out and swiped at Ange.

She ducked just in time and thrust her sword into its body. The blackness gave way, and the cut bled the same swirling ethers as the eyes. She slashed again. It screeched at such a high-pitch her ears bled.

"How do I kill it, Lido?"

"You cannot but you must defeat its strength."

The creature turned to her and hissed as the wound healed in its torso. It picked her up and threw her, but she landed upright on her feet. She leapt up at the Ondraack and slashed and stabbed until the ethers of colour bled into the chamber. It screeched and contorted but would not relent as it met Ange blow for blow.

"Lesser one you stain the purity of the shadow with the density of light within your flesh. Be gone from my realm." Ondraak spoke. Its voice was so thick with ancient power that Lido and Ange both collapsed as the words ate into their forms. It grew to its full size, towering over Ange. The colour swirled around making everything glow in magnificent rainbows but the rays cut anything they touched. It scooped Ange up and thrust her far out into the slate grey rocks. She landed with such a thud that all the wind was knocked out of her. She got up gasping. She sprinted back to the cave. Her legs pumped and threatened to give way, but nothing stopped the resolve and strength she felt. She remembered faces of people whose names she did not know but filled her heart with courage and not fear. Ange Tsaed had never felt so alive and invincible then when she ran with the thoughts of those people smiling at her. The eyes of Norbu filled her bones and the smile of a girl like herself and a man and a woman different but the same. She ran with the faces of Tessi, Mata and Bensah smiling at her. She remembered Nekoda's bark.

As the entrance of the cave drew near, she heard hissing behind her. She did not remove her gaze from the black mouth of the cave knowing what chased behind. Racing into the den she launched herself at the cage of Lido and hacked at the stone bars.

"What makes stone? What made the mountain and what made the sand beneath my feet? How were the great spires of palaces and cities hewn from their beds? How did the stones gifted from a riverbed come to rest in my hand? From time and the will to create and to know. I have no time, but I wish to re-make this cage. I wish to know how the light was made into stone and then unmake it." Ange whispered as her blade began to slice through the rock and within in an instant had managed to destroy one of the columns. Then the talon of the Ondraack wrenched her away. She stabbed at its claw, and it let go. Stepping away she looked at its eyes.

"Do you see me creature? Do you see that I have come back? I am of this world and the world of the clayborn. I can rule light and will it to change. I stand staring at a creature ancient and never wearied and full of powers and strength. I am young and weak and yet you still must battle me. Don't you see I shall never be defeated here? Why is that you must battle me? Because we are made of the same thing, and we fight for the right to rule its power. Now stand away, the custodian needs to be free of your bonds."

The Ondraack hissed and Ange felt the venom of its malice sting her mind.

"You see much lesser one and the Ondraack seeks your will to break it."

"You cannot creature. Don't you see you are formed from the very thing you seek to destroy? Feel this and then see yourself."

Ange stepped forward and slashed. She jumped into the gaping wound and was swallowed into the corona of colour. The Ondraack attempted to capture her before she disappeared, but it was too late. It looked inside its glossy black hide and turned inside itself.

Two consciousnesses chased each other through the miasma of churning colours. Ange could not feel her body but suddenly remembered who she was. Then the sorrow of all that had been lost came to her and then anger. She stopped moving and turned. The black shape followed, it contorted in resistance to the light but neither it nor the shadow could swallow the other.

"Behold me Ondraack."

The creature stopped.

Ange and the ancient creature from the first wars floated in light and colour. Soon the colour began to nibble away at the edges of the dark shape, tickling it and then gnawing.

"You shall remain here if you do not let me pass through your realm. My battle lies elsewhere in my world. Let me pass with the prisoner you hold captive before you are utterly annihilated."

Ondraack reached for Ange and grabbed her. It tried to devour her but could not as the colours pushed its away.

"Let it be Ondraack. You walk in a realm that is no longer your dominion. Our paths were never meant to cross. We are unknown to each other. We are neither enemy nor ally."

The huge black jaws opened revealing fangs razor sharp dripping with black oil. But as it tried to devour Ange it was pushed back again and again.

"Stand down!" Ange warned. She saw her blade be made and remade as if the bonds of light understood where the metal blade had come from.

Its massive head expanded to three times its size and towered over Ange. She did not move.

"Stand down Ondraack. You are matched by a creature of newer light and caged by fewer memories."

She held her blade in the roof of its cavernous mouth, the black bile from its fangs sizzled on the steel.

For an eternity they remained like this, staring into each other and each seeing that neither of them would win this battle. It shrunk back to its normal size as the heat of the swirling colours abraded the hide of the creature.

"Interloper of Caemeris, the Ondraack were made from the death of stars and shun their light. You were made from the gaze of our enemy the First Star. It shall not be borne that you tread in our realm again. But neither can we defeat you for our paths are chained to their own destinies. You shall remain until the spirit is freed by your own hand and then you must leave. If the scent of you passes again into the pits of the Ondraack, then your fate shall be to battle us until the death of all things."

Suddenly Ange found herself sitting in the gloom of Lido's prison. The hand of the custodian touched her shoulder. She jumped.

"If I free you, we can leave unhindered."

"Hurry Ange" spoke Lido.

Ange started to cut the stone column of the cage. As her hacking neared breaking point of the column the blade would go no further. Ange began to weary and soon slumped against the wall. The Ondraack were nowhere to be seen.

"Lido, I don't know what to do."

"Keep trying Ange."

She got up again and stared intently at the columns of rock. She ran her hand over them to feel them. Was there sorcery in them? She felt nothing only a cold hardness. She sat again and swigged some water. She noticed the cask was empty. Lido watched her test if there was any left and reached forward. The god touched the cask and it instantly swelled with liquid. Ange sipped some more and as soon as the sweetness of the water ran down her throat, her mind filled with memories of the grove and with Nekoda, Bensah and Gildas. Ange gasped as she remembered Nekoda's name and Bensah's beaming smile made her laugh and weep. The water tumbling over rocks in the caves.

"I remember now."

She stood more resolute and swung her little blade into the stone. The chopping made more of the rock chip away. As the last blade stroke cut through the pillar it crumbled into tiny pieces for a moment. Lido went to leave but as the spirit stepped through the space, the pillar reformed preventing her from escaping.

"No!" cried Ange and began to cut the column of rock again. Lido stood ready to leave and once again the rock shattered into a thousand pieces but instantly reformed. Ange screamed her frustration. The anger welled up and she flew into the colonnade again with her blade. Eventually it began to weaken. She stopped. Her hands bleeding, she looked at the spirit. Her face was streaked with tears.

"What will I do?"

"I do not know. I am caged here in this place, my brethren created it. I am protected from death, but my power lies weakened as it has been placed into the prism and the shadows of Baachelaus eat at the power of caemeris."

Ange placed her blade down and sat. She drank again and instantly felt refreshed. The smell of the grove suffused her senses as if she were there. She brought Bensah's face to mind and Nekoda. There were others but they remained shadows to her. She drank again to make the shadows in her mind reveal who they were, but they remined as foggy forms on the edges of her sight. Then she looked at the water cask and the cage.

"You were made to care for my world, Lido. Is this true?"

"Yes Ange."

"But when you and the custodians are united you form the same realm. This realm of Caemeris?"

"Yes, I think so. Norbu, Ascendant and Descendant bring all together."

"I am not of this world, but you are because it is the ruins of your realm. The Ondraack understood this. I think I understand. This is the place where everything in my home is made. You and the stone are made from the same thing. Just as you moved the stones in the river and ocean and make sand from mountains. You and stone are the same thing, one stops the other while one changes the other. How did you shape the rocks in the riverbed and mountains into sand? How did you make your cave?"

"With the wind, Aerean, I can make the stones small, or I can crawl inside and set them free back to their beginnings before they became stone."

"Come to me. I am made from the clay of Norbu's stones. Let us remake stone as we do back home."

Ange drank a huge mouthful of water and spat it over stone bars. They shattered into a thousand pieces but instead of reforming they remained suspended in the air.

"Hurry Lido!" she called.

Lido stepped from her cage and gathered Ange in her watery arms. Far away a screech came across the gloom.

"Hurry, before Ondraack returns."

The tree stood large and alone in the middle of a yellowed desert. In the sky swirled clouds thick and angry, yellow like the sand but tinged with grey. All the time they threatened to unleash a massive storm below. The tree could be seen from a thousand leagues away. Its trunk was the span of ten other trees lined up together and its withered gnarled branches stretched for a half a league in each direction. The bark had been contorted in an upward spiral by eons of battering storms and winds. It was dying but so slowly that in the end the land and the tree waited to see which expired first. Her feet stood on the highest branch of the great tree. The bitterness of the winds around her had begun to erode her flesh. It stung like the little creatures had stung when she had awoken in the end realm. This place bound her more and she could not overcome the wounds in her flesh and the insults to her heart. He was here and he knew she was but again they remained apart. She stood looking far in every direction waiting for the one to fetch her and make this existence end. Nothing in the emptiness; not him or her she thought as she stood still, the beauty now decayed by time's implacable motion.

"Where am I and why am I here? she asked.

In her memory she saw them walking together, Norbu, Lido, Aerean, Seraf and Descendant. On Descendant's head sat the light of Magmeris and on hers Belmaris - beacons of pure light formed from the First Star. There luminescence lighting their path as they journeyed the realm of the brethren of the Caemeris. Surrounding their corona sat a shadow of their dooms. Their path stretched before them, never dimmed by anything other than the light of the stars bestowed upon them. They gathered all the brethren to them and enthroned the custodians of creation between them. Seraf, Aerean, Lido and Norbu bowed in devotion to the last of the brethren formed. As the six brethren stood together, they watched eternal day grow ever more. Golden arches formed into columns around them as the temple of light was built from the seven colours of the eternal. As they entered the great sanctuary of light in the distance stood the throne of Descendant and at the other, the seat of Ascendant. Each chair raised upon a dais of golden hues, shimmered as the light of the First Star touched their surface. The walk seemed interminable as the light of the star jewel guided their paths. Together across the vastness of the lighted realm sat, Descendant, changer of light to dark and Ascendant, changer of dark to light. The forgers who bring form to the light and its return to the edges of the unknown. Their thrones forming the boundary between Caemeris and the abyss of the void.

Descendant and Ascendant watched each other as eons passed and the colours of Caemeris scored the marks of the third Age of light into being. Then the mighty Aracnine appeared. First took the light shimmering from the Star jewels of each of the gods and drew an image. When the two jewels shall become one, the First Star will be reborn and like the void that was broken by the spears of light so shall all that are sustained by it, be destroyed at its rebirth. But until then the first among the brethren shall remain in awe of one another until the return of Caemeris.

The Aracnine receded to the edges of the realm to watch and wait to be called again.

Ascendant stood looking across the barren vista which stretched beyond the petrified limbs of the tree. Doubt and sorrow came to her again but no tears formed as the arid winds simply sucked the moisture from the eyes which had been made in the realm of the clayborn.

She closed her eyes and searched her ancient memories to the moment before the breach. The aching she felt to be enthralled again made her gasp. Their constancy was strong and unbreakable until the glance at something that moved upon the edges of time and consciousness. She had watched Descendant's gaze wrench away as it if had just happened at that moment. Her cry across the ages rebounded like an echo in the deepest wells of sorrow and despair. She tried to see what ruptured the balance and there in the fragments of her decaying memories she had seen the shadow, more ancient, more potent rise upon the infinite dawn, and she knew that this had usurped Descendant's purpose. The pain welled in her. The sound of the chains dragging him away as the emptiness of the void tore through her heart and mind. The sanctuary of Caemeris stood on a precipice of destruction. Too much had been endured for it to be restored.

"Let it end. Let it end. Come to me. We will destroy the shadow and all that is created as well. Come, we will kill all that has been wrought and restore our places again." She screamed across the howling winds. The magnificent and beautiful god stood regally upon the great tree. Her flesh began to peel from her face and arms. The white bone beneath soon yellowed as the sulphur began to scour away the last remains of the body which now caged her.

Far away Ange looked at the steep descent into the desert below. Lido stood behind her. Ange tasted the salt on the wind and spat it out. She took some water to wash her mouth. Lido roused slightly as if hearing something on the wind.

"Assumpta" she called. But there was no answer.

A gust of wind came racing up the cliff face bringing the sand with it. She noticed little sparks of light dancing on the translucent form of Lido.

"Is she across the desert?"

"Yes, but I cannot go with you. I will bring more harm to you. This is the basin of binding. Where the custodians forged new creations. The salts will ignite if I tread upon them."

Ange's heart sank with fear again.

"I will meet you at the Gate of the Dead star. Ascendant will know where to find it. Ange, I fear my sister's despair has clouded her purpose. She will need you to be strong to bring her back safely" spoke Lido.

"What will happen to Norbu? The dead god will kill him."

Ange felt her fear spill into her words and eyes.

"Nay, none can kill the other, our doom if we fail is to live caged and denied our purpose and death. It is no blessing to live forever, lost to unending dawns and darkness. The brethren are long lived but not eternal only a few have been bestowed that fate. Make haste, your world dies every day that Voloc remains unchallenged."

Ange stepped to the edge of the cliff and placed her scarf around her face so that only a tiny slit around her eyes remained. As she descended into the desert, the thought that she had done this before came to her but that time she looked across a sea of red sand. She noticed her water cask refilled each time she drank from it. A tiny smile formed as she looked back at Lido on top of the cliff.

The desert gouged at her throat and eyes as the grains embedded themselves into her flesh. Her legs ached as the sand grew softer and deeper making each step more difficult. Soon she had to use her sword to steady herself as she sunk deeper and deeper into the sand. Each muscle wrenched every time she heaved herself up onto the surface. Eventually it became so hard that she lay panting on the hot grains. Her chest wheezing as the yellow dust burned inside her.

She took some water and felt her strength return. Just as she stood a slow wave rippled across the sand. She waited for it to reach her. She saw columns of sand rising behind the wave in perfect formation. They reached high into the swirling clouds and stood frozen. They were innumerable and for a league they stretched before her. She walked amongst them. Placing her hand on one of the pillars it instantly collapsed sending a shockwave through all the others. A scream came across the winds as Ange stood frozen with fear at what may happen next. She turned in the direction of the scream trying to decide if that was Assumpta's cry across the empty plain.

The wave came again, and this time Ange was careful not to touch the pillars. The sand was firmer underfoot allowing her to walk more easily. Making her way through the maze she saw figures sculpted from the grains. One of them turned towards her. It was like a massive spider. Its grainy mouth roared when it saw her. It began to run towards her. She started to run but her legs began to give way from exhaustion. She could hear the creature's footsteps behind her. Turning she saw it had long legs and arms with large head covered in a crown of spines. It seemed familiar to her. In the distance the shadow of a tree stretched along the sand, as if beckoning her to it. Ange turned in that direction. She touched one of the pillars to make it collapse hoping the creature would also disappear. The colonnades fell but the creature did not. She turned to face it. She readied her blade as it sped into her. Her sword simply slid straight through the beast's body without making any wound. The large claws scooped her up, crushing any air in her chest. She stabbed at its arm, but it was futile, the grains simply fell away with no affect. It threw her into the air. Her mouth became buried in the dirt when she landed. Choking she rolled over. She reached for her cask of water, but it was not there. Barely able to breath she stood looking for the black leather sack. The creature was making its way towards her quickly. Her eyes scanned frantically for it. A black spec amongst the yellow caught her eye. She ran towards it. Just as the creature swiped for her head she dived onto the sand and snatched the cask. Gulping down the liquid her burning throat eased and she caught her breath. She got up and began to sprint towards the shadow of the tree she had seen. The creature pursued her and was quickly catching her. The branches of the tree soon began to thicken above her head. She saw the mighty trunk sitting majestically among the dunes. Her heart leapt as another sight met her eyes. She saw Assumpta; ragged and decayed but none the less it was her standing upon the very highest branch.

"Assumpta, it is me Ange."

The god's head turned and for a moment Ange hesitated as the skeletal face which stared at her resembled the dead god upon the throne.

"Run Ange, hasten to me. My mind is clouded by the venomous air that scours the land. It poisons my memories and brings them to life, warped and malicious."

Ange could hear the crunching sound of the creature's footsteps as it neared her. She managed to get to the trunk of the tree. She scrambled up the knotted bark. She saw a hand reach down for her. Then she felt the pain of the claw as it latched onto her leg. It was her weak leg. It pulled hard and twisted it. She felt the bone snap. She screamed with pain. She reefed herself away as Assumpta pulled her up. The creature let go and screeched at her. It began to climb but as soon as its legs left the ground it disintegrated.

She clung to Assumpta as the god walked to the top of the tree. Her broken leg dangled beneath. The pain tore through her every time it swung against a branch.

"Ange, do not wane now, we still have much more to do." Assumpta gave some water to Ange. She woke again as the pain eased a little.

"How will I walk?"

Assumpta took the leg in her hand and pulled the bones together. Ange screamed in pain. "Ange gather the sand and the water and place it over your leg. This is the basin which binds the light. It is where the first threads of the Clayborn are formed. When the colours of caemeris are bonded and become dense."

Ange scooped some dirt and poured water onto it. She made a paste and placed it on her leg. She felt an itch and then a sensation like ants crawling inside her leg.

"Get up and try standing on it." Ange stood half dazed. The leg held but the pain was horrendous.

Ange collapsed onto a branch of the tree. "Why did you choose me? I can barely walk. And now I lay here even more wounded and in great pain, and still, you urge me to save you. What sort of god are you? Gildas, yes that was his name, the giant man who wanted to kill everything, he was suspicious of you." Ange glared at Assumpta as the stabbing pain of her broken leg washed over her like the blasting winds off the sand.

"You are right to mistrust me, but I can only say that if we remain this way, then Voloc will devour your world as ours. Feel the life in the tree Ange. It never let's go; it never gives up. It sits on the edge of destruction but still it keeps the sand bound to its roots and remains. Heal your leg with the prism. It was forged for the clayborn by Norbu. You were made by the colours wrought by Caemeris. We are the first forms of those colours. That is why we are shapeless, and easy to bend into the shadows and out of them into the formless vista of the ocean of light."

Ange pulled the prism from the pouch around her neck and placed it on her leg. It pulsed. She thought she could see her bones knitting together. She stood up, the leg felt stronger, and the pain eased. She peered into the tree and inside stretched an eternity of living. It had once existed on Arglethium but now remained in Caemeris.

"How did it come here?" asked Ange.

"As we forged, we become part of the creations, and this seed grew as Arglethium grew. It bound us to the world of the next age of light, as bond, an anchor of dense light. It was the roots of our work. It withers now but does not die. If it dies, then it means the third Age of light has ceased and we are forgotten. It is the tree of hope, lost and fulfilled."

"We are to meet Lido at the gate of the dead star. She said you would know how to find it."

"Lido lives and what news of Norbu?"

"He is chained by the dead god and the spirits of wind and fire."

"Yes, his strength is mightier from his time lost in the void. It would take all of their wills to contain our brother."

Ange stood. The pain was less but she mistrusted her leg, fearful it would give out.

"We must go. Which way to the gate of the dead star?"

"We will need to take the stairs of Ruin."

Ange climbed down the massive trunk towards the sand. As she neared the ground, she hesitated, wondering if the creature would leap up and grab her again.

"It will not return."

Assumpta climbed down around Ange and helped her make the rest of the distance.

Ange stood catching her breath letting the pain subside. She looked up at the magnificent dead tree.

"What place is this and what was that creature that chased me?"

"It is the plateau of Ghord. The creature was born out of a mirage of my birthplace; a mimic of the great guardians called Aracnine. It saw you as an intruder and attacked you."

A memory stirred in Ange of being in a cold dark place with one of these creatures and with another who could speak to them.

"Are you ready? The stairs of Ruin are the climb out of oblivion from this realm. Descendant is not free yet of his cage and this makes the trek to the gate more treacherous. The stairs will try and stop our escape as this world is the creation of Descendant's corrupted gaze."

"Then how does the dead god not know where we are and come take us prisoners?"

"The gods mind is lost, and the confusion blinds it from much that exists here. From within the void were made fell creatures who possess a power which Descendant could never wield. Not even the first star held sway over these first born, most of all the shadow Voloc. This is the deception of the great deceiver, to make Baachelaus think it is he who reigns and not the true purveyor of despair and shadow."

Assumpta broke a branch off the tree. The snap echoed for a league in each direction as if the tree wept at being wounded in such a way.

"Here Ange this will help you."

Ange took it and placed one end under her arm and used it as a crutch.

"We will walk with our backs to the plains of Ghord until we reach the stairs. The gates of Magmeris lie at the highest point of them."

Ange limped behind Assumpta. It seemed slow but she nevertheless kept up with the god. Ange looked at the rotted and chewed flesh of the god's body and the torn rags she wore. She realised that if she had not come when she did, the god would have remained lost in her daydream of memories until the flesh and bones had been scoured away.

"What is our purpose Assumpta? Do we go back to the world I come from and destroy the lord that lays waste to my kind?"

"Yes, for the dead god as you call Baachelaus cannot assume the throne until the chains have been broken. Voloc has not freed the servant. Voloc has only freed itself from the tether of its own shadow. It now exists unfettered and blind with power fed by the bonds of dense light which form the world of Arglethium. We go there to kill Voloc, free your world and then the Ascendant and Descendant formed from the First Stars light shall retake their rule of destiny until the end of time calls. This world is an abomination and can only be killed when Voloc's claws are torn loose."

Ange thought of Norbu's words how the custodian's world was meant to end. She was about to ask Assumpta but thought it better not to. Ange wondered if any of the custodians understood what was happening. This thought sent a jab of fear into her, as she wondered if there was any way out of the mess, she and Arglethium had been entangled.

The yellow lands and scouring winds soon gave way to the reprieve of thick forests. The trees were densely packed together, and the sky had disappeared above them leaving them in darkness. The shape of them was familiar to Ange, large bulbous trunks with a canopy of leaves. Where had she seen them before? A memory of drinking from one of them formed in her mind. Her body was in pain like now. The juice of the tree had revived her, and she had got up to walk then just like this time. Then she remembered the boabs near her home. She touched a trunk briefly to see if more memories would come but only a sense of deep sorrow washed over her. So much destroyed. Anger welled inside her, so much destroyed because of these gods and their war with Voloc.

She pulled away from the tree and continued behind Assumpta. Each step Ange took plunged her leg into painful waves.

Assumpta strode ahead of her without looking to see if she kept up with her. Beginning to tire Ange called out to the god to ask her to stop and rest a little. She turned and looked at Ange and for a moment in the gloom all Ange could see was a pale eyeless face like the dead god. Her heart skipped a beat until Assumpta spoke.

"Of course. I will go ahead a little bit to see how far the stairs are."

Ange sat against a tree and swigged some water.

"Lido are you here now? It would be safe for you to tread amongst the forest."

There was no answer only the stillness of the towering trees around her. Ange sat back and tested the broken leg. Pressing it gently a bolt of pain went through her. She sat back against the trunk panting as the pain ebbed away. Closing her eyes, she tried to think about the animal that would come to mind or in her dreams wishing it were here now. What was its name again? She drifted off thinking of running through grasses along the river. The animal bounded alongside. Her eyes closed and she slept. Around her the trees grew closer and thicker and the path she walked upon disappeared.

There was a snap of a twig. Eyes wide awake she looked in the gloom and saw Assumpta standing with her back to her.

"I have left you something to eat, roots. Take your fill and follow me."

Ange took a root and bit into it. It was bitter but edible. Her stomach growled with relief at the food. She ate quickly as she saw the god begin to walk again into the gloom. She looked at the forest around her and realised the path had gone. Her feet now touched a tree trunk where before it had been open around her.

"Wait Assumpta."

Ange got up limping and followed.

"I have been calling Lido. She could come now and join us" spoke Ange.

"Yes, that is good. Call her."

Ange was almost running to keep up with Assumpta but was swiftly losing her.

"Please slow down, Assumpta."

Assumpta disappeared behind a trunk. Ange began to grow wary. Her mind raced what should she do?

"Lido, Assumpta where are you? Lead me to the gates of the dead star."

She gripped her sword tightly. The gloom and silence of the woods gave nothing away.

"Where are you going, clayborn?"

The face and voice appeared out of nowhere. It was the god of fire.

Ange screamed and then toppled over. The god persisted and threatened to burn her as it stood over her. Ange composed herself.

"You know where fire god. You heard me call out. Where is Assumpta?"

"She flees my flames, but I will burn the forest and reveal where she hides."

Ange managed to get herself up. She stood on her broken leg and despite the pain it did not give way. She slashed at Seraf and felt her hand burn as the blade touched the flaming hide of the god. She did not drop the weapon but persisted in her attack.

"You can't kill me."

She turned and ran as fast as she could. She snaked her way through the forest and never-ending tree trunks. Their branches clawed at her. Suddenly a great burst of heat exploded around her. She fell to the ground to avoid being burned. Overhead the roaring sound of the flames deafened her. When it had finished, she got up and ran again. She remembered running into a river when fire had blazed across the land once before. Someone had plunged her under the water. The river had stopped her being burned.

"Lido, come now, quell your brother."

Nothing answered. Another burst of incendiary rage spread through the darkness incinerating the trees. Suddenly the sky appeared above her. In the distance she saw a great wall of mountainous rocks. At the base of them stood a figure, translucent causing the cliff to ripple. It was Lido. Ange felt the heat from Seraf behind her and knew she would be incinerated in a flash. She took her cask and unstopped it. She took her leather belt and doused it in the remaining water and turning she flung the leather slingshot at the god. It caught around its torso and knees. She pulled on it hard until it buckled. She leapt onto the smouldering figure and wrapped the leather belt around tighter and poured the rest of the water out of her cask onto the god.

"Lido!" She screamed as Seraf spat fire at Ange and almost overwhelmed her with its strength.

A wave of water suddenly appeared over her head and doused the blind fury of Seraf.

"Be dimmed brother by your brethren."

Lido formed into herself and stood over the fire god. Seraf shrunk to his normal size but struggled with bursts of white sparks. Ange held tightly onto the wet leather bonds.

"Did you find Assumpta?" Lido asked Ange.

"I did but she wandered into the forest to find a path and when she returned, she would not look at me. I lost her among the trees."

"We must continue to the gate. The forest will always lead to the stairs. We will find her on the way."

"What of the fire god?"

"Seraf is to come with us. The Stairs of Ruin will break the chains of Baachelaus. They will break the will of many. Keeper this will be your truest test for it is the gateway between the worlds and the potency of the Descendant's memory lingers the strongest here."

"How is it the dead god can do this and none of you can?"

"Because Descendant stared into the mind of Caemeris and has been touched by the void. Lido, Aerean and Seraf were the custodians shaping the colours of making into being, not their death. By staring into the makers of light and dark Descendant can rule both. Assumpta being the custodian of light to dark will allow Descendant to bring its vision to reality. Ascendant brings purpose and meaning to the making. That is what makes the stone you carry strong. It holds the memory of both. It holds what Descendant saw and Ascendant brings the will to make it happen. And they both contain the memories of the first light, the light of Caemeris. It holds the will to make life or death happen."

Ange wondered if this is what Norbu meant when he said Custodian's time had ended. He had placed their power into the stone and with its power could be wielded by others, like her.

"Come fire god." Ange called to Seraf gripping the leather bond tightly.

"You shall not survive this weakling." Seraf spoke as a spark of flame shot out towards Ange. She ducked in time, so it missed her head.

Soon they came to the base of the stone wall. A gap in the rock revealed a staircase carved into the mountain. Ange looked at Lido and nodded.

"Step boldly and wisely Ange."

Just then a rumble sounded across the plains and in the distance. They could see the ripple flatten the huge forest they had just come from.

"You see Norbu is free and Baachelaus chases him. You shall not escape the dominion of our brother Lido" spoke Seraf as his eyes blazed blue.

"Hurry Ange, they come" called Lido.

Ange reached the first of the stairs and saw they went up in a spiral fashion. She dragged Seraf behind her and each time the god caught a ledge she reefed the spirit; each tug causing her broken leg to shake with unsteadiness and searing waves of pain.

She approached the top of the first set of stairs but noticed that she never reached the final step. As she would place her foot on the last one another would form. She stopped, panting with exhaustion realising that sorcery was at work.

She pulled Seraf closer. With her dagger dipped in the water blessed by Lido she placed its tip near the god's eyes.

"Your master must know the secret to the stairs."

"You need to defeat them clayborn or you will never leave."

 Ange sat back and looked at the stairs. The ledge above which seemed to be the only way out of this part of the climb was so close Ange could almost touch it. She stood and placed her foot on the next step and then the next but made no ground.

"Lido, there is no way forward."

"I know Ange, I do not know how to overcome them."

Ange stepped back and walked down two stairs. She noticed that the steps disappeared. She walked them again and they reappeared. She reached up and tried to touch the ledge, but it seemed to disappear as her hand neared it. She thought of the world. She cannot be destroyed only trapped. Why? Because the world was not meant to exist and was ruptured from its purpose. Caemeris itself does not exist as it was made to form other creations, like Arglethium. Now it exists on the whim of a brittle and broken mind. Here was the realm before creation. It was how the bonds began before they were shaped into being. Creation could be retold anyway who chose to command it. Ange looked at the stairs and spoke.

"Stairs to the ledge."

A staircase formed to the top of the pathway. She walked on it dragging Seraf behind her. She stepped onto the last step and placed her foot up to what appeared to be the pathway and instead of another stair forming it was just the smooth surface of the ledge.

She hoisted the god up. Below Lido had her back turned to her. Ange looked beyond the god to see what she was watching. On the bottom of the stairs, she saw Assumpta. Then the booming call of Norbu made her look across the plains. In the distance Descendant rode a creature made of bones. In his hand he held a long spear. It was hunting Norbu.

"No!" Ange called.

Her heart breaking at the thought of the great and loving god being tormented in this way.

"Hurry Ange, they will catch us" called Assumpta. Her face was shredded, and her hair was hung in long smoking tendrils. Ange wondered what had happened to the god in the forest.

Ange ran along the path until it ended with a wall of rock. There was no way through it. She tapped on the rocks to see if there was a secret passage but there was nothing. The rumbling from Norbu's thunderous steps grew stronger. The surface was completely smooth. She stood back and saw the top of the flat wall and stepping back further she saw that another wall sat above it. The wall was the stair.

"Let me walk on stairs to the gate of the dead star."

Nothing happened.

"Creation is not magic, and it is not whimsy. Purpose, need and boundaries are what is needed to forge Ange." She heard Seraf speak.

"Let me walk on stairs to the dead star." But still nothing happened. "I don't understand. It worked before."

Her heart sank wondering how she would scale the perfectly smooth surface. She thought of her blade and her dagger. She turned as she heard a sizzling sound behind her. Seraf was burning through the sling she had bound him in. She saw Lido and Assumpta coming towards her.

"Lido your brother escapes my bonds."

Instantly the water spirit soaked him in another spray of water. Seraf roared his frustration.

"Baachelaus, release this servant. Let me breath my breathe of destruction and raze the lands." Seraf's voice echoed across the plains and lands.

Assumpta went to the smooth rock wall near Ange. She took a leap into the air. Lido helped her with a wave of water. But suddenly the rock grew into a hand and thrust her down. She lay stunned on the gravel path.

"Assumpta, are you alright?" Ange asked.

"It seems the stairs are impenetrable Ange" Assumpta spoke as she got up.

Ange looked again. Seraf was chuckling behind them.

"You will not escape."

Ange took her dagger and her axe and plunged them both into the rock. She steadied herself and hoisting herself up onto the dagger she pulled the axe and stabbed it in higher. The wall did not respond to the injury inflicted by her weapons. She continued. The weight of Seraf began to drag as she neared the top of the first stair. She heaved with an almighty surge to rollover onto the edge of the step. Seraf lay swinging. She threw a rope down to the waiting gods. Assumpta went first. The rock seemed to allow it. As Ange watched Assumpta climb, it dawned on her that she must do it first or they would never escape. But why, she wondered?

"Because the prism you hold contains the power of forging of Caemeris" whispered the voice of Norbu in her mind.

Ange turned over and the sight that met her eyes made her hope fail completely. The steps went so high she lost sight of them. She heaved Seraf up. Norbu's voice bellowed across the air; the force of it almost knocking her over. She saw the god fighting off the minions of Baachelaus as they clung to his body ripping and tearing with claws of bone and iron. Around him she saw a figure, in spinning whirlwinds, so strong they tore at Norbu's form. Her pity turned to anger in an instant. She turned to the custodians.

"Lido, Assumpta can you help your brethren. I will forge the path forward to the gate. Save Norbu."

The two custodians looked at one another. Seraf sat against the rock.

"Which shall go?" Lido asked.

"It cannot be me." Assumpta replied.

Ange looked at her wondering why Assumpta could not go.

"It will be the end, Keeper. It is his quest to capture me before it is time. It will be the end and he does not see that. My quest was to restore him to his throne not to be with me. We will equal the power contained within the prism. It will mean no end to this torment."

"Then how will you do that if you cannot be near him?" asked Ange.

"We brought him here to break Voloc's bonds, but something still thwarts us. He is still chained. We thought that your world would survive once Voloc lost its hold on the Descendant, but its power remains as potent as ever. You are the path back now Ange. I called you first to use your strength and tenacity forged in a world full of hatred for one such as you and now I need you to be the pathfinder to your realm. You are the Keeper of this long sorrowful quest that has spanned eons. Become the custodian of memory and shadow. Find the way to restore the custodians to their realm so that they are ready for the return of Caemeris. Break Voloc's chains here and in Arglethium" replied Assumpta.

"I will go and follow you with Norbu" spoke Lido. "Aerean will be formidable and may overcome me. It was with her strength with my great oceans, that we shaped your world Ange."

Seraf looked at them all. His eyes blazing with vermillion flames and sparks. He had heard Assumpta's words and distant memories stirred but the darkness clouded his mind again as the whispered echoes of long ago disappeared.

Ange turned and looked at the next stair and plunged her dagger in and then her sword. Assumpta and Seraf waited as she climbed the smooth surface. She had forgotten that every move she made mimicked that of Gildas and Sa-Tuc in their journeys to hide the prism in the Graan icelands. Getting to the top she hoisted Seraf up, each aching bone and sinew in her body screaming with exhaustion. She looked and saw the shimmer of Lido making her way to the forest below. As she pulled Seraf up onto the ledge, her foot slipped, and she fell into the fire god's body. She held her breathe expecting to be incinerated but instead she found herself looking into the belly of the sun. At the very centre she saw a tiny spec of gold flame amongst lava flows of red. She touched the flame and suddenly she saw the essence of Seraf staring back, bound in black threads. She reached out to break the threads, but she felt herself beginning to burn. Some of the thread reached toward her but then retracted. She stared intently into the dark strands. She saw the echo of the sun in Seraf's flames and bound within it lay the heart of death and emptiness as well. The sun makes mischief as well as the shadow.

"Who seeks to destroy the custodians and Arglethium Seraf, god of flame? The shadow eats at the heart of the flames of the sun as much as it does you Seraf" Ange spoke into the furnace surrounding her.

"The void was first clayborn" came the answer from an unknown voice.

Pulling herself out quickly she was stunned by the gloom of the corrupted world of the prism. Gasping for air she saw Assumpta standing above her. She looked at Seraf who lay still not moving.

"Seraf is dying. We must hurry." spoke Ange.

Assumpta concerned at Ange's words plunged her hand into the chest of Seraf and instantly the bile of Descendant met her. She collapsed under the malice and hatred there. She plunged deeper to find the flame of Seraf and free her brother, but the shadow engulfed her further.

Ange looked at Assumpta shrivel and turn a shade blacker than the night. Her eyes dimmed and black ooze dribbled from her eyes and mouth.

"No!" Ange screamed and wrenched Assumpta's hand out of Seraf. The colour returned to the god's body slowly as the black poison sizzled on the grey marble.

"Can you walk? I cannot carry both of you the burden will be too heavy."

Assumpta nodded dazed. Ange remembered the black threads retracted from her but not Assumpta.

The roars and bellows of Norbu and Baachelaus faded the further they climbed. Ange's legs and arms shook from weariness but at least she was able to ignore the pain from her broken leg as the exhaustion she now felt dulled it. Reaching the next wall, Ange peered up and thought for a moment something dark and silvery shimmered inside the stone. Its surface was not as smooth, and the ridges were broken with slits. It reminded her of rows of teeth. Hopefully, it will be easier to climb she thought. Looking beyond the edge of the wall, she saw the yellow clouds of the sky and a mountain tip.

"Please let it be the last" she pleaded.

Below spears of light and the roar of wind and water echoed in the cliffs around them as Lido and Norbu battled with Descendant and Aerean. Assumpta stood behind Ange waiting.

Ange began the climb again, sword then dagger and then sword. She could feel the rumble of the battle. She stopped to catch her breath. Just a few more she said to herself. Then she felt the spear stab into her leg then another appeared just under her arm and then one shot out towards her face just missing her eyes. She was so startled she lost her grip and fell on top of Seraf. She checked herself but did not appear to be wounded. She looked at the wall above her and saw the spears retract into the stone. She sobbed with anger and exhaustion.

"No! Give me passage."

She heaved herself up again and began to climb. She braced herself more firmly waiting for the spears to come. One of them shot out and pushed her back to the ground. She lay looking at Seraf.

"You will not escape clayborn."

"You are strong, and I am weak so why is it that you remain my prisoner. Break free and end this futile quest that I remain bound to. If I am to die here, then end this now and we will both be free."

She taunted Seraf knowing he could no more escape then, she could.

"You are wise to see this truth. Think then what may sustain you and what thwarts the dead one. What did you see that drew you near to its bosom and lies within mine? What lies at the heart of your world that without its gaze upon us would send me and the clayborn to oblivion?"

Ange stared at the god mesmerised by its eyes. She did not notice the leather bond fraying strand by strand.

Ange remembered the golden flame inside Seraf's chest and the memory of lying among grass staring at the yellow disc in the sky. She plunged her hand into Seraf and searched for the heat of the bound flame. She took a piece and withdrew her hand. On the tip of her finger sat the tiny flame of gold; strong and vibrant. Its potency flowed through her. Assumpta sat near her to look at it and smiled.

"It is a tear of Belmaris, offspring of Caemeris. I once wore a crown in which was seated the light of Belmaris."

"Why did you help me fire god? You are almost free now as I have no more water and cannot hold you. By the time I climb this last stair you shall be free to do the bidding of the dead god."

"I am dying. The poison of Voloc eats me alive and I shall not be restored to my glorious self unless I am plunged into the heart of Belmaris."

"Then if you desire, you shall be thrust through the gate of the dead star to find the blood of your maker."

Ange took her sword and stabbed it into the wall. The spears shot out as expected. She then placed the flame on her finger near her mouth and blew across the stone surface. It burst forth in a fireball as it if had been ignited by the sun itself. The spears melted away almost instantly. The wall began to buckle as the flame left its incendiary kiss on the granite. Little crystals shone brightly when Ange stopped blowing as the ancient minerals within the stone were forged into jewels.

The flame died on her finger. Suddenly the booming voice of Norbu came across the sky. It rattled the cliffs and the bones of Ange.

"Hurry Ange, the gate must be open," called Assumpta.

Ange stabbed the wall with her weapons and began the climb. As she climbed, she looked at the sparkling crystals and began to pluck them out of the wall and place them in her tunic.

"They remind me of a gift I once had. They were stones that looked like the eyes of the great god Norbu. Now I have jewels forged from the heart of Seraf, the god of fire."

Reaching the edge of the wall she heard a low humming noise. She peered over the top and saw far into the distance a stone monument in the shape of an arch ornately carved with lips of flame in contorted patterns. The humming came from the arch. She pulled Seraf up and Assumpta followed.

"That is the gate of the dead star. Hurry now. Sister Lido and Brother Norbu, make haste we are almost free" Assumpta called across the winds.

Ange looked at Seraf.

"If I free you, to whom shall you run, your maker or your dead brethren?"

"You can no longer carry me Keeper. Free yourself and me. Flee to the gate and let the final battle begin. Where I run is for my choosing alone and neither path will decide what fate has already set for each of us."

Ange looked at Seraf and knew the custodian spoke the truth. None of her life was of her making but here she still stood in the face of the makers of the world as equal friend, enemy and liberator. She took her blade and cut the bonds. Instantly Seraf exploded into his glorious self.

He towered over Ange and Assumpta not moving. Ange braced herself for any attack as did Assumpta.

"Brethren I am still the higher one. You are weakened by Baachelaus and Voloc's poison" Assumpta spoke in a threatening voice.

Seraf suddenly plunged his fiery claw into his chest. On his finger rested the small flame of his heart. He moved toward Ange and touched his finger to her forehead. The flame disappeared. As he pulled away on her skin remained a tattoo of it.

"You have been marked with the heart of Seraf. I will return to where the first flames were made but in you shall be the memory of my potency and existence."

Seraf bolted towards the gate. Ange and Assumpta followed. After a few paces a roar shook the stones beneath their feet. Ange looked back and saw Baachelaus standing on top of the ridge and behind the god stood a legion of creatures first made of the void unknown to the light. Norbu and Lido were racing ahead towards she and Assumpta. They quickened their pace but before them and behind

Seraf a tornado formed. It quickly grew in strength so that it pushed Ange back. Seraf stopped.

"Aerean, come with me or you will die."

Seraf stepped into the maelstrom and instantly a fireball of wind and flame burst forth. The vortex was so powerful it began to distort the arch of the gate.

Lido and Norbu caught up to Ange. Norbu scooped Ange up.

"Hurry Keeper, the dead one grows angry."

Lido stopped and turned toward Seraf and Aerean.

"I will gather them both to me for I have created and destroyed with each of my brethren, Norbu" spoke Lido.

Assumpta felt something pull her back and noticed a lasso around her. Norbu grabbed her before Baachelaus could, but she became caught between the two. Norbu pulled with all his strength, but it would not give way.

"Run! Destroy Voloc!" Assumpta screamed.

Norbu and Ange ran towards the gate. Seraf wrestled with Aerean as Lido formed a huge translucent wave around each of the custodians. Ange touched the tattoo on her forehead and instantly the flame came to life. She blew onto it towards the fiery tornado. She heard a scream as Seraf was flung out towards the gate. The god disappeared into the mouth of Magmeris' tomb.

"You shall be re-born brethren once the flame of the great star Belmaris has cleansed you of Voloc's venom" spoke Norbu.

Lido and Aerean remained together in a tornado of water rather than flame. They smashed into the rocky cliffs. As the gate neared, Ange looked back. She saw Assumpta being surrounded by legions of shadow and death with Baachelaus coming towards her.

Ange could see the custodian standing ragged and decayed but magnificent in her strength and failing beauty. How wondrous these gods must have been when they first came to be, she thought as she watched Ascendant take her sword and cut down the bony stead the Baachelaus rode upon. Descendant rose from the rubble of the horse and smashed Ascendant into stones. She rose again and so began the battle between the ancient Diarchs of existence.

"He will kill her" Ange cried. Norbu and Ange stood at the gate.

"Nay they will kill you clayborn, for they were made to be the custodians of the last created and when their time ends so does yours. They are the changers of light and darkness, of memory and shadow back to light. They give purpose to the creations of Caemeris. Hasten there is no time left. We must return to weaken Voloc" spoke Norbu.

Norbu and Ange dove into the mouth of Magmeris and into the tomb's silence.

Ascendant saw them flee as Descendant rose above her again. Their swords clashed in powerful and destructive strokes, but each could not gain victory over the other. Blow after blow rained down on them with neither conceding any ground.

Lido and Aerean separated and warily edged closer to Baachelaus and Assumpta. Their brethren battled and none not even the mighty Norbu could stop them.

Descendant roared in frustration as they smashed into the cliffs of Ruin.

"Who are you?" the dead eyes looked at the wretched creature who was impervious to his strength.

"I am Ascendant. I am the other that gazed at the one called Descendant across the expanses of time. Our thrones remain empty and the created existence that we are all a part of now hurtles to its destruction. Will the Descendant being take its place and restore the realm of Caemeris?"

They landed on the ground and instantly the army of Baachelaus gathered ready to pounce at any moment. The creatures dredged from their fell spaces in the void began to overpower Assumpta.

"Baachelaus remember me" she pleaded.

The specs of light in the eyeless sockets revealed nothing. He stood looking at Assumpta scouring his ancient memory to find any whisper of what the god spoke of, but nothing came.

He raised his spear and plunged it deep into the bony chest of Assumpta. She stumbled but taking her sword she stabbed Baachelaus in the ragged wound where the ancient bonds of Voloc lay torn.

"My tear was forged into the prism so that your memory and destiny remained safe from the shadow and malice that took your heart. Search your realm find what my tear captured. Remember."

The prism, the gift of Norbu whispered in the god's memory. It held a power, seek it and the power of the Caemeris will be yours.

Descendant removed the spear and stepped away from the blade of Assumpta.

"Stand down legion."

The creatures retreated away. Aerean and Lido crept closer to Baachelaus and Assumpta.

"Norbu and the wielder of the prism have escaped. They go to the realm of dense light and Seraf to his death. They seek to destroy the shadow" Aerean whispered.

"No, Baachelaus, remember. Remember what you were and the colours which we used to make" Lido shrouded Baachelaus in her lightness to open his memories.

Baachelaus roared in anger. He had been so close to uniting the brethren and seizing the rule of the custodial power and now it had been taken from his grasp again. Taking his spear, he snatched Lido, Aerean and Assumpta.

"You have thwarted me for the last time. I shall watch your annihilation in the cages of the void. To be left to rot with these beasts for an eon."

"It is not us that thwarts your purpose. It is Voloc. It wants the power for itself and uses you to find it. Once it devours the world it will devour you as well Baachelaus. Destroy Voloc and you shall be free."

Assumpta pleaded feeling her spirit ebbing away as the shadow began to devour her. "Search your memory Baachelaus. Find the prism and look into the vision that it has protected all this time."

Just then Assumpta found herself along with Aerean and Lido thrust into darkness.

"Assumpta where are we?" asked Lido

"I do not know Brethren" replied Assumpta. She moved and found herself surrounded by walls. The walls were transparent but solid. Dim light pervaded in the distance. A figure moved in the shadows, vaguely she saw it held a spear. Aerean and Lido touched the invisible wall. They felt it vibrate and their energy seep into it and back into them. But as they tried to push through to escape, they felt the energy rebound back doubly. Assumpta touched it and felt nothing. I am not meant to exist here; I exist in the hearts of the clayborn. Rising panic consumed her.

"Baachelaus, search your memory" she screamed into the emptiness around her.

"Sister it is all doomed" came Aerean's whisper. Assumpta did not answer as the sorrow engulfed her again.

Baachelaus stood at the gate of Magmeris with the words of Assumpta ringing in his mind. Faintly in the distance he saw the plains of Ghord form into a cathedral with two figures sitting at either end. He saw it collapse and the guardians chaining a creature and dragging it away. He saw a figure scoop something up, it sparkled. It was the jewel.

"Bring it to me creature" the god commanded. The figure walked towards Baachelaus on the ridge. It resembled the brethren Norbu. It placed the jewel in the palm of Baachelaus and disintegrated.

Baachelaus held the jewel up and peered into the perfectly carved stone and gasped. As each memory flashed before him his flesh re-made itself into the image ordained at his creation. The dead legion around him cringed but the god that existed then did not last as the dead flesh and eyeless face returned. Through the eyes of Uchala's blood Descendant realised all Caemeris had forged and all that had been destroyed by the desire of him to usurp Caemeris rule. It was Voloc's invasion which had ruptured the realm of the second age of light.

"Can the Descendant be restored? Can the light of Caemeris be ruled once more?"

In the echoes of the past and future across the expanses of the time came the answer.

"The vision is lost."

"Then who is the usurper of my throne?"

No answer came to this question. The desire to rule all, that had first swelled in the god's heart when the chain of destiny was sundered stirred again along with the words of Assumpta "Destroy Voloc!"

Baachelaus looked at the black mouth of the gate. Raising the spear of death, the dead god bellowed to the fell creatures gathered around it.

"Forward Legion!"

# PART THREE

# SCIONS

## of

# A NEW COVENANT

# 10

# The Shroud of the Old Maid

The gentle breeze brought with it the smell of burning wood. Tessi swallowed her need to cough as she climbed over another scorched stump among the tangled mayhem of the forest. The black of the night had begun to lighten to grey as the sun moved across the dawn sky. Angette grizzled as the grit of the smoke penetrated the muslin clothe that covered her mouth.

"Shoo Angette, we will need to be quiet. There may be more soldiers" spoke Tessi.

I don't know where I am Tessi thought as she scanned around her. Her tunic and trousers were covered in soot and all she could taste was ash. She unbuttoned her tunic and began to feed Angette. She tested the weight of her water cask. It still was half full.

"I am at least walking in the right direction. The sun always set on this side of the Palace towards the warming forests and rose on the other side toward my home" she spoke into the silence.

A shiver went through her at the thought of returning to the Bay of Tears. But the nightmares were so real.

"I am coming Noab." Tessi sighed convinced that each day it took to reach the Palace was another day of torment for Noab.

After Angette had finished suckling, she placed her over her shoulder and gently patted her on the back. Tessi drank some more water and nibbled on an oat biscuit. Angette dozed off.

As she continued the stumps began to thin eventually turning into burnt fields. She stared across the ashen vista and her heart sunk. Her heart ached for the sands of her home. The clean air and dry freshness of the straw in their huts; the clear water of the mighty Choasa. The memory of the taste of goat milk made her mouth water.

A crack echoed across the windless plain. She froze too afraid to turn around to see what made the sound. She saw a dense patch of trees to her right. She began to sprint toward them. Angette woke from the jolting of Tessi running.

She saw a hollowed-out log just inside the forested patch. She slid in underneath. The charcoal of the timber swathed her in blackened ash. She placed her veil over Angette's face to stifle the whimpering.

She heard footsteps crunching on the grass. She looked through a small crack. Nothing.

Then she heard voices. Her heart froze. Guttural and fierce. That is not Matavian she thought. Angette struggled but Tessi hugged her fiercely desperate to stop the baby from giving them away. The voices slowly faded.

"We wait Angette. We wait again until the moon rises to make sure they do not return."

She took a swig of water. Deep tiredness entered her body and soon in the silence and warmth of the tree trunk she fell asleep.

Noab sat on window ledge. He was screaming for someone to take him. Below it was a hundred spans to the rocky shore. The moon was full reflecting into the languid tide. It ignored the child as he teetered along the wall. No one came. Then a wind swept up. It was strong and tipped a moored boat over in the bay. Noab suddenly fell over the edge from the force of the wind.

A face appeared at the window. Shall I save your child, or will you? What mother leaves their child? It was the Queen. Her face snarled as her talons stretched down to grab Noab.

Tessi screamed and lashed out to snatch Noab away from the Queen. Her hand connected with a face. She woke and then the hand smothered her mouth. She pulled back hitting her head on the inside of the log. Her heart pounded as she tried to make out the face.

"Shh, it's me Nene."

Nene's hand eased off her mouth.

"How did you find me?"

"Luck. I came to the fields of Vran and saw the Unstaadt camp further ahead. I stole into this patch of trees for cover. I heard your crying as you slept. You are lucky I found you dear heart and not those beasts."

Tessi hugged Nene.

"You shouldn't have come. The Queen will kill you m'lady."

"Call me Nene. Now we must try and leave these fields before we are discovered."

Nene helped Tessi up out of the log.

"Where will we go?"

"I know a way."

"Ushan, come" whispered Nene.

There was a low growl in the dark. Angette squeaked slightly at the sound of the lion.

They crept along stumbling in the pale shadows of the moon.

"I cannot hear anyone following us" spoke Tessi.

"No, the Lioness has watched over us. What made you scream Tessi?"

"I dream of Noab. He is in danger. It is like I am there with him and always the Queen watches with her claws ready to kill or snatch him away again. It is so real Nene. I cannot bear it any longer. I don't care if we all die together but we must be together. I will not let him think I abandoned him."

Tessi shook as she sobbed from exhaustion and fear for Noab. Nene held her gently.

Nene wondered about the nightmares and Tessi's words 'like she was there'.

"There, there. I sense there is more at play here than the fear the night brings in its shadows. Come I know where we can find sanctuary and food."

Soon the moonlight gave way to a pale sunlight. Tessi followed Nene silently relieved to have company.

"Nene I will go to the White Palace and not be stopped."

"I know Tessi, but I want to go there more prepared. Besides a little food and rest will be better than none."

"Yes, I agree. I need to bathe Angette, she is soiled, and it is beginning to burn her skin."

"I may be able to find some stores of salve to help."

Nene stopped walking suddenly and began to tap the ground with her foot. Angette giggled as she watched the chubby woman move.

"Ah here it is."

Nene bent down and felt along the ground. She suddenly heaved aside a metal door hidden beneath earth and ash. She stepped down into the tunnel.

"Wait here and keep watch while I see if it is safe." She spoke to Tessi before disappearing inside the trapdoor.

Nene slipped down the steps until she landed heavily against the wall with her feet stopping on the ground. It was dark except for a tiny shaft of light breaking at least hundred paces ahead where the ground had caved in.

She took a flint stone from her trouser pocket and a bunch of twigs. She bound the twigs with the cloth used to carry the flint. Striking the flint, she lit the twigs. The torch created enough light to let her walk forward. She whistled. It echoed along the tunnel and back again to Nene. She waited. There was no answer or sound.

"Tessi, come down. It is safe. Tread carefully the stairs are very steep." She held the tiny flame up toward the entrance. She saw Tessi carefully begin to descend toward her.

"Thank you, Nene." She steadied herself with Nene's outstretched hands.

"Where are we?" Tessi asked.

"An escape tunnel beneath my lands. They were built in my great-great-great grandmother's time when we were at war with Matavia. They were used as a way of getting food and messages in and out of the city secretly. This one leads to an old sanctuary where we would hide if the city were under siege."

"How will you know where to go?"

"Well, you see as a young girl I was a bit of a scallywag. I would get dressed in my riding clothes. I would memorise the maps made from the scholars of all the tunnels and then test my memory by exploring them. I did it until I learned where every tunnel led. There are over one hundred of them. My memory has never failed me Tessi."

Tessi smiled thinking of the Queen walking around the tunnels trying to find where they led and then finding her way back.

Angette cooed quietly until she realised her noises were rebounding off the stone walls. Then she started to coo louder until it became a shrill warble. Ushan replied with a roar of her own.

"Shh Angette" spoke Tessi.

"Shh Ushan" spoke Nene.

The baby laughed and began in even greater chorus.

"Nene she will give us away."

"I think we would have been found by now. We are almost there."

Nene saw the rubble against the door. She gave the torch to Tessi, stooping she pulled two large bricks which had been dislodged away from the frame of the door.

"Ok let's try that." Tessi helped Nene up as she shoved the last piece of wall away.

Nene pushed the door, and it gave way. Stale air wheezed out into the tunnel. It was pitch black inside.

Nene felt her way along until her hand brushed an oil lamp which sat on the wall. She took the torch and lit the wick. Dim light greeted them, and a dusty room filled with scrolls on two long tables and scattered litters made of mulch and straw for beds.

"What was here?"

"It was like our war room, and it was also my secret archive. Come we are in for a treat." Nene walked into another chamber behind a torn curtain. Inside were bathing vats with withered roses and glass jars filled with coloured liquids.

"It is a bathing chamber" spoke Tessi.

"Yes. It was also used to treat wounded soldiers after the many battles with our neighbours."

Nene stooped and saw that there were stones beneath the large vat. She took an urn and poured a liquid on it. She lit it. Flames burst up the side.

Angette squealed with delight.

Nene reached up and turned a wooden key. Angette's squealing barely drowned out the grinding of a stone wheel as it moved across its gutter. Water began to trickle from the large stone reservoir set into the rock wall and into the vat.

"There. We are in for a grand pleasure. We will wait for it to warm and then we shall each have a bath in roses and lavender."

Tessi could not believe that such luxury existed under the earth.

"I remember before all this happened, the brides of the villages would bathe in the mighty Choasa. The waters were crystal clear, and all the colours of the earth would sparkle under the water. I have not felt the blessing of those waters for so long. I hope one day I may show Angette and Noab that river. Do you think it still flows or has this demon spirit poisoned it as well? I know the dawns are paler as if the sun is being eaten by the buzzards of our deserts."

"I believe Tessi if we succeed, we will enjoy once more these memories of the beauty and generosity of our lands which brought joy to our hearts and bodies, or we will die with those memories of happiness. Either way, I believe we are blessed."

Tessi looked at Nene.

"I am not sure I would be so happy, but I understand what you are saying. But I would be sad to think that Noab and Angette will never know what I have known."

"Come while we wait for the water to warm, we can find some food."

Tessi placed Angette on a table and took off her clothes.

"Do you have any salve? Her skin is raw."

"Yes, there will be some in the other chamber. Have a look in this chest Tessi. There should be some preserved fruits and vegetables and flours to make bread."

Nene kicked the chest over to Tessi and then went inside to the baths. Nene made her way over to a large table with mortars and pestles. She saw a jar with an unbroken wax seal. She carried it over to Tessi.

"This is from the oil of sheep fleece. It is soothing and protects the skin."

"There is some flour and corn meal. And some jars full of fruits Nene" spoke Tessi.

"Ahh good we can make some dough."

Nene strolled into the bath chamber and checked the water in the vat. It was warm and almost full.

She undid the tap. Water began to flow into one of the copper tubs.

"Tessi the water should be warm enough for Angette. When it is full enough simply turn the tap this way and it will stop. The vases on the table are medicines. While the ones near the tubs are perfumes. Choose whatever you like. I will bake some bread."

Tessi sniffed the perfumes and put a drop of lemon myrtle and lavender into the water. She placed Angette in the water and let her splash.

Nene put some logs in the hearth and lit a small fire. She hung an iron plate over it to warm it. She then took some the flour and water and it on a clay disc until it formed a lump of dough. She rubbed some salt, rosemary and thyme into it. She placed the disc on the iron skillet to bake. She took some wooden platters and put the fruit and pickled carrots and artichokes on them.

She nibbled on a prune.

"Now let me see, where are my books?" Nene strode into an alcove hidden behind shelves of pots. The little room was laden with old leather bound and parchment books from floor to ceiling.

She stood on a stool and reached up to second shelf from the ceiling. She pulled down the book.

Tessi had come out with Angette wrapped in clean cloth and placed her on one of the tables She was putting the lanolin on Angette's rashes. Deftly she tied another nappy and swaddling clothe around her.

"Here I will cradle her while you bathe." Nene took Angette from Tessi.

Tessi went back in. Nene heard more water pouring into the vat. She checked the dough. With a fork she flipped it over to cook on the other side.

Tessi poured some lavender and rose oil into the water and stepped into the tub. The water covered her to her shoulder. For just a moment the terrors of the last cycle of moons washed away. She scrubbed her head and hair and body all over. Instantly the aroma of the oils and warmth of the water made her fully awake. Cuts on her arms and legs stung momentarily as the fragrant water oozed into them. She could not believe how calm and silent it was. It was as if nothing had happened or was happening around them. A dull lump of pain for Noab and Ange sat within her heart, but for the moment, her body did not heave with exhaustion.

She closed her eyes. Noab's face was before her. He was crying. His eyes were hollow, and his cheeks were gaunt. Look mother look what you forsake. Cowardice starves your child. The malicious whisper of the Queen floated through dream.

Tessi whimpered as the image grew and the chilling claws of the Queen latched onto his head. Blood oozed down the face of Noab.

"No!" Tessi screamed and lurched up out of the tub. She saw Nene standing at the doorway. She held a burning twig with a strong odour of gantwood. It made Tessi gag.

"Send the memories far into the sky for the eagle to pluck the heart of malice. Be gone, be blind to all and one. Be gone, be blind to other's dreams. Leave to watch your own screams and the eagle to feast on your desires."

Tessi saw Nene's eyes glowed a light blue like the sky.

"There I think you should be safe for a while from these terrors. I fear the Queen has grown in her sorcery. The charm of night dream is very old and very powerful, and few can wield it. If she can place terror into the very depths of your heart, then her talons have grown in their sharpness and reach."

Nene left Tessi once more. Tessi shivered not wanting to close her eyes again. She washed the soot from her body.

"Is Noab safe?" she walked out into the kitchen where Nene sat eating with Angette on her knee. Beside her platter Nene had a book opened.

"I cannot see that far. I will ingest the herb of sleep and will see where my dream eyes take me. Ah good now my turn to bathe. Now there is preserved fruit which we call jam and is delicious on the dough cake. And the carrots and artichokes are still good to eat." Nene handed her Angette back.

"Are you a witch?"

"Let's just say I am a better Queen than I am a witch. My ancestors come from an ancient line of sorcerers. Long dead but I kept the books of learning from those times and occasionally dabbled but I was never successful on the more potent hexes and incantations. Giandra comes from a similar line but one which was our enemy. They breached the rules of the order and were condemned for their perversions."

Nene looked at Tessi. She saw fear on her face.

"You have seen these depravities first-hand Tessi. I will not harm you and am not practiced in these arts anyway. At most my dreams provide me with glimpses of the future or unseen action or the unheard word but nothing else. I believe you have been ensorcelled by Giandra. She has forced you to come to her before Gildas for an unknown purpose. We must be on guard." She squeezed Tessi's arm to reassure her as she went into the chamber. Ushan followed curious where Nene was going.

Tessi heard the splash as Nene got into her tub. The Queen began to sing. It was sweet and off key but full of happiness. Angette joined in as Tessi ate greedily the bread and jam. Tessi giggled at Nene and Angette's singing.

She looked at the book Nene had open. The text was indecipherable to Tessi. Writing was not part of their learning, but they knew the counting for trade and were sent to Ancrid to learn some of the Western and Drax symbols when they reached their first cycle and before betrothal. She preferred the stories they learnt when the village elders would gather. The stories were how they learned together. It was better she thought. The books looked like bricks in a wall and only allowed some into their knowledge. At least she thought we all learned together in her home.

"Ahh that is so much better." Nene spoke walking in with her long hair combed and washed hanging down her back. "I will keep reading to see if there is anything else which may help us when we arrive at the dreaded fortress." Nene put some garnish of herbs into a kettle and some water. She placed it over the fire to brew.

"Have you ever been betrothed and had children of your own?" asked Tessi.

Nene nibbled on some figs and began to run her finger over some text inside the large book.

"No to both." She smiled at Tessi's question "I will die without an heir. My kingdom is gone. My brothers were the hope for the sceptre of Aeserea to remain within the Des Vries line and now they are gone as well."

"Why not? I mean why didn't you marry when you knew it was important to keep the rule of your country. We are all betrothed by our sixteenth summer. I was betrothed to Liet before the plague came. I would have been wedded on the following cool season festival of the long night."

"You must tell me of your lands and ways Tessi. I have never seen the Eastern Deserts or the route of the Mighty Choasa. I have sailed past your lands once on a voyage around the Middling Isles."

"It is so strange for all of us. I fear there is no time for us to speak of the past when tomorrow seems to be fading with each pale dawn that rises" spoke Tessi.

'I know. I have no words of comfort. My lands are razed to ash and even if we succeed on taking back your child what then?" Tessi watched Nene staring into the room as if she was dreaming of something.

Tessi sat Angette up to burp. Nene looked at the child and the faintest sense of gladness and hope came to her heart. If one such as this daughter of the desert can live through the torment of a plague and then the tyrants of Matavia, surely there will be a way to defeat this darkness which consumed the world.

"You never told me why you didn't marry" spoke Tessi.

"Oh, I didn't find any suitable contenders. There were many very keen to sit closely to the sceptre of rule but none I thought I could bear to spend my days with or even have children. In my heart of hearts as well I think I didn't really want to be a mother or wife. It doesn't mean I didn't want to love but I just really didn't desire those other things. I couldn't just do it for the sake of duty." Her mind drifted to Medret. Her heart ached for him still. "And when Draved and Dronagh were born I thought I would step aside when they came of age, and they would rule. I always wanted to pursue scholarship in the old ways of healing and sorcery and our knowledge of the skies. But it was not to be. It's not that there aren't nights when I am haunted by my choices, but I felt they were the right ones at the time Tessi. And now with what has happened perhaps a deeper wisdom was at work. After all I would not be here with you now if I had children to care for which were my own." Nene smiled serenely into the flickering shadows of the chamber.

Tessi could see she had a genuine heart and love for people around her.

"I am glad you found us Nene."

"So am I Tessi."

"You must have a deep well of love in you Tessi to care for your children so much in the circumstances of their fathering."

"I am torn at all times when the memories of their making return in my dreams. As we say in my village my heart is not the desert meaning it is not at peace with itself like the desert is. If I were in the village there would have been salts, I could take from the elder of Ancrid to stop their birth. But there was nothing I could do in the Palace. When I saw them and their mixed skin, I thought they are as much mine as they are the King's. And I could not leave them to the fate of the Queen either. I both love and hate my children. I understand why our mother did not kill Ange my sister, her form brought shame to our father, and she was shunned because of it. But our mother was protective and loved her regardless. These babies born of violence shall know I am their mother as I knew mine. And I will give them their story beautiful and ugly as it is."

"Ah you indeed strong and pure as the desert. It must be a wise teacher to make people with such loyalty to their own and the strength to endure its lessons."

"It is not as fruitful in its giving as the forest and fields. We must be like this to survive" replied Tessi.

"I can see you are weary. Are you afraid to sleep?" asked Nene.

"I will dream of Noab again. Are you sure it is a curse from the Queen?"

"Yes, I sense her menace here. I will enact the charm of the old maid's veil, around us tonight so you at least may rest."

Nene gathered the platters and wiped them off with a cloth.

Tessi went over to a litter near the fire and lay down with Angette.

Nene began to speak.

"Old maiden, shrouded in the forest, quiet upon the moss, silence among the leaves, carry the nightshade with you, bring us the quietude of peaceful sleep, hide us among your misted fold, lead the dream wraiths away, keep them at play until the break of day."

"Can you see Noab, Nene?" Tessi asked as she began to drift to sleep.

"I will seek him out, but I can't promise anything" Nene replied.

Tessi fell asleep. Ushan was swishing at the door. Nene got up and let the cat out. She went back and stirred her tea. She turned each page of the large spell book until she saw the title: Laws of Adriaan Fire. Her heart was fearful. She knew she was no match for Giandra. They were going to their doom.

Her finger pulled away with blood on its tip. She looked at the smudge on the page. She saw the charm of change. Next to it was written "Quickening of blood and fire". This always frightened her. These were the laws which were never to be infringed at pain of expulsion. She remembered the book of the condemned listed the sorcerers who had breached these laws. Giandra was the daughter of Lord Mor Daast. His knowledge wielded the power of the starlight and fire mixed with the blood of flesh and bone. It was potent and deadly to those who did not have the will to control it.

"Have you found your strength Giandra? Have you mastered the charm of change and quickening of blood? Have the gods which now destroy our lands shown you how? Why do you desire these children so much and Tessi? What is it that you are seeking?"

Nene closed the book and opened another one. She found the page titled "Velleity of Dream Voyage."

"Dream wanderer, wayfarer, voyager and seeker of the unseen. Show me the hunter of my dreams and all those who rest close to my bed, pry out the spectres of nightmare and shadows."

Nene took a vial of gogangal root powder made from spores dug from beneath the soil and poured it into the mug of hot water. She sipped the bitter tea and sat back.

She slumped against the chair. She felt her body disintegrate like spores release in springtime carried by the breeze. Nene saw her lands burned and blackened to ash. She saw soldiers and their captives walking in lines toward the ocean. She saw the white palace and red eyes peering across Matavia, the Bay of Tears, over the ocean and toward the southern lands. She saw the sleeping child in the pristine white walls. The boy was peaceful. Nene saw the fierce light connecting the blood of the child and the red eyes. Nene looked back and saw the old maid's veil remained opaque, keeping Tessi safe from Giandra's eyes. Nene saw the fierce flames within the Queen as she stood on the balcony and how they did not burn her.

"You wish to be more powerful than your father. That is your desire." Nene spoke in the dark silent chamber.

She drifted seeking a way to protect herself, Tessi and the children. Nothing. They were naked in front of such strength. Then she saw the fine white streak on the edges of the flames surrounding Giandra. It was star light. It had been the first lessons learned at the time of studying the skies. Starlight permeated all light. It was the oldest of all light. Nene remembered it was the first book of the books of learning. She saw the red eyes surround the starlight and begin to chew at it. She saw figures moving on the edge of the light. Something pulled at the shadow around the red eyes and dimmed the starlight. Who are you? What are you to rule the light and shadow together? She slumped further letting herself drift on the winds. This time she asked to go back to her memories, when she was happy and the mighty forest of Vran pulsated with outstretched limbs protecting them all. The Lioness sat upon the great rock watching and waiting.

Nene woke suddenly. She stood and went to the bookshelf. She pulled out a book wrapped in wax cloth and went to the table. She saw Tessi was asleep, but Angette was awake playing with her hands and cooing. She briefly waved at Nene but continued to watch her fingers as they splayed out and then made a fist. Nene smiled.

She carefully opened the book. It was so old.

This must be at least ten decicycles or a thousand winters old she thought.

There on the first page was the text she needed.

*"Of all light that we know and feel, starlight is the oldest light and the first of all light. Older than flame and older than sunlight or moonlight. It has the power to draw all things together and bond them into the world we see. How was this discovered? The deep delving of our ancestors' memories showed times when the sunlight was extinguished, and the night sky died, and all things died here. In the translucence of water or crystals deep within the caves of*

*mountains, light still penetrates and breaks into the colours of the world. And when we watch with the crystals our vision changes. The light is distorted and changes the binding of the world and how we see it.*"

She went toward the last the paragraph of the first rules.

*"Starlight can be used to shield dark flame or shadow. It is impenetrable and exists within all things. Even darkness cannot destroy it because without it none can exist. Even if the darkest of shadows were to come to life, they would need this light to remain.*"

"Yes, but how do I use it to protect us?" Nene asked frustrated. She turned the next page and saw a drawing. It was of a diamond with lights beaming from it. It sat within a map of the southern lands.

Nene looked at Tessi and remembered Gildas story of why the shadow invaded this world. The crystal or jewel Tessi's sister carried was the key to it. Giandra wanted the children as a bargaining tool between the shadow and the jewel to obtain the power she lusted for.

Nene closed the book. Starlight is the first light and the most aged of all light. For shadow to exist in this world it would need starlight. Nothing can destroy it except itself. Nene sat back in her chair and fell to sleep peacefully thinking on the meaning of these words.

Tessi stirred. She saw Nene preparing dough.

"Did you sleep well Tessi?" Nene placed another pancake on the skillet.

"Yes, but did you rest at all Nene?" asked Tessi seeing a pile of already made bread on each plate with fruit spread on it.

"Yes, I did Tessi. Noab is safe."

Tessi burst into tears at hearing the words.

"But we go to a doom I am not sure we will be able to escape from. There is much darkness and strength awake in the world and I am not skilled enough to combat it. But you and your kin are needed, and I feel the safest thing to do is to go into the jaws of the beast and show it the strength of what made us flesh and bone."

"Ange said the same thing. I think that is why she did she what she did."

"I believe Giandra will take us to your sister. But I will keep the charm of the old maid's veil in place until we get there. It will keep our strength up, so we not weakened by Giandra's malicious nightmares."

"It will be dangerous along the roads" spoke Tessi as she began to nurse Angette.

"We will be underground until almost the coastline. Then we will be in Matavian territory. If we are captured, they will take us to the Queen, or we will make a surprise visit. Eat up Tessi, the next adventure begins." Nene gave Tessi a cup of herbal tea. They toasted to their journey ahead.

Ushan wandered in from the tunnel. She began to preen herself near the fire.

Nene noticed a piece of cloth stuck on large fangs. She pulled it out. It was embroidered with a vulture.

I hope that Unstaadt soldier was not too tough to chew thought Nene.

# 11

# Steppes of the Jun

Kado eyed General Laotian. He was a dangerous man. He reminded Kado of Sa; deceptive in every way on the outside, an unsprung coil waiting to explode with repressed fury.

"Do you follow me into battle?"

The General did not respond. Kado had summonsed all the generals of the twelve Kingdoms of the Drax. They stood before him each of whom had derided the son of the Emperor Ko at one time or another and no less now.

"You are here at the whim of a spirit Kado. We would walk to our death behind you. You are a wraith that has come to curse the lands of the Dragon even more. The dragon is patient. It will rise again once the shadow has exhausted itself."

"We go to our death now General. The Hill of Jun will fall. Already the Unstaadt gather their momentum to attack. To live like housed rats, waiting for the vulture to come and devour us is hardly worthy of the people of the Dragon."

Kado circled General Laotian watching his every move. He knew about the knife contained in the soldier's sleeve and the poisoned tip upon it. He knew if he strayed within the reach of the General's arm he would strike like a viper and that the old Kado would be dead before he hit the floor.

Kado wondered for a moment if he should test the gift of Vipax by walking more closely to Lao. He noticed the twitching jaw muscle; the miniscule movement the only sign of the tension that belied the face of stone.

Kado breathed in the air and for the first time felt the adrenaline of being in control of other people. He had received the message from Jarrod and knew that thousands of Graan had already marched upon Shadaraq and were on their way here. He would join them with the few still loyal to the Ko Dynasty.

"I need an answer Lao."

Kado walked towards the General and as he was about to pass by, he stepped towards Lao. In an instant the dagger had been produced and raked across Kado's neck.

Kado felt the pain of the cut and then the poison work directly into his body. He collapsed on the floor. His chest would not move as he tried to breathe and as the venom paralysed all his muscles, his body became completely still. Lao stood over him and spat on him.

"Son of Ko, you have and always will be unworthy to fly the banner of the dragon into battle."

Everything began to go black as the remaining air in his lungs was used up. He noticed as he closed his eyes three of the Generals were trying to wrestle Lao and remove the dagger from his hand.

"You have killed the Heir to the Dragon's Throne. You have cursed us for a thousand generations" General Tat shouted.

I have found my warriors Kado thought as his body gave way to the poison. As his last breath was expelled Kado shut his eyes. He sensed the presence of Vipax.

"How long Vipax?"

"Do not amuse yourself with my gift Scaletryx. It is given so the world will not be destroyed by the shadow. And it will ask for sacrifice as it did of the Sentinels who were bestowed this gift at their births."

Kado felt himself being thrust away. He woke and sucked in a breath. Launching himself upright in a swift movement, he took a sword out of the hilt of General Laotian and held it to the General's throat. A small trickle of blood ran down onto the collar. Kado saw the stunned look in Lao's eyes.

"I have seen who would be loyal once more to the Drax. Tat, Sai and Woansa bind them and take them to the gathering wells below. You have shown your disloyalty to the emperor, now restore yourselves by your deaths. Feel the fire of the dragon in your bellies."

The disgraced Generals were bound and dragged by their feet on the granite floor down a long ramp carved from the mountainside. Below bustled the remains of the Ko Empire in the form of villagers and farmers and soldiers. The cavern expanded almost a league in each direction with only a few tiny shafts of light poking through into the gloom.

Kado followed and pointed to the ledge that jutted out over the people below. Kado thumped the sceptre on the stone sending echoes across expansive ceiling of stone. Everything became silent as thousands of faces looked up at their ruler.

"People of the Dragon's fire behold your ruler and Emperor. I have found my warriors who are loyal to the Dragon and its sceptre. No more shall we live like rats hidden beneath stones, but we will go to war and die in glorious battle or relish a victory that the scholars shall write about for a thousand harvests. All of you are now called to fight for the survival of the Kingdom and all our lands. I ask for those loyal to show yourselves and those who are not. Know this, the breath of the Dragon will only enflame the hearts of those loyal to the Sceptre. For those who cannot swear this oath then redeem your disloyalty and remove any curse that may follow your treachery by taking the honour of the Kiss of the Dragons Fire. See here."

Kado gestured for the Generals to be dragged forward and hung over the edge of the ledge.

"These are traitors to the Dragon. Show the people Generals how you remove the curse you bring with your treachery."

None of the soldiers moved, they only struggled against the bonds. General Lao's face began to redden as the blood filled his head. He reached trying to pull himself up the rope and then realising there was a ledge beneath he began to swing himself back and forth to try and grab the rocks. Suddenly the general sprouted wings and a tail. His body transformed into a tiny dragon. The bonds loosened around his limbs, and he fell. But before plunging into the crowd the dragon flew up in a sharp arc toward the roof of the cavern and landed on a ledge of rock.

"For those loyal to the traitor, follow him to his doom," commanded Kado. His eyes glowed with tiny yellow specs.

Suddenly the other generals transformed into the dragons. The other six Zhang flew to the ledge and formed a row. They hissed at the people below.

"Make your choice! The dragon or its heir!" shouted Kado.

Below he looked on and saw people and soldiers falling while others began to chant as they made their choice. Another hundred Zhang flew up into the shadows.

While below the chorus "Drax! Drax!" rose up toward the roof of the cavern.

"General Tat, we are ready for war. Gather the soldiers and anyone who can wield a sword. We go to the Iron Coast where the demon dwells."

Tat looked at Kado and nodded. Kado's eyes dimmed. He took the sceptre and raised it above his head and shouted across the cavernous space.

"Ready for War, bring the breath of the Dragon to life and cleanse its lands of the fetid stench of the Unstaadt and Matavian. Long live the Dragon, Long live its Emperor!"

The Hill of the Jun shook with the sound of the voices responding to Kado's call to war. He turned and made his way back to the throne room. Princess Yan met him along the passage. She smelt of flowers and honey. She continued ahead of him. He became mesmerised by the smell that wafted towards him. Every move of her body seemed to be intoxicating and he felt himself become aroused.

"Princess you are more alluring than usual."

"It is the oils that I brought with me Emperor. Do you like them? They are my special creations for occasions such as these."

Kado nodded as he continued to walk.

"Walk with me Princess."

He watched her closely as she obediently fell to his side. She turned her head to look at him.

"Watch your step Princess."

Upon reaching the chamber he placed the sceptre on the throne. Clapping his hands, the chamber cleared of servants and guards.

Princess Yan bowed and made to leave.

"Not you Yan."

He took some water and drank.

"Those oils, they are strong. Where did you get them from?"

"We made them in my palace. The mistresses kept them for their bathing rituals when the masters came for their visitations."

"How much of it is there?"

"I had all the stores brought here, forty canisters."

"How much have you used here today?"

"Why do you like it Kado? This is merely a drop" she giggled flirting with him.

"I do like it Yan. I like it very much. It seems to pervade all my senses and rouses them more than I would like."

He strode slowly over to the Princess. She smiled waiting for his touch. His hand slid around her soft pale throat. He moved behind her and pulled her closely and gently placed his other arm around her waist. He smelt her hair and skin and felt instantly the effect of the essence magnify his attraction to her. He began to stiffen with desire.

"It's almost bewitching Yan." She let her body relax into his letting him know of her consent.

He kissed her throat and moved his hand lower to find the opening of her robes. Suddenly his other hand tightened holding her firmly. She tried to struggle but Kado was too strong.

"If I let you go will you ever try your sorcery on your Emperor and Ruler again? You think you can wield the sceptre of the Dragon through me and an heir? Know this Princess, the Kado of your memory is no more and will not be weakened by his desires or need to rebel. Do not attempt this sorcery again or you will feel the sting of Dragon fire."

He let her go as he saw the skin around her lips begin to turn blue. She collapsed onto the ground grasping her throat.

"The generals are still loyal to me and my father Kado Kodrax. You are foolish to think that they will follow you. They will seek my patronage and wealth." She spoke back viciously.

"I have dealt with the Generals who wish to betray the Dragon and its Emperor."

Stepping over her he clapped his hands and sat at a table where a meal had been left for him. The servant Wan bowed and looked nervously at the Princess on the ground. The guards filed back in.

"Escort the Princess to her chambers so she may rest. Wan take your men and remove all the canisters of essence that are stored there. I have use for them. Do not spill any of it on you; if you do bath yourself and your clothes."

"No, it is mine" Princess Yan protested.

"Get her maids to wash her down" ordered Kado.

Kado finished eating. He took out the message that Jarrod had sent him. They would arrive at the pass of Shadaraq in the next quart moon. All the clans had gathered. Unstaadt sighted on all roads south.

He took out some parchment and wrote to Gildas.

"Sceptre taken and sanctified in the blood of traitors. Dragon's breath is lit."

He decided to go down to where Vipax had left him. He needed a suit of armour.

The stairwell was still and cool. His mind began to clear from the fragrance of the enchanted essence of the Princess. He would need to watch her if he survived what was to come. His mind drifted to Sa. He longed to see her and hear her counsel. As he entered the vault he began to sift through the piles of armour. He found a set of leather britches and the ornate overall to match them. It was made of deep burgundy leather. Cured and stitched with three layers the suit was virtually impenetrable. On the front were embroidered in gold thread intricate designs meant to reinforce the vest for strength but also exuded the opulence and wealth of the Ko Magisterium. The helmet sat nearby. He noticed the insignia of a dragon with Draxanus Deathflame embroidered around it. The first Drax ruler.

He tried it on. The helmet was slightly too large but could be altered, the vest and trousers the same.

He placed them aside and selected a shield and daggers. There was a crossbow adorned with the same markings as the vest and was died the deep bloodred of the rosewood tree. Looking at the vast cache he wondered how many generations of Emperors had been adding to the pile. His father had been the most prolific. The warmonger knew how many enemies he had made over the life of his rule. Not all could be dispatched when it suited the emperor, and a day would come when the ruler would fight the ruled. Now though, all this metal and leather would be used to fight against an enemy unknown and unseen and virtually indestructible. Would it be enough? Kado thought. He saw the tear of Vipax lying near the water's edge. He picked it up and put it inside his tunic.

"Where are you Sa-Tuc? I need your steady hand to guide. The indolent Prince may have found his courage but his skill in battle is yet to be seen. If I survive to rule the Kingdom, will I be any better than my father?"

"I see this one you call Sa-Tuc in your heart Scaletryx. This clayborn is hollow unlike the rest of your kind and you will not fill the chasm that lives there. Ready to battle, the dragon has heard the cry of the children baying for war. Its bones are shaken."

"What do you mean, Sa-Tuc is hollow?"

"Another time Scaletryx. The war begins!"

Kado felt something push him towards the entrance to the cavern. He took the suit and made his way back up to the winding stairs. Upon entering the throne room, he saw that it was empty of any guards but noticed the canisters of essence near the wall. He took the suit to the table where he dined and spread it out.

"Wan."

The servant came in straight away.

"Take this, alter it to my size and fetch General Tat."

"Yes Emperor."

Kado took out the tear of Vipax and peered into it. It is by this power I have become powerful and not my own merit. This will be the foundation of the new land of Drax if it survives the shadow of Voloc. The tear of the serpent and the flame of the dragon. What might and curse has been bestowed on me and my kind thought Kado.

Kado picked up a staff and began to perform his defensive manoeuvres. He had practiced a thousand times in his life but never used them in a battle. Sa-Tuc had known this was his weakness and had taught him ways to be a lethal adversary, but subtlety would not be enough for this battle. If the Kingdom is going to survive then his skill on the battlefield will need to be shown, otherwise the people would overthrow him making all this in vain.

General Tat arrived as Kado stood musing over his doubt.

"Emperor."

"General are we ready to ride. I have received word from the Graan Elder-Chieftain that they will be at the Shadaraq pass in the next moon. I want to cross the land bridge south from Hosiaan together as a force."

"We have sent soldiers out to force the remaining peasants with wit enough to wield a sword or axe. They can be the shield against the onslaught if the Unstaadt attack before the coast."

Kado went to the canisters and gestured to the General to come over.

"Breathe General."

Tat took a deep breath and instantly felt giddy and a desire to visit his wife.

"Well General, do you think the barbarians may learn to show affection toward their enemy instead of malice? Douse the peasants and lay people in the perfume and have them walk to the front line. Place some in our cannons and aim for the heart of the Vulture.

Smother the rancid hide in flowers and honey. Empty the caves below; make sure everyone is armed."

"But there is no honour in this Emperor. We will meet them in battle and know we die with strength worthy of our lands and ancestors. This deceit is for sorcerers and mages not soldiers.'

"I know General, but another battle awaits us in the south. A battle which we have no way of knowing how long it will last. Even the march to the battlefield will be a battle as the desert will be hungry for our flesh as well. I need as many soldiers as possible to survive the journey. I do not want any wasted on petty skirmishes in these lands."

"I understand Emperor." General Tat left.

Kado sat and picked at a carrot and some pheasant. In the deep recesses of Kado's mind a memory came back to him. He must have been no more than five winters. He was walking behind his father, and they were both dressed ready for battle. The warriors were in perfect formation as their emperor inspected them.

"Drive the dogs into the ground!"

Ko had picked his son up and strode back towards the gates of the Palace. In the distance he could see large gatherings of people holding picks and axes. They were the farmers that tilled the fields to supply Drax City with food. Previously the peasants had been given special status as the custodians of the harvests. But his father had demoted them and called them the peasant class after one of the largest land holders had asked for water rights from the wells where the prized breed of battle horses drank. Even with the lower classes and the farmers starving due to failures of the harvest in a dry season Ko Paidrax had felt that this was an impudent request indeed and from that day, the farmers had been relegated to the same caste as peasants.

Kado thought of the warriors as they doused the peasants in oils of perfumes and set them ablaze. The scent drew the mountain bears to finish off those who had survived. His father had made him watch from safety. He remembered his father's bellowing commands vibrating in his chest as he watched and heard their screams.

"Kill the rebellious and undeserving rats!"

Kado remembered he had wondered at the time what the city would do for food. However soon the fields had been replaced with slaves and those kin left from the dead rebels. Would his father be proud of him now that it was this memory which may help them reach the final battle for the Kingdom relatively unscathed?

Kado walked to the tunnel that led to the roost of the vultures. There was a faint odour of rotten flesh on the breeze. He checked the nests of the birds and saw that they were empty.

He looked across the fields and in the distance over twenty leagues away he could just see the ocean between the middling lands and the Iron coast. In between lay the lands annexed by the Unstaadt. He could see the small funnels of smoke rising in the distance where they either razed the villages to the ground or set up their humpy camps. The Unstaadt were barely civilised, a tribe of fighting barbarians. They killed their old men when they could not fight and their women when they could not breed. The children were kept either to become fighters or breeders. Trained from a young age even to the death as children those who survived to become their generals were formidable foes.

"Kado Kodrax"

Kado startled when he heard General Tat's voice.

"We are ready to begin the exodus. Have you sent word to the Graan?"

"I will send word to meet us at the Steppes of Jun."

Kado watched the sunset knowing that by dawn he would be riding to the destiny his father had ultimately aspired for him to fulfil; to lead the Ko Kingdom into battle and his probable doom.

# 12

# Eagle, Bear and Lion

Gildas stared at Polax sparring with Tyl and Axl. The thought occurred to him for the first time if his son had lived then this perhaps would have been him. Would he have tolerated a son whose prowess may have surpassed his own? Would he have been willing to let go of his right to rule for the sake of his youngling? Would his road have ended here if the child had lived?

He stopped his musing and made his way back to the camp. He saw General Medret greeting another soldier. The man's coat was torn and covered in dust, but the ornate embroidery was still clear on the collar and sleeves. They place too much on the eye these Aeserean. I hope they put it into the wielding of their swords he thought.

"Ah Gildas, this is Lord Jonas Warick. He has brought the garrisons safely through the blades of the scum from the borders of Irasia and the southern coast" spoke Medret.

Gildas nodded not speaking.

Warick hesitated upon seeing the brute size of Gildas.

"I remember the legends of Gildas Gol. My father while not liking your methods, understood your strength and respected your skill in battle. I am glad at this desperate time, that your blade lies next to ours and not against it."

"Ay, it is dark times for all; the sight of any lands lying in the hands of the Matavian cannot be borne with a blind eye and idle blade" Gildas replied.

"Gildas is now known as the Keeper of Tarentess, the great fang of the Lioness as we call it in our lands Jonas. Have the men been camped?" spoke Medret.

"Ay Cotus, we have five legions strong with the addition of the southern Doanda tribes and a coalition of people who wished to fight rather than accept the fate of being enslaved" replied Jonas.

"We go to battle on the morn. We have enough to take the Bay of Tears and their ships" the Knight replied.

Gildas sat down and lit his pipe. Warick and Medret joined him along with Polax, Tyl and Axl. The Graanar acknowledged Lord Warick who stood to greet them.

"Lord Warick this is Chieftain Polax of Clan Timmo and his kinsmen Tyl and Axl" spoke Gildas.

"Gildas, we should wait until Jarrod and Olac have united with the Drax." Polax had overheard Medret speaking of leaving on the next dawn.

"Their battle will not join ours until the end. They will destroy the Unstaadt and we the Matavians. It is a fair fight for all and the black blood of these scum, will feed the dirt for next year's harvest. The lands with the most bountiful harvests will be called the victor." Gildas spoke with a grin on his face.

"After the Bay is taken, how will the ships bear our numbers to the Iron Coast? If the Matavians attack they are just as likely to burn their ships if they know we need them." asked Lord Warick.

"Polax," Gildas signalled the chieftain to speak.

"The Clan Timmo are as much of the sea as ice and will bring our mighty vessels. There is a channel of water that is a gateway to the western oceans. Word has been sent. So far, the raging storms that afflict the northern waters have not moved to the west. We will be waiting from the waters to protect the ships but also carry our hoards south. Has the bird god returned?"

"Not yet Polax. We will leave the protection of the Forests. We will be open in our attack Lord Knight" replied Gildas.

"We can go by the Hendra Vale; it is dangerous but will be a quicker route. The creatures that live there will be easily succumbed with this many blades" spoke Medret.

"Nay, the valley is mine," replied Gildas.

Medret looked at Gildas wondering what he meant.

"We will go in the open plains until the plateau below the Point of Isthmus. The forces will meet on the salt of the vale that lies above the city," continued Gildas.

"Why there?" asked Polax

"They can surround us from all sides" spoke Medret. "The point of Isthmus is exposed, and we will be seen from there? They can attack at any time, and we will be spread thin until we reach of the plateau."

"It will be the same for them, there is no land that will give them traction. They have no stealth in their battles, it is always open and on the field. If they are going to attack it won't be until we reach the plateau. When we are near, I will take Axl and Tyl to the Palace. Faad will know I seek the child leaving our entourage exposed as it crosses the plateau. He will take a chance to destroy our forces in one easy blow. But it means leaving his Queen free to die upon my blade. With her dead he will capitulate. Faad is weak compared to Ranik. He will not be able to control the Generals. If for some reason the Queen and Faad are true to the pact made and agree to join us, then it will be of no loss and an easy road to the south. But at least from that position on the plateau the graanar will be ready" Gildas nodded satisfied with the plans.

"You still hope that you can force them to fight along with us Gildas?"

"Perhaps, but mostly it is to stop too much time spent in battle here. The Generals are tenacious. I believe even this shadow that drives the stink of battle in the air would be thwarted by the iron will of the Matavian overlords especially in the heat of battle."

"I would rather spill my blood here now then fight in allegiance with those beasts." Lord Warwick spat on the ground as he grumbled his disgust for the Matavians.

"Ay you will have your vengeance Knight, but we must take the ships and Bay first. It will be better if they can be subdued and commanded to save as many of us before we reach the lair of the demon. I do not know how long we will need to lay siege in the Iron Coast" replied Gildas.

"Have no fear Jonas, you have not seen all there is to see yet, especially from Gildas. I too feel your twitching at such an alliance. But there is no more Aeserea with no heirs the rule of the Des Vries is finished on the death of the Queen. The lands are ravaged and sacred forests all but destroyed. We are landless and now have no choice but to fight a common enemy to all of us, even the Matavians." Cotus spoke as patted his old friend on the shoulder. He saw the veins pulsing on Jonas's head, a signal his long-time compatriot was about to explode with fury. The thought of fighting alongside their mortal enemies was enough to make the man gut himself like the Unstaadt.

"Ay, it is for the final clash that we march Knight. The battle at the Bay of Tears is just a way to sail to the shores of the red lands of the south. When we draw nearer General you will need to lead the legions to the centre of the battle. If needed make it a swift kill."

"One of the fatal flaws of the Matavians is that their soldiers are loyal out of subjugation. The skill and lust for battle belongs to an elite few who Ranik used to protect himself. Kill the Generals and the rest of the dogs are like a fevered rabble" Medret added.

"True. Even the Unstaadt are tougher in their approach, as one captain is killed, another one steps up. Jarrod and Kado's path will be more difficult" spoke Gildas.

"There is one more thing Gildas. When we reach the Iron Coast, the lands are arid. The dust is fine red grain parched of water for many hundreds of deci-cycles and for many leagues. The march may well kill us if no stores of water can be found," spoke Medret.

"Aye Knight, I have thought of this. Our allies the Orynth will need to drop water to us. There is no other way."

"We will need them for battle though?" spoke Axl who had become enthralled with the mighty Orynth.

"Some yes, but we will perish without even having to face the wraith if we have naught to drink." Gildas replied. "I want all the men ready by dawn tomorrow. Axl and Tyl I want you to hand out the blades to everyone who marches with us. Knight you may select your Captains to hasten the blade swearing."

Just as Gildas finished speaking, he looked up "Ah just in time. This is a new ally Lord Warick, see the great mysteries of the world reveal itself."

Warick looked at the Orynth landing on the ground. They placed massive bundles of swords , arrow shafts and cross bows at the base of two giant fig trees. They then left without acknowledging anyone.

"Take your blade Jonas. It is the gift of Gildas" spoke Medret.

"How so many? Have the Graan been stashing weapons for a war Cotus? Who are those creatures?"

Medret could see the soldier bristling thinking that some attack had been planned on the Aeserean Kingdom, but for Ranik's onslaught.

"Nay, hold ya temper man. There is much to tell you, but it would mean nothing unless I could show you as well. Any hope for victory now lies with Gildas."

"Ay until he decides he wants the power that these despots all seek at the cost of everything around them." Jonas retorted.

"I think not Jonas. He is different. I remember meeting Gildas on the battlefield when I first soldiered under King Erdene. If all we had to cling to was Gildas Gol of those yester days and this demon, then I would ride to my death now. But he has been cowed. I can see a man willing to bend his own mind to something more than himself. It took a spirit of the netherworlds to do it, but it has been done. The Graan do not align with him, they have made him exile. His brother Jarrod now rules the northern tribes and he begrudgingly agreed to follow Gildas since all our doom now lies within sight. But any hope we have defeating these dark days lies with him, of this, I am sure."

"I will take ye word for it Cotus. The spirits of the soldiers have lifted since being here. They know that death lies in their sight and seek their own glory. And now that I see more than just our blades goes to war with us, my own shadow of doom lifts as well. How are they wrought so quickly?" Jonas had picked up a sword and began inspecting it.

"After the battle is won Gildas may take you on a tour of his Keep."

"The horses will not trek the great deserts of the lands south. I have heard legends of their expanses and heat, as if the sun lay claim to it as its own above all other in the world."

"Nay Jonas, it will be ships and then by foot to this fortress in the desert" replied Medret.

Gildas walked among the gathered legions of soldiers. Graan and Aeserean mingled in small groups here and there but for the most part they remained separate. All of them he thought would know that their lives were here or in chains with Matavian whips to flay the flesh from their bones. He thought of Kado. The kite had come with news that Kado had seized control of the Feudal Lords. He wondered about the assassin. EY had not returned to give news of her whereabouts. He knew in his mind what would happen when he reached the Bay of Tears. Gildas breathed the anticipation of the battle to come, and his blood roared with the need for it to begin. Never had he felt so alive as when blade and blood would mingle. Even more now that the enemy he faced was almost beyond his skill to defeat. If he died it would be a worthy death. Gildas Keeper of Tarentess, clansman of the mighty Graan dead at the hands of the demon god created at the beginning of all things. Nekoda had come up to him and sat panting by his side. He patted the scarred and loyal dog. Puffing on his pipe he watched the sun set in a glory of magentas and reds.

"Bring the dawn soon. My blood, flesh and bone scream to ride forth to begin the feast of death."

The entourage snaked its way down into the passage of Yullaan. It was the densest part of the Forests of Vran and the northern tables that skirted the feet of the great ranges beneath Tarentess. Gildas looked back through the dense foliage of leaves and branches made by the ancient oaks, figs, and elm trees. He vaguely heard the falls of Udana and Adana that ran through the table where the water spirits grove was found. It seemed a long time ago since the demon had hunted him into the pool. The memory of the restoring power of the water remained vivid.

Behind him flew banners of bear and lion: white with a black silhouette of the ice bear head with fangs bared and the green and gold of the Lioness. Forty thousand followed him. How many would survive, he wondered.

Suddenly the forest thinned where the ravaging fires of the battle for Esteron City marked the footprint of destruction by the Matavian invasion. He heard a low cheer building behind him. Looking across to the west in the distance stood a lonely burnt statue of a lion. It was one of the four pillars at the borders between Aeserea and Matavia. The massive mane and mouth frozen in a warning roar carved from the green and black marble from the base of Tarentess. The cheer was caught by the wind and carried the voices of the Aeserean people.

"Hail to the Lioness. Her grace still blesses these lands."

Then the song of the Icebear chorus rose into the crisp morning air.

*"Dig the snow and claw the bone,*

*roar your song across the cold*

*Great Spirit fill our meat*

*Fill our chest with ice and fire*

*Let the claw and blade crush the enemy's huts*

*Spill their blood on dirt and stone*

*Ram the gate with their screams of pain*

*Victory, Victory, to the Raging Mother,*

*Hear your cub's battle cry, feel the axe and blade."*

Gildas began to jog.

"Forward, we race to victory!" he roared back to the army behind him and then broke into a sprint.

Cotus and Jonas called together "Aesereans form your ranks."

The foot soldiers went into perfect unison and the cavalry rode on the flanks. Soon the forty thousand began to race towards the plains of Isthmus.

# 13

# Scent of the Serpent

"Bring the axe up and over in a large arc and with your other hand bring the blade to the belly." Jarrod showed the clan maid Ina, the manoeuvre for fighting. She was tall for her age but not sturdy.

Ina nodded and mimicked the move. She felt the blade connect with Jarrod's waist and nodded in satisfaction.

"Good, keep practising that move. Your blade hand will protect your flank but can be lethal while your axe blocks the downward thrust of your adversary."

"Thank you, Chieftain." Ina nodded and went back to the rest of the group.

Jarrod watched the rest of the younglings practice. Caelwyn came to mind. She would have had the baby by now. Han and Jano had been instructed to stay to help her but also if he did not survive then they would be next chieftains of the Gol clan. But if we lose our nation, what would they rule? Even the ice was being chewed away by the black ocean beneath it and too many of these younglings have no experience of war he thought.

"We will need to start our march south again on the morning Jarrod," spoke Brago.

"Ay haste is needed. Many more skirmishes and we will be too depleted to even meet Gildas in the southern deserts. I still have the stains of the battle at Shadaraq."

"How do the younglings fare?" asked Brago

"Ah they are strong and eager but too young in my mind. I fear of the loss of the graanar. We will not survive this battle Brago."

"Ay, it is our doom we run to. Our forests wither as the salty water from beneath begins to reach their roots."

"Any word of the Draxus?"

"Ay, a hoard has been seen leaving the feet of the mountains to the east."

"We will head down the western flank of the Drax lands to ensure nothing chases us from behind or from the Western shores."

"We found a group of Aeserean merchants as they were fleeing Shadaraq. They have asked to join us."

"Can they fight?"

"As well as any plump westerner Chieftain," Bregt replied in a matter-of-fact tone.

"Ay, I take your point. It has been many cycles of the moon since I stayed in the city of Esteron and Irasian temples. I learnt much on the finery of things and learning how to keep records and the lessons the past gives us. They also began to see the ways of the Graan and our knowledge not just as blood thirsty hunters scavenging a living out of the ice."

"And what would be wrong with that?" laughed Brago. Jarrod slapped him on the back half agreeing.

"Ay when we face the complete destruction of everything you wonder what the point was of knowing where to place of a comma in a writ or even for that matter how to find a place of shelter when the winds of Raajn would scream across the ice."

"Chieftains, the boars are roasted and dripping fat flavoured with the dirt here."

Jarrod and Brago looked up at the voice of Olas, one of the older women who had come to fight. She held a leaf with steaming pile of meat on it.

"Ay, we come now," replied Jarrod.

"On the dawn Brago, break the clans down into smaller numbers. We are too large to move quickly. If we each spread across the western flanks from the Bay of Drax to the citadel we will topple any hidden Matavian or rogue Drax. We will move faster to the Hosiaan bay. It will also give the younglings a chance to battle before we head into the southern lands."

"Ay Chieftain."

Jarrod watched the dawn to the west as he ran with the graan behind him to make their way to the rendezvous with the Draxus.

At the height of the sun, they passed the crater where the Emerald city of Drax once stood. He remembered the story Gildas had told of the awakening of the god of stone. He didn't really believe it until he saw the devastation of the great city. He had only been there once in his life but remembered the glory of its wealth and ancient history. For some reason the empty crust of rubble which sparkled with gemstones among the ruins, made his heart ache for Caelwyn and his homelands. The purity of life on the ice, the crystals sparkling on the large expanses when the sun was at its zenith. Was this what the great lands of the Ice Mother would become, swallowed into the black ocean, destroyed beyond memory. He thought of Gildas and wondered how his journey had been. He remembered the time of he and Jesse as youths and how happy they had seemed. He had been blinded by Gildas' strength and protector as older brother to his will for power which lay beneath that façade of guardianship. Why did Jesse choose you Gildas? She could have been anyone's clan wife or ruled in her own right.

Jarrod's musing was suddenly interrupted by the sounds of yelling. A skirmish had broken out behind him.

"We will go to help them Chieftain. It is a group of Draxus" called Ina.

"Nay I see picks and axes. They are not soldiers. Probably starving farmers."

Soon the graanar had surrounded the small group of Drax. Jarrod strode toward them.

"Chieftain, we have a few. I think they are not dangerous" spoke Ina.

"Are there more of them?" Jarrod asked

"Not that we can see. But they sprung up out of the ground between us. So more may lay in wait."

"We are allies of Prince Kado, heir to the Drax Empire, son of Paidrax Ko" spoke Jarrod to one of the group. They were filthy and looked half starved.

The man looked at Jarrod and replied in the Drax tongue. Jarrod did not understand the words but heard the name Kado just before the man spat on the ground in disgust. A woman made a hissing noise as well.

"Cursed son of Ko" she spoke in the trader tongue.

"Ina, take a group and search for other places where the ground looks disturbed. Brago can some of your clan run ahead and keep a look out. Graanar keep an eye. Picks and Axes can still cause a wound and make you lame. Take these ones, give them food and water and leave them with supplies. We continue our march south." Jarrod ordered to the gathered clans.

"Did you see that Chieftain. They do not like this prince we go to meet" spoke Brago.

"Nay Brago, we may be going to the southern lands alone. Emperor Ko was more a tyrant than a ruler, but he was brilliant. His son did not impress me as the same. More of a scholar type than soldier." Jarrod replied. He wondered at Kado being called cursed.

By the end of the third day the Graanar had reached the edge of the valley that led down towards the coast. Jarrod saw in the distance the dark shadow of Kado's forces moving over the undulations of the Hosiaan Province. Further still the blue ocean which stretched between the Middling lands toward the southern coast. He could just make out a break in the blue waves where rubble had formed a land bridge to the closest tip of the southern coast. On it was a dark shadow. He realised there would be no time for parlance or rest. Their enemy stood ready.

"Forward Graanar! Friend and enemy await to do battle. Graanar! Graanar!" Jarrod shouted across to the hoard who followed him.

He heard the roar of the Graan battle cry behind him spurring them on to an even faster sprint.

Dragon and Bear met a league before the ruins of Hosiaan Citadel. Before them stood ten thousand Unstaadt warriors, their black and red leather tunics and helms dimming the green lushness of the fertile lands. Kado sat on his horse and beside him walked Jarrod, so tall that his head sat ear to ear with Kado's stallion. Along each side of them the Graan chieftains and the Generals of Emperor Kado Kodrax ready to launch their attack.

Kado raised his sword and shouted "Send the first wave. Release the essence."

Jarrod watched as thousands of farmers and peasants dressed only in rags with pickaxes were forced into the frontline of the battle and made to run towards the Unstaadt waiting.

Jarrod thought they will be slaughtered.

Then as the peasants neared the waiting enemy volleys of arrows with small bundles attached to them flew into the air and exploded just above them.

Kado and the Generals watched along with the Graan Chieftains as the vicious blows of the barbarians began to give way to indolent strikes with little aim, giving the remaining peasants a reprieve from the killing field they had been forced into.

"To battle!" screamed Kado.

The legions of the Dragon Dynasty and the Graanar raced to the Unstaadt and when they clashed, they fought drug addled fiends that slashed at air. Jarrod looked down at all the dead farmers and became infuriated at the waste. He tore his way forward along with graanar. Soon however the effect of the perfume had worn out and the Unstaadt resumed their lethal assault.

Jarrod saw Kado fighting blow for blow with two Generals. One of them caught him on his back and sliced off the flesh at the shoulder blade. He did not flinch as he brought his sword down in a graceful arc and decapitated one of the Generals. The clansman watched, mesmerised, as the bone and sinews moved in unison on the body of Kado. No blood came from the wound. He has been taken by the shadow he thought or is it a gift of Gildas?

Jarrod resumed fighting thrusting his way forward in the melee of battle. He realised he could hear the roar of the ocean all around him. He stopped to see where his Chieftains were positioned and saw that they had managed to make it halfway across the land bridge. The waves turbulently washed over the edges of the rubble.

Suddenly the fighting stopped as the Unstaadt turned and raced toward the south. Behind them lay a league of dead bodies.

"Graanar answer the bear, Gol, Clotte, Bregt, Nimmo, Hadraan and Kaan!" shouted Jarrod.

An almighty roar moved across the sea of fighting drowning out the ocean around them.

"Follow the stench of the Vulture, pluck its hide and break its bones, feed the Ice Mother with its flesh" shouted Jarrod.

He looked at Kado's wounds, half his face had been carved off and one of his arms had lost its skin.

"We will follow them into the desert lands Prince. No peasants or potions to hide behind now but your bewitching may come in handy if we had the time to watch you kill them one by one. You are your father's son, terrorize and oppress with a mirage of power behind the glamour of your riches."

Jarrod laughed as he slapped Kado with his blade playfully. He took off with dozens of graanar following. General Tat rode up to Kado.

"Kado we will ride ahead. I have sent the rear to kill off any remains of the enemy, so we are protected from the back."

Kado said nothing as the words of Jarrod echoed in his mind. The doubt that had never left even with the gift bestowed by Vipax sat like a spear in his heart.

"Emperor, you are wounded badly but do not bleed, are you able to ride on."

Kado turned to Tat and looked at him "Ride on General. Kill the scum. Make haste to the Iron Coast."

The Graan and Drax caught up to the Unstaadt as they climbed the cliffs formed from Norbu's awakening. Kado got off his horse as he saw the three chief Generals of the Unstaadt fighting and slaughtering his people. He took his blades and launched himself in a frenzy of blows at them. They met him at every swipe and arc and clash of blade. He roared his frustration at not defeating them. Jarrod and Brago watched him but were caught in a vicious bombardment too far away. Jarrod saw that none of Kado's warriors came near him.

They believe him to be cursed as well, he thought as an axe landed near his feet.

Kado landed his sword into the back of Malack the Great. He roared at Kado like a bull as he fell, but even before his body hit the rubble Zitnash the Savage came with a powerful lance to Kado's back forcing him to his knees. His arm was wrenched by the force of it dislocating it from his shoulder. Suddenly, he was buried under the blows of the Unstaadt barbarians. Kado could see the flesh of his body being stripped off, but he felt nothing.

"I have become a wraith of the underworld. Vipax kill these barbarians for I cannot. The shadow will feed off my un-death and make our enemy stronger."

"I know Scaletryx. That is why I created you, for my ancient enemy is the dragon and now it rises again to meet me in battle. These custodians have brought destruction to this world I have guarded since its beginning. I have raised Scaletryx and brought an army to destroy these offspring of Caemeris and Voloc, while I shall have my final battle with the dragon. Run now to the Iron Fortress of Voloc, let the destruction begin. Take my armies to battle. Kill the Keeper who brings the power of Caemeris here. Destroy the Custodians and the shadow together."

"You gave me this power to kill Ange and Gildas."

"Yes. For they are now the inheritors of the Caemeris. And its light is what drew Voloc here. They must be destroyed like Voloc. If not now then in time, the battle will be between Scaletryx and the Keepers of stone and light."

Kado's heart sank as he realised that Vipax had connived to make its own desires come true.

As Vipax rose out of the water the Graan and Unstaadt stopped their fighting.

The great yellow eyes glittered in the sunlight as the magnificent creature rose far above them. It hung in the air momentarily.

"Run. Run Now!" yelled Jarrod.

Vipax opened its massive jaws, and its fangs were like magnesium spears of light. It flipped over in the air and came crashing down onto the ocean surface, sending a tsunami of water towards the land bridge.

The Unstaadt soldiers stood back snarling at the creature. Kado saw his chance. He took his blade and decapitated the two brutes who had attacked him. He let the wave of water wash over him becoming entangled in the dead bodies of the Unstaadt. The Graanar and Draxus managed to scrabble to safety on the shores of the Iron coast along with the remaining barbarians.

The waves of water splashed against the cliffs and spilled over the top onto the red sands of the desert. A massive stream flooded into a gully its narrow path funnelling the water into an ever- quickening river.

Vipax saw that Kado had been washed away and dived into the water to find him. Scooping him up it carried Kado to the coast. Vipax spoke as the Graan and Unstaadt raced far into the desert away from the cacophony of waves.

"Follow the stream clayborn. It will bring the desert to life and lead you to the destroyer of all things. Battle well. Fight with the heart of Vipax. Let its glory sit in the memory of the great Belmaris. Go Scaletryx, you know what you must do."

Jarrod came to Kado as Vipax retreated under the water. Upon seeing that Kado's flesh had healed without a mark, Jarrod knew that Kado could not wield the power bestowed on him and now it had almost destroyed the Drax and Graanar. The Elda-Chief wondered if the prince, needed to be defeated as well.

# 14

# Desires of Stone and Flame

"So young mother, you want your child back?" Giandra saw Tessi at the crib where Noab lay.

"He is mine not yours." Tessi did not turn around but reached over and took Noab out. She placed her shawl over him.

"Stand away Giandra." Nene stood at the doorway with Angette in a halter and Ushan straining on a leash. Giandra saw the blood dripping off the lion's jaws.

Giandra glided over to the window to look out over the bay. It was a full moon and the water reflected it perfectly.

"Nene, why did you give up the knowledge of your grandmothers and not learn the laws of Adriaan fire?"

"Giandra, let us be. Battle comes and our time maybe limited. Let the girl be free if only for a short time to be with her children. Tessi come over here."

"Nay Nene, you cannot leave. I wanted you here for a reason."

"What use are we and my children to you?" asked Tessi.

"You are no use to me other than the blood of children sustains my flesh. But the dark shadow which rules over our lands has need of you and your kin. It seems to seek for you and these others, the Graan clansman and the Draxus. It is strange to me. My ancestors found wisdom in the shadows and pain of the flames of Adria and yours Nene found them in the light of the spirits who sit in the sky at night. I wonder who this shadow is? The power it wields is stronger than anything I have ever sensed but a simple desert dweller thwarts its purpose. The blood of us here seems to stop it from consuming all around it. Why do you think that is Nene, Tessi?"

Nene pushed Tessi and gestured for her to try and leave.

"I don't know Giandra. I know the old knowledge seemed wise at the time, but the sorcery of your father made you a beast to be reviled. My ancestors understanding of the lights of the sky were not understood as well and it led to superstition, some of it silly and other times lethal when it turned against those who challenged those beliefs."

Nene felt a blade near her ear. She grabbed Tessi's arm to stop her in case they killed her.

"I have no intention of killing you. Faad take them to the turret and lock them in. I will join them soon."

Faad escorted Tessi and Nene along with Ushan up spiral staircase. He opened the door, and they went inside. Just as he was about to close it Ushan swiped towards him. Her claws catching his throat. He pulled his blade to slash the cat's paw. She let go and growled.

Nene pulled Ushan toward her to stop Faad stabbing her. Tessi and Nene saw the sinews in Faad's neck. He should be dead thought Nene. Faad looked at Nene.

"You are too loyal to your masters Faad. You were born from a long line of great sword masters. Now you skulk in the shadows threatening babes and their mothers."

"We all have our price to pay," spoke Faad. He closed the door. The sound of the locks imprisoning them echoed loudly.

"What will we do now?" Nene tried the door. It was bolted from the other side.

"We wait for Gildas, Nene," spoke Tessi hugging Noab.

"Yes, I can't see what else to do. Giandra hopes to make a pact with this shadow spirit, but her mind is addled as always."

Giandra heard Nene's words.

"I will do more than make a pact she whispered into the cool air. I can see far into the shadows Nene. Come with me and I will show you what you abandoned. Perhaps when it is done, I will take you as co ruler, and we shall be the Queens of fire and light and a new age shall begin."

Suddenly Nene fainted. Tessi quickly put Noab on a chair and snatched Angette from underneath Nene.

"Nene wake up, what is the matter?" pleaded Tessi. Ushan stalked around Nene growling.

Nene vaguely heard Tessi calling to her, but she was being pulled into darkness. She saw Giandra watching into a huge void.

"Look at what awaits. We could rule the power which destroys light."

Nene did not feel fear at what lay before her. It was silent darkness. In the distance she saw a face. It was like Tessi's. Are you, her sister? Nene asked

The face nodded.

"What is happening?" asked Nene.

"Leave here," replied Ange.

Giandra loomed in front of Nene.

"Voloc seeks a way into the world. It seeks the power this one has been given, and the bonds in the blood of the clayborn. I will bring them all here and with that consummation of Voloc and the deep memories laid down in the making of the clayborn I will rupture the bones of the world and let the shadow sink deep. In that moment I will plunge into the blood and shadow and bring to birth the new flames of Adria. Stronger and more potent."

Nene looked at Giandra.

"You will fail. You do not understand the world or your own heart. You will fail. This shadow is not the wellspring of power you seek Giandra. It only understands the power of light and seeks to end it. Your desire is to conquer your father."

"No Nene my desire is to rule fire, and this shadow will teach me. It knows how to extinguish light. It is the way to rule the power of the sun and moon, to kill light and to make light. Imagine in one thought I could bring night to the world and with the next un-ending dawns."

"Leave here. Voloc is not something which can be ruled. It was made before the light. Leave here." called Ange.

Suddenly Giandra found herself being thrust back into her chamber. "It will be mine desert-dweller." She smiled sensing the power Ange wielded.

Nene woke in the dim light of the room. Tessi was watching over her.

"Are you alright?"

"Yes, I am Tessi. I saw your sister."

"Ange, is she ok? Where is she?"

"Deep within the shadows of this demon. Giandra is lost. But I fear if she succeeds even just a little, she will be unstoppable."

"What can we do though?"

"Nothing Tessi. Your sister wields great power and was able to command Giandra. If there is any hope it lies with her. Oh, the darkness Tessi which lies beneath our sight. We are blind to it."

"You do not seem frightened though Nene?"

"No, it was strange, as though this is where everything begins, in the endless silence."

"Come look out this window. I think there may be more hope. Look over here Nene." Tessi pulled Nene over to the window.

"See there in the distance." On the plains towards the north small specs of flame progressed across the plateau. Underneath could just be seen the movement of a large shadow.

"Ah, it will not be long now. Our forces have gathered. Soon we may be free and even if it all ends you are with your children Tessi."

Tessi smiled at Nene, "It is not so little that I hoped for that Nene, but my heart aches with sorrow that I do not hope for a life beyond this nightmare."

"I know Tessi. It is just so sad, and not even of our own making. The world, sun and stars have revealed their faces, and it is not kindness that greets us but the indifferent and majestic strength of life and death."

Gildas, Axl and Tyl stood on the edge of the plateau above the city of Matavia. It had been a swift ride with no Matavians to greet them. Medret came up to the large clansmen.

"So, we part here. I fought on this plain many summers ago. My father still lived, and our King Erdene the Wise sat on the throne. It is a trap for us Gildas. We will be wedged in here if all the might of the cursed is thrust at us. The plains further north have deep gorges in their centre so once the Matavians push back we will be trapped like hares in their burrows."

"Hold your ground Knight is all I ask. This is just a step to the real battle that awaits us," spoke Gildas.

"We could ride to the shores and commandeer the ships in a day," Medret replied as his heart and mind filled with battle lust.

"Polax the Graanar are to surround the Aeserean. Form the mother and cub and bring it to life."

Medret snorted at the thought of being protected from battle by the Graanar.

"Nay Knight you will understand why we Graanar fight this way. Hold to Polax's command."

Medret felt the icy steel of Gildas pierce into him as if the warrior could read his thoughts.

"Ay, Gildas." Medret said relenting.

Gildas clasped hands with Polax and Medret. They stood and watched as Gildas, Axl and Tyl took the path to the vale of the hunted toward the Palace.

"Come, Knight" called Polax.

Medret led his men down into the valley. The moon was on the wane and the few stars that shone were obscured by patchy clouds.

The Aeserean horses neighed as their masters let them go. The Knight General wondered what had become of his beloved mare. He hoped she had outrun the scourge of Unstaadt when the bird gods had rescued, he and Nene. Not wanting to think about what may have happened if the mare had not escaped, he pushed the thought of her out of his mind.

Soon they had reached the middle of the plateau. The Graan had spread out around the Aesereans in a thinned circle of three men deep. Medret noticed the greatest of the graanar stood on the outer circle of fighters while inside the smaller ones armed with sharpened axes and daggers of bear teeth stood ready to impale.

"Sit ya hides" yelled Polax.

Everything was silent except for the occasional cough.

Medret could see Polax coming towards him.

"When they come, hold ya blades up high above ye heads. Skewer the chunt-bastids as they land. T'is how the Ice bear feeds her cubs. It gives them something to play with while it still lives but weakens it so they can feast."

"We need to get to the Generals, Chieftain. They will each lead a flank towards us. They need to be killed or we will lose too many," spoke Medret.

"Ay, Knight, do yer think the three of us; you, the other Knight and me will be enough?"

Medret noticed the grin on Polax and nodded in agreement. Suddenly a low beat of a drum echoed across the skies and seemed to instantly thicken the air.

"Blades ready, hold em high. Graanar claws ready! Bring death to all" shouted Polax.

In the darkness came screeching followed by a shadow spilling over the edges of the cliff like an ocean of black water.

"Fight with the bear and the lion's hearts" called Polax.

Medret heart raced as he made his way to the eastern edge of the gathered mass of warriors. Briefly he saw a glimmer of an eagle's head on the tip of a massive spear; the Generals were the only ones who carried them. The beak a razor tip that would shred the innards of an enemy, while the poison it was laced with ate the flesh.

Medret gripped his sword and pushed his way towards the General. His eyes never strayed from the head of the eagle in the darkness.

His mind cleared as it always did before battle. He felt a faint pulse move through his arm the tighter he gripped his blade.

A growl rose around him as the black swarm of Matavians met the Graanar. The clash of swords and axes soon began to be drowned out by the screams of the Matavians bodies as they flew in the air to be stuck on the tips of the swords of his people. As each body became skewered a cheer went up followed by the shrill song of the steel blades of Tarentess pulverizing the Matavian scum into nothing but pounded meat.

As the Knight General neared the edge of the melee, he became drenched in blood making him blend more into the darkness of the night. Unseen he broke through into the last row of Graanar. Medret saw the General slashing three Graan down with an axe in one hand and then skewered another with the spear. He gripped his sword and launched himself at his mortal enemy and landed his blade into the body of the General. Suddenly a surge of power went through him forcing the General back. Medret flowed with the momentum stepping forward he raised his sword in an arc and decapitated the Matavian. He screamed with delight as he saw the head roll. The spear came down and landed on the body. Medret looked for the General's head and snatching it he placed it on the spear and screamed,

"For our Kingdom, dead brothers, and sisters, for the Lion and the ancient trees of the Vran. Kill them, Kill them all!"

Cotus Medret flew into a dozen more of his accursed enemy and with each blow brought them death and freedom from the bonds of the shadow that ruled their minds and hearts.

Gildas heard the clash begin. He clenched the sword in his hand and knew that the power in him flowed in the blood of the blades formed in Tarentess.

Tyl and Axl looked back wanting to join Polax and their clansmen.

"There will be another chance Graanar to fight beside yer kin" spoke Gildas.

They sprinted around the outskirts of the villages that sat along the road to the city. Soon the white turrets of the Palace glowed in the distance. Gildas pointed to a patch of forest that buttressed the western edge of the Palace walls.

"It is a whoring bitch of bush that grows there but will hide us until we reach the walls. When inside kill anyone, servants, and guards alike. Spare no one."

Stealthily Gildas made his way towards the walls. He headed towards the sewer culvert that led underneath to the gaol. The smell soon began to waft to them.

"At least this stinking shit isn't from Ranik" Gildas whispered to himself.

A small scuffle broke out behind him. Looking back, he saw Tyl easing a dead guard to the ground. He placed some branches over the body.

Axl came over as well wiping his hands on the grass.

"I think they were expecting us."

"Ay, it was my fear that the witch of this place would sense me."

They moved into the even blacker darkness of the tunnel making them crouch low. Soon the stairwell that led up into the kitchens came into view. Creeping up the spiralled staircase like silent giants they reached the opening. Expecting to find it full of people they were met with walls and floors drenched in blood and gore.

Gildas signalled to keep moving up. They strode into the massive banquet hall. Alone at the top of the great feasting table stood Faad, he did not move or draw his blade. One hand rested on the back of a leather chair bound in the skin of a slave and the other rubbed his throat. Blood trickled between his fingers.

"You have come early Gildas. Did we not agree to meet as allies and tread the road to battle against Voloc?"

"Ay, we did Faad. But I am ready now. The shadow grows too strong and the final call to arms cannot be delayed any longer. I come only to claim the child. I will spare your life Faad, you will perish anyway. The claw of the shadow fits well into the skin of your Queen."

Gildas looked at the wounds inflicted and saw they were deep, fatally deep.

"We are all going to perish Gildas. Why do you waste these men's lives on this futile battle? Let them go and live what life they can while the sun still touches them. The shadow will break the girl's hold once it possesses all of her kin."

"Coward Faad, skulking in the shadows like all the vermin of your lands."

Gildas hefted his sword to kill the captain once and for all.

"Hold your blade Keeper."

The voice was silken, but Gildas could feel the venom of the words and where they came from. Turning he saw the Queen. She looked almost translucent like a wraith released from the underworld.

"Where is the child?"

Gildas voice was low and menacing. He could feel the blade in his hand baying to be wielded to spill the blood of the witch that stood before him.

"You cannot have him. He belongs to me now and calls me mother."

She launched herself at Gildas. He readied himself to meet her attack. Her claws dug into his flesh as she thrust him against the wall. Her eyes flared into a brilliant red and her teeth bared like a wolf about to eat its prey.

He rebounded off the stone and with a massive arc of his blade he brought it down with all his force to cut the head off the deranged creature. But then her hand grasped the sword and instead of it cutting her he felt the power surge away from him and into her. Giandra's eyes flared brilliantly and beneath her skin her veins darkened with the blood of Tarentess. Gildas realised why the Queen had lured him here; to drink on the power given to him from Tarentess. He pulled away but she disappeared sending the sword into the stone and cracking the flagstones in four directions. Shards of granite exploded cutting into his flesh.

Guards began to spill into the room to attack.

"Take them Graanar!" he roared.

Tyl and Axl within a few strokes of their blades had covered the walls of the feasting hall in blood. Gildas stood heaving looking for Faad. He was nowhere. Gildas sped towards the stairs that led to the main turret. His mind raced back to the first time he took these stairs and the satisfying memory of cutting off Ranik's head. Barging into the chamber he stopped dead as he saw Tessi and Nene each holding a child with swords ready to attack. A lion reared up on a leash tied to Nene's waist. Its golden fur was covered in blood.

Faad stood ready with a sword. Suddenly a maelstrom of wind began to form in the room. Giandra appeared with her skin and eyes glowing. Gildas could feel her power and his pulsing between them.

"Come to me. Now!" he shouted but it was too late as he leapt to grab them, they vanished. Axl and Tyl raced to find Gildas standing alone.

Gildas roared in frustration.

Tyl and Axl stood back as they felt the black blood of the earth and stony ice of his eyes pierce their hearts and minds sending the rage and fury that flowed in Gildas' veins into theirs.

Gildas' mind filled with the images of the witch that called him, the cell of Banrock, the dead body of Jess, Ange being taken by the Demon and most of all the red eyes of Voloc. Its malicious laugh tormented the great warrior again and again. All of it tore through his mind. As he raced down the stairs of the tower, he swung his axe and sword in huge lethal blows, smashing the walls and cracking the stone steps he trod on. As he tried to destroy the visions in his mind with each swing, he shook the foundations of the palace deep into its bedrock. He thrust his sword so hard into the floors that the great stone pylons the palace sat upon began to give way. Axl and Tyl barely got out of the tower.

The sinews everywhere in his body pulsed with tiny rivers of black as the power and menace of the mountain coursed through his body. The sword hummed its song of destruction and his body pulsed with its chorus. He looked at Axl and Tyl.

"Kill all of them. Kill them all. Destroy this place. Destroy every dwelling. Destroy Matavia!"

Axl and Tyl nodded and fled to the fields to rally the Graanar and Aesereans. Tyl looked at Axl.

"He is a man no more Graanar."

"Nay he is not."

Behind them they heard the rage of the Keeper of Tarentess bellow into the night amidst the sounds of the crashing ruins of the White Palace of Matavia. As each wall fell, a thousand sighs of children and slaves, sacrificed and tortured to death were released into the night, free of the demented rulers of Matavia who had terrorised the lands for ten generations.

Giandra stood in the cavern deep beneath the great writhing fortress formed from the salts of the Iron coast deserts. She felt the ripple of power surge as Gildas unleashed his strength, the strength of Norbu, ancient of Caemeris.

She saw the two children, and their mother and Ange lying in the dirt of the cavern. Ange lay wrapped in the blood of the clayborn and the bonds of stone and light.

"You see, dark one, I bring it all to you. I have unleashed the mountains heart and the heart of the world to let you in, now let me see. The heart of our world lies open for you." She called across the chasm of darkness.

Silence.

Then Voloc rose.

"Ah, I see the light of Caemeris, unleashed more into the world of clay. It surges from deep within the heart of this world and its voice is a whisper in the echoes of my existence. What do you wish to see pale one? What power do you think Voloc seeks? I hold all I need here now and have no need of you. I know the calls of Norbu, and the light which birthed the custodian. I know Norbu's blood flows in the flesh of this clayborn you have enraged to bring more destruction. I have the bearer of the stone which binds the memories of caemeris, and the blood bound in the flesh of these others you hold prisoner as well.

Giandra reached inside the darkness "Give me your strength."

"It would kill you pale one. Don't you see what I am?"

"No, let me see!" pleaded Giandra. "I want to see beyond the flames, beyond my flesh, beyond my desire and my need to feed. Let me see." She fell in further into the darkness. Giandra saw nothing. Her flesh crumbled before her as she reached out hoping to touch something.

"Why is there nothing?"

"What do you think Voloc is, clayborn?"

"No, you hide your power, you hide it from me. I hold the charm of change. I can bring the power of blood and the flame of Adria and the shadow to destroy dawn together."

"Your flames and sorcery are nothing more than the stars which I devour. Even Caemeris memory will fail before me."

Voloc left, Giandra hung in the darkness, her hand reached out but there was nothing there.

Nene looked at Giandra's wild eyes staring into something she could not see. Giandra's hand kept reaching out grasping at an invisible object. Nene knew that desire, that unfettered and insatiable desire to know and to rule. But Giandra did not understand what she dealt with now.

"You will not conquer this enemy Giandra. Let it go and let us be free of this prison."

Giandra did not hear Nene's plea. Faad went to his Queen and grabbed her face.

"Look at me, Giandra!"

"Faad, I have looked into the heart of the shadow."

"And what did you see?"

"Nothing but I do not believe it. The girl was watching me. The one there that lies still on the dirt. If she can be there, why can't I?"

"Let it go Giandra. Let us be free. These gods that war cannot be defeated by us" spoke Nene.

"Ange knows what it will take" Tessi sat sobbing with the twins near Ange.

Giandra's eyes flared to life. She sneered at them all "I will rule the shadow and the light."

"It is the light which caused chaos to begin. Voloc is the destroyer, and no other will bring the death of the makers of light and their progeny, the clayborn" the voice of Voloc trembled through them.

Tessi whimpered as its emptiness gouged into her heart. Nene hugged her as hope died within her at the words of Voloc.

# 15

# Blue Smoke and Brown Dirt

Tamatjera watched the plump janabaal nibbling on the leaves. They were fatter here and the meat richer. His mouth and stomach missed the taste of their meat from his lands; the taste of red dirt not the sweetness of trees that dripped their juice. They are too fat to run he thought as he began to drain the blood of the janabaal he had caught. He missed the chase of the hunt. The animals here did not flee at the slightest crack of a twig or crunch of a stone like the fleet desert rats and lizards of his own country. He skinned the carcass carefully and put the hide aside on a rock. Then he placed the body on the flames to roast. The smoke may alert the tree dwellers that there was a wanderer about in their lands he thought. So far, he had found none of the kin from the land of trees and brown dirt. He went to the edge of the cliff he sat upon. The rock jutted out allowing Tamatjera to survey a valley which stretched as far as he could see. Four stone pillars broke the vista of trees in the direction where the sun rose. The sky was clear, and the air scented with oil of the leaves, creating a blue haze over the valley.

He heard a noise come from where he had made camp. He went back to see what it was. The sound came from the pouch hanging from the branch of the tree. Tamatjera hit it again with the end of his spear. The movement in the pouch stopped. He sat down to wait for the meat to cook

On his walk he had seen the great iron cave that the beast was building. He had felt the urging of his dead ancestors in his mind as he had silently made his way south. He wondered if anything would be left when he returned. Their warning cries from the depths of the spirit world spoke of the ending of his time and the land itself. His bones had shivered in the night as he lay trying to sleep. Even the eyes of the night skies had disappeared, smothering him in a dark veil of emptiness. The creature in the sack had flown at him in the night when the rain spirits had covered the moon making the lands even darker. It had clawed at his face and arms. It was made of the metal the northern traders used in their weapons but moved like the bone and sinew of the bats that dwelt deep within the caves where he lived. Eventually he had knocked the beast to the ground and beat it until it stopped moving. He had looked at the deformed and unnatural creature. He watched as it greedily sucked up the blood from his wounds that had spilt onto the sand. In his heart he knew that the beast who had invaded their lands wanted to eat everything, not just rule the dirt and oceans, but devour it as well. He had thumped the creature again to make sure it was dead and put it in his pouch. This would convince the peoples of the blue smoke of the undead spirits awakening and that destruction was near.

The fire crackled dwarfed beneath canopy of trees. He finished eating the janabaal. He lay down as night fell. Tamatjera dreamed of a red dawn creeping over the horizon. His woman and daughter were gathering berries and he walked with a dead lizard on his shoulder.

The world was clean and free of the trouble that now beset it. He was taking his son to the initiation rites neither of them speaking only watching the great wave rock rise in the distance. It was here that he would make his son hunt alone and learn the harshness and providence of the red dirt. The spirits of the sands would take the child and leave the warrior and hunter behind.

The crackle of the sacred fire to bring the spirits to life echoed in his mind. He watched as the smoke obscured his son walking into the desert. For some reason Tamatjera felt an ache in his heart, like a wound that had not healed. It was the fear that he would never see his son grow and that the red earth that had sustained his people for as long as their elders remembered would become forged into iron and metal. Under foot was not red dirt but black metal, torn from the grains of the earth and placed there as the massive fortress of the demon spread, smothering lizards and janabaals. His son kept walking towards the ugly mountain of steel lost to his father and tribe. Tamatjera called to him, but it was too late as the iron walls grew taller trapping his son forever.

He woke with a start as the sun rose above the valley, breaking into the shade of the bush where he had made camp. The fear of his dream remained real and hung on his chest like a rock. Worst of all he knew the dream was no dream but something which was happening now.

Walking to the edge of the escarpment he scanned from left to right across the valley. Something caught his eye. It was a thin wisp of smoke at least a league away. Gathering his spear and the pouch hanging from the tree he walked towards the stone stairway he had come up. He saw one of the trees that dripped its juices down its bark. It was in full blossom which meant in his lands the heat was coming soon. He wondered if the people here set the great fire to burn. There were a lot of leaves on the ground. He kicked the mulch that lay there and saw a black layer of soot. It had been two seasons since the fire spirit had passed. Taking a twig, he scraped off some of the honey from the tree and ate it. Its sweetness revived him.

The steps down were slippery in places where the dew had settled from the night. The sack lay heavily over his shoulder and was limp. Perhaps the creature had finally died wondered Tamatjera. It would be at least a day's journey to the place where he had seen the smoke. Down into the valley Tamatjera strode. The canopy above was thin enough to allow the sunlight to stream enough to light the shaded pathway. The acrid smell of the trees helped keep Tamatjera's mind clear from the images of his dream. Soon he could hear the trickle of running water. He had reached the bottom of the valley. He drank some and began to follow the creek. It flowed in the direction of the smoke he had seen.

The creek turned from a small stream to a deep slow river by the high point of the sun. Tamatjera sat on a rock trying to see a way across. He decided he would have to swim. He was not sure if the waters here hid the great lizards like they did in his own lands but there was no other way. He plunged into the river and let the current carry him as he swam towards the other bank. The water was cool and deep as his feet paddled freely not detecting the bottom. He grabbed a branch and hoisted himself up.

The bush was denser on this side with no path cut out to guide the wanderer. The rocks stuck out at awkward angles so that Tamatjera had to scramble rather then walk through the bush. His shins and feet bled from the jagged edges of the stones. Night fell again and he made camp. He had become disorientated and wondered if he was nearing the place of the other tribe. He was too low down in the valley to see where he was. He would know on the dawn as the sun had risen directly above the smoke.

As he slept the same dream came to him. His heart raced as he saw his son disappear behind walls of metal and the land go from red to black under his feet. He prayed the spirits would come and remove the curse from the land but there was no answer. The birds lay dead on the ground, oceans of them falling out of the sky their rainbow feathers dull and grey from the soot of the black dust that rose from the fortress.

He had seen the great red spirits that had chased his people so many moons ago when the dead god had risen and killed his father. They had returned but were ruled by another. The eight spirits and their ruler had walked into the red sands toward the valley where myrtle and the lizards of the leaves dwelt. He had followed them until they disappeared into the darkness of the cave at the bottom of the valley. It had been on his return from that place that the iron creature had attacked him. It had been following the red spirits as well. His mind reeled as it jumped from memory to dream and back again, but all the time the shadow of the demon remained in the distance, like the sting of the red and black spiders who lived beneath rocks. Only this time it had bitten the heart of the world; its venom poisoning everything it touched.

A twig broke. Tamatjera woke to see the shapes of people standing around him in the darkness. One of them poked his thigh with a spear. He got up.

"I am Tamatjera Widjera. I have walked from the lands of the red desert to find the people of blue smoke."

"We will go to the elders. We have seen you wandering lost in the bush for most of the last moon. What are you doing in these lands?" spoke one of the shapes.

"I will only speak with the elders of my purpose."

Tamatjera gathered his spear and the pouch.

The silence of the night was only broken by the crack of twigs and leaves beneath the feet of the group as they lead Tamatjera to their elders. No one spoke. Tamatjera followed closely the footsteps of the man in front of him so he wouldn't stumble on the rocks.

On the dawn the wisp of smoke was closer. They had crossed up hill and downhill and now walked along a ridge which slowly took them to a lake fed from the same river he had swum across.

The tribe gathered around them as the group neared the main huts of the elders. Tamatjera wondered how many lived here. The land gave more in food and water than the red desert, but the bush still held rule with little or no trace of people living within it. Three people sat near a fire, two men and a woman. People came out from their huts to look at the stranger.

"We have found him, Yutinn."

Tamatjera sat near the fire. The group that had found him retreated behind the elders except for two who remained standing behind Tamatjera. He pulled the sack forward. One of the younger men put his spear out to warn him. He pulled the creature out cautiously expecting it to move but it lay still. The metal shell was unnatural to Tamatjera, and he wanted to throw it in the river to be rid of it.

"I am Tamatjera Widjera. A demon spirit has risen in the lands of my people. It destroys the lands and all that it sustains. This is one of the beasts that is born from its loins and devours all that it finds. I have come to ask your kin to join with my people to battle this spirit. Its gaze will find the lands here and it will be well fed on the people. My people have decided that it is better to die in battle then to die in bondage to the demon and watch the desert die beneath it. We will fight with spear and rock so that when the spirits of the sky come to take our souls, they will remain free. I have come as elder of my kin to ask the people of the blue smoke and brown dirt to join us to keep the lands sacred and water pure."

There was no response. One of the elders picked up the creature. Its body glinted in the sunlight. Its eyes were closed. It had razor sharp claws and a head like a bird.

Yutinn nodded to one of the young men. He left and went to a humpy. He came back with something. He flung it onto the ground. Tamatjera saw it was creature like the one he had carried. The claws of the demon had stretched far.

"We know the demon rises in the red lands. It hunts us also. Tribes that live on the edges of the bush have been taken. That is why you have walked this far and not seen our people. If we do not fight the demon, we will belong to it for longer than the memory of our peoples. Better to run to our deaths as free people then remain as wraiths walking in shadow. We will gather the peoples of the blue smoke and walk to battle on the red dirt."

Tamatjera was relieved that the elders agreed so quickly to go to fight. But his heart remained heavy at the thought of so many going to their deaths.

"Search for the peoples of blue water beneath. Their elder is Sanaoya. Gather them near the rock of Ungara!" called Yutinn to the two warriors that stood behind Tamatjera.

A young man came over with a couple of lizards. He placed them on the fire to roast.

"We will eat and then begin the walk to battle Tamatjera Widjera. This will be the end of our lives in this bush."

The lizard meat was sweet and fatty to Tamatjera's tongue. He looked at the plump bodies of the tribe. They were large not lean like his own people. The woman had big hips and stomachs. They would suffer in the lands of the red dirt. Perhaps it was wrong to make them fight but it could not be borne that any of their kin should die in captivity to this creature.

That evening Tamatjera prayed to the spirits of the great serpents, lizards and spiders of the dirt asking that they rise and fight with them. He prayed to his ancestors and fathers to welcome them when they died. The headiness of the eucalypt made him alert and strong. He carved a new spear to match the one he had brought with him. They would gather their rocks as they neared the black humpy of the demon and he imagined destroying the walls with his stones and spear. He remembered his son and knew that he would not let the stone and metal build around him and leave him to a fate worse than what death would bring.

The sun rose in a formidable array of pink mixed with the blue mist of the valley. Tamatjera walked into the bush behind Unginnan; a man of his own age and son of the elder Yutinn. They left the elders and older woman and children that could not carry their spears. They moved silently along a trail which could not be seen by Tamatjera's eyes. Unginnan knew every branch and rock underfoot like his own hand and never hesitated once in his steps or direction. Soon they began to climb up a steep hill and Tamatjera had to scramble. He stopped and looked back down the gully. Below for a league came a trail of people. It stretched as far away as the four pillars of stone he had seen in the valley.

The weight of the fear that had clung to him since the death of his father Widjera lifted a little. He turned and continued behind Unginnan. Three nights they made their journey to the edge of the forest when the heat of the desert began to be felt on their face and skins. In the distance the great rock of Ungara stood rising up out of a sea of green. Tamatjera could just make out a line of shapes moving towards the base of the rainbow granite formation. It was more of their peoples gathering. His heart leapt again with a faint hope that perhaps it would not be the end of them all.

The leaders of the tribes stood at the top of the rock and looked toward the red lands that stretched for a thousand leagues before them. Ever since the last great heat when Tamatjera had set out to gather the tribes, the Iron Fortress had grown so that now its central spire was just discernible in the haze of the horizon.

"There lies the dwelling of the demon. It grows stronger with every sun and moon. My people walk from the great water above us. We will meet them and battle together at the edge of the valley where the black janabaals live" spoke Tamatjera.

Unginnan gazed at the black shape and thought it looked like a fang of one of the great water lizards.

"You have called us to our death Tamatjera of the red dirt. The people of blue smoke will thank the lands that have fed us and then make the walk to meet our ancestors in the sky."

"We will remain free until the great water comes and floods the lands. It is only then that we will rise to tread the dirt and stone again" replied Tamatjera.

The white and black and red smoke contrasted against the green of the bush as the smoke and chanting went on into the night. The celebration was one of thanksgiving and preparation to die, not to seek glory. The flames dancing fingers imploring the sky for admission to the dwellings of their ancestors. The women's chanting resounded through the night's silence unchallenged. The stories remembering the beginning of creation and how the first tribes separated into the people of the blue smoke, the red dirt, and the sand of the oceans, echoed deep into the earth. Each of the warriors gave thanks for the life they had lived for unknown generations and now asked to be taken back from where they had come from. The rhythm of their stories and cries pierced the dirt and far into the bedrock of the great southern lands. The blood of their ancestors that had soaked into the soil over the millennia had bonded the soul of the tribes to this land. They asked to return to it to wait for the time when water would come and revive the desert and bring seed to life. The earth slumbered silently as its own creator lay bound by chains, but the memory of Norbu was not dead, and it heard the chants of the people above and let them echo through its ancient foundations.

Sa-Tuchala opened her eyes. The blue shone forth into the darkness of her den. She felt the heart of the peoples beat in unison with her heart, the heart of Uchala. She saw into their souls and how their blood flowed with the same colour as the dirt that raised them. She heard their chants and cries for freedom after their death and the death of the shadow that had come to devour the desert and its richness.

"First I hear the cry of battle against the shadow and the cry to die free from its chains. Blessed are the clayborn for even the eternal must remain bound to their purpose. It is the cry of the first who trod this world. Shall I answer and seek to do battle against this undefeated enemy? Perhaps the time has come for this place to be destroyed as is with all things. Will Uchala's spirit be diminished by my loyalty to the blood that first ran in my body; the blood of the clayborn?"

"Only you can answer this Majestic Sa-Tuchala. The Aracnine will follow and serve their queen."

Sa-Tuchala rose. She stood the same stature as before, but her eyes shone blue, and her fingers were longer. Her fangs remained hidden until the venom of life was called for rebirth.

She pondered all that lay in her ancient memory, the wars of creation to the time she stood as clayborn as the assassin of the Drax. She peered into the blackness and knew that the heart of the lands rotted. She tried to seek the great custodians of the world, but they were gone. The clayborn lives on earth were one fine strand of web compared to the eternal existence that Uchala had endured. But they were favoured by the memory of Caemeris and bore the same chaos that the ocean of light held within it. Then she remembered Ange; fragile and untested but was now the key to stopping the shadow from defeating all in its wake including herself.

The chant of the tribes came to her again and set her ancient blood pulsing. She stood as a spectre of blue in her den with the guardians.

"Sa-Tuchala shall answer the call of the clay-born. She shall fight the shadow along with them and if victory is not destined then she will release the ancient ones to their ancestors as free spirits to be called when their ancestors deem it."

The eight Aracnine rose and bowed to their Queen.

As Sa-Tuchala woke and the chanting pounded into the depths of the red desert of the Iron Coast deep beneath the Fortress where once sat Seraf the custodian of fire lay the darkness of Voloc. It chewed on the dirt and bonds forged by Norbu in between the grains. It tasted the blood of the peoples of the desert from the creatures who had feasted on their flesh.

In the silent void Voloc heard the songs of the clayborn penetrate and rebound in deafening quakes. The ripples of the calls tearing at the very heart of Voloc. It remembered the misery which the chaos of light brought with it. In the distance shone the blue threads of Uchala's inheritor. Ancient and unknown even to Voloc, the sentinels awakening disturbing the slumber of darkness.

So now Voloc must defeat the bonds of light and the bonds of ancient memories it thought as it lay among the hectic roars of creation.

Voloc pulled upon the waves of singing and the blue light of Uchala, the blood of the clayborn embedded in the grains of sand and formed its legions of creatures. The Iron Fortress spilled its claws out over the altar of Seraf where once the custodian of flame lay in suzerainty over the desert. Forcing the black ooze deeper and further into the earth.

All are bound together but it was the void which existed first whispered Voloc.

Sa-Tuchala heard the whisper and deep in his meditation so did Tamatjera.

The chanting stopping as the sun rose. With the dawn the desert burst forth with blood magenta and gold signalling the great storm to come.

Unginnan could feel the sand burn his feet as the fingers of the sun crawled across the land.

"This will test the people of the blue smoke. You will grow used to the ways of the red dirt. Your thirst will lessen, and your body grow stronger. You will be ready for battle when the time comes" spoke Tamatjera.

Tamatjera began to dig until the sand became darker and moister. The water welled to the surface.

"Dig around you," he called.

Soon, the legions of red dirt and blue smoke were drinking out of the sand.

"There will be more as we walk around the cursed cave."

Tamatjera resumed his trek through his homelands, his eyes continually scanning to watch for any movement. As each league passed the unnatural shape of the black fortress was clearer. Suddenly a whooping noise flew past Tamatjera's head. He ducked down. There was a screech and then a thump. A slingshot of rocks had brought down another of the bat creatures. Then came another and another. A hundred of the tribe brought down the iron bats. Black ooze dribbled into the dirt, making puddles of metal from the blood. Tamatjera watched it writhe and then disappear into the sand.

That night the vanguard of the southern tribes did not light fires, chant or sing. They sat in darkness silently waiting to see if more creatures came.

"I see now that even if we defeat this invader, the blood of the beasts which attack will flood the lands like the great rains" spoke Tamatjera.

"Our blood must stain the land more and protect it from the curse the demon brings with its beasts. Let our ancient ancestors' blood nourish the desert" replied Unginnan.

As the dawn rose again, Tamatjera called to all that sat waiting to walk again.

He whooped across the vast emptiness calling the others to join him in their cry of battle.

On the third dawn since the people of trees and blue smoke left their lands, they met the kin of Tamatjera. The two peoples stood looking at the plump and wiry alike. Each made to thrive in the great land's diversity and capricious ways.

Unginnan and Tamatjera met with Sanaoya the warrior of the coastal plains.

"We are ready" spoke Tamatjera. "The peoples' blood will bless the dirt and hold it in covenant until it is freed of the venom that now seeps into it."

Suddenly there was a commotion towards the southern end of the huge league of tribe people. Tamatjera watched and held his breath as the sight of the thick cloud of bats came towards them.

The tribes spread themselves out to meet the tirade that raced towards them. Rocks shot up into the sky. As the creatures fell to the ground, they spat their black poison at the legs of the dirt warriors and clawed at their legs. The warriors in turn shot their spears into the hearts of the beasts to finish them. Wave after wave came across the skies as the red blood of the warriors mixed into the sand with the black bile. Tamatjera readied his sling and brought down three at a time. He threw his rocks in a frenzy. The venom burnt and scalded his flesh, but he did not relent and neither did the beasts. He tripped over a body and saw that it was his brother Ginajera.

"Sing to the spirits brother, I will join you soon enough." He spoke as he moved forward to stab a clutch of bats gnawing on another warrior. His arms and legs did not weary and neither did his courage. He stopped for a moment as he realised it was dark. They had battled all day. The stars shone until a black spectre blocked them. He realised it was more of the beasts coming.

He cried into the night as he readied himself again for the next onslaught. Then he saw it. The blue glow of Sa's eyes dispelled the darkness of the night and the hordes of Voloc of creations screeched their hatred at the ancient power that had returned. The creatures flew away shunning the light. The eight Aracnine stood fully restored from First to Last. They glided through the glut of people as if they did not even see them standing there.

Tamatjera gripped his spear and slingshot of rocks.

"I sense your fear and love clayborn. You remember the night the dark one awoke and the Aracnine walked with the beast. They are no longer bonded to the shadow and are now ruled by Sa-Tuchala, reborn of the ancient one who dwelled here from the beginning days" spoke Sa-Tuchala in Tamatjera's mind.

"We are here to stain the land with our blood so that the dirt maybe kept clean from the curse that the shadow brings. We will protect the lands until the great rains wash it clean and our people can rise again."

"I know ancestor. I heard your calls deep in the wells of my memory. I too seek the death of the Shadow. I will aid you in your calls to keep the lands clean and rid this world of its malice and destruction. First to Last kneel to the ancient ancestors whose blood formed the covenant with the brethren Norbu."

The guardians all stooped to bow to the peoples of the red dirt and blue smoke.

Tamatjera's heart lifted when he saw the ancient and mighty creatures bow down in homage to them. He took his spear and held it aloft with a screeching cry of war. It was matched by the legions standing around he and Sa-Tuc. He called to the spirit of Widjera and Ardana, his father and mother to wait for their son, whose own spirit shall soon be released.

Suddenly the cacophony was broken by a piercing cry. The melee of fighting stopped. First had stood and was screaming into the sky. It stood at full stature; the other seven guardians swayed in unison with their elder. Tamatjera felt the ripples of the guardian's scream move through his body.

"They release their sorrow at all that has passed and their own bondage to Voloc but call for the end to come so that all created may fulfil their destiny. Come we will go to the Fortress of Iron and call our enemy to come and find its destruction" spoke Sa-Tuchala.

She began to walk over the sand. Tamatjera noticed she barely made an imprint in the fine grains. The Aracnine followed her as did

Tamatjera, Unginnan and Sanaoya and their people. Their ears still rang from the noise of First's cry.

Tamatjera heart thudded with fear. In the distance came another black shadow of creatures but larger and with maws open. This time they had the heads of the great lizards of the northern waters. The Aracnine grabbed them and them flung far into the sky and deep into the earth.

Sa-Tuchala eyes blazed to life draping everything in a veil of blue as she launched herself at the flying lizards.

"I see you Voloc. Let the battle of the ancients begin."

Her voice shook the ground beneath Tamatjera's feet. His warrior heart swelled with fury and peace at the readiness to die. His spear pierced three bats at a time their fangs and claws gnashing wildly as he drove them into the ground. Rivers of blood, red and black, flooded the land seeping far into the parched grains of dead dirt.

# 16

# Legion of Tarentess

XI flew over the red sand with the leather pouch full of water. It had deposited another six throughout the trek from the coast for Gildas to follow. As it sped across the skies it saw a dark shadow moving over the arid plains and changed its direction to investigate.

XI saw the legions of desert dwellers walking across the sands from the southwest. They walked to battle as well. XI saw that they dug the earth until pools of water formed. Flying away it went to find Gildas.

Gildas was climbing a rocky hill cursing the prickly spinifex grass as it inflicted tiny cuts on his legs. The flies collected on his back and neck, and he spat out just as many as he sucked in, as his breathing became more laboured from the climb.

"Chunt bastid flies. They must shit their young."

"The bastids stick like the gum we use on the ships" panted Polax alongside Gildas.

Cotus Medret walked further behind. He was remembering his time as a youth when he had ventured south before taking his duties as a soldier for the throne. The memories of the accursed heat of this place had returned vividly. What he did notice was there were none of the unusual creatures that hopped alongside him on his travels so many summers ago. Neither were there any of the colourful birds that would call out across the perfectly blue sky in waves as vast as the ocean.

He stopped and waited for Warick to catch up to him. He saw the trail of the Graan and Aeserean following for a league behind. Knowing that they probably walked to their deaths he did not know whether it would be kinder to die from the sting of the desert or in battle.

"Cotus, we have only trekked seven nights and we already have soldiers succumbing to the harshness of the lands here" spoke Lord Warwick.

"I know Jonas. Perhaps our quest will be in vain."

The shadow of XI flew overhead. It alighted in front of Gildas. It had dropped the leather bucket further back. It squawked at Gildas. It stood and began to scratch the ground ripping up the hard rocks.

Gildas had sucked the last of his own cask dry. His temper got the better of him as he watched the bird god looking like it was building a nest.

"What are yer doing?" he asked spitting out a small swarm of flies clinging to the drops of moisture on his lips.

XI ignored him as the pit around the Orynth deepened so that the walls were almost the same height as the orynth's shoulders.

Suddenly dark liquid welled up from the middle. As it drove its huge talons in further the liquid began to flow freely.

"Drink dirt walkers. I will dig more." XI alighted and flew towards the rear of the vanguard.

Gildas scooped the water up in his hand and tasted it. It was gritty but wet.

"Drink!" he called back to those in earshot. Soon the soldiers gathered around the well in the sand. Once they were sated, they replenished their leather casks before continuing the trek.

Cotus threw up after drinking the muddy liquid but after the third attempt his belly accepted it.

I am going to kill this fiend for turning us into scavenging animals in the filth he thought as he refilled his pouch.

That evening after journeying another a league Gildas rested letting the cooler air of the evening sooth his burnt skin.

"Bastids" he cursed when he saw there were dead flies in his pipe as he took it out to smoke. XI landed near him covered in mud. It began to preen its feathers.

"XI what did you see on your journey?"

"It has made creatures from the hard salt found in the dirt, not flesh or feather but hard and enduring like your weapons. They fly like the great swarms of the locust when they seek the harvests. They would shred the hide of the Orynth in such numbers. Our battle will be a true test of our strength against the malformed of Voloc."

Gildas nodded appreciating the warrior heart of the great bird.

"Any news of the Prince and Jarrod?"

"My brethren have seen your kin. The great serpent Vipax watches over them, and they have forced the barbarians towards the shadows keep. They now run to the battle."

"Good, Kado succeeded."

Gildas was pleased with the thought of the mighty serpent fighting alongside them.

"The Orynth see that the poison of Voloc has scarred the mighty serpent. We shall keep watch."

"What do you mean XI?"

"Its' sight is clouded" XI responded.

"Will it also be an enemy which needs to be overcome?" asked Gildas.

"The Orynth will keep watch. But your ally has been stained by the great sentinel and much may come of the creature now called Scaletryx."

"Scaletryx, another foe?" Gildas slowly sucked on his pipe perturbed another enemy had been forged by Voloc.

"Your ally, has been renamed Scaletryx, by Vipax the sentinel."

Gildas did not respond. So Kado has changed in more than his standing with his people he thought.

"We will need to meet to make a plan for the battle Gildas" spoke the Knight General as he walked over to Gildas and XI.

"Ay. XI can you carry myself and the Knight to meet my brother and the prince?"

Before XI answered Polax interrupted "We will not win a full-frontal attack, Gildas. As much stealth with force as the Ice mother is needed."

"Ay graanar. I have considered our approach but will need to see this fortress to be certain. XI how far is it 'til we reach the battle ground?"

"By your strides another three sunrises."

"XI take us to the camp of Kado and Jarrod."

"Now Gildas?" asked Cotus.

"Ay, now. We are rested enough. I would have us walk night and day if not for the fact we would lose our way in the dark. The stars are unknown to me here and I will not risk wandering lost in the festering heat" Gildas replied.

XI shook his feathers. It gathered Gildas and Medret up and took them into the night sky. The cool breeze was soothing on the wounds of each of the men. Gildas nursed a gash in his flank from a surprised Matavian who was hiding in the gallows of one of the ships they had taken to the southern shores. The memory of Clan Timmo in their magnificent vessels swelled his chest – a hundred vessel formation with huge white sails adorned with the face of the Ice Mother. It looked like the great white mother walked on the ocean herself. Gildas peered ahead in the night searching for signs of Kado and Jarrod. In the far distance he could just see the black turret of what must be the Keep of Voloc. The days when he ran frightened through the forests to the sacred pool of the water spirit came back to him. Back then he was broken and ready to die but now he chased the shadow with a heart full of desire to battle regardless of what fate awaited him.

PO flew up to XI as it neared the encamped warriors of Kado and Jarrod.

Landing silently, Kado and Jarrod stood. EY walked over with Kado and Jarrod. Gildas embraced his brother. Turning to Kado he clasped his arm in a gesture of peace.

"Well done Prince to make the Unstaadt run like mice is no small feat."

Kado smiled "I had help from a powerful ally."

General Tat came over when he saw Gildas and Medret land. "Emperor Kodrax, there are more of the creatures coming."

General Tat acknowledged Gildas and the Knight General. He eyed them cautiously having heard of both men before more as enemies then allies.

"Splash them with the essence and flame. Send a perfumed gift to the demon. His foulness may yet be doused."

"I have come to talk of our plan to attack," spoke Gildas.

Jarrod and Kado looked at one another.

"It knows we come Gildas. There is no surprise now. The Unstaadt were not destroyed merely forced further into the desert."

"Ay, but I would like to see the fortress before we arrive. EY, can you take us over the fortress without being seen or will the demon sense us?" spoke Gildas.

"Voloc's strength grows the more it feeds on Arglethium. It senses all who dwell here. Most potent are the gifts of the sentinels and the blood of Tarentess which will give it more power, especially now it is mixed with the ancestors of the first clayborn who made covenant with Norbu. There is nothing which remains hidden."

"Ay, I know this but there is no choice. I think it is better to see this fortress and find a way to stave off our doom until Ange brings the custodians back. I sense her at times and know she is not yet defeated."

"Will the sentinels help us EY?" asked Kado urgently, remembering what Vipax told him of his purpose.

"Uchala the ancient has been reborn and walks to battle also. The guardians walk with the first of these lands. Vipax the mighty serpent, has passed its gift to you Scaletryx. You must decide."

"Is this Uchala an enemy or ally?" asked Gildas instantly alert to another creature they did not know about.

"Is it Sa-Tuc the one that walked with us?" asked Kado.

"Yes" replied EY.

Gildas smiled at the unforeseen boon in this news. The assassin was a formidable adversary as herself, what now that she has become a god; she would be almost indestructible.

"EY take us over the fortress," commanded Gildas.

EY, PO and XI gathered Jarrod, Gildas and Medret and launched into the air.

Kado walked with VA and AX giving each a canister of oil to throw on the creatures. As the Orynth alighted Kado stood on a ridge watching the volleys of flaming arrows set the creatures alight. They fell screaming into the dirt forming pools of metal that soaked into the sand as if the grains were drinking.

Medret watched Kado below as he broke the masses of creatures that came towards the encampment.

"Elda Chief why is the Draxus so unscathed by his battles?" asked the Knight General.

"Ay you noticed Knight. He was ripped to shreds by the Unstaadt Generals and his wounds healed as I stood watching. I fear that the emperor walks between life and death. It is yet to be seen if he is friend or foe. The shadow may yet call another servant."

Gildas listened to the conversation and remembered what EY had said to Kado about it being his decision. Perhaps the shadow's poison had sunk further and farther than he had considered.

Gildas' breathing became laboured the higher they went. Soon the shadow of the Iron Fortress came into view. It was surrounded by a black crawling mass of beasts interspersed with mingled hordes of all people of the lands. Its central spires were like jagged pieces of metal screaming for the sky. Gildas felt like he was being drawn into its shadow. The fortress was alive; its malice spewing out over the lands and swallowing the pale light of the moon. The half-made walls resembled jagged fangs and claws ready to devour anything that neared them. He saw that the creatures were bursting out of the spires and walls, like it gave birth to them. Looking at it his mind saw an image of the fortress forming into a beast of death and utter degradation, rising out of its tomb to chew on the remains of the lands until everything had been consumed.

"EY show me all of this leviathan of iron" Gildas watched keenly but he was too high to see what he was looking for. "Take me closer."

As they neared within half a league of the fortress both Gildas and EY could feel a wave of malevolence wash over them.

"That is what you seek Keeper. There lies your battle bed and path to victory and death of the clansman Gildas of Gol. This is the price Norbu's well will extract from your bones ice born" spoke EY.

Gildas nodded his heart thudding as the same fear that had pierced his stubborn hide when the wolf had hunted him struck again. He saw deep inside the fortress Ange and Tessi with her children, Queen Nene and Giandra, and most of all he saw the void of Voloc. He saw the path he needed to take to reach them.

"I have seen enough EY. Take us back."

As they neared the encampment, Medret, Jarrod and Gildas saw that the last invasion of beasts had been quelled. Kado stood over a carcass of a creature half metal and flesh. It resembled a large lizard with wings and razor-sharp spines covering its hide. It screeched as the black ooze seeped out of its thrashing body and into the earth.

Kado nodded at the group as they landed near him. Gildas saw that Kado was surrounded by a pale indigo glow in the moonlight.

"Jarrod we will come from the western edge and you from the east" spoke Gildas.

"The sleeping clan wife seems best Gildas. There is too much to cut through to easily reach the lair without being reduced to a few raiding thieves," spoke Jarrod.

"Ay, brother. Those were my thoughts as well."

"How far are you from the Keep?" asked Kado as he wiped his sword clean of filth.

"We are another three dawns according to the Orynth."

"We will reach the Keep before you. We are only half that time and our path clearer."

"Hold steady at your camp until the second dawn and we will meet at the fortress together. I will make my way into the centre of the rotten cave and attempt to battle the demon and find the desert dwellers and the Queen."

"I will come with you Gildas. I will seek Nene as well" spoke Medret.

"Ay, Knight."

Gildas stood and embraced Jarrod.

"Sturdy axe and may the battle heart of the ice mother be with you. Farewell Elda Chief. Emperor Ko, the serpent, and its memories courses in your flesh. Meet poison with poison kill all that stand in the way of the legions of Tarentess." Gildas held out his arm as a sign of loyalty and bond in common purpose.

Kado nodded at Gildas. The warning of Vipax to seek the destruction of Gildas and Ange hung on his chest. He did not understand why the sentinel wanted them dead. Was it because their power now only fed Voloc and would not defeat it? He took Gildas' arm and shook hands. They both sensed the strength given to each of them as they looked at each other, neither of them daring to speak of what may come between them.

EY and XI gathered Gildas and the Knight General up into the night. Gildas watched his brother shrink as he flew away. His mind flashed back to the time of his youth when he, Jarrod and Jesse would hunt and fish together. His heart grew heavy at the memories. A life he would have surely sent to the same destruction as they faced now had he remained as Elda-Chieftain. He and this demon spirit were one and the same in their essence.

"Jesse may your loyalty to the Ice Mother bless this unworthy graanar once more as he meets the demon and each of us gaze at their own lust for destruction. Grant your betrothed one last boon of mercy that his warring blood may not be spilt in vain."

Suddenly a sight on the lands below lifted the veil of sorrow from his heart. In his musing he had not noticed that the Orynth had headed towards the south. In the moonlight below he saw ten thousand warriors of the red lands being led by Sa-Tuc and her guardians. A shadow flew towards them; it was more of the creatures that had attacked Kado. With lightning speed, they swooped down onto the entourage below. A blue light lit the whole desert. Gildas and Medret saw shapes dart up into the air and bring the bats and lizards crashing to the ground.

Gildas sensed the power within the Assassin and saw a glimmer of victory spark in his heart.

The bats instantly changed their direction and began to aim directly towards Gildas and the Knight.

"Make haste EY they have seen us" called Medret. "Is that force friend or foe Gildas?"

"Friend Knight and a mighty one at that."

The Orynth sped away with their cargo with such pace that the Knight General blacked out. Within minutes XI and EY had outflown the deformed creatures and deposited Gildas and Medret on the ground. Nekoda bounded up to Gildas missing his friend.

"We will draw them away from here so you will be unhindered in your journey. We will only meet in battle. Enough water has been dug for you by XI. The pits will lead you directly to the Keep. For feather and flesh, may our battle be mighty and worthy of those whose blood has already been spilt and wing broken" spoke EY.

EY embraced Gildas. "Keeper of Tarentess fight bravely and be worthy of the throne that must be won from the great lord of the earth."

Gildas looked at EY and wondered what the creature was talking about.

EY and XI flew away into the night. Gildas wondered if he would see them alive again.

The pink of the next dawn rose over the rocks and sand.

Gildas called across the dunes "Make haste brothers. We run to war!"

As the thousands of soldiers and graanar trekked in the empty lands nothing could be heard but the sound of their feet crunching on the oceans of dirt around them.

On the third night they rested. The hum of the Iron Fortress could be felt beneath the grains of sand as they stopped only two leagues away from the edge of the maelstrom of living shadow. Gildas gathered the Graan chieftains and Aeserean Lords. He saw their pale skin had burnt and blistered in the heat. But he also saw that all the men's eyes were bright and ready to fight.

"Brethren I have called ye here to make our plans known. The graanar will lead the front of the attack. I have seen the slaves and beasts that corral at the foot of the lair. We look like them. When we arrive, you are to smother yourself in filth and stink and like the wretches of the Matavian dungeons we will walk in amongst them silently and then awaken with screams of battle. We will kill the hordes from within their nest and our friends, the westerners, too pretty to be mistaken for legions of the maligned and chunt ugly." Gildas smiling at his bluntness continued "They will meet the demonic hordes from the desert."

"What of the demon Gildas?" asked Polax.

"My battle is with the wolf. The hunted has become the hunter. The Knight General and I will make our way into its lair to steal the desert-dwellers and the Queen away.'

"Who will be the victor Gildas?" asked Jonas.

"This battle I believe will end nothing. I only seek to prevent the shadow from gaining its full strength and tipping the world into a wraith like existence, neither alive nor dead. I remember my father saying to me when I took the chieftain rule on his death bed, 'Hatred will always drive a man to take the next step until the edge of the cliff is found when he will need to decide to jump or turn away. But a man who despairs and surrenders to his own weakness will never take any step and his bones will lie where he falls with certainty of death,' either way we men die but I have chosen to jump for there is no way back. This Shadow will not be so kind to let our bones melt into the dirt that fed them and I will not walk for an eternity with regret and cowardice as my bondage."

"None of us want that fate Gildas," spoke Medret.

Tyl and Axl came over to the war council. They were sweating and covered in dust from their journey from the coast.

"What news brothers?" asked Gildas.

"The last of the ships o' our clan has walked upon these shores but bring grave news. Our lands are breaking as the ocean churns with deadly force. Not only that, at the mouths of the great maelstroms the cries of the ocean are dimmed with something else being birthed from deep below. I fear our homelands may not be there to return to.

It is also rumoured the mountains including your Keep are breaking free of their stone feet. They are cloven into many pieces."

"What of the clan wives and the children?" asked Polax concerned at the news.

"They have retreated to the forest of Enan. The ice is thick and sturdy and lies far from the claws of the water."

"It is truly the end of all things. All lands are now destroyed or have been so fouled by this beast that no person can live there" spoke Polax.

 The Knight General stood and lit his pipe. The night was completely still around him as though nothing else existed in the world. He thought of Nene and wondered if she was still alive. If he died with his queen, it would not be such a difficult fate to bear. He thought of his mare and wondered what had become of the magnificent beast.

"There is no time left Gildas we must run day and night. It will be to no avail to be rested for the battle. The war will last an age or a moment, either way all our bones will break in the end" Medret spoke.

"Ay, Knight. Axl and Tyl will ye legs carry you further."

"Our axes and blades grow weary from lack of use graanar" spoke Tyl. "Will ye lead Gildas or should we?"

Gildas stood and offered his hand to Tyl and Axl.

"Lead us to death and glory. These wastelands need to hear the roar of the ice mother coming. We will become the sleeping wife as we approach."

"I'd like a wife or two now" spoke Tyl not thinking. All the chieftains and Gildas and the Knight burst into laughter.

"I will lead the rear vanguard. Chieftains your men will follow our footsteps?" asked Lord Warick.

"Ay, tell them the oath of the bear abides now with the Lioness. They will obey your battle cry Knight" replied Polax.

Nekoda whined sensing that they would be moving again. Gildas rubbed the dogs scarred head. He looped a leather strap onto its neck.

"The girl will not forgive me if you die needlessly. Lord Warwick, it is not as pretty as a lion, but the courage and loyalty of the dog cannot be doubted."

Lord Warick took the leash and patted Nekoda.

"Be ready for when the moon's crescent lies high in the sky. It is then the war cry is to go out."

Running into the darkness Gildas held his blade close by. He could feel the land sing to him. He also sensed that this place was older in its memories. It was where the first steps of the custodians trod when all things had been created and the eternal relinquished their rule to the custodians. Most potent to him was the blood of the peoples that dwelt here. Much had been spilt over the thousand generations and had become bound to the land and dirt. It had protected them from complete destruction. Even now with the demon claws ripping their lands apart as it built its nest, the red lands had not succumbed or broken like that of the ice or mountains. The ancient covenant still held sway and thwarted the strength of the shadow. For the first time Gildas felt humbled to be aware of such ancient forces and their tenacity. Sorrow and humility had been strangers to the great warrior, and both had met him this night when strength and battle lust were needed most.

It was nearing dusk as Tyl and Axl crawled over the edge of the glass dunes where Seraf's altar once lay. The hardness of the scorched sand tore the flesh on their legs. They were spent. Their throats and lips were cracked and bleeding from the heat of the sun and sand alike. Before them, lay the seething mass of creatures, slaves, Unstaadt and Matavian. All who appeared to be digging at the dirt and hauling great rocks which they dragged back towards the black tower and were forming a massive wall of iron. As the rock was dredged up the iron creatures who stood three graanar tall, would touch the rock and shape it into a black metal. They appeared in the same form as the red beasts called the guardians. Then the slaves would haul it to the wall being built around the bulwark. Tyl saw the eyes of the slaves; they were glassed over and white like clouds. Their bones stuck out from their flesh, but they still moved. He knew in his heart that if they did not thwart the shadow then this would be their fate also. One of them a child, by the size of the body, fell over and the creature stood on it crushing its body into the quagmire of the pits they dug from. It picked up the limp form and blew on its face. It awoke and then the guard's claw elongated into a whip of chains with spines and lashed the child. Its cries lasted only momentarily and then it just hung like an empty sack from the talons. The beast put the child down and it began to mechanically collect the rocks to bring to the pile near another of its gaolers.

"Eternal misery and pain will be our fate brother" he said to Axl.

"That beast is mine brother."

They crawled back down to the waiting legion.

"Ready yourselves. Once the sun sinks below the land then we will begin our invasion" Axl called across the waiting graan.

The paste made from the sand stung as it sat over the blistered skin of the pale graanar. They hid their blades beneath their tunic. Fortunately, the battles and then trek to the lands had shredded their clothes like the rags of the enslaved.

"We will need to kill the Unstaadt and Matavians first, as they will know by our tongue, we are not slaves."

Gildas nodded. He watched the sun inch its way closer to sleep. His heart was calm and hand steady. It was always this way before battle. He soaked up the power in the dirt and felt the throb of the consecrated blood within the memory of the grains. He could hear the low hum of the subjugated souls caught by the shadows power and craved to release them. He blew into his blades handle and whispered "By the might of the Custodian, and the clay of Arglethium may the strength of Norbu, stone forger, be with all who seek life amidst death. Death to shadow."

Tyl, Axl, Polax, Medret, Warick and all the warriors of Tarentess felt their weapons come alive with the potency of the world they were born from and seep into their flesh.

As the last cerise finger of the sun let go the graan moved quietly over the crystalised sand dunes in the darkness.

Gildas, Tyl, Axl and the Knight General felt the first sting of an iron spike hit their flesh only a few rows into the living dead surrounding them. Gildas saw a group of Unstaadt carrying blocks of steel to the wall. Walking up behind he slid his blade into each of them. The clot of bodies was so thick that carcasses were crushed into the muddy filth unseen.

Cotus Medret stole a glance around him and saw the graanar immersed everywhere picking off soldiers. He followed Gildas silently around to the northern edge of the walls. He saw a slave slip over and saw that he wore the tunic of the Aeserean lands. He stooped over him, but the face was not recognisable only white eyes and torn flesh. He glided his blade into the flesh of the man.

"Swiftly now to the lioness, she awaits you, faithful brother."

As they rounded the curve of the great wall Gildas peered into the sky and saw that the crescent moon was high in the sky. He looked back towards the eastern ridge and watched the black shape of the gathered masses of the Draxus and his graanar brothers. Suddenly he felt the prick of a blade in his thigh. He whipped around to see who it was and stared straight at Tyl and Axl.

"Brother, it is time to raise the cry of the ice mother and wake the wrath of the sleeping wife" spoke Tyl.

"Ay it is," Gildas replied grinning "Knight the gate to enter the fortress lies a few paces ahead. It is time."

Axl and Tyl climbed onto a stack of rocks. Three of the metal guards stood and readied their whips to pull him down thinking him a slave.

"The Ice Mother calls! Fight! Fight! Fight!" they roared across to their comrades.

As Gildas raced towards the opening in the wall he heard the battle cry echo around him. Then there were more responses back. Suddenly the voices of Axl and Tyl stopped. Gildas turned and saw the three whips of the guards wrap around the graanar and pull them to the ground. He lost sight of them as they fell into the melee of bodies and creatures.

"Your flesh and blood bless this ground, brothers," Gildas spoke.

Nekoda strained on the leash held by Lord Warick. He could sense the danger Gildas faced and wanted to run and defend him.

As the battle cry moved across the skies the leash snapped. Instantly Nekoda sped into the night to find Gildas. He streaked across the dirt guided by the scent of Gildas and Ange. Ange was near and nothing would thwart the fealty and courage of the dog as it went to kill the demon and protect its pack.

"To war! To war, bring the Lion and Bear to arms! Raise your blades and claws" called the Aeserean Lord running behind Nekoda towards the Iron Keep

.

# 17

# Voloc's Lair

Tessi sat with Nene and Ushan near Ange.

"Oh, Ange we were too late." Tessi sobbed as she cradled Ange's broken and decaying body in the dirt.

Nene patted the tiny figure as she shook with grief. In the distance could be heard faint echoes of the babies crying. Nene looked at the empty swaddling clothe around Tessi and wondered how they would flee this accursed place with the children.

She saw the ragged child lying in the dusty floor. In the hands of the dead body sat a jewel. The fingers were entwined around it firmly but were burnt as if the power contained within it was slowly eating them away.

Ushan got up again and prowled the edges of the cave they sat in. Her tail flicked warning of her agitation at being caged. The great cat hissed at Ange and shunned her by walking away from the place where the body lay.

"We need to find them Nene. I won't let them die here."

Tessi's eyes were as large as the moon in the darkness. She sat up and looked around the cave. A faint red glow pierced the darkness allowing them to see their prison. Its walls ran straight up from naturally formed sandstone and seams of coloured rock. Nene had seen the black, red, and white minerals with flashes of gold forming the layers of stone and understood the wealth that lay here.

Tessi stood and began to inspect the walls. They could climb them. There was an entrance at ground level, but the passage was heavily infested with creatures that shredded anything that came near them.

She turned back towards Ange. Tessi removed her scarf and shawl and placed them reverently over Ange's body. She sobbed lowering her head.

"I am so sorry Ange. I don't want to leave you here all alone, but I must find Angette and Noab. Angette has your spirit. She will be strong like you."

Her heart felt like it was going to explode with grief and anger at all that they had endured. When would it end?

She got up and strode to the wall and began to scale it. The craggy surface offered many gaps to place her hands and feet. She climbed easily and quickly reached a large hole half-way up the wall that promised another way out of the lair.

Nene watched keenly readying herself in case Tessi slipped and she needed to catch her.

"Careful dear one" she whispered.

Just as Tessi felt as if her legs would give way her hand reached the opening. Climbing up she managed to get herself on top of the ledge. Quietly she cinched her way against the wall until she could peer into the dark mouth of a tunnel. A cool breeze flowed through the tunnel. She slowly craned her head into the space and was met with darkness and a vague outline of walls for a few paces until the faint glow from their prison was swallowed by shadow.

She moved back to the edge.

"It is a tunnel but dark. I cannot see beyond a few paces. We have no choice" Tessi whispered down to Nene.

Nene swallowed wondering what to do. They would be left here to rot like the child that lay on the ground. She looked at Ushan.

"Come here Ushan" called Nene. The lion went cautiously over to Nene. Nene hugged her carefully and then tried to lift Ushan. The lion growled and slipped out her arms.

"We cannot take you pet. The climb is too steep for you, and I cannot lift you. Take the passages we came through; your mighty roar and claws will destroy the maligned creatures that dwell there."

Nene hugged Ushan weeping at the loss of her pet and then began to climb.

Ushan roared at the Queen and tried to climb but kept falling. Nene sobbed as she rose higher and higher. She hissed at Ushan to stop trying to follow her. Eventually reaching Tessi, Nene lay flat against the rock her chest heaving with exhaustion. Ushan's cries could be heard from the bottom of the cave.

"Quickly Tessi before our courage fails."

They both crawled into the tunnel. Nene stood slowly testing the height of it and found she could stand straight without hitting her head.

They walked cautiously as the blackness engulfed them. Nene felt the fear rising in her chest as if she would be suffocated from the lack of light. It never ended. They walked until the air grew thicker and the walls were warm to touch. There was no sound from anywhere. Ushan's growls had disappeared. They both sat weary and fearful that it would lead nowhere.

"We must keep going Tessi. There is nothing back the way we came."

They got up and continued. They felt a rise in the ground beneath. Suddenly Nene put one foot forward and knew it was a mistake. There was nothing underneath. She tried to grab a wall, but the momentum of her steps thrust her forward. Nene plunged into the dark not knowing where she would land and if she would live to find out.

"Nene, no! Where are you?" Tessi screamed.

Tessi groped blindly hoping to find the Queen but there was nothing. She sat down too afraid to move. She sobbed wondering if the Queen lived. She reached out tentatively trying to move forward. She continued slowly until she felt a breath brush her face. She froze. Then deep malicious whispers grew around her. She did not want to look up because she knew what stood before her. Angette and Noab came to her mind. The sorrow and guilt at not being able to protect them from the Queen enraged her fragile heart.

"I will die along, with my children before you can have their blood."

"You are strong and persistent and the fire in your belly shines brightly. But you will not defeat the shadow before you."

Suddenly everything flared a brilliant red revealing where she was.

The Matavian Queen stood in a far corner of the den. Captain Faad held Nene with a knife at her throat. Her face was bloody from the fall. The babies lay asleep hanging in what looked like cocoons.

A roar echoed from deep below them. It was Ushan. Her mind flashed to Ange's body lying down there alone. She sobbed in anger and fear. She launched herself at the witch. She clawed and screamed at her. The thought of killing her pulsed in every vein just to end the torment she had suffered. The Queen thrust her back against the wall with such force she blacked out momentarily.

"The babies shall live or die in my arms not yours" Tessi screamed with such ferocity that the Matavian suzerain hesitated to land the lethal blow. Suddenly Nene turned and clawed at Faad's face. He grabbed her around the neck and began to squeeze.

"Die maiden, neither mother nor monarch!" he roared.

Then the air thickened, and everyone's movements seemed to slow as if the air clung to them like mud. Voloc entered and everyone felt their hearts and minds freeze with fear and pain. It stood as a shadow on the wall in the form of anything that came to mind of those who stood close to it.

"Ancient one you fight the weakling for no reason. You want your children back and you shall have them."

The shadow flickered, and suddenly a gasp came from Queen Giandra.

"Servant thy will is mine to command and not by your own desires shall yours be fulfilled."

Giandra raised a flame from her hands and thrust it at the Shadow on the walls. Voloc chuckled as it let the flames of Adria dance around itself.

"You bring your lessened light to the creature of the void. It dies as it nears the maker of shadows as did Caemeris. Understand your light brings neither the colours of creation nor the calm of darkness. It is the feeble whimsy of an ignorant mind. Voloc has existed before any flame and cannot be maimed by the clayborn. Only the Caemeris has usurped my rule and it is and its creations that I shall destroy."

"I brought you the ancient blood you desired."

The Queen began to gasp for air. Faad went to grab her as she fell to the ground.

"Yes, you did, but they would have been mine anyway. All the custodians have done is hastened my purpose to destroy everything Caemeris formed. Their blood was tainted with the jewel of Norbu and anything it has touched draws me to it. Their blood does not give me power. It merely strengthens yours so that Voloc must grow stronger to devour it."

"So, until the jewel is destroyed your purpose is thwarted?" Tessi asked.

"Ancient one I feel the hatred and malice for this one's perversions. You cry for death to find her and hope it will lessen the stain of revenge in your heart. Shall I snuff out this servant?"

Tessi looked at the Queen and knew she wanted her dead like the King. Her mind felt the presence of the demon and the fury and rage at all that had happened well in her chest.

"Kill her!" Tessi ordered.

Instantly the Queen lay paralysed in agony her glassy eyes pleading to Tessi to relent. But Tessi did not. She took her dagger and plunged it into the heart of the depraved witch.

Faad grabbed Tessi to stop her doing it again. Nene thrust herself at Faad and pushed him into the wall to stop him hurting Tessi.

"Enough Tessi, she is dead. Do not let the essence of the woman's demented soul poison you as well," spoke Nene.

Tessi dropped the dagger and stood. She reached for the children and carefully unstrung them from the roof of the cavern. She gathered both into her arms and cradled them fiercely.

"Now that you have your prizes bring your sister to me" ordered Voloc.

"You haven't answered my question. If it is only that we draw you to us because of this Caemeris, why do you need the jewel? We cannot give you the jewel it was given to Ange and only she can relinquish it." Tessi asked half sobbing heaves fearing what Voloc may do to her.

There was silence. No answer came.

"Let us go Demon. We neither, hinder nor help you. Leave us in whatever peace remains for our lands and people" spoke Nene.

Faad lay sitting over the queen on the ground. Her face withered quickly, and her body decayed as he held her. She disintegrated into dust as he lay her back on the ground.

Voloc suddenly materialised in front of them. Its eyes shone a blood red, and a miasma of black formed its body. Its claws hung loosely from its side and its mouth breathed the stench of death itself. There was no face only the eyes whose vision had spanned the eons of time and pierced all that they gazed upon.

Nene began to weep blood as the sight of the utter depravation of the creature bombarded her mind and body. Nene's hair turned white. Tessi collapsed onto the ground and could not breathe.

"See the shadow and destroyer of the first light, the one called Voloc. When your blood kin returns you shall bring her to me or I shall take the life of your children and consume them before you."

"She will not turn from her destiny for the sake of my children. She knows our fate will be death to all if she does. If you will not set us free then kill us now Demon, for I made it my purpose to be with my children until the end. They will know their mother lay with them and did not abandon them. We will walk to our peoples and to

Ancrid our god together." Tessi took a deep breath. "Take the jewel yourself if you are so powerful."

Tessi trembled uncontrollably waiting for the lethal blow from Voloc. Instead, only a laugh of malice that reverberated into the walls of the cave and earth met her.

"Voloc cannot answer your question nor can Caemeris. Our paths were set in motion well before your memory or ours. I will not let you die clayborn, for Voloc seeks to reap all that exists into its shadow from every age of light. You will live but the grief you shall feel will never wane and the pain will cut like a blade renewed and sharpened with every waking moment."

An image formed on the cavern wall. Nene, Tessi and Faad felt the waves of pain and sorrow and agony wash over them and saw their fate under Voloc's reign. They felt the chains of its bondage tear their skin and fester into oozing wounds.

"You will not stop me. You will make the Keeper relinquish the tears of Ascendant and bring the memory of Caemeris to me or you shall live in a cage of sorrow and subjugation to relive the torment of seeing them perish. But if you do this for me, if you deliver the custodian of the jewel to me then I will grant the freedom of death to you."

The demon rose before them all and took the babies close to its face. Tessi ran forward to snatch them away from it. Nene raised her sword to stab at the beast, but it grew red hot and she had to drop it as it seared her flesh. Faad merely watched stunned and mute. He knew that it had been a mistake to walk with Giandra for it had only given the demon more power and weakened Gildas armies to fight. He thought of the great army that could have walked upon this lair and at least glorified the bravery of men. Instead, he had let his debauchery for a fevered and demented sorcerer, bind him to her perverse desires.

"Nene, I remember once your father telling me that I had been a true soldier and warrior, a glimmer of talent in a sea of dishonour and insanity."

"Then help us Piotr, your rulers are dead. The empire is dead. Be worthy of the praise my father bestowed. His words were never spoken lightly."

Faad stood with his sword and slashed at Voloc's torso. The demon laughed at the futile attempt but it only enraged Faad more making him whip into a frenzy of stabbing at the shadow before him. His mind reeled with images of dead and tortured souls at the hands of his suzerains. Voloc picked up the broken captain of Matavia and plunged its malice deep into his heart. Faad screamed with the agony of it.

"You shall rest in the barbs of pain inflicted upon the ones you ruled. Voloc's desire is fulfilled with you."

Faad woke in the dim light of a tunnel. At the opening a pale sun set across the Hendra Valley. He walked toward the opening slowly waiting to see if anything was lying in wait to attack him. Suddenly he heard whispers. Then tiny yellow eyes appeared in front of him. The whispers grew louder and then he felt the claws on his neck.

Voloc took Angette and Noab and touched their foreheads. Its claw singed their skin, but they did not scream as they remembered the first touch of Voloc when they were growing inside their mother. It drew on the strength of life within them and began to chew on the bonds of light which made them.

"Put them down Shadow and bow to the keeper of Ascendent's tears. Gaze upon the custodian of memory and death."

Ange stood with Ushan on a leash. Her sword shone brilliantly, and her body had remade itself.

Voloc dropped the children as it turned and hissed at Ange. Nene and Tessi dived to capture the babies before they hit the ground.

"Run Tessi, Run far. The battle begins and I must fulfil the quest given to me."

Tessi wept openly in great heaving sobs at the sight of Ange being alive.

"Now sister! Run!"

Nene pulled Tessi.

"The great cat will lead you out to freedom" urged Ange.

Nene took the leash from Ange and led Tessi towards an opening in the wall.

Tessi looked back into the lair and saw the tiny figure of Ange standing ready to face the demon towering above her; her mind reeling from everything happening.

"Now it begins Demon." Ange hissed back at the shadow. It swiped at her.

"I have faced the Ondraack and defeated them. I have caged a god and set it free. I have peered into the heart of flame and seen the death of light and still live. I have stood in front of your servant Baachelaus and escaped his destiny. And now I seek to destroy the master of destruction."

Ange stabbed at the shadow and her sword connected. It drew the blackness away but instead of light existing beneath only more shadow lay there.

"I am not borne of the light clayborn."

It slashed at Ange and knocked her against the wall. The prism fell out of its pouch onto the sand. Voloc seized it. Ange flew at its talon and knocked it back out. She snatched it back just as Voloc latched onto her and squeezed her so that she almost blacked out. She remembered the flame of Seraf. Touching her forehead, she relit the tiny light and blew on her finger towards the shadow. It ignited into massive burst of sparks and fury. Voloc opened its mouth and swallowed the flame whole. It laughed at her attempt.

Ange stabbed with the blade of Norbu and managed to get herself free of the claws. Her mind raced. Nothing defeated the creature until she thought of the tears. She peered into it. Inside she saw the cathedral of light the way it was meant to be. She blew the flame of Seraf again but let it pass through the jewel. The flame burst into an explosion of white light and engulfed Voloc. The demon roared as it felt the incendiary heat blister its hide. Ange was thrust against the wall as Voloc let her go to escape the great heat. Voloc strode towards her. She blew again and this time baptised her sword in the heat of the fire. As its claw neared her, she swung her blade down and cut off its talon.

Voloc stopped. Its eyes glowed even redder as its talon grew back as if nothing had happened. Ange slashed again and again drawing the demon out of the lair and into the tunnel. The metal bats fluttered as their creator walked amongst them. Voloc reached for Ange, but she sprang away and once again doused it in the flame of Seraf. She took one of the stones and sling shot it into its eye. Voloc roared as the crystals of Seraf ate their way into its eyes. Ange ran as fast as she could before the demon recovered. Just as she went to plunge her blade into Voloc, its talon wrapped around her neck. Her eyes peered into the eyes of Voloc, and both wept at the sight that met them. Voloc saw the rupture of the void and its essence shredded by the surge of light and the chaos of creation. Ange peered into an unending prison of stars and creatures laid to waste by its power in ancient memories and tombs that stretched forth into Ages that had not yet come to pass. One thread of light shone brightly, and a deep fear chilled her bones. She pulled away her heart exploding with rage, she jabbed her blade again and again into the rapacious vision of destruction. Voloc let go. Suddenly a massive shudder ran through the tunnel dislodging the creatures. The walls cracked and the ground began to open underneath. The bats flew in frenzied confusion around Ange and Voloc.

"Voloc, thy servant has come to defeat thee and usurp thy throne."

Baachelaus' voice pierced the darkness of the cave. Voloc laughed when it heard.

"Keeper you have brought the wrong one back."

It snatched her up. Ange could feel her body breaking under the power and her heart failing. She took the prism and held it high.

"I call the light of Caemeris, the memories of the custodians of making to thwart this creature that forsook your rule. Destroy it in the name of the Keeper that now guards all that had been wrought by your eternal sight."

The crystal did nothing as Ange began to black out. Voloc plucked it out of her hands. Ange held her breath waiting to see what would happen. Suddenly the prism burst into a raiment colour like a rainbow.

Baachelaus heard the call of Ange and saw the prism burst the light into its elemental form.

"The first Custodians have forsaken their destinies. So now we rest in the hands of this mighty but clay-bound mortal. Usurper and most unworthy of the vision, it shall not be borne that neither the clayborn nor the shadow rule the light of Caemeris" spoke Baachelaus, his voice thundering deep into the bedrock of the world.

"You are the usurpers of what existed first, and you shall be destroyed" roared Voloc as the lights seared its hide causing it to turn to smoke and ash. It dropped the crystal. Ange snatched it up as Voloc raged in burning contortions. She bolted towards the entrance of the lair.

She met Nene, Tessi and Ushan fighting their way through the cacophony of bats as they made their way out of the tunnel. Ange slashed her way forward and began to clear a passage for them to escape by. They were bleeding and torn to shreds from the fangs and claws.

The children's screams joined the sounds of the deformed beasts. Another shudder ran through the labyrinth along with a roar. Ange looked behind her to see if Voloc gave chase. The memories of staring into the pool of darkness contained within Voloc remained vivid despite the melee around her. For an eternity they stretched, and her steps shadowed the same path as Voloc. A lead weight hung on her heart at the thought at what may lay before her. She had seen herself in that single thread of light.

"Hurry to the entrance. I will lead you out and then I will return to hunt the beast."

Suddenly Tessi was hugging Ange, weeping. Noab struggled between them.

"What happened to your eyes Ange?" Tessi looked at the white discs that shone out from her sister's face.

"I have seen much, sister, and believe I am no longer what I once was and weep for that. If this ends and victory is ours, then we shall run by the Mighty Choasa again and lie in the grass beneath the sun and sky."

Nene came forward with Angette.

"Ange this is Nene, the Queen of the Aeserean people." Nene looked at Ange and the tiny stature unbelieving at the strength that lay within.

The rumbling came again and this time the roof of the cavern began to crumble.

"Quickly, follow me."

Ange led them through the maze of red sandstone. The creatures had thinned so that now Nene, Ushan and Ange easily plucked them off before they attacked. The black blood burnt their clothes and skin. The tunnel grew smaller until they had to squeeze through a hole. Nene was almost stuck but Ange and Tessi managed to pull her through. As they turned their hearts sank when they looked upon a vast cavern stretching down to a still pool of water. On the other side was another entrance that led away but it was a dozen lengths of men and too far for them to reach. A rock tumbled over the edge and plopped into the pool below. Ange noticed smoke rose as the liquid seemed to eat the rubble.

"It is not water Ange. It is something vile" spoke Nene.

Ange stood looking at the immense space. She could not leap that far. She heard a clunk of metal as she went to step closer to the edge. Looking down it was a dead bat. She picked it up and felt it humming in her hands. She realised that the creatures were all connected to Voloc and could be harmed like it and remade through the prism.

"Gather as many of these things as you can."

"Why?" asked Nene.

"Just do it and I will show you."

They gathered the unnatural beasts into a pile near the edge of the rock. Ange touched the flame of Seraf and blew. In her mind she pictured a bridge she and Bensah had crossed over on their journey to Lido's pool. The iron reshaped itself into the image in Ange's mind. It stretched across the vault beneath until it connected to the edge of the other side.

Ange trod on the structure to test its strength. Steady under her foot she stepped forward and led the others across the bat-bridge. It hummed beneath their feet. She willed it to stay underfoot.

"Hurry."

"Nearly there" called Ange but as she looked ahead her heart froze.

A growl drifted across the air towards them. Nene screamed and gathered Tessi and Ushan to her.

"What is it?"

The creature snapped its gaping maw at the wanderers of its lair. Its head was covered in spines and its claws were long and thin and razor sharp. Its fangs glinted as they managed to capture the dim red light that suffused through the cavern. The hound stood the height of a man. Suddenly it broke into a frenzy of barks and began to walk onto the bridge. A massive crack like thunder suddenly shot through the earth. The bridge shook violently knocking Ange and Nene over. Tessie shrieked.

I made you as well thought Ange looking at its huge jaws which resembled Nekoda's.

Ange saw Tessi was barely hanging onto the edge of the bridge with Noab. As Ange and Nene dived to snatch Tessi from falling another thud rippled through the cavern. They managed to catch Tessi. Ange gripped a gap in the moulded iron. She heaved to pull Tessi up but stopped as the beast's breath washed over her. She looked up and saw the red eyes and glistening fangs above her.

If I destroy you, will I destroy the bridge? We will tumble and everyone except me will die thought Ange.

Ushan prowled towards the hound ready to attack. But the dog growled menacingly at the great cat. It eyes glowed even brighter. Ushan sensed a fiercer beast than herself and stopped.

Ange felt Tessi slipping in her other hand. The air stilled when the beast turned back to Ange relishing the death it was to inflict upon them. Then she heard the voice of a friend cut through the foul air that surrounded her. Nekoda raced in barking. Its crisp sharp calls echoed all around them and Ange could feel it vibrate in the bridge itself.

The dog launched itself at the hound and its great jaws ripped through the iron hide. The hound turned and let off a brutal snarl. As Nekoda drew it away from Ange, she and Nene hoisted Tessi up. Ange swung around with her blade and drove it straight into the demon dog as it wrestled with Nekoda. It screeched as she and Nekoda slayed the foul thing. Its black blood causing the deformed creatures to sizzle and melt away weakening the bridge.

"Quickly the bridge will give way. Get to the ledge!" she called to Tessi and Nene. They dashed past just avoiding a swipe from the claws of the beast. Ange landed a mighty blow to decapitate the creature and then leapt over it to reach the ledge. She grabbed Nekoda by a tuft of mangy fur behind his ears heaving him toward her as the poison cut its way through the last of the bat bridge. Ange heard the crack and knew it would give way. Tessi and Nene leapt onto the ledge as the bridge gave way. Ange flung the dog and herself towards the rock but knew instantly she would not make it as the rest of the bridge broke apart. She felt herself falling with Nekoda alongside her.

"Not yet sister and dog."

The mighty hands of Gildas caught her tunic and the contorted skin of Nekoda. The dog yelped as its flesh wrenched. The Graan Lord heaved them both up effortlessly. He placed them on the rocky ledge. Ange stood before him. He looked at her and saw the same crippled body, but scar ridden and with the white eyes of a wraith who has seen more than was deemed wise. Ange felt no fear toward him, nor did she see any loathing in his eyes. Each stared at the warrior before them.

"Is the jewel still with you Keeper?" asked Gildas.

"Yes, Keeper but I have not destroyed Voloc" replied Ange.

"Ay it will take all our strengths warrior heart" spoke Gildas.

Ange turned from the gaze of Gildas as Nekoda came up to her.

"My friend forever." She hugged the great dog as tears welled in her eyes.

"My lady you are alive."

The Knight General raced in his face covered in filth and his clothes tattered.

"The cursed vermin in the tunnels now know the strength of Aeserean blades my Queen."

Nene went to Medret "I knew you would come."

Ushan sat preening her fur. She growled at Nekoda when he barked.

Another shudder tore through the cavern sending an avalanche of boulders careening from the roof.

"Knight you will need to take them to safety. We still have enemies that have not been destroyed." spoke Gildas.

"Ange come with us. Flee this place. The jewel is safe now and the demon cannot seize it" pleaded Tessi.

"No Tessi. I must remain. Go now. If Voloc is defeated, then I will find you otherwise we are both doomed. The jewel is needed to defeat the Shadow."

Tessi let a gulp of sorrow escape.

"Take the children and be safe. Hurry there is no time."

Ange kissed each of the babes and Tessi.

"You were my third protector after Mata and Norbu."

Tessi looked at Ange wanting to speak but only joy and sorrow overwhelmed her.

"Come" called the Knight. He took Nene by the arm and led her out through the tunnel with his sword held high ready to kill all.

"Run to the road of Jarrod and the Prince" called Gildas.

"We are in your hands. May the Lioness' roar follow your footsteps and sharpen your blade. I will return to fight with my brothers once our Queen is safe."

Cotus Medret tipped his sword to each of them. Ange and Gildas watched as they fled into the darkness of the tunnel and disappear. Ange wondered if she would ever see Tessi again.

"There is another way which will bring us out to the heart of the destruction that surrounds this place. We will work our way out until Voloc is found" spoke Gildas.

"The battle needs to be finished brother before all grow weary and are devoured by the unyielding lust of the shadow."

Ange clasped her hand around his as a bond of strength and purpose. Gildas could feel the power in Ange and knew he touched the spirit of creation. He both feared and craved the wellspring of possibility which dwelt within her flesh and the chance to rule it.

"Ay, sister bonded now to this realm called Caemeris."

"And bringer of our destruction" Ange replied. She stared at Gildas, and he saw the flicker of shadow that passed between them. "It will not be finished here, brother."

# 18

# Reunion Part II

Norbu stood on the ridge soaking up the earth beneath him. He watched the minions of Voloc spew out of the great Iron Fortress and could see the birthing of a creature ready to eat everything its gaze landed upon.

The father of Arglethium relished the warmth of his world and for a moment felt a twinge of sorrow that perhaps this would be the end of his reign here. This dirt was old but potent in its strength. He took a deep breath pushing the great chest of Norbu out. He gripped his sword and raced towards the melee of death below. His booming steps connecting with the rock and stone as his sacred form pulsed in union with the land. The faces, fangs and blades of his enemy turned to watch the custodian of Arglethium racing towards them in readiness for the onslaught.

First of the Aracnine saw the custodian and screeched its cry of welcome across the skies. Tamatjera cringed from the noise again; his ears were still ringing from their march to the battle. He kept his eyes fixed on Norbu not wanting to lose sight of the great spirit that had just appeared.

Norbu's blade slashed and tore through the masses of iron beasts that gnashed at his legs and arms. But as the pile of destroyed beasts rose so more would swarm around him taking their aim at the custodian.

As his blade cut down the iron guards fashioned in the form of the Aracnine, Norbu heard a noise underneath all the hissing and screams. His ancient memory flared to life. The spiked whip of a guard caught him around the neck, but he wrenched it easily and pulled the creature towards him. He crushed its head to dust and blew it into the wind. The sound came to him again and this time he stood still. Iron bats and lizards gnawed while the guards and hounds whipped at his flesh. But none of the frenzied attack distracted Norbu as he stood listening.

"There it was" he whispered. A low dull roar and the sound of beating wings.

He looked up as the shadow of EY, AX, PO, VA and XI caught his gaze above him in the sky. He took a hound that had latched onto his throat and broke its neck.

"Brethren, our ancient enemy has awoken. We must see its end for the shadow seems indestructible and never ending in its power. It dredges all its progeny from their tombs to torment and destroy" called EY.

"Mighty Orynth, lead me. My spear wrought from the heart of Belmaris is ready to meet it once again."

Norbu followed the great birds as they flew towards the east; his bounding steps cracking the molten black sand where Seraf had battled Baachelaus. In the far distance, he saw Vipax shoot out of the ocean and into the sky towards a white shape. Out of the white shape shot a crystal flame. Vipax roared as its golden scales were singed with the heat of the fire.

"Mordraak, the slayer, come to me. I have not given thee leave to flee thy tomb" ordered the custodian of Arglethium.

The dragon heard the voice of Norbu and roared its acceptance across the sky.

Kado heard the call of the dragon and the voice of Vipax in his mind.

"The first dragon Mordraak has awoken Scaletryx and comes to meet us in battle."

"Show me."

In his mind he saw the winged behemoth spewing out of the ocean rupturing the icelands and splitting the earth beneath the ocean. Its massive body blocking the sun, its white scaly hide dazzling as the light rebounded off it. Its jaws opened and the flames shot out. Kado felt the pain as the flame seared Vipax's skin.

"Come Mordraak, eons have passed since I doused your fire. It is time to finish it" Vipax lashed in the ocean daring the leviathan to attack again.

"General I will race to find Sa-Tuc. Another enemy looms in the distance. Stay and fight here and hold the legions of Voloc at bay" called Kado to General Tat.

"Yes, my Lord. What else besets us?"

"The first of all dragons has been awoken by the shadow" replied Kado.

Kado searched across the warring bodies until he saw the streak of blue light in the distance. A dozen hounds smelt his flesh and bolted directly towards him. He leapt over their fowl breath and fangs and with one easy stroke, they fell beneath his sword. He streaked towards Sa as more of the rabid dogs gave chase. He could hear their snarling just behind him.

"Assassin, we must race towards the ocean. A great enemy rises."

Suddenly the talons of First swung past him and gathered two of the hounds up. It flung them high into the sky. Kado ducked as the Aracnine scooped another handful of beasts.

"Its name Scaletryx?" asked Sa-Tuchala.

Kado hesitated at being called this name. How would she know?"

"Vipax called it Mordraak."

Sa-Tuchala made a hissing sound at the name and bared her fangs.

"Make haste Scaletryx your progenitor has been reborn!"

Kado and Sa-Tuchala arrived on the knoll of rock near the coastal plains. They watched as Mordraak swooped from the sky to meet Norbu as he launched himself into the air. The clash resulted in a fantastic shower of sparks and flame. The Orynth darted in and out plunging their talons and beaks into the dragon trying to open a wound in the pure white hide for Norbu to thrust his spear.

EY and AX caught a glimpse of the red eyes that sparkled like rubies and dove directly into them, pecking and scratching trying to blind the dragon. Mordraak pulled away and vomited molten lava out of its mouth. EY and AX did not release themselves in time and were caught in the fiery river. VA, XI and PO flew to pull their brethren free but the down draft from the great lizard forced them back. VA's wing broke as Mordraak's claws tore through the feather and bone. The Orynth was driven into the ground. EY and AX plummeted behind their brethren with plumage ablaze.

"First call all the Aracnine and we will surround the beast" ordered Sa-Tuchala.

Kado began to aim arrows at the eyes of the creature and managed to stick one. Its claws frenziedly dislodging it. It shot flame at the emperor. It barely missed him. Suddenly Norbu swung up onto Mordraak's neck and began hacking at the thick hide to dislodge the foul head.

The Aracnine swayed and chanted as Sa stood in the centre of the guardians. In her hands a ball of blue light began to form gathering size and power. She shot it at the underbelly of the creature and made a direct hit. It spun over from the force. Norbu clung by one hand. It rolled over again and again until the custodian let go. It then shot flame at Sa and the guardians. She met it with blue pulsing light as the Aracnine held her aloft giving their queen their strength. The blue flame met the white in an explosion which quaked through the earth.

Kado continued aiming his arrows at the soft gourd beneath the jaws and the eyes. The bombardment of arrows distracted it enough that it stopped its onslaught of Sa. PO and XI flew at the dragon's head again and again.

"I remember your kind. So many died to lay me in my tomb, and I have arisen again, and you have not" roared Mordraak.

The voice was thick and low and jarred the ears of the ones fighting below. It lunged at the two remaining Orynth and managed to snatch XI. It ripped the great bird in two. PO screeched with grief at the death of its family. Its heart broke as it realised it was the last of its kind.

It launched itself at the face of the great lizard and managed to pluck one of its eyes out. The dragon roared and lashed at PO. It shattered the bones of one of its wings. PO managed to fly away out of reach with the eye of Mordraak still in its talons.

"The wound inflicted by the Orynth will remain as a mark on eternity's memory. Destroy the beast father and avenge your servants and brethren." PO called as it threw the dragon's eye to Norbu. Catching it easily Norbu stood and waited for the dragon to come to him. PO landed in the ocean floating in the waves waiting to see the death of its mortal enemy.

"Do you remember me Mordraak? You still bear the scar I inflicted when we last battled. Now a new one will be given for you to dwell upon in your watery tomb."

He tossed the dragon's eye in his hand to taunt the creature.

"The rays of Belmaris cannot thwart me now Stone Forger. The shadow of the void has awoken and with it all its progeny cry their birthright across the eons of time."

It spat out is molten ash and flame and covered the sky so thickly the sun and stars were blocked out plunging Arglethium into darkness. As the winged behemoth landed the thud cracked the cliffs of the northern coastline sending an avalanche of red sandstone into the ocean. Its tail swung in a massive arc for half a league.

Norbu raced towards the ancient worm and as he neared, he drew on the dirt, rock, and stone with all the power he could muster and brought his blade down on the neck of the dragon. Sa approached as did Kado. They gathered around the beast. They met it with a frenzy of blows and barbs and stinging arrows. The Aracnine screeched their chorus of battle and scraped their talons along the impenetrable scales. Mordraak hissed and spat and stomped unrelenting in its quest to destroy everything that was an abomination to the dark.

As he slashed against the dragon, Norbu felt a zephyr of stale air brush across his flesh. Turning he saw on the far horizon the tomb of Magmeris open and Descendent ride into the world with his minions of death following. The god rode a stead of fleshless form and thorned head. The black sockets within its face shone with the aquamarine light of Uchala's and Vipax venom. His long, blackened talons gripped the sceptre of bone and iron.

"Voloc, thy servant has come to defeat thee and usurp thy throne" called Baachelaus across the fighting hordes of beasts and clayborn.

Sa-Tuchala and the Aracnine were pulled to their knees as the chains that had bound Baachelaus were remade. First screeched its rage as the guardian watched the chain reform within its own chest and into the other seven.

"How can this be? They have found their queen and she has given herself to them," called Sa-Tuchala as she felt the weight of the bondage crush her.

"Voloc the deceiver, the descendant comes to defeat his gaoler. The custodian remembers his purpose and sees where his throne lies and now seeks revenge upon the one who denied him his destiny" spoke Norbu.

Norbu stood and watched his brethren return from the realm of Caemeris but did not seek to do battle with him for that duty lay with others. He shut his mind quickly though when he felt the fowl worm Mordraak pierce his thoughts. Turning back, he gripped his sword and began the second battle of the dragon. Kado ran to his aid, but the serpent flung him back into the desert with one flick of its tail.

"Vipax help me."

"I cannot. Aid Sa-Tuchala. The dead minions of Baachelaus chase the shadows of Stonthrax as the custodian draws strength from the sentinel" ordered Vipax.

Kado ran towards Sa seeing the black shadow of Baachelaus' army race across the dunes towards them.

The Aracnine lay writhing in pain as the yoke of Baachelaus restored powers grew menacingly more lethal. Kado saw the chains between them and Sa. The cadaverous forms from the realm of the Descendant reached ever closer.

"Sa-Tuc, be free!" he yelled as he dove into the minions with the speed and grace of a viper. He slashed the chains between the Aracnine and then Sa and continued to pile the bones of the already dead around him.

"Arise Aracnine, slay those that should be dead and have been re-woken by the lost one. I shall face Mordraak the slayer and see its bones are once more laid to rest" ordered Sa-Tuchala.

Sa strode to where Norbu fought viciously with the dragon. The custodian was met blow for blow, yet he did not falter. Norbu knew as he weaved and made his cuts that the victor would not stand until the others battled and all their fates were decided.

"Sa-Tuchala, we have much to do here until the final blow is made by the new custodians."

"We do. Let us thwart this lizard until the Keepers do their work."

Tamatjera watched the god appear from nowhere riding a massive stead made of bone and nothing else. It rode to the Iron Fortress oblivious to the battle around it. It was the same god that had awoken so many moons ago when his father Widjera had gone to call the spirits to take him. The god was strong and had bought with its hordes of the dead. Tamatjera knew the moment drew near when all would die for even if the demon was destroyed the dead god would live. He struck out at the lifeless creatures and the iron fangs of the bats and even though his spear splintered, and flesh lay gaping he felt nothing, only the satisfaction every drop of his blood poured into the dirt.

"Bring the end soon so renewal may begin," he prayed to the spirits of his ancestor.

"Voloc show yourself! Meet your servant's call for revenge" roared Baachelaus across the heaving mass of destruction.

The air thickened and the darkness seem to drain as if something drew on it. Silence then moved across the lands and sky as everything stilled. Voloc rose from its fortress and stood upon the spike that reached for the sky. Its presence only seen by its piercing red eyes entering the hearts and minds of all who stood watching.

"Progeny, hold thy course as I meet my servant, born of Caemeris and bonded now to Oblyquixiton" Voloc's voice rippled across the world.

The thick clouds of ash that had shrouded everything darkened further. Mordraak stilled its thrashing and glowed even brighter at its maker's command. The bats, lizards and hounds spouting from the fortress slowed. The free who battled could feel their weapons become like boulders of iron as the potency of the shadow pervaded everything.

Descendant rode towards his gaoler; the pounding strides of his stead cracking the bedrock beneath and echoing into the sky.

"I have seen what was stolen from me, great deceiver. I have seen my throne and come to claim it."

Voloc hissed at Baachelaus. The custodian raised his spear and with lightning speed shot it at Voloc. As the spear of dead light pierced the emptiness Voloc screeched at the wound.

"You are not restored until the other throne is filled."

"I have the changer of dark to light. The balance is restored, I hold the Ascendant's power now as well" replied Descendant.

Voloc suddenly appeared in front of the god. The horse reared up in fright. Voloc wrenched Baachelaus to the dirt.

"You become more like the land you devour shadow" spoke Baachelaus as his blades struck the hide of Voloc, half metal half shadow.

The sound of iron on iron rang in the night sky as the blade of Descendant struck Voloc. The shadow caught his prisoner by the throat and raised him high.

"Ahh, I have wounded thee, eternal watchers, I have perverted the great vision you deemed should be the destiny of those formed by Caemeris" taunted Voloc.

Voloc drew on the vastness of its realm, the void, unlit from the First star's rays. The power was so strong the sky broke, and the moon was pulled toward the earth making the ocean rise to the top of the lands.

Baachelaus raged at the arrogance of the shadow. The custodian dredged the vision to mind of what it had seen in its realm of the lost; its power and glory stolen by the fiend of the void. He plunged his claw into the chest of Voloc sensing the power draining away from him into the shadow.

"Take what I have been given usurper. Take the poison that you bled into me and made the god that now stands before you."

The world stilled as the equal forces met, light dimmed, and shadow faded. The forces converged and froze the gods of destruction in a marriage of revenge and ancient malice.

Ange saw her opportunity along with Gildas as they watched from a large iron spire that rose above the main turret of the fortress.

"We have them sister. All else waits for this moment to be finished. I shall take the shadow and you must cage the god. Will the same thing happen as it did when Norbu captured him?" spoke Gildas.

"The tears belong to me now. The vision is mine to keep. The god does not see this. It only sees its own desires as does the shadow. They know not who their true enemies are. I am the changer of light and dark now. I am the custodian of death and memory. You are the protector of stone and rock."

"Ay, sister. I bow to you in this moment of destiny."

Nekoda stood between them waiting to be commanded to battle again. Ange stroked behind his ears wishing she could hug him. The memory of all the times Bensah would visit with the great ugly dog came to her. The moments of lying along the riverbank watching the waters of the Choasa flow silently past with Nekoda loyally sitting near her. The sorrow of it all broke her heart and tears streamed down her face. My beautiful friends she thought to herself. I do this most of all for you and Tessi. How had this all happened rumbled through her mind as her chest thumped with a pounding heart. How would she defeat these leviathans of ancient rule and creation? She a villager, an exile in her own home from the red sands of the mighty Choasa river.

"Gildas, I have no fear, for I can do no more than this but let it be over so that I may see the mighty Choasa and Tessi again, so the world may live again."

"Ay, sister. It is a great boon indeed for fate to change her gaze and open another way for us. I was scorned by the cuts of my own blade but yours was borne by hands your kin. Now we stand here, chosen by gods tired from an ancient war ready to do battle. We stand to save those who would have seen us dead. Your strength lies in winning the greatest battle, surviving a world of hatred, and still seeking the goodness that lies here. Mine was given by the lands I was birthed. Together it is a mighty storm that comes towards these destroyers. Those who scorned us shall fill scrolls about the glorious legends of the new covenant forged by the clay born of Arglethium."

"I will walk to this moment of doom with the memory of those I love; for it is for them that I do this and no other. I have no other fate other than this moment, what came before is forgotten. What comes now is taken and borne with a heart ready to bear it" spoke Ange.

Gildas wondered if he did this for himself or the people below who battled the fell beasts. He remembered the moment in the Keep of Tarentess when Ascendant had shown him what lay between him and annihilation. It was the devotion of Jesse and Jarrod that had saved him from certain enslavement from Voloc but even at this moment of life and death he still thought more of his own glory then of them. It is for that reason Ange was chosen to bear the Tears of Ascendant's lost hope and not I he thought.

Yes, Ange replied to Gildas in his mind. I only asked to live and now I seek to understand. You wanted power but now before you lies power in its true form, not the flimsy desires of a clayborn ignorant to the very thing that made him.

"Keeper of Tarentess command the dog to go to your clansman until the end" spoke Ange.

Gildas whistled into the air. Nekoda sat up right.

"To the ice mother dog!"

Nekoda hesitated not wanting to leave knowing that Ange and Gildas were walking to danger. But their insistence could not be disobeyed. He ran towards Jarrod and Polax standing amongst the beasts spewing out of the guts of the earth.

Gildas and Ange began their descent. As they neared their quarry, they felt the potency of the forces weigh them down. Their swords and shields felt like lead in their hands. Ange held the Tear in one hand. She noticed it became cooler as she neared Baachelaus and Voloc. She felt herself merge with the memories laid down and the watching eye of a great conscious, ancient and far seeing but gone now. Its legacy left to all the creatures it thrust into existence. She watched with the sight of Caemeris and knew this was not the end either. Before her she saw the light dispersing and the ending of that existence in great empty stars and dead suns. Ange wondered why she had been given the power to rule light and shadow and wondered who watched from so far away.

Baachelaus wrenched himself away from Voloc unfettering the earth and sky. The battle around them resumed more viciously than before.

"Die shadow."

Baachelaus hefted his blade above him and swung while Voloc drove its talons into Descendant. Ange bolted forward with the tears held high.

"Bring forth the light of the vision of Caemeris" she commanded.

The raiment of colours that was the placenta for the birth of the First Star broke forth scorching Voloc and breaking the darkness Mordraak had released. Gildas flew at the demon as it turned its hide from the lights. Descendant roared at Ange and snatched her to its face. The empty sockets sucked in the light. She held if aloft closer and closer.

"You could not chain me in your realm Baachelaus and now you stand upon the dirt and rock that birthed me. Take your throne Descendant, see where it lies" spoke Ange.

Ange felt the power of the prism fill her and the lights dance in her soul and in the withered heart of the god. Neither could step away as they were swept together in the maelstrom of power.

Gildas plunged his sword into the head of the Voloc and felt the strength of the prism wash into it from his sword. All the power of the custodial brethren, the seven colours of light began to claw away the shadow's grip. It lunged once at Ange to grab the jewel. As its talons connected with it, Ange's eyes glowed white and the blood of the earth from Gildas joined the custodian spirit of hope. The field of power cloaked the four crushing them together. The spirit and the blood coursed in unison pulling the corrupted ancients together.

"I will not be caged again! Deceivers of the eternal light. My wrath will seek you and find you until the end of all things!" Baachelaus voice echoed as the tears of Ascendant swallowed the god into itself. Voloc's hide began to break down as Gildas sinew and muscle pulsed with the blood of the earth draining the potency from the demon. Suddenly the rainbow of light ended.

"Die you beast of shadow and death!" he roared.

Suddenly Voloc's eyes blazed red until a burst of yellow tore the shadow to a thousand pieces. Gildas became engulfed in the flames and felt every part of his body burn as the blood of the earth ignited. Ange fell to the ground and shielded herself from the heat.

An almighty boom cracked through the earth and rippled across the world. Nene, Tessi, Medret and Ushan felt the earth give way beneath. Vipax rose out of the water forcing the ocean into a tsunami. The wave raced towards them.

"Cotus what will we do?"

"Run! Run as fast you can."

Vipax saw the clayborn running frantically from the wall of water approaching.

"It is too late, the earth ruptures as the Caemexa and Oblyquixita are bonded" spoke Vipax.

Tessi screamed in desperation. "Ange save us, we will die. We cannot make it."

Ange heard her sister's cry amongst the ash and ruin.

"Sa-Tuchala, I have saved thee from the bonds of Descendant and now bear this burden. I command thee to save the blood kin of the Custodian of shadow."

Sa and the Aracnine had felt the release from Baachelaus the moment the god had been consumed by the prism. Ange's command came to them.

"Aracnine to the clayborn. We have been called." First screeched and all eight of the guardians raced towards Tessi and Nene.

Kado saw Mordraak suddenly awaken as well and take Norbu in its jaws. It flew far into the sky as Norbu stabbed viciously.

"Vipax your enemy flees with your brother of the earth" called Kado.

"Yes Scaletryx. I smell its foul breath and stinking hide."

PO rose, battered and torn. It had seen the maligned dragon snatch Norbu. As it flew into the sky its feathers fell away revealing the lethal blows of the dragon. PO's call of grief and revenge broke the emptiness of the sky. The Orynth chased until it could see the white hide of the dragon. Vipax had risen from the ocean's depth waiting as well to snatch the worm back to its tomb. The red blazing eye of the creature saw the Serpent and opened its jaws dropping Norbu into the thrashing water. PO flew directly into the dragon. Mordraak let its spittle of fire lick the Orynth.

"Mighty servant and brethren. Thy valour remains unequalled." Norbu captured the Orynth gently as it fell into his arms.

Nene and Tessi were pulled up to the highest rock they could find by the Knight. They stood huddled together watching the ocean draw away and the wave gather, protecting the babies as best they could.

As the roar of the wave neared Tessi sang to the babies to calm them before they died. The spray of the ocean touched her face making her heart skip with fear and sorrow.

"Oh Ange, we will see you again with Mata."

Suddenly she was being pulled up. So strong was the grip she lost her breath. She opened her eyes and saw the face of Last the Aracnine. Looking around her the eight guardians stood chest high in the ocean. Nene, Angette, the Knight and Ushan all safely held above the water. Noab had stopped crying mesmerised by the face of their rescuer.

"Oh Ange!" Tessi sobbed as the tears of relief flooded into the sea around her.

Vipax bared its fangs and leapt out of the ocean. Mordraak spat another flame at the serpent, but the great snake latched onto the dragon's throat and pierced its hide with venom. It pulled the beast down into its watery nest. Mordraak screeched and railed against the serpent's strength but could not release itself.

Under the ocean they battled. The water hissed and bubbled as the flame of Mordraak boiled it, such was its strength that not even the waters of the world would douse its fire. Then suddenly the dragon launched itself from the roiling waters and into the skies. It flew directly up and broke through its clouds of ash and smoke. Vipax hung from its thorny hide tenaciously not letting go. Flames burst again and again over the sentinel as Mordraak tried to kill it.

"Enough ancient. It is gone. The shadow is defeated. The fell beast goes to find its father. It is defeated."

Norbu called to Vipax as he reached up and grabbed the tail of the snake. Vipax let go at the command of Norbu.

"The fell creatures still do not reign in our dominion. We are victorious again Custodian" Vipax hissed vehemently at Norbu raging at not devouring Mordraak.

"Indeed, ancient one, you are still ruler of your domain," replied Norbu.

He strode across the shattered lands towards the Iron Keep that had begun to sink back into the earth. Around him the last of the legions of Descendant and Voloc were being killed off by the clayborn who remained. A melange of flesh, iron and bone carpeted the dirt. He felt the ruptured land and earth and the poison seeping in from the breach of Voloc. He looked ahead and saw the tiny figure standing in amidst the smoke and utter destruction. Her eyes shone brightly against the darkness of death surrounding her. He saw the faithful pet run to her, and she hugged it. In her hand lay the jewel the custodian had forged with his hands so many eons ago. He had placed his own hope there as with that of the Ascendant when the realm of light had been breached.

Norbu lay PO down on the dirt gently and then walked to Ange. Kneeling on one knee the custodian still towering over the figure of Ange clasped the jewel in her hands between his.

"Custodian, you have captured my brother until all is restored. The shadow lies dead at the hands of the ice warrior. You have both done what I could not. But the strength of the earth lies weakened and will fail as the poison of Voloc has run deep and needs to be cleansed. For now, though let your heart and body rest for the valour and courage of the Custodian of Shadow and memory has triumphed and caged the deceiver and the destroyer."

"My kin live as do I, but the shadow still lies before me Norbu." Ange looked deep into the eyes of Norbu and saw herself as she now stood but she also saw with the eyes of the custodians all that had passed and was to come. "Will you remake the jewel for it has blackened from the battle? It will be needed again" she asked.

He looked at it and held it in his hand. Norbu gasped at what lay inside the blackened stone, as his hands reforged the crystal to perfect clarity and shape.

"Changer of dark and light and to dark again. You are chained to the first ones, born even before Norbu of the realm of colour and light. Long will be your journey."

Jarrod, Axl, Tyl and Polax came running. They were covered in soot and the black blood of the creatures. Jarrod frantically searched the charred dirt and rocks.

"Where is Gildas?" he asked.

# 19

# Destiny's Footfalls

The Orynth lay on shards of crystal deep within the den of Sa-Tuchala. Around them stood Sa, Kado, Norbu, Jarrod, Tamatjera, Nene and Cotus Medret. Ange and Tessi were sitting further back against a great spire of pure diamond that reached to the roof of the cave. They were holding Angette and Noab. The babies slept soundly having been lulled to drowsiness by the light dancing amongst the crystals.

Ange felt at peace; she was here with Tessi, and alive. The weight and unending sense of doom had lifted so that everything seemed clearer. She looked around the cave and could see every facet and tiny particle that had grown over the eons to form the magnificent sculptures of the cavern. Seeing Norbu her heart was filled with love for the custodian whose hands had helped formed all the beauty and terror of Arglethium.

Norbu walked towards the bodies of the Orynth.

"Brethren, you have returned deep into the memory of ancient visions of colour and the first bonds of creation. The valour of your hearts and the sturdiness of wing and feather shall be remembered for a thousand generations of the clayborn and in the binding light of the Caemexa whom you so valiantly defended."

The custodian laid his hands on the torn and broken bodies. Nothing happened for a long time but very slowly Ange saw the bodies begin to fade. The small stones underneath the gods glimmered just slightly as their splintered wings and bloodied feathers disappeared.

"Where will they go Norbu?" she asked.

"Wherever they deem their spirits should lie Brethren."

He turned towards the gathered warriors.

"Dwellers of ice, sand and clay, Arglethium lies poisoned and dying even with the destruction of Voloc. Its venom runs deep, and the beast Mordraak has broken the lands of the great Ice Mother so that new paths and mountains have been forged. The clayborn have been decimated."

Jarrod thought of Caelwyn and their children. Instead of feeling triumphant at their victory, he felt a doom wash over him.

"Mighty Lord, do our lands survive?" he asked.

"Ay, they do. All is not lost Elda."

"Does Gildas live?"

"Elda Chieftain, The Keeper of Tarentess lies in the ruins of battle. His blood now mixes with the decay of Voloc to protect the dirt rock and stone. Pay homage in your legends to the one called Gildas Gol. I remember the taste of blood spilled upon my earth by his hand at one time and now his own shall cleanse the world of the great enemy that besieged us."

Norbu gestured for them to gather around closer.

"I call you all to a new covenant. Ten millennia ago, the first peoples that walked the land came here at my call. Each swore an oath when the time came that the peoples of this world would gather in legion to defeat the rise of the shadow. The descendants of these ancestors stand here today. The tribes of the red dirt were given the sacred duty as Keepers of Magmeris' gate. That shall remain their purpose. Tamatjera of Widjera come forward. Sa-Tuchala and the Aracnine walk with him also."

All of them came towards Norbu. He plucked a crystal stalagmite from the floor of the cave effortlessly. He drew a diamond on the forehead on each of them standing before him. The Aracnine groaned at the touch of Norbu as did Sa. Tamatjera looked at them wondering what the guardians had seen. He felt the sighs of generations of his ancestors, echo in his thoughts. What else may befall the people of the red dust?

"You are now bound to guard the gate until times end. Sa-Tuchala, ancient and potent with the will of the first created you are granted the most to bear. Keep watch and do not pervert your purpose even for those clayborn you served loyally. Your oaths remain to the Custodian, the one called Ange Tsaed. It is for her to decide when things end or remain. But you must answer her when she calls. Tamatjera, your hide is tough and lean from the whims of the red deserts. Pay homage to your ancestors to keep the shadow from issuing from the gate until all has healed. Sa-Tuchala lives for the ancients not you and while her dwelling remains in your lands it is not yours to hold. But you may be called to defend her den of diamonds from the unending lust that dwells within the hearts of the clayborn. Her strength is yours if you need it."

"The peoples of the Lioness and Bear come forward."

Jarrod and Nene walked up to Norbu. Norbu scarred their foreheads with a diamond.

"Your peoples are now bound to the covenant remade here. When called you are to gather and defend the gate and the lands of your birth. Servants of the Lioness, you are bestowed custodians of the great trees of your lands and across the world. Bring back the mighty forests made with my brethren, Lido and Aerean. Use the bones of the dead as nourishment, so their memory will remain among the living and give life back to the world."

"Great Lord of the Mountain and Lands, I request that the covenant for the peoples I rule be made with my heir. To bear witness shall be the Knight General" Nene interrupted "Tessi come forward with the babes" Nene gestured for Tessi to come forward.

Tessi hesitated and looked at Ange. Ange nodded her approval for she had guessed what the Queen was about to do.

Tessi carried the twins over. Noab lay asleep on her shoulder while Angette wriggled in her other arm.

"The blood kin of Ange, defeater of the shadow demon; Tessi Tsaed and her children Noab and Angette I name as my heirs to the

Kingdom of the Lioness. I will not bear any young of my own, but fate has shown a way where the great lands of Aeserea shall have its suzerains. I also bestow the lands formerly known as Matavia to the keeping of the Tsaed kin as once our thrones were ruled by one suzerain and were joined in allegiance to the Lioness. Now the thrones may be ruled as brother and sister kingdoms; a new bloodline loyal to the Lioness and the god of the desert Ancrid and beyond that the Custodians of this star Caemeris. When their mother so chooses or when she passes, whatever comes first, the rule of the Kingdoms shall be given to each; The Serpent and the Flower."

Tessi was overwhelmed with this announcement by Nene. No words came as her heart filled with fear at the thought of them being made heirs to thrones. She longed for the simple days of her village life with Ange beside her. Ushan purred in the corner and winked her approval of Tessi.

"Knight General are there any objections to my choice as rulers of our lands?"

"Nay my lady, I speak for all the people who remain. The scourge of Ranik shall be removed from the lands of Matavia and a new era shall dawn of peace and prosperity between Matavia and Aeserea. The evil deeds exacted upon you Tessi cannot be forgotten but in the glorious rule of Noab Tsaed the First and Angette Tsaed the First a new wellspring of hope will grow. The Aeserean people pledge allegiance to the Serpent and the Flower."

The Knight General thumped his chest with his sword.

"It is done then" spoke Norbu.

Norbu went to Tessi and the babies and marked them with the crystal. Neither of the children moved or cried at the touch. Tessi noticed the slight frown on Norbu's face as he marked their forehead. She remembered Voloc touching them and wondered what may lie ahead for the children. Their heritage was awash with acts of evil and honour. She wondered which would lie closest to the hearts of the babes.

"Your peoples stand outside, ready to walk to their lands to rebuild. It will be long and difficult after such destruction. Go now and remake my dominion. Remember your oaths, for the caemexa are bound to the clayborn as you are to Arglethium. If it dies you die."

Jarrod, Nene and Tamatjera looked at around to see who would leave first.

Ange stepped forward and went to Nene and Tessi "Come it is time to go to your new home Tessi. My heart leaps with joy at the love the people of the lioness have given you."

Ange took Noab and began to lead them out of the cave.

Polax, Tyl and Axl had entered the cave waiting for Jarrod.

Jarrod saw them but hesitated "Does Gildas live Custodian?"

"Pay homage to your brother and remember this deed above all other deeds. Remember the exile and protector of stone and not the barbarian murderer."

"Come we need to leave. The sun rises and I want to watch the dawn over the lands of the red dust." called Ange hurrying them all.

Kado watched them leave. His heart and mind were weary, but his body felt alive and strong. He had not heard from Vipax since the white dragon had escaped. He went to where Sa Tuc stood near the altar of crystals. He touched them and felt an energy diffuse into this flesh. He pulled away knowing that it was not for him to know this ancient knowledge. He looked at Sa. She seemed as contained and unreadable as always. He knew she was not the same Sa-Tuc that he had known.

"What oaths shall be asked of Kado Kodrax, emperor of the Dragon empire mighty Custodian?"

"You have been baptised Scaletryx by the ancient serpent Vipax. The venom of resurrection is only for those born of Caemexa or shadow. It is not for the clayborn to imbibe this cudgel of strength. Vipax has perverted its birthright and now cursed you among your own and ancients alike. Long and weary will your life become. Maligned and mistrusted by all. But as the shadow diffuses further into the middle of Arglethium then it is the ones with both shadow and light which may to help rule its power. In my binding you were not seen Scaletryx, but Norbu was not given the gift of seeing all things. The torment caused by this corruption of light and dark ruptures the history of making and Norbu's purpose. Your torment is mine, but it may serve to slow Arglethium's death and aid my brethren in her quest."

Norbu stood before the altar completely still. His words were not threatening but matter of fact. Kado's heart reeled at words of the great custodian.

"No covenant can be made with one such as you Kado Kodrax. Mordraak is the purveyor of your father's blood. Your peoples betrayed the first covenant that was wrought and began to seek the power of the jewel. It is why I slumbered for so long beneath the earth to hide the jewel from the eyes of Mordraak. Now the serpent Vipax must sleep to cleanse itself of Voloc's poison. Its sorrow will be great when it awakens and sees what it has done to desecrate this most sacred of all power given to it."

"So, what of me, I have not asked for this inheritance. I have been plagued all my days by the misdeeds of those with more strength to steer the fates of others then myself and yet I continue to be bound by their lack of wisdom and vision. If it was not my father, it is now a fevered and blind god" Kado spoke with suppressed fury at what Norbu said.

"Indeed, you have. That is why I will allow you to remain an exile amongst the clayborn neither dead nor alive and unable to die. If any progeny is borne, then they shall be cursed with no death but with memories of long eons of waiting, the curse of the sentinels of Stonthrax."

"Nay, I will rebuild an honourable kingdom. I will restore the banner of the Drax Dynasty and let the world know of its greatness, honour, and mercy. Sa-Tuc will you not join your friend and lover once more. The Kingdom, that saved you and made you?"

"I cannot Kado Kodrax, Sa-Tuchala lives now within ancient thoughts and memories and will soon forget her origin. I am grateful for the keen eye of the general that saw my skill, a talent that I now know came not from my parents but the ancient power that formed me. I will live in covenant with the Custodian of shadow and memory until it is deemed, I no longer exist."

"The people of the Drax Empire shall not be forgotten for their sacrifice and courage in the battle to end. They fought shoulder to shoulder with all the peoples of these lands as brethren and now you relegate them to dishonour because of the demented mind of a god's foolishness. It will not be borne that this shall be the fate of the people of the Dragon. Norbu the Custodian, Sa-Tuchala of the Aracnine do you seek more enemies to battle? Do you now call the rage of the beast Mordraak again against you? No, I will not have my name and dynasty stained so easily by those who climbed to their glory upon its flagstones. I will raise the Drax Magisterium again and it shall be known across the lands. Covenant or not, the dragon shall be sought again for its strength."

He struck his sword against a crystal shard near him and smashed it to a thousand pieces in his anger. One of them cut his face but no blood came from the wound. He smashed more and more as a frenzy of rage overtook his mind. He crushed the stones into his flesh but all that remained was the white bone beneath.

He stopped heaving as the grief of everything had befallen him, the loss of Sa and the wound of being ignored at the very moment when at last Kado Kodrax had shown his courage and valour in battle consumed him. When he could show his face with pride amongst his people and destroy the memory of the indolent prince.

He collapsed on the ground clutching his sword. He could not escape he knew that.

"Vipax snatched me from the Keep of Lido, and I died. I did not ask for this fate."

"I know which is why we have not destroyed Vipax nor banished you" Sa spoke. "But know Kado, the breach of the serpent is a grave one and you are a witness to this. If Voloc had known of the weapon that stood ready in you, then victory may not have fallen where it did. Leave and take your people with you. Rebuild you Kingdom if you must."

Kado looked at Sa, his heart torn with grief and anger. Taking a shard of crystal, he plunged it into his chest to kill his beating heart.

The pain lasted only a moment as everything went black. But then his eyes opened to reveal the cave again. He stabbed again but the same happened.

His scream of rage echoed throughout the cave. Ange looked back across the barren plains as his cry of frustration floated across the sand. She knew what had happened to Kado and her heart out went to him. She had seen him strive so hard to learn and he had walked with her in her journey and showed kindness to her. He too had been an outsider like her and known the scorn of those supposed to love them. She sent her mind to his and felt the sorrow wash over her.

"Kado Kodrax, the custodian calls you to an oath. If she calls for the exiles blade, will you give it to her? Will you come if the Custodian calls?"

There was silence in her mind as she watched the dawn rise in a corona of gold and cerise over the dead lands.

"Vipax has set me on a path to become your enemy Ange and now Norbu has strengthened this with his denial."

"I can promise that redemption may await even the abomination Scaletryx at the side of the changer of light and dark. I am ruler of the shadows and memories of the realm of light and here in Arglethium. Your curse is mine as well and will not be forgotten. Again, I ask, will you come if the Custodian calls?"

Then as fragile as a butterfly's wings flutter the reply came to her "Yes."

Kado stood and removed the spike of diamond in his chest. He did not look at Norbu or Sa as he walked to the entrance. As he emerged General Tat greeted him. He looked at the torn flesh on his Lord's face.

"Gather the army, we go back to rebuild the Emerald Palace."

"Yes, my lord."

Ange continued with Tessi and Nene. Noab rested easily in her arms; her white eyes mesmerising him. Nene and the Knight General followed.

"Cotus, send a few to guard us as we make our way. You will need to rally our men and bring them home. I will gather the people from the grove for a hearty welcome and celebration."

"Ay my lady." Cotus whistled to a group of soldiers who lay resting against some rocks. They bowed when they saw Nene with him.

"Men you are to escort the Queen and her companions back to the grove of the Lioness. Be vigilant I don't think all these creatures were slain and may dwell in the darker places."

The look of relief to be leaving the lands spoke their willingness for such a task. They tidied themselves up and swigged the last of their water. All of them were bloody and dishevelled.

"It is good that we will march to the grove with such medallions and arms of service as what we wear." Nene spoke with a wry smile on her face as she looked at the ragged looking entourage including herself.

"The Queen of Aeserea bedecked in ripped and torn britches. My father would never have believed it."

She looked at Cotus Medret, her heart ever devoted to the Knight. On impulse she hugged him. He did not know how to respond again and was glad that the light was still weak and did not reveal his flush of embarrassment.

"Soon the throne of the Lioness will be restored," he spoke.

Ushan roared ahead urging them to keep going.

"And so, the great protector calls us to our journey home" Nene spoke pulling away.

They turned and followed Ushan who was teasing Nekoda as he nipped at her tail and barking every time, she swung it at him.

Tessi and Ange naturally fell in close together enjoying the peace and silence.

"You must leave again Ange?"

"Yes, I will return though."

Tears began to spread down Tessi's face.

"I cannot believe that only two summers ago we danced with the sun bride in the tunics our mother made for us. Oh, how it has all changed, sister. I want you to see the babes grow. You can teach them to be warriors full of courage and mercy. Does the jewel give you sight? Do you see what may become of them?"

"I do not know. I have been too busy capturing gods and slaying demons."

Tessi snorted at her sister's gentle chiding through the sadness that lay over everything. Angette struggled in her arms wanting to walk.

"They will be walking and running soon. The children have seen and been touched by more than is right for babies. I do not know what will happen. But I will return Tessi, please remember that. This is not farewell forever. I promise you that."

Ange knew in her heart that she would return but she did not know when.

"Please can you not stay a little while more. Until the wounds and memories fade and the summer comes again, and the days are brighter."

Ange saw the pleading in Tessi's eyes and wanted so much to throw the prism into the ocean and forget everything that had happened.

"That would be so nice Tessi. I would long for that."

"We will walk to the land bridge and rest overnight. I know there is shelter there to rest after sunset. We will reach it by nightfall" spoke Nene as she walked up to them. She saw the tears in Tessi's face.

The girls nodded as they watched the red dirt stretch ahead.

Gildas stood on the great table of ice that lay to the west of the Forest of Enan. He watched two figures walking towards him. The wind whipped around him in a blizzard. It was cool and soothing after the heat of the red lands in the south. He saw that the figures were a woman holding a child and a great bear. The bear stood taller than himself.

The bear's jaws opened emitting a massive roar. It loped over to him with unnatural speed and knocked him over. He had no sword and could not defend himself. He looked at the great white face and fangs and knew he stared straight into the eyes of the Ice Mother.

"The mother calls you Gildas and wishes to know what you choose."

He started as he realised it was the voice of Jesse. He pushed and the bear stepped aside letting him get up. He looked at her and the child.

"How are you alive?"

"We are not but we live in a realm between life and death. The Ice mother takes us to her until the time comes when all existence ends."

"It is completed now. We defeated Voloc," replied Gildas.

"No, it is not. More is to be done. That is why you must choose between walking with me until the end of all things or take your place upon the throne of Norbu."

The Ice bear began to grow impatient swinging back and forth waiting for Gildas.

"What choice is there? I live with you in a place where no harm will come but neither will death release me. I remain an exile wherever I stand. So do I sit in readiness for the call by the Custodian Ange and restore the lands and purge the dirt of Voloc. The rock and stone are beneath me now. I cannot forsake the clay and ice of the world which birthed me for the faintest of hope of a life which it seems was never meant to be. Can you not come with me Jesse, and live by my side in Tarentess? Can the strength of Norbu and the will of the Ice mother not grant one boon at this time when the world almost breaks?

Jesse looked at the bear, but the bear growled at the question.

"Keeper of Tarentess, blood kin of the graanar, you must decide. The ancients do not sway from their paths for it would mean the death of all. You must walk alone or with me that is what has been ordained since the paw and foot have trod together."

Gildas stared for a long time at Jesse and the child in her arms. He remembered her blue eyes, so vivid, warm, and welcoming, not the cold white of his own.

"Why did you choose me Jesse? You would be alive with younglings around you. Like Jarrod and his wife."

"Because the roar of the ice mother pulsed within me but with me her paw nurtured fealty to the ice and its ways rather than the brutal lust for conquest as it did in you. I was your bond to the lands which made you so you would not give over completely to the shadows which chased you in your dreams. I wanted you Gildas because your strength met mine."

"Can I ever see you again?"

"Lost cub of the Ice Mother when all things end you shall be called to me. Rock and stone may flow in your flesh for now, but it was the ice that first birthed you."

The bear rose upon her hind feet and bellowed her oath across the lands. She turned in readiness to leave.

Gildas saw the eons of time ahead as the lands healed and new rock and stone were built. His heart lay here in the ice, but he could not rest his bones yet. He turned and saw a path stretching ahead and knew that he had decided.

Jesse stood watching ignoring the impatient stamping of the great bear.

"You know that this would not have been if not for you" he called to her.

"I know. The mighty warrior has a heart that needs protecting after all. Fate in its wisdom gave it to me to hold safely until you return." Gildas walked away with the hope that at the end of all things he had a place where he could finally rest.

Norbu waited amongst the rubble of the battlefield. It was dark again with the moon on the wane. It had only been three dawns since the destruction of Voloc. The stars were still dimmed from the smoke and fumes that poured from the decaying fortress. Its black walls and spires were sinking back into the dirt, but it was slow and malignant in its destruction. He could hear the cries of the creatures of Voloc underneath as the caves collapsed filling with the bile of the shadow.

He could feel Sa-Tuchala and Vipax slumber. He searched the emptiness of the night watching and waiting. The last of the clayborn had made camps far away from the scorched battle fields. Tamatjera's people had marked the ground as cursed but vowed to return in five wet season's time.

He saw what he was looking for. The form began to rise out of the dirt slowly; a slight shimmer surrounding the shape. Norbu began to stride towards him. Then as he neared, he saw the blade materialise in the darkness and readied his own. He ran towards the shape as it stood in the darkness above the grave of Voloc.

"Keeper of Tarentess prove your blade and right to my throne!"

The great warriors for rock, earth and stone met on the grave of Shadow's death. Sparks flew from their blades, showering everything near with such heat they melted the sand into glass. The thunder of their battle rippled into the desert and ocean.

Ange was making her way from the coast near the land bridge. She had left Tessi asleep with her children nestled beneath a great boab tree. It was warm and safe for them. Queen Nene had woken but Ange bade her not to wake Tessi.

"Tell Tessi I will return but there is more to be done."

Nene nodded.

"I will treat her and the babes as if they were my own. Brave one you have given us a reprieve from evil and destroyed our enemies near and far. Your name shall be hallowed in the lands of the Lioness."

Ange had left with fresh vigour for the journey ahead. Nekoda followed behind, sniffing for any trace of the creatures borne of Voloc.

Suddenly the dog shot off in the night towards something unseen to Ange. It was barking madly in the silence in pursuit of something to hunt.

As she smiled at Nekoda she suddenly felt a thunderous boom ripple across the skies and into the ground. It came from the fortress. Panicking she began to run. She passed a camp of men who had stood looking toward the sounds of metal blades striking.

As Ange climbed the ridge that overlooked the blackened valley of the Iron Fortress, she saw Norbu and Gildas fighting. Gildas had the advantage and was driving Norbu into the ground. Two men came running up behind her weapons ready. She noticed they were graan.

"Has the shadow taken hold of the gods?" asked one of them.

"Nay but I do not understand this madness" replied Ange.

She swept down towards them with the prism ready and her blade.

Suddenly Gildas rose in the air in a great sweeping arc.

His voice boomed across the night, "The throne is mine as is leaf, dirt and stone."

His blade came down on Norbu and stabbed the mighty custodian and father of Arglethium in the chest.

"No!" Ange screamed as she saw Norbu collapse to the ground. The force of his body falling shook the land around him. She flew at Gildas with her blade and with all the strength she could muster she thrust him to the ground away from the broken body of the Custodian. She lassoed her rope around Gildas neck and wrenched him toward her. She stood over him glaring at the clansman. The faces of slavers and Ranik and all the men who had spat on her and leered at Tessi and imprisoned the girls and women. All the people who had been slain by Gildas Gol rose before her. She took the shadows of Voloc and made them rise before Gildas.

"What have you done? Why have you killed Norbu?" the anger and grief in her heart swelled so much she felt it was going to explode. Gildas gently pried her blade away.

"Stand away sister. This is the way fate has chosen as it was for you. It was by the mighty Norbu's will that we should fight."

"I hate you with all my heart and being. I hate the men who are like you. I hated the tyrants who chained my people and sold my sister. Why would the maker of all things choose you Gildas? Why was I chosen? We are nothing to these rulers of light and making. Why?"

Ange pleaded pulling the leash tighter around Gildas neck. "I have the strength to slay you and now I have the will to do it." Her words spoken with venom.

"I believe you sister. I ask you to heed what Norbu has willed. We are both born of the clay."

Ange placed the prism on Gildas forehead and let it burn him.

"See now your bond to me. For if I will it, I will end you just as the deserts were once mountains. You are bound to your Keep and to me."

Gildas nodded knowing his fate now lay bound to two oaths.

Ange got up and went to Norbu. She cradled his head in her arms.

"Oh, mighty Custodian and brethren, you loved me more and gave me more than my own blood kin. Know that I go to bring all that was wrought in the first moments to be restored again so that your memory shall never be forgotten or lost."

She sobbed over his body.

Axl and Tyl came walking slowly towards Gildas uncertain of what was happening.

"Are you a wraith of the underworld or graan?" Axl asked Gildas wary of what they looked upon. The memory of seeing their clan brother turn to ash was still strong in their minds.

Just as he was about to answer five shadows landed around the body of Norbu.

EY spoke to Gildas.

"Keeper of Tarentess, we have returned to take our places as servants to the Custodian of the lands. We shall protect the body of Norbu, so it is not desecrated by the darkness until his blood is drained into the earth. Then he shall be placed in a tomb as memory to the second Age of Light and custodian to the third Age of Light."

"Ay mighty warriors. This is indeed worthy of the first stone forger."

Ange gently lay Norbu's head down. She knew that this is what Norbu wanted but did not understand it. Norbu dying hurt more than when Mata and Bensah had died. Then the anger returned as she thought of all she had lost and still must do. She let out another sob again.

"Oh, protect him well, brave and valiant Orynth. My sorrow lies most deeply here at this sight and the death of these lands."

"It is time Ange" spoke Gildas.

She nodded. She looked once more at Norbu and saw the blood trickling down his chest and into the sand. It did not drain as if it was lifeless but rather like a snake with purpose forcing its way into the grains of dirt.

Ange squeezed on the prism. "Bring forth the mouth of Magmeris!" she commanded.

In the darkness the tomb of Magmeris opened silently. Gildas peered into the gate and could see only an abyss of black. Just faintly a cry floated out of the emptiness. But it was cut short as Nekoda barked.

"There sister your loyal legion is ready" spoke Gildas.

"Remember you are bound to me now Gildas. You will come when the Custodian calls." Ange looked at Gildas and the Orynth.

"Claw and iron will come sister," replied Gildas.

"Come Nekoda. Whatever awaits us now, we need to always remember Arglethium is our home, and we must protect it."

Ange jumped into the black mouth of the gate. Nekoda barked once at Gildas and then sped into the black hole following Ange.

As the gate closed Gildas heard the cries of sorrow and rage growing stronger. His warrior heart longed to follow and fight whatever may lie on the other side.

"Much lies ahead of you sister." Gildas turned to Axl and Tyl "Come Graanar, I will journey back to my Keep and slay as we go what is left of Voloc's reign."

"Which path Graanar?"

"Hendra Valley. My heart still burns for a fight with an enemy that lies there."

# Belmaris Speaks

"Belmaris remembers the light and the shadow cast at its birth. Caemeris has passed and left its progeny as ruler of two realms. I have been the witness to the rise and ruin of the creatures which come from the realm where no light exists. In its emptiness and silence the void had held dominion over all that it touched, while at the heart of fire and light existed chaos and noise. When the light and silence collided Belmaris awoke.

The creatures spawned after my awakening by the caemexa called custodians, thrived in the warmth of the star they called the sun; Belmaris of Caemeris. They are deemed clayborn of the third age of light and in their hearts Belmaris sees the turmoil of my birth also.

How did it dawn that Belmaris became ruler of creations that rage against themselves?

At the very first thought of Caemeris, light ruptured the void piercing the sleeping conscience. In that breach the First Star laid suzerainty over the silence, not to control it but merely to exist in all things. Discord seeped into the stillness of the abyss the more Caemeris grew in knowledge of shadow revealing the void's emptiness to itself. Despair became the igniting spark birthing

Oblyquixiton, the unlit star, subjugator of flame, annihilator of creation's pain. As the eons of time passed, discord between the unlit one and Caemeris birthed an insatiable malice, and the wars of creation began.

My progenitor unable to be thwarted from its vision brought the colours of existence into being. It was then Magmeris and Belmaris were issued into existence, the first Age of light. After bestowing us life the First Star continued its quest to fill the emptiness and destroy the silence.

Unknown to each other, my sister and I grew in our glory and raged our birthright, across the abyss, filling its solitude with beings known as the created. Magmeris and Belmaris offspring of the First Star; beacons at each end of the great chasm of darkness.

When the first wars of Caemeris and Oblyquixiton ceased, Belmaris and Magmeris desired to be fecund like Caemeris. Our spawn grew with our spirit, fed by the sparks and explosions of new life. Our fiery hearts stabbed all the darkest recesses cleansing the shadows and giving new dawns to things deemed dead. Our brightness etched its mark across the void in harmony but fated to never meet to keep a balance deemed wise by the First Star. Oblyquixiton raged against its gaolers and began to pull the first birthed of Caemeris closer until in the magnificent chaos Magmeris' rays struck Belmaris.

It was then I sensed the potency within the sister and its greatness. I saw that it had become a larger and greater sentinel to that of Belmaris. I called to the First Star, but it did not answer. In its quest to conquer the dark it had thrust the first colours further and farther so that now our creator had vanished from our sight.

Magmeris grew as the eons passed and with it Belmaris saw its death. This could not be borne for with time comes knowledge and the desire to devour existence so that only the light of Belmaris remained. This desire burned brighter than the First Star's spark and soon overcame the purpose given at the time of my awakening.

Then in the emptiness I sensed a creature of Oblyquixiton's making. Deep and potent from its pits it rose stridently bellowing its presence. The silence that held it was broken as it spewed forth its deadness. It speared the smaller stars and lanced them in their flames of colours so that tombs and dens were made for its progeny. Then it sensed Belmaris and called its offspring to gather and destroy the great sentinel.

'Servant, you will not destroy me. I am made to remain until times end.'

'I am no servant of thee. I am the void aware and all seeing. You are the progeny of the usurper who has fled my gaze. You and all that is wrought will be undone and the defilement shall end. My dominion remains mine to hold and it is by my will that it shall return to the stillness of the dark.'

Potent and rich with the power of the void, it doused my spears of light and killed their enlivening touch.

'Come to Belmaris, for I seek to know and see all' I commanded.

The servant pierced my fiery form with potency strong and matured from the ancient battles. Belmaris took all that existed within the mind of the creature and drew the darkness into my luminescent heart. Light stilled and became un-violent at the presence of the shadow with in me. The two became one as the flame of Belmaris burned with the chill of Oblyquixiton. But the first vision laid down for Belmaris would not be doused and in its heart sparked the desire to rule all that could be known. In my quest to know the dark, silence ensued and stilled the wars of creation for eons, dimming the Shadow's malice and Belmaris' fire.

Then Magmeris spoke.

'Brethren of the First Star, I sense something has been lost for too much light now lives for the darkness to remain. It will dim those born of the First Star as the young are birthed again and again. No elder stars or shadow to quell their rage to exist. I also see a new vision dawning; an era where the First Star has shaped yet more creatures. Greater and with the purpose to rule even the first offspring: a realm brighter and more eternal than our own; a second Age of Caemexa. Are Magmeris and Belmaris to be relegated to the rule of these others?'

Belmaris woke from its slumber at the voice of its sister. The noise felt like a quickening lance of death as it woke the conscious within. The memory of the first rupture of the void woke with it and Belmaris' heart felt the pain of creation as it consumed the peace of Oblyquixiton. This union forged an unquenchable desire to dim mighty Magmeris who had grown in my dormition. I took a spec of Caemeris that lay within me and thrust it across the emptiness to kill my twin; the stabbing blow ripping it in two, sending my sister to its eternal tomb. But the strike was made with such rage that the spear of Belmaris shot across the emptiness to search for the new realm of light unseen and unknown to its memory. And as my rays streaked on their murderous path, they tore the sleeping conscious of the dark from me and birthed it into the chaotic world. Baptised in the stained and defiled light of Belmaris union with Oblyquixiton, Voloc the Destroyer was born.

Further and further my rays screamed their victory across the silent eons until they met the second born of Caemeris. Belmaris rays became frigid at first touch with these different and more sublime creatures. Their light was awash with all the colours of making. They could dim the starlight or raise it high. Belmaris heart tore in two at the betrayal of Caemeris to forge the Custodians of light. And in my rage Oblyquixiton saw a way to rule the chaos.

As Belmaris struck the new realm of light it saw its death. It could not be borne by the mighty progeny of the First Star that its dominion would be usurped. It ripped the edges of the realm open and let the darkness bleed in. It stole the rulers from their thrones and gave one to Voloc to cage. But Belmaris was thwarted by those borne of the second Age of light. A memory of its greatness remained. A tear of sorrow shaped into a jewel holding the colours of making. Belmaris saw once again its death imprisoned inside the stone.

Now again this relic of the second Age of light and bringer of my death has been lost.

Voloc, you have returned to the heart of Belmaris. You have forgotten your time before Belmaris, the time of the unlit star and now your purpose lies with mine. The heart of Belmaris is unsated. Its final conquest has been denied.

"Servant, awake! Belmaris wills that nothing shall remain of the second Age of Light or the progeny it formed. Voloc, the Destroyer, seek the Custodian of memory and death! Destroy the descendant of clay! Bring the tear of Ascendant to me!"

Ange watched across the barren plain of sulphurous dust in the basin of binding. The tree of lost hope was a tiny spec in the distance and the thrones of Ascendant and Descendant lay empty. Nekoda stood by her side. Suddenly the abrading wind ceased as its howling was replaced by a scream of pain rippling across the horizon. She steeled herself as the birth cry of Voloc pierced her heart, flesh, and bone. The prism flared against her skin as the voice of the great shadow struck it.

"You are not defeated Voloc, and the Custodians are caged once more. I must find what made you and the custodians to bring an end to these wars which seek to destroy Arglethium. Come Nekoda, the real battle for our world begins" Ange spoke as she held the prism up and peered into the eye of Caemeris.

The story continues in Book Four
## SEER OF LIGHT

∞

# Appendix

## THE CLAYBORN OF ARGLETHIUM

Ange Tsaed: from the village of Kensai in the lands of the Mighty Choasa

Gildas Gol of the Graan: former warlord and Chieftain of the Graan Clans of the Northern Icelands

Sa-Tuc: Assassin to Emperor Ko

Kado Kodrax: Heir to the Drax Magisterium

Bensah El Bunani: Trader and family friend of Ange and Tessi

Tessi Tsaed: Sister to Ange

Nekoda: Wild dog / hyena cross breed, companion to Bensah and Ange

Angette (Mordraag) Tsaed-Ranik: Daughter of Tessi Tsaed

Noab (Tias) Tsaed-Ranik: Son of Tessi Tsaed

Queen Nene Des Vries: Ruler of Aeserea

Prince Draved Des Vries: Brother of Queen Nene

Prince Dronagh Des Vries: Brother of Queen Nene

Lord Cotus Medret: First Knight and Commander of Aeserean Forces

Lord Jonas Warick: First Knight of the Cavalry

Lord Kyle Yonan: First Knight of the Cavalry

Jarrod Gol – Elda - Chieftain of the Graan, brother to Gildas

Caelwyn Gol – Elda Clan Wife of the Graan, wife of Jarrod

Polax of Timmo – Chieftain of Clan Timmo

Tyl of Timmo – Clansman of Timmo Clan

Axl of Timmo – Clansman of Timmo Clan

Queen Giandra Ranik: wife of Lord Ranik, Queen of Matavia

Captain Piotr Faad: Knight Captain of the Matavia Garrison

# CAEMEXA BORN OF CAEMERIS

## The Custodians

Baachelaus (Descendant): Diarch of Caemeris, spirit of the unknown, binder of yearning & fulfilment

Assumpta (Ascendant): Diarch of Caemeris, spirit of the clay born, binder of light & shadow

Norbu: Elder of Creation, Custodian of Arglethium

Lido: Water Custodian

Seraf: Fire Custodian

Aerean: Wind Custodian

Belmaris: Sun

Magmeris: Dead sun, sibling to Belmaris

## Progeny of Stonthrax

The Guardians, Aracnine: eight in number, jailers of Baachelaus

The Orynth: YU, EY, PO, XI, AX, VA. Friends to Norbu

Uchala: Sentinel, Spider in form

Vipax: Sentinel, Serpent in form

## Oblyquixita born of Oblyquixiton

Voloc: Dark Custodian, Born of Oblyquixiton

Mordraak The Slayer: Dragon formed from the first wars of creation

Ondraack: Fell Creature of the Void

## About the Author

CLARE ROLFE is an Australian self-published author. Her first novel was the dystopian fantasy Ten Letters to Delacroix's Tomb, released in 2016. Her inspirations for writing include philosophy, the natural world and science. She dabbles in poetry and flash fiction and is a routine blogger of her work. Find her on her webpage www.clrolfe.com

Descendant's Throne continues the story of the Legend of Caemeris and the mystery behind the prism forged from Ascendant's Tear.

Stay in Touch

www.clrolfe.com

Facebook: Clare Rolfe / CL Rolfe

Twitter: @rolfe_cl

Mickey Martin has done it again!

*Soul Keepers of Glenormiston South* is one of my favourite stories *ever*. It delivered everything you'd want from an urban fantasy romance.

Magic … hot sex … excellent plot twists … but left me with one thought.

What about Max? What was his story? *Obsidian Souls* delivers *exactly* that and has joined the ranks of unputdownable reading!

Another excellent story that pulls you into our beautiful Victorian countryside and leaves you gasping and wondering to the very last page.

The chemistry between characters is amazing, the plot captivated me with every page turned, and I don't want to spoil any of the storyline … but the outcome is *brilliant!*

Now I'm just wondering about Red? I need to know her amazing journey. Spill it, Martin!

**Kelly McDonald**
**Garden Babies Fine Fairy Art/Portraits and Photography**

The stakes are raised in this sequel of *Soul Keepers of Glenormiston South*. The story continues at a crucial moment in the earth's and characters' history, and it pulled me right in. It was hard for me to put the book down, as Martin masterfully created thrilling moment after thrilling moment. There were so many twists, I couldn't keep up. The book was dynamic and captivating. Can't wait for the next one!

**Sonee Singh**
**Author of *Lonely Dove* and the award-winning *Soul Seeker Collection* of poetry**

Mickey Martin weaves the magic of good, evil, despair and love into another amazing story that keeps you turning page after page. If you have read *Soul Keepers of Glenormiston South* then you know that what you are about to read comes from a place of imagination that is second to none.

**Sue Croft**
**Contributing author in *The Colours of Me* and *Historian***

Mickey Martin's *Obsidian Souls* had me hooked from the first page. After reading *Soul Keepers of Glenormiston South,* I was a fan of all things 'Soul Keepers', and couldn't wait to read Max's story. As expected, Martin held my attention with the perfect combination of relatable characters, intriguing plot twists and a gripping storyline set in a stunning location, Noorat, in our vibrant state of Victoria. Congratulations, Martin. I look forward to what comes next!

**Taylah Manna**
**Avid reader**

Martin has done it again! Obsidian Souls, is an exquisite journey returning to the magical essence of the Victoria Collection and the mesmerising characters from Soul Keepers of Glenormiston South - who protect all life and Mother Earth. An incredible read, that I could not put down. I want more from this author!

**Jess Fowler Art**

Yet again Martin captivates the reader with all the twists and turns in the much-anticipated sequel to *Soul Keepers of Glenormiston South, Obsidian Souls!* Revisiting the beloved characters introduced to us in *Soul Keepers, Obsidian Souls* delves deeper into Max's journey and takes us on a spell-binding roller-coaster through every unputdownable page! Yet another gripping novel from this extraordinary author.

**Sally Taylor**
**L2P Project Officer – Frankston City Council**

## Also by Mickey Martin:

### The Given Trilogy:

The Given

Dark Angel

The Guardian

### The Victorian Collection:

Soul Keepers of Glenormiston South *Glenormiston South 3265*

Obsidian Souls' *Noorat 3265*

Chilling Summer in Inglewood *Inglewood 3517* (COMING SOON)

Sweet Water Creek *Frankston 3199* (COMING SOON)

•

Sweet Delights – A GUMNUT PRESS ANTHOLOGY

MESSAGES from the EMBERS – BLACK QUILL PRESS

## Writing as Michelle Weitering:

Thirteen and Underwater

The Power of Knowing – K P WEAVER – MMH PRESS

The Colours of Me – with Kez Wickham St George – MMH PRESS